UPCOI

Never miss a new title!

Keep up with Jeff Buick's new releases and sign up for his newsletter at JEFFBUICK.COM

CURRENTLY AVAILABLE TITLES

BOBBY GRECO SERIES

No End of Bad Guys

One is Evil

CURTIS WESTCOTT SERIES

A Killing Game

The Wrong Side of Murder

* * *

COMING SOON

AJ COSTA SERIES

Size Four

COMING SOON

STAND ALONE TITLES

The Krubera Conspiracy

Bloodline (re-release)

The Art of Deceit

The Reluctant Truth

This book is entirely a work of fiction. All characters and their names are from the author's imagination. Places, events and incidents, while often based on reality, are used fictitiously. If there is any resemblance to a real person, whether they are living or dead, it is purely coincidental.

Cover and interior design by Christina Curkovic.

Cover images courtesy of the following contributors:

- SB on Unsplash
- Life Of Pix from Pexels
- Jacob Morch on Unsplash
- Max Kleinen on Unsplash

ISBN: 978-1-989727-02-7

THE WRONG SIDE OF MURDER

CURTIS WESTCOTT CRIME THRILLER SERIES: BOOK 2

JEFF BUICK

To Danielle

Hope you enjoy this one!

All the best.

January 2022

NOVEL WORDS INC

CHAPTER ONE

The crime scene crew figures the body has been there a while.

Aislinn Byrne slipped into her car and tapped the steering wheel with a chewed nail, the dispatcher's words echoing in her head. Aislinn hated the rotting, bloated corpses – they were hideous and smelled awful. But there was no choosing which murder you worked, it all came down to whether you were at the top of the rotation. She started her car and pulled into the midday traffic.

Google Maps was dormant on this trip. Jamaica Plain was her backyard, had been since she was a red-haired tomboy racing down hills on her tricycle. She knew the building where some unfortunate had stumbled onto today's murder victim – an old red brick three-story on the corner across from the Purple Cactus Burrito Bar. Maybe she'd grab some lunch after checking out the scene. Then she remembered the dispatcher's warning and thought, maybe not.

A forensics unit was already on site and the uniforms had secured a half-block perimeter with crime scene tape. She rolled her window down and held up her badge for the officer guarding the street, then drove under the tape and parked behind the CSI van. She clipped the badge to her belt as she walked toward the door, eyes scanning the crowd from behind her sunglasses. *Perps love to watch the cops fuss over their work,* Westcott had told her. That had proved to be good advice. She'd solved a murder once by watching the CCTV footage of herself arriving at the scene and seeing a guy in the crowd whose body language was all wrong. Nothing twigged with her this time and she tucked her sunglasses in her blazer pocket and entered the building.

It was dark and the air felt cool after the warmth of the late spring sun. She shivered slightly as she took the stairs to the third floor, where another officer was blocking the hallway. Aislinn flashed her badge and he jotted the number and her name on his notepad, then shuffled aside, throwing her a look as she passed. She'd seen that look before at some of the messier murders – he'd seen something that disagreed with him. The worn hardwood squeaked slightly underfoot and Aislinn noted the names on the closed doors as she passed. An accountant, a PR firm, and a beauty supply distributor were neighbors to the open door at the end of the hall. She pulled on latex gloves and stood in the doorway.

The space was in the midst of a major renovation, with fresh drywall in places and a few wires hanging from the high ceiling where tiles had been removed. A bank of windows fronted onto Center Street, flooding the space with natural light, and the scent of freshly cut wood hung in the still air. The old floor coverings were a mess, crisscrossed with lines where walls had been torn out to create an open workspace. They likely hadn't expected to find a body in one.

Five people were in the room – two crime scene techs, a photographer, the coroner, and a uniformed officer. She headed for the CSI crew with one eye on the coroner and photographer. Their motions looked choreographed – this was a seasoned team going through their routine. A crime scene technician nodded to her, then went back to searching for and collecting evidence. The coroner was standing next to a drywalled pillar in the center of the room that had been cut open. She glanced over her shoulder as Aislinn came alongside, then pulled down her mask. Her eyes had a look that told Aislinn that this call was something special.

"Hey, Aislinn," Rebecca Carlisle said. "You got this one, huh."

"Yeah."

Carlisle moved aside slightly and Aislinn could now see the head of a body that had been crammed into the tight space. It set her back on her heels for a split second.

"It's been here for ages, but it's not going to smell," Carlisle said. "It's dehydrated. Mummified, almost."

Aislinn took another step forward. The body was wrapped in polyethylene but still clearly visible, and it wasn't pretty. The corpse's skin had stretched tight over the skull bones and the mouth was frozen open, like the victim was in the middle of a perpetual scream. The eyes were little more than hollow sockets and what had once been a beautiful head of hair looked like brittle straw.

The pillar was an electrical chase, filled with wires that fed current from the main panel in the basement to the lights and plugs throughout the room. The drywall had been cut along the edge of the chase, then snapped off at a height that exposed the corpse's head. Whoever had pulled off the drywall had stopped immediately, which was hardly a surprise.

"Who found the body?" Aislinn asked.

"A couple of tradesmen," Rebecca said. "They're in the adjoining room, pretty shook up."

"No wonder." Aislinn took another look at the tortured face, then made her way to where the workers were sequestered with an officer in a small office off the main room. They were both in their twenties with tool belts hanging off their hips. "Detective Byrne. Which one of you found the body?"

The taller, thinner of the two lifted his hand. "I did. Well, we both did, sort of."

Aislinn took a good look at the pair – the man with his hand up was visibly shaken, his eyes darting about quickly as his mind processed the reality of the situation. The second man had dark hair and seemed more at ease with the whole thing, his droopy eyes giving him an almost-bored look. *Mutt and Jeff,* she thought.

"Please state your name and then run through what happened," she said to the thin man.

"I'm Ryan," he said in a quick staccato. "I was cutting into the edge of the chase, being careful not to slice any of the electrical conduits, and when I was about five feet from the floor I gave the drywall a yank and it snapped. And there it was."

"A fucking mummy head, staring at us," the dark-haired man said in a slow monotone. Then he added, "I'm Jeremy."

"Where were you when all this happened?" Aislinn asked Jeremy.

"Standing behind Ryan. Watching. Didn't expect that." Every sentence was delivered separately, like a waiter bringing individual courses.

"Did you touch anything inside the chase?" she asked Ryan.

"No," Ryan said. "I jumped back, it scared the shit out of me. Some bits of drywall might have fallen inside, but I didn't go anywhere near her – or him – or whatever it is. We called you guys right away."

"Preserving the scene, we were," Jeremy said.

Aislinn stared at Jeremy, trying to figure out if he was serious or mocking her. When she realized he was being entirely serious, she said, "Well, good work, guys." Ryan seemed pleased, Jeremy remained deadpan.

She turned to the attending officer and said, "Get their statements, please."

Aislinn returned to where Rebecca Carlisle was preparing to slice open the remainder of the pillar and expose the rest of the body. She had a drywall saw and a utility knife in hand and was calculating where to make her cut.

"Are you okay with me opening the chase?" she asked Aislinn.

"Yeah, nothing on this side of the wall of any value."

"It's been years since she was put in here," Carlisle agreed.

Carlisle started with the razor-sharp knife, cutting down about six inches on one side, then the other. She made a deep incision across the drywall at the bottom of her cuts, then she grabbed on and gave it a sharp yank. It snapped off cleanly, exposing the bare shoulders of the corpse and giving the coroner a better look at what was inside the chase. She peered in with a flashlight, then said, "I can cut all the way to the floor without touching the poly wrapping the body."

Aislinn didn't respond and Carlisle made the cuts, then gave the large piece of drywall a tug. It snapped on the cuts and broke away. The corpse came lurching forward and Aislinn grabbed it by the shoulders, its head jerking about like a bobblehead. Carlisle set the drywall aside and got a good grip on the poly near the feet.

"Let's lift it out and lay it down there," Carlisle said, motioning to a clear spot on the floor with a drop sheet already in place.

"Right." Aislinn lifted, surprised at how light the body was and set her end down on the sheet.

They could see the corpse clearly now – a woman in a full-length, strapless red dress. The details of the body and the dress were mostly obscured by the folds in the poly, but the color drained from Aislinn's face and she took a step back.

"Jesus," she whispered.

Carlisle snapped her head around and asked, "You okay?"

"Yeah, all good," Aislinn said, not sure she was. A very dark image was forming in her head and she backed off and sat on the window sill while the coroner and her crew dusted the poly for prints and talked about how to cut it open with the least amount of damage to any potential evidence. After a few minutes Carlisle plodded over in her booties.

"I can cut open the poly here or take it to the morgue," Carlisle said."

Usually, the body would be taken to the morgue and the poly cut with CSI and the lead detective in attendance, but since they were all present Aislinn decided not to wait. It was bucking protocol, but she had her reasons.

"I'm good with you doing it here." Aislinn figured the photos and Carlisle's report would give her any DNA traces or fingerprints on the plastic.

Carlisle replaced her mask, dug in her toolbox and pulled out a razor knife in a sealed bag. She ripped open the plastic, removed the sterilized blade and cut a slit in the poly from one end to the other, then made shorter slits at each end and pulled it back. The body was that of a woman, dressed in a red satin gown with a matching sash around her waist. The thick, dark hair was like spray-painted straw and had fallen across the face. Carlisle pushed it back, once again revealing the grotesque open-mouth scream and hollow eye sockets. Carlisle glanced up at Aislinn, whose face had gone even whiter.

Vertigo threatened and Aislinn swayed back and forth, fighting to stay on her feet.

"It's going to take me a while to figure out how long she's been dead," Carlisle said. "Even then it will likely be a guess."

Aislinn struggled to catch her breath and grabbed for a nearby chair. She sat down heavily and focused on the floor. She closed her eyes, images of teenage girls sweeping around the room flooded in, their new dresses swirling about, their voices young and excited. *Oh, God, it's so red. I love it, love it, love it.*

Aislinn swallowed, her eyes still shut tight. "Twenty years, give or take a few days."

Everyone within earshot stopped, the only sound a low hiss from an air conditioning duct.

"That's pretty specific," Carlisle said, standing. She waited a minute, then said, "Care to explain?"

Aislinn didn't respond. Her emotions were churning like an angry sea and she couldn't keep a straight train of thought. It was threatening to derail her. Long forgotten memories, now as vivid as sharply focused pictures, flashed through the darkness, bringing that day back as if were in the moment. *So this is where you ended up. All that wondering, and here you are.*

Eventually, Aislinn opened her eyes and said, "Darina Volkov. She disappeared on prom night, June 2001."

"You knew her," Carlisle stated.

"Good friends," Aislinn uttered, turning away from the hollow sockets that had once held dark, mischievous eyes.

She needed to get out of the room and stood on weak knees. "Please send the report to District A-1, Homicide."

There was nothing of value here, not after twenty years of office workers spilling coffee and dropping bits of their lunch on the floor. Anything of use in the investigation would come from the CSI team's search inside the electrical chase and from Rebecca's examination of the body and the poly. Even then, hoping for trace materials on either was optimistic, time had a way of destroying evidence.

"When can I expect it?" Aislinn asked, struggling to keep herself together.

Carlisle gave the corpse a long look, then said, "I can have some preliminary data by tomorrow afternoon. Tissue samples will take longer."

Aislinn nodded. "That's fast."

Carlisle stood with her hands at her sides, dressed head to toe in scrubs, her mask hanging askew around her neck. "Sorry about your friend, Aislinn."

Aislinn was close to tears and managed a crooked smile. "Thanks."

Aislinn spun on her heels and headed for the door. She kept moving, one foot in front of the other, not making eye contact with the officer guarding the scene, her hand wiping at her eyes as she walked down the hallway. She took the stairs and stopped at the second floor to regroup.

"Darina," she whispered, her friend's tortured face forever burned into her memory. "Oh, god."

Five minutes slipped by before she could stop the image from banging around in her head. Finally she put on her professional face and made her way to the street. More onlookers had gathered by the tape and all eyes were on her as she walked to her car. She slipped in and pulled away, driving slowly until she had cleared the scene, then merged in with the traffic.

Her anger was building, trampling over the grief and shock. Aislinn's hands were shaking with rage and she gripped the steering wheel so tightly her knuckles were white. She could hear her teeth grinding and forced herself to relax her jaw before she snapped a piece off one of her teeth. She pulled off the main street and drove a few blocks then steered to the curb and turned the car off. Aislinn sat without moving, one thought running over and over through her mind. Then she said it aloud.

"I won't let you down, Darina."

CHAPTER TWO

Curtis Westcott gave Aislinn a hard look. Assigning a file to a detective with a personal connection to the case had backfired on him in the past, especially if they were too close to the victim. Underlying feelings crept in and skewed their logic, they saw things that weren't there, missed things that were. The investigator needed to be rock-solid and able to block out their anger. As the head of Homicide for Boston, which included Jamaica Plain, he needed to be sure Aislinn had been cleared of any involvement in the girl's disappearance, and that she could keep an objective eye on things before he gave her the file.

"You and Darina Volkov were friends in high school," Curtis said.

Aislinn nodded.

"This is going nowhere until you're out of the box," Curtis said. Even if Aislinn was nothing more than a witness to the events, she was still on the list of suspects. Pushing that aside without vetting and clearing her could taint the investigation and bring Internal Affairs down on the department. "I've set up an interview with another detective. You can head down after we talk."

"Okay." Aislinn got the drift. She was going to be put across the table from a seasoned interviewer who would look for the tiniest hole in her role the night Darina went missing.

"Tell me what you know about the day she disappeared," Curtis said.

Aislinn shifted in the chair facing Westcott's desk and swallowed. It was amazing how vivid her memories of that day were, even after twenty years, and her emotions were in high gear. Still, she had to be careful, Westcott was evaluating her ability to deliver a solid investigation and every word counted.

"Darina dropped by my place to pick me up about nine in the morning. We were both starving so we raided the fridge and took the food to my bedroom." Aislinn could almost taste the cold chicken and potato salad. "Darina was so excited about the prom and the after-parties. With Shane, the guy who was taking her, not so much."

"Why not?" Curtis asked.

"Our dates weren't anything special. Just guys we knew from school. There were four of us that hung around – Darina, Kayla, Sofia and me – *none* of us had steady boyfriends." She surprised herself, putting extra emphasis on *none,* like it mattered.

Curtis smiled. Aislinn was all business, his go-to detective on tough cases, and he'd never really pictured her as a high school girl with crushes on boys and all the insecurities that go with being a teenager. "Got it," he said. "So you and Darina had a bite to eat then headed out. What next?"

"Typical girl stuff. We were all in for the prom, super stoked about getting glammed up. You know, the fancy dresses and getting our hair done."

Curtis raised an eyebrow at that.

She ran a hand across her short, spiky red hair. "It was a *lot* longer and thicker then."

"Okay," Curtis said.

Aislinn grinned and stayed on her game. This was when she either sold her boss or watched Darina's file land on another detective's desk. "Darina was the outlier that day. The rest of us were happy to settle in at Kayla's, but as usual she was all over the map."

"How's that?"

"Darina had her own car, so she was the cool one. She'd drop by and pick us up and a lot of the time we did what she wanted."

"I remember those days. Got car, got control," Curtis said.

"Right. Here's how the day played out – we started at Kayla's place and then headed to Julia's on Center Street to get our hair done. It was a small shop and there were only two stylists, so we played rock-paper-scissors to see who went first and it ended up being Darina and Kayla. Sofia and I had to wait, which kind of sucked."

"What time was this?" Curtis asked.

"We arrived at Kayla's around 10:00 and were at the hairdresser by 11:00. Darina and Kayla were done by 12:30, then went next door to have some lunch. Sofia and I were cut and set by 2:00 and that's about when Darina and Kayla showed up from lunch. I think something happened while they were there, both of them seemed a bit off, but I never found out what it was."

"Off?" Curtis asked.

"Yeah, like something had gone wrong while they were eating. Darina was all wound up. I'll find out, Kayla Walsh still lives in Jamaica Plain."

The name was familiar to Curtis, there had been a sergeant named Walsh who had retired about five years earlier. "Any relation to Arnie Walsh?"

"She's his daughter."

"I knew him." Curtis smiled. "He was at A-1 precinct when I first started."

Aislinn nodded. "He came over from Jamaica Plain, one of my dad's crew."

"Okay, so this is all happening at Arnie's house."

"We went there a lot." Aislinn couldn't help a sheepish grin. "They had a swimming pool."

Curtis caught her drift. Teenagers always headed for the house with the best toys or the laxest parents – or both. "Then what?"

"That's when Darina went rogue on us. She always did shit like that. She jumped up and said she needed a beer and was going to Cody Hall's place. Headed out the front door and was gone."

"Just like that."

"Yup, she liked him and was going to make damn sure he knew it."

"But you said she was going with Shane, so Darina and Cody weren't going together," Curtis said.

"Right, Cody had already asked another girl so Darina asked Shane."

"Got it," Curtis said.

"So there we are, sitting around with our hair done, waiting for the esthetician to show up and do our makeup. Kayla's dad had headed out for his shift mid-afternoon and her mom was working as well so we had the house all to ourselves.

"The makeup lady showed up on time and got started, then Darina comes flying back in around 4:30, maybe a bit earlier. She's in some sort of tizzy, hauls Kayla into the back yard by the pool where they had a really heated conversation. They ended up yelling at each other."

"What about?" Curtis asked.

"No idea, but that was Darina, always going off on someone. I'll find out when I talk to Kayla."

"Okay, it's around 4:30. Then what?"

"The aesthetician left and we split up to get dressed. Kayla's bedroom wasn't very big and Darina was still angry, so Sofia stayed with Kayla while Darina and I went into the master bedroom. We changed and that seemed to calm Darina down quite a bit. She looked like a dream. She had a red strapless gown that fit her like a glove – you get the idea. I snapped a picture. Hold on, I gave it to the detectives so it's probably in Darina's original file."

The file was on the edge of Curtis's desk and he opened it and flipped through the contents. He came to a handful of photos, leafed through them, then held one up. Aislinn nodded and Curtis had a long look. Darina *was* stunning – she could have been a cover girl for a teen fashion magazine. Her gown was snug in all the right places and she seemed much older than seventeen with her dark hair pulled up off her bare shoulders and the professionally applied makeup. She looked out of sync with the bedroom setting, with its shag rug, wood dresser and floral wallpaper.

"She was a very beautiful girl," Curtis said, slipping the photo back in the file. *The kind that could drive a young man wild,* he thought.

"And a bit of a drama queen," Aislinn said. "Totally impetuous about a lot of things, but serious about her studies."

"A dichotomy of sorts?" Curtis asked.

Aislinn considered that, then said, "No, she was pretty consistent – usually flighty, with everything being a crisis of some sort. Except about going to college. She was level headed and excited about that, told us that she was getting out of Jamaica Plain, going to a good school."

"She had the marks?" Curtis asked and Aislinn nodded. "Okay, you were in the master bedroom getting ready."

"Right, we were sitting on the bed talking and in walks Kayla. She takes one look at Darina and then makes some catty comment about the girl Cody was taking to the prom – that she was really pretty or something like that. Darina snapped back at Kayla, then jumped up and jerked her head around and..." Aislinn paused, unsure of how to describe the look. "Her eyes were really wide, it was weird. Then she got up and stormed out. She didn't say another word, just went straight out the front door, got in her car and left us there."

Curtis waited.

"That was the last time I saw her," Aislinn said slowly, willing her voice to remain calm.

"That seems a bit callous of Kayla," Curtis said. "Mean, like it was deliberate."

"Oh, Kayla could be a bitch," Aislinn said. "She definitely had a mean streak."

"Hmm," Curtis said, considering that. "Okay, where did Darina go when she left Kayla's?' he asked.

"Kristin Sanders' house. Shane was best friends with Kristin's date so they had it worked out that they would all meet at her place and go to the prom together from there."

"Did she make it to Kristin's place?"

Aislinn nodded. “Kristin said that when Darina finally showed up she was upset and asked to use the phone. She made a call and then went storming out. Told Kristin she’d meet them at the dance. That was the last time anyone saw her.”

“Except the killer,” Curtis said.

“Yeah, except the killer.” Aislinn set her mug on the desk.

“What happened when she didn’t show up at the prom?” Curtis asked.

Aislinn’s brow furrowed ever so slightly, a hint of the guilt she carried. “We joked about her not being there – it didn’t seem sinister. She was angry and it wasn’t out of character for her to disappear. We figured she’d stood up Shane. Everyone felt sorry for him and miffed at her. Things didn’t really heat up until the next day when her mother started phoning around to find her.”

“Wasn’t Darina’s mother at the grad dinner?” Curtis asked.

Aislinn shook her head. “Our dinner was the week prior, this was only the dance.”

“Okay,” Curtis said. “So the prom was normal. No one acting strangely.”

“Nothing out of the ordinary. At least, not that I can remember.” She took a deep breath. “It was a long time ago.”

“It was,” Curtis said.

Aislinn looked him in the eye. “I really want to go back over the movements of everyone who had any involvement with Darina that night. Cody, Shane, Kristin, and Kayla especially.”

“What about Sofia?” Curtis asked. “She was with you all day and was at the prom.”

“Sofia’s parents picked her up halfway through the night. They were flying to New York to catch a redeye to London. I’ll confirm her alibi between the last time Darina was seen alive and when Sofia’s parents picked her up.”

“Well, if that checks out she can be struck off the list.”

“Right,” Aislinn said, feeling a bit strange at viewing her school friends as potential suspects. She shook it off – that was exactly the sort of emotional baggage Curtis would be watching for. "Actually, it's weird her body showing up now."

Curtis raised an eyebrow. "How do you figure that?"

"Our twenty-year high school reunion is in a few days."

"You going?" Curtis avoided reunions like the plague – you were either the type who got hyped up or hated the thought – he was definitely the latter.

Aislinn sat up. "Am now."

There was a moment of silence, then Aislinn said, "One more thing. Darina's father, Alexi Volkov, was murdered six months before she disappeared."

Curtis leaned forward slightly. "Seriously?"

She nodded. "Right before Christmas."

"Was it solved?"

"Nope."

"Now that's a shade more than interesting." He settled back into his chair. A minute passed, then he said, "You need to be sure you want this one. Things you didn't know are going to come out of the weeds. The kids you knew back then may not be the people you thought they were. Darina may not be the person you thought she was. Bad stuff will find its way to the surface, Aislinn."

"Not my first rodeo, LT," she said.

"Yeah, but this is personal. Darina was a friend at a time when that was really important."

"Yeah, I'm good."

"Just warning you," Curtis said. "It could get messy."

She stood and straightened her gun under her blazer. "They all get messy, boss."

He couldn't argue with that.

A text buzzed on his phone and he gave it a quick look. "Okay, Aislinn. Kevin Hurd is waiting for you in Room Six. Clear the interview, get yourself out of the suspects' box and it's all yours."

"Kevin Hurd." Aislinn grimaced. "Shit."

Curtis wagged his finger at her. "We'll be under a microscope if things fall apart. Having Kevin on the other side of the interview will cut any speculation off at the knees." He left a long gap in the conversation. "You need to be in the clear before you so much as *touch* that file."

"Yeah, I know it." She plucked her mug off the desk and headed for the door, then stopped and asked, "Are you going to Dad's retirement thing?"

Curtis grinned. "What do *you* think?"

She laughed at that.

"Brandy's in for the weekend."

"Nice, glad she's in town." Aislinn had met Brandy and found her smart, funny and gorgeous - *perfect* for Curtis.

"She coming?" Aislinn asked, hopeful.

"Wouldn't miss it, I'm sure."

"It'll mean a lot to Dad that you're there."

"Cian's a good guy. Damn fine cop."

"Yeah, he's that," she said and started down the hallway to the interview room where Kevin Hurd was waiting for her. As she pulled the door open and sat in the hot seat, she was sure of one thing. Curtis Westcott was on his computer pulling up the file on Alexi Volkov.

CHAPTER THREE

Darina Volkov's father had been a gangster.

Curtis scrolled through what they had on the twenty-year-old cold case. It wasn't much, but enough to warrant requesting that the paper files be retrieved from the archives and sent to his office. The facts were straight forward – Volkov had been shot in the back of the head with a small caliber gun five days before Christmas. He was murdered in the driveway of his house in Jamaica Plain, and his daughter remembered seeing a figure dressed entirely in black walk out from beside the hedge earlier in the evening, around eight o'clock. The girl had gone in through the front door and didn't see her father's car in the driveway at the side of the house. At ten o'clock his wife went out the back door with the trash and looked down the side yard. Volkov's body was face down in the snow next to his Audi.

Alexi Volkov's car door was still open when the police arrived at ten-fifteen and his body had remained untouched. The coroner estimated he'd been dead about two hours. Some attention was paid to the daughter's witness statement, as she had seen the figure about the time the coroner figured her father was murdered. She was a credible witness, saying the intruder had worn a balaclava and had a dark parka over a black shirt. Two things stood out – a wristwatch and a silver pendant that she could see under his partially open coat. The most significant part of her statement was the time, as it jibed with the coroner's estimated time of death.

What interested Curtis most was that Volkov had been murdered while on trial for racketeering, perjury and obstruction of justice. It had all the markings of a mob hit – a decision to keep Volkov from flipping and testifying against his mob connections.

Curtis had a quick look at the detectives who worked the file – Tony DeMarco and Bill Nyson. He recognized DeMarco's name, but not Nyson's. That wasn't a surprise, he had still been in law school in 2000. A lot of the guys working cases back then had already retired by the time he took over as Chief of Homicide for Boston. He exited the database – the paper file would likely yield a lot more information. Still, speaking with Bill Nyson, if he was still around, would be a good starting point. He picked up the phone and dialed Stan Lamers.

"Hey, can you find out if an of old-timer is still on the job?" he asked when Stan answered.

"Sure, boss."

Curtis glanced at the notes he'd scribbled on a Post-It note. Tony DeMarco was at the top, but he didn't bother giving Stan that name. "Bill Nyson – he was working out of Jamaica Plain back in 2000."

Curtis was well aware that Tony DeMarco wasn't on the job. DeMarco had been shot and killed in 2003 while responding to a burglary in progress. Curtis was still in law school at the time, but when he entered the department he was brought up to speed on every officer-involved death.

"I'm almost at the precinct," Stan said. "Give me an hour or two. Anything else?"

"Nah, not right now. I'm out of here."

"Cian's retirement bash?"

"Yup, you going?" Curtis asked.

"I'll try. Didn't really know him other than he was Aislinn's dad."

"Maybe we'll see you there." Curtis hung up and gathered his laptop and sunglasses. There were a lot of cops in the Jamaica Plain precinct he had never met, which meant Curtis expected to see a lot of new faces at the pub.

Jamaica Plain was a different world from central Boston, grittier despite its recent gentrification, and with more of a sense of community. Locals from JP, as it was affectionately known, tended to stay and the neighborhood had a vibrant, colorful feel to it. Aislinn was no exception, she'd grown up in JP. She knew every alley and backstreet bar, and had an enviable list of contacts she could pump for information. Aislinn worked a lot of the JP murders and her intimate knowledge of the neighborhood was part of the reason he had decided to let her take the Darina Volkov case, providing she cleared the interview. All of that, and the fact that he didn't see her emotions getting in the way of running a thorough investigation had him hoping she cleared the interview.

He spotted Stan in the parking lot walking from his car to the precinct door and veered toward him. The man was hard to miss – six-four with a shaved head and eyes so intense a vampire would think twice about biting.

"Aside from digging up info on Nyson, you got anything else on the go?" Curtis asked.

"Nothing pressing. Why?"

"It's Friday. How about I give you a lift to Cian's party. It'll mean the world to Aislinn that you made it."

A few seconds passed, then Stan said, "Aw, what the hell, why not."

"Great, I just need to stop by my place and pick up Brandy."

Stan raised an eyebrow and grinned. "Well done, LT."

"Hmmm," Curtis said, not sure exactly how to respond.

The drive from downtown Boston to Back Bay was quick and while Curtis ran in to get Brandy, Stan texted a contact at the precinct and requested the information on Bill Nyson. He shifted to the back seat and watched Brandy as she came down the steps from Curtis's brownstone toward the car. She was full figured, tanned from the Napa Valley sun, and walked with just the right amount of sway. She broke into a wide smile when she spotted Stan in the car, and when she got in she twisted and leaned over the seat.

"Stan, so good to see you."

"You as well," Stan said, staring into her eyes. Deep teal, almost translucent, they were captivating. "Good flight?"

"Long, but worth it," she said, grinning at Curtis, who had slid in behind the wheel.

Back Bay to Jamaica Plain took half an hour and parking was impossible. They found a spot two blocks away and hoofed it back to Galway House, where a uniform cop saw them approaching and blocked the entrance with his arm.

"Private party," he said.

Nothing about Curtis, with his thick, jet-black hair and Brandy on his arm, said *cop*. "So me and my buddy can't come in?"

The cop took a look at Stan's jeans and untucked Motley Crue T-shirt, then doubled down. "Like I said, private function."

Curtis and Stan both pulled their creds at the same time, waited for him to have a good look, then laughed and pushed by the unfortunate sot who got stuck on door duty. Inside the place was packed with half the Jamaica Plain police precinct. An upbeat tune rocked the sound system and everyone was talking loudly to be heard over it. Stan recognized a coroner with whom he'd worked on a recent case and tapped Curtis on the arm. He pointed at her.

"Hey, I'm going to get a few minutes with Janet. I never get to talk to her unless we're at a crime scene."

"Right," Curtis said. "We'll find Aislinn and Cian."

"Talk to you later," Stan said, heading off and squeezing his massive frame through the throng.

"This is fun." Brandy beamed as they threaded their way to where two bartenders were moving fast, sweating just trying to keep up.

It was Curtis's first time in the bar and it seemed like the perfect place for a proud Irish cop to have his retirement party. The walls were deep red and a row of filled-to-the-brim booths ran parallel to the long, wooden bar where cops in their civvies were queued up three deep. Hundreds of bottles of every imaginable hard liquor lined the wall behind the bar and they were going down fast.

After a wait in the queue they backed off, drinks in hand, and found an open spot not too far from the bar. Curtis gave Brandy a welcome-back kiss. "Missed you."

"Missed you, too," she said. "Did *not* miss this weather though. Too humid."

"Nah, this is good. Napa's too dry," Curtis said, pulling her tight against him as a guy tried to squeeze through. "Maybe crowded places are a good thing."

She pushed in ever tighter. "Oh, they definitely are."

Curtis scanned the room for Aislinn and spotted her standing next to a picture of Johnny Cash on stage, middle finger up at whomever took the picture. They started over, subtly elbowing their way through the mostly-male throng of cops and ex-cops.

Aislinn was talking with a group of men about her age, all of whom were hanging on her every word. There must have been a punch line because they all started laughing and she looked pleased her joke had gone over well. She shifted her tall, lean frame slightly and looked Curtis's way, like she could feel someone was watching her. He nodded and she broke into a wide grin when she saw Brandy, and waved at them to come over.

"Brandy," she said, giving her a hug.

"Everyone – my boss – Curtis Westcott," Aislinn announced. "And his definitely better half, Brandy."

"Boston brass in JP, must be a big deal," a guy named Chad crowed, looking like he'd had a few too many.

Curtis wasn't going to bite. "It's Cian's night, wouldn't miss it."

"Be nice," Aislinn said to Chad, her tone shutting him down on the spot.

"Your dad around?" Curtis asked.

"Yeah, he's in the back. Let's go." She threw Chad a piercing look as she spun to leave.

Curtis tailed her and saw men's eyes flick around to have a quick look as she passed. He wondered what it would be like to go through life with the opposite sex always checking you out. By the time they reached a nook in the back of the bar he had decided it would be a royal pain in the ass.

"Hey, Dad." Aislinn kissed him on the cheek and then moved back a touch so he could see Curtis.

"Lieutenant Westcott," Cian said, grasping Curtis's hand.

If there was ever a case of the apple not falling far from the tree it was here. Aislinn's shock of short, red hair was exactly the same color and length as her dad's, and both had thin faces with sparkling green eyes. A few wrinkles creased the elder Byrne's cheeks and forehead, but for sixty he was still pounding it.

"Cian." Curtis tried not to wince at the strength of the man's grip. "It's Curtis now. You're retired – remember?"

Cian had a hearty laugh at that. "I'm already bored. Need another detective up there in A-1?"

"Nah, nobody ever gets murdered in Boston," Curtis said, glancing at Brandy. "Cian, this is Brandy Eagleson."

"Brandy, you're the gal from Napa, the one who helped break open the Charlebois case." Cian gave her an approving look. "Aislinn told me all about that one. God, what a monster."

"He was a bad guy alright," she said, shuddering. That was an understatement. "I just helped out a bit, it was all Aislinn and Stan and Curtis."

"My girl, the detective." Cian grinned and hugged his daughter, pride emanating from every pore.

The music changed and the new song, *Welcome to the Jungle* by Guns N' Roses, was loud enough to shut down the conversation for a minute. Cian finally stuck his head around the corner and yelled for the bartender to *turn the fucking music down*, then tucked back into the corner with Curtis and his daughter.

"Oh hell, here comes trouble," Cian said, grinning as a group of three men about his age appeared out of the crowd.

All three were dressed retro for Cian's big night – bell-bottom pants, open shirts, and flashy pendants on thick chains. The rail-thin one was even wearing a long-hair wig. They looked completely ridiculous.

"Curtis, Brandy, these are the mongrels I'll be golfing and playing cards with. Ken Smith, Arnie Walsh, and Larry Toews. Nothing but a waste of skin, these three."

"Arnie, good to see you." Curtis motioned at the man's drink. "Still nursing the whiskey, I see."

"You got it, baby," Arnie said, clinking his glass against Curtis's beer bottle.

Curtis couldn't help smiling. Arnie was well known at A-1 for his stylish clothes and the ever-present drink in hand when off the job, and people joked that he reminded them of a blond-haired Dean Martin. He turned to the other two men. "Were you guys on the force?"

"Dorchester," Ken said, brushing aside strands of hair from the wig. "Retired five years ago, thought the ticker was going to pack it in." He patted his chest. "Worried my wife wouldn't even notice I wasn't around."

That got some laughs and Curtis shifted to Larry, the only one without a drink.

"Spent some time in Central," Larry said, "but transferred to Roxbury about twenty years ago."

"Before my time," Curtis said. "Open bar and you're not drinking?"

"Training for my next triathlon."

"He's an *elite*," Ken said, making quotation marks. "But he only does it to stay in shape so he can keep up with us on the golf course."

Larry grinned, revealing slightly crooked teeth. He gave Aislinn a playful elbow. "What's on the books now?"

Aislinn glanced at Curtis and he nodded. "Darina Volkov. Her body showed up today."

That stopped the conversation in its tracks and Cian took a step back. "Darina."

Aislinn nodded, watching and taking the temperature of the room.

"Holy shit." A pregnant pause, then Cian said, "I remember there was talk that she might have committed suicide."

"Yeah, not likely," Aislinn said. "Unless she drywalled herself inside an electrical chase."

Even talking to her dad she kept the fact that the body had been encased in poly under wraps. It was holdback, an intimate piece of knowledge that only the investigators and the people at the crime scene were privy to.

"Jesus," Arnie said. "Does Kayla know?"

Aislinn wasn't surprised that Arnie Walsh's first thoughts were of the effect this could have on his daughter. "Not yet, but I'll be in touch soon. We need to piece together Darina's movements, and she spent time at your house on prom day."

"That whole thing really messed Kayla up," Arnie said. "Hell, all of us."

Cian took a long, hard look at his daughter. "Brings back a lot of memories." He leaned closer to Curtis and asked, "Is she all right to work it?"

"Not sure," Curtis said. "She's in the box right now, had her interview, needs to be cleared." He didn't need to explain any further, everyone knew that if Aislinn was a witness she needed to be vetted prior to working the case.

Cian touched Aislinn on her shoulder. "You need to give this some serious thought. A lot of stuff is going to come out when you start digging."

"Yeah, I know, Dad. Big girl now, remember?"

Curtis glanced at his watch, then stuck out his hand and said, "Cian, the department just lost a great guy." He jerked his head toward the group of three. "Good luck playing cards with these sharks."

Cian fake-grimaced. "Lose money to these bandits? No way."

That drew some raucous comments from the crowd and Curtis took the moment to detach himself and Brandy from the group. He gave Aislinn a quick nod of the head for her to follow them, and when she caught up, he said, "Kevin gave me a call."

"And..."

"Said he grilled the hell out of you."

"And..." Aislinn's heart was pounding.

"He cleared you. Congrats."

"Jesus, LT," Aislinn said, letting out a lungful of air.

Curtis just smiled and took Brandy by the hand. They worked

their way through the crowd until they found Stan entrenched in a noisy group, and looking like he'd had a couple.

"I'll grab an Uber tonight," Stan yelled over the din.

Curtis and Brandy stopped to chat a couple of times on the way out, then escaped onto the street. They started walking to his car, talking quietly, her hand warm in his.

"That cold case, the one with the girl Aislinn knew," Brandy said. "It sounds awful."

"They're all awful," Curtis said. "The difference is, this one's personal for Aislinn."

"That has to be tough," Brandy said as Curtis opened the car door and she slipped in.

"Well, that's her job. It's going to shake her up a bit, but I think she'll be okay." Curtis hoped he was right.

CHAPTER FOUR

After being cleared to work the case on Friday, Aislinn created a case file and sent a request to the records department for information on Darina Volkov's June, 2001, disappearance. The response from records arrived early Saturday morning – Lieutenant Westcott had been sent the original file and he had given his approval for her to access it from his office. She walked down the hall and found it on his desk, right where it had been the day before. She took the folder back to her cubicle, holding it tightly so the photos didn't fall out.

Aislinn headed through the deserted bullpen to the coffee room and got a pot going, then sat at the window while it brewed. The view was mostly a handful of faceless government buildings, but she focused on the squat, ugly one that housed the US Immigration Court. It was a modern day Ellis Island for immigrants trying to gain a foothold in America, a feat much more difficult in 2021 than five years before. Everything had changed, and in her opinion, not for the better. She wondered if her father, who had come from Ireland clutching his parents' hands at three years old, would get the green light now. Nothing in her life would be the same if they had been denied entry almost sixty years ago.

Thinking about it all depressed her and she shuffled off to pour her first coffee. Mug in hand, she settled into her chair and flipped open the file on Darina Volkov. Four photographs slid out and landed on the desk. Aislinn picked them up and took a long, hard look. There were two prints from Sofia's camera, and two from hers, all taken on the day of the prom. Sofia's shots were in the back yard by the pool, one with Aislinn bent over and laughing at Kayla's shoes, and another of all four of them posing. Sofia had used the timer on her camera to take that shot.

The last two, the pictures Aislinn had taken, were not as generic as Sofia's. One had Darina sitting on the bed, and then there was the one she and Curtis had looked at on Friday, with Darina standing and posing in her dress. It had been snapped a few moments before Darina ran out of Kayla's house, and there was little doubt it was the last photo of the girl before she was killed. Aislinn stared at it for a long time, intense feelings of sadness washing over her as she thought back to that day. *If only I'd known what was coming, I could have stopped you.* It was a ludicrous thought, and eventually she set the pictures aside and dug into the paperwork.

The cover page, duly filled out in blue ink, explained the basics – Darina Volkov was seventeen years old at the time and had gone missing on Friday, June 15, 2001. Her mother insisted it was out of character and that Darina was not a runaway. Her father, it noted, was deceased, although the cause of death wasn't listed. That struck Aislinn as odd, considering he was murdered six months prior to his daughter's disappearance. There was another annotation on the file, that Tony DeMarco and Bill Nyson were assigned to the case as they were the team who had worked Alexi Volkov's murder, and if there were any links they would be most likely to notice.

The file showed that Darina had some college money with her that day, but no indication of the amount. A handwritten sidebar said that it was possible the missing girl had used the cash to leave Boston and hit the road. Aislinn highlighted that and made a note to follow up on the missing money.

The address of the family home was listed and Aislinn could still picture the pale blue two-story house with its white trim. She'd be seeing it again soon, when she visited Darina's next of kin, Tania Volkov. What wasn't listed was the pink, stuffed unicorn sitting on Darina's pillow, the Linkin Park posters on her walls, and the bright blue backpack filled with her schoolbooks. The case file was clinical, with very little personal information about the missing person. The investigating detectives concentrated on only the relevant facts, but it seemed callous. She straightened up and gave her head a shake – her subjective voice was creeping in already. She got up and wandered back to the coffee room to clear her head.

When she returned, Aislinn went to the second page of the report, which was filled with handwritten witness statements. Darina's mom, in subsequent interviews, had shed surprising little light on things, simply saying her daughter had left the house early the morning of the prom and hadn't returned home. There was nothing suspicious about that, as Darina had told her mother she was getting dressed at Kayla's. The neighbors on one side were in the garden and saw her leave in her red Mazda, noting that she'd waved from the curb, gown in hand, and smiled. That was consistent with the sort of mood a teenager would be in on prom day, and the detectives noted that it indicated her state of mind.

The next witness statements were from school friends who had been with her that day. The first was Kayla Walsh, the drop-dead gorgeous one in the group with her long blond hair, Barbie doll body, and perfect white teeth. But she was sketchy – a liar and manipulator who would throw you under the bus in a moment if it suited her. She used people, especially boys, twisted them to get exactly what she wanted. That had always struck Aislinn as odd, since Kayla's dad was a well-liked cop who worked out of the same precinct as her own father. Aislinn had never trusted Kayla and was immediately wary of what she had told the detectives.

Since Aislinn had actually been there on the day, she brought a critical eye to the reports. According to Kayla, Darina had shown up at her house with Sofia and Aislinn around 10:00 and they had killed an hour before heading to the hairdresser. She and Darina had gone first, then headed next door for burgers and fries. The talk, she said, was about the upcoming dance. Kayla noted Darina wasn't happy about going with Shane Collins and called it a mercy date. Darina had laughed and said he wasn't getting anywhere with her, no matter how much he spent. They finished lunch, linked up with Aislinn and Sofia, then drove back to Kayla's house. Kayla made a best-guess that it was around 2:15 when Darina suddenly announced she was going to Cody Hall's house for a beer. Then she was gone.

Cody Hall. Aislinn sat back and closed her eyes, picturing him with his wild, curly hair. Cody was into smoking pot and drinking, which set him apart from the rest of the group. Still, he had this incredible charisma and a great sense of humor, and that kept him in the mix. Bottom line on Cody was that anyone and everyone liked the guy and he was welcomed everywhere he went. While Darina always worked hard and kept up her grades, she also dabbled in drugs and loved a drink, all of which played well with Cody. He could be talked into cracking a beer anytime of the day, and Darina sometimes called him and hooked up for an afternoon session. Apparently, prom day was one of those occasions.

Cody's statement jibed with Kayla's, in that she arrived at his place around 2:30 and turned down an offer of homemade nachos, saying she had just eaten. They had a beer and talked about the upcoming dance. Darina mentioned that she wished they were going together, then left to check in with Shane Collins, her date. Cody figured she left his place at about 3:30.

The next interview on the page was with Shane, whom she remembered well. Aislinn felt a wash of empathy course over her as she thought of Shane and his nightmare of a home life. Mother drunk by noon, father showing up every now and then to beat his wife or his kids, Shane fending for himself. He left home right after he graduated and enlisted in the army. No surprise there, he was in cadets during high school and looked just like the marines on the posters. The last she heard of him he had been deployed to Iraq in 2003.

Shane's witness statement was concise, matter of fact and to the point, and the first one to shed some light on Darina's mental state. It was obvious he knew he wasn't her first choice as a date. She was upfront about what to expect that night, and it didn't include a romp in the back seat of his car. More importantly, he felt Darina was still struggling with her father's death and graduation had exacerbated her upset. The bottom line according to Shane Collins – she was depressed.

Aislinn set the report on her desk and sipped her coffee. Shane's armchair diagnosis of where Darina's head was at the time of her disappearance was believable. If anyone could grasp depression and angst it was Shane Collins. If he was right, the initial direction the case had taken – that she may have committed suicide – was sort of understandable. Still, that tack had led to a less than stellar investigation, and it was obvious now that suicide should have never been an option.

"Suicide – that's ridiculous," Aislinn said out loud. "Darina looking like a million bucks, ready to show up at the dance and give Cody a taste of what he was missing. No chance she would miss *that* opportunity."

She kept reading.

Shane offered an answer to the obvious question of how he had reacted to Darina standing him up. He admitted to being miffed, angry even, but had gone to the dance fully expecting her to be there somewhere. When she didn't show by halfway through the dance, he left and went home. His parents were having a brutal fight and he took it for a while, then ducked out and headed to the after party. That left a huge gap in his timeline for the evening with only his parents as his alibi. Aislinn spent a few minutes searching for them and when she came up empty she tried the obits in *The Globe*. Both of them were there, his mom dead almost fifteen years and his dad less than two.

"Shit," she whispered.

Shane was angry with Darina when he left the dance, which gave him motive, and now he had an unsubstantiated alibi. That went to opportunity. He easily had the strength to drag a body up three flights of stairs, which gave him means. Means, motive and opportunity –

the three essentials to committing murder. Still, she knew Shane and he wasn't the kind of guy to lose control like that.

"Keep it objective," she said to herself. "He's a suspect."

Aislinn picked up the report and stared at the name on the next witness statement. *Aislinn Byrne.* It felt odd to read what the detectives had jotted down from the interview almost twenty years ago.

Byrne was in the group of four friends and present for much of the day. She attended the hairdresser and then returned to the Walsh residence with the other girls. She did not accompany the subject when she left the Walsh house at 2:30 to visit Cody Hall. Byrne was at the Walsh house when Darina returned at 4:30 to have her makeup done, then spent time with her while they were dressing for the upcoming dance. Darina changed from jeans to a red dress and high heel shoes and left immediately after for Kristin Sanders' house. Byrne said she noticed the subject was "upset" when she left, and thought the reason may be that Darina was unhappy about who she was going to the dance with. Byrne considered a reliable witness.

Aislinn reread the words. *Byrne considered a reliable witness.* She got up and walked to the window and stared out. The sky had darkened and the clouds were low and threatening. She crossed her arms and rubbed her shoulders, shuddering as she thought back to the moment when Darina jumped off the bed and bolted out the door. She closed her eyes and the scene played out like it had happened yesterday.

* * *

Friday, June 15, 2001

PROM HAD FINALLY ARRIVED, and the girls were all in. Fresh back from the hair salon they were ripping the cellophane off their dresses and unboxing their shoes.

"No, not there," Kayla said when Darina set her dress on the bed. "No room."

Darina snatched her dress off the bed. "C'mon A, let's find somewhere else to change." She threw Kayla a sideways look, sharp as a dagger. "The big cats can't be in the same cage."

She huffed off and Aislinn grabbed her dress and shoes and trailed her down the hall. Behind them Kayla was loudly staking claim to her bedroom and insisting it was the best place to get dressed. Darina veered off into the master suite, dropped her high heels on the rug and stood in the center of the room, one hand on her hip the other holding her shimmering prom dress.

"Now this is better," she declared. "Right, A?"

Aislinn nodded, her thatch of red hair moving about with the motion. "Much better."

Darina tossed her dress on the bed and stretched her arms over her head. "All this fuss." She spun on her heels to face her friend. "I'm not sure Shane is worth it."

"Maybe not," Aislinn said, "but you look beautiful. I think a lot of guys will be checking you out."

She kicked that around for a few seconds, then brightened. "You're right. My last shot at knocking some socks off before I leave for college."

Aislinn sat on the bed and started unbuttoning her blouse. "That's going to be great – you heading off to college."

Darina's smile was contagious. "Oh, it's going to be the best, A." She plopped down on the bed. "I have my tuition money and offers from four of five colleges I applied to. I'm getting out of JP."

Aislinn's smile faded a bit. "Nice for you."

Darina grabbed Aislinn by the shoulders and stared straight into her eyes. "You don't have to stay. You're smart and have good grades. You can get out of here."

"JP's not so bad," Aislinn said. "Twenty minutes to downtown Boston."

"I like Boston," Darina said without letting go. "But it's not New York."

"Is that where you're going?" Aislinn asked, snuggling her toes into the shag rug.

Darina finally let go of Aislinn and grinned. "Not sure. I have options."

She jumped to her feet and shed her top and jeans in two decisive moves, then slipped into her dress. “Zip me, A.”

“Sure.”

The zipper was a bit tricky because the dress fit so snugly, but after Aislinn got it through the tough spot it went to the top no problem. Darina turned around and posed. The satin fabric hugged her curves and the deep red color was vibrant against her black hair. She threw back her shoulders and gave her friend the toothiest smile she could muster.

“Oh, my God, you look fantastic,” Aislinn said. “No, no, better than fantastic. Like a dream.”

“Thanks, A. Put on *your* dress.”

Aislinn slipped out of her casual clothes and pulled on her gown. Her father had balked at the price tag, but her mother had put her foot down hard. *Graduation happens once, Cian.* And so she had left the store with the nicest piece of clothing she had ever owned. Sapphire blue with a handful of tiny cream-colored embroidered beads, it *was* stunning. Her body hadn’t filled out like Darina’s or Kayla’s, but her slim waistline and shoulders suited the dress.

“Oh, A, look at you.”

Aislinn blushed and stood, giving her new gown a twirl. “Feeling good,” she said.

“Looking good.”

Darina sat on the edge of the bed and slipped into her shoes. Aislinn sat beside her and picked up her camera, then snapped a shot. “Hey, you need all of me in that picture,” Darina declared, standing up.

Aislinn stayed on the bed and lined up the shot. “Perfect,” she smiled as Darina sat down to fix her other shoe.

The door swung open and Kayla burst in. “Ah, here you are, in my parents’ room.” She gave Darina and her dress the once over with a disapproving eye. “Little tight isn’t it?”

Darina craned her neck around and shot Kayla a nasty look, which only served to fuel Kayla’s mean girl rant.

“Too bad Cody’s going with Emma and all,” Kayla crowed. “I’ll bet she makes Cody *really* happy tonight." She winked at Aislinn, whose freckled skin took on a tinge of color.

Darina jumped up and stopped dead in her tracks. She seemed unsure, then her eyes widened and anger lit up her face. She stormed past Kayla and gave her a solid shoulder bump, then slammed the front door on her way out. Kayla stared down the hall for a moment, then looked back at Aislinn, still sitting on the bed.

"Looks like someone can't take a joke." Kayla turned and disappeared down the hall, in the direction of her bedroom.

Aislinn sat on the bed, alone and wondering what the hell had just happened.

* * *

Present day

AISLINN'S EYES flashed open and she let out a lungful of air as the final images of that afternoon played out in her head. Twenty years had passed and it was all still so vivid. God, some things never left a person.

Aislinn finished her coffee and hoofed it to the staff room. She poured another coffee, added cream and sugar and stirred it in, then returned to her desk and dove back into the file. The final witness who had seen Darina on the day she disappeared was Kristin Sanders. A shiver ran up Aislinn's spine – Kristin was an ice queen, cold and calculating, who never took on anything without an agenda. She had few, if any, close friends, and was more of an interloper than a member of the group. Interloper or not, Kristin had played a central role on prom night because Shane and Kristin's date were best friends and the two couples were riding to the dance together.

According to the notes in the file, Darina had shown up at Kristin's house around seven o'clock. She was decked out for the prom in her bright-red satin strapless gown with matching high heels, upswept hair and fresh lipstick. But Kristin described her as "distressed", fumbling about and shaking, unable to settle. Shortly after arriving she asked to use the phone and made a call in private that lasted a few minutes. When she returned to the living room there was no masking her anxiety. She told Kristin she had to leave and ran out the front door, squealing her tires as she pulled away from the house.

Aside from the killer, it appeared that Kristin Sanders was the last person to see Darina alive.

Aislinn spent another hour on the file, making notes on how DeMarco and Nyson had worked the case. They had chased numerous leads, all dead ends. Even the phone number Darina had called from Kristin's house, possibly their best angle, was thought to be untraceable at the time. Aislinn sat back and thought about that. Technology had changed, but even back in 2001 the phone company likely had the tools to track calls and Aislinn was leaning toward the lack of a trace on the number as sloppy work by someone involved in the investigation. She made a note to follow up on that.

Eventually, DeMarco and Nyson had pushed the file to the side of their desks as new ones rolled in. Aislinn couldn't fault the detectives, they had to move on in order to keep up with their workload. It was how things worked in missing persons and homicide. Not every case got solved.

Aislinn took one last look through the photos, lingering on the two shots she had taken of Darina at Kayla's house, then she closed the file and signed onto the website for The English School in Jamaica Plain. She clicked on the link for the upcoming reunion, now only a week away, and entered her details. Her finger hovered over the *enter* button for a long time. All the memories of high school flooded back – feeling awkward, self-conscious of her flaming red hair and being so skinny. Puberty, adolescence, boys, drugs, drinking, one of the popular girls warming up to her and then telling everyone that Aislinn was her bitch. All the fun and the tears of her teen years about to be resurrected. But now, she was a murder cop. She asked the questions, she had control.

Aislinn hit *enter*.

"Nobody's bitch now," she whispered.

CHAPTER FIVE

Saturday morning Curtis made breakfast in bed, complete with pancakes, eggs, toast, and steaming coffee. Brandy elbowed her way up on the mattress as Curtis stacked the pillows against the headboard and tucked in beside her.

"Sleep well?" he asked.

She gave him a nod and a grin. "I was tired from the flight and then Cian's party."

He smiled. "Thought you might be."

She put a touch of jam on the toast, took a bite and when she was finished chewing, said, "That's kind of creepy, Aislinn getting called out to the scene and being confronted with her friend's corpse."

"Yeah, it is. I can't remember anything like that happening, not since I've been with the force."

She finished one of the eggs, poached medium to perfection, and said, "Her dad is nice. And those friends of his. Goodness."

"They're characters all right." He chuckled. "Back in the day Arnie Walsh was a sergeant, Ken and Larry were officers, working the beat."

"Well, the party was fun. Thanks for taking me."

"Hey, you fit in so well."

She managed a hint of a smile. "I don't know how you do it, Curtis. I really don't. The whole thing with Renee, it was so horrible."

Curtis thought back to the case he was working when he met Brandy – Renee Charlesbois had been abducted by a killer on a mission – and figured Brandy was right. Pretty much everything about murder was ugly – the corpse, inconsolable family members, the lies, the dirt they dug up – but then there was the solve. The one thing that made up for all the wear and tear that went with working the cases. Retribution for the victim, the one person who couldn't do anything to bring their killer to justice.

"It *was* horrible," Curtis said. "But you were awesome. Wouldn't have cracked it without your help."

She smiled at the compliment. "And now this one with that girl who went missing on prom night."

"Darina Volkov," he said. "Her father was a bad guy, into a bunch of illegal stuff. He got himself shot in the back of the head and Darina saw someone in black clothes and a balaclava leaving the scene. It's probably what got her killed six months later."

"That's sad."

He stretched out beside her, careful not to spill the coffee or tip the tray. "I have to go in for a bit today if that's okay."

"Of course." She broke into a wide smile. "If you drop me off at Copley Place I can walk home if I wrap up before you."

"Done," Curtis said. "Sure you don't mind?"

"No, take care of things then call me." She picked up her fork and dug into the remaining egg. "I'd better eat, I'll need my strength to carry all those shopping bags."

They finished breakfast and Curtis dropped Brandy at the upscale mall, then drove to District A-1 with Barclay, his black Lab, hanging his head out the rear window. Every Saturday morning Barclay was at the front door, tapping a paw on the carpet, waiting. He loved the car and the precinct was even better, a virtual cornucopia of treats and affectionate pats on the head. This week was no different and by the time they reached Curtis's office, Barclay's belly was full and he slipped under the desk for a well-deserved snooze.

Curtis sat in his chair, careful not to tread on Barclay, and signed into the Boston Police database. Aislinn had submitted her request for Darina Volkov's file on Friday, before she left for her father's party. No surprise there, he thought, glancing at the empty spot on his desk where Darina's file had been sitting. A new email was waiting and it was the file on Alexi Volkov, Darina's father. Curtis opened it, sent it to the printer and leaned back in his chair with his dog curled up at his feet as the document rolled off the LaserJet.

Tania Volkov, wife to Alexi and mother to Darina, had seen her share of grief. Husband murdered, daughter missing, the woman must have been shattered into a thousand pieces. Now, adding to her misery, the missing daughter shows up murdered. Curtis didn't believe in coincidences – when things looked like they might be linked they often were. Alexi Volkov being shot in the back of the head had all the markings of a gang killing, and his daughter getting murdered and plastered inside a wall six months later was too much of a coincidence. Curtis had a gut feel they were related. How and why were the obvious questions.

Mob hits were designed to scare people into submission, deliberate in execution with the body left in a highly visible spot. It was rare for a witness to step forward and everyone knew if they crossed the gang they would pay for it. Somehow, Alexi had pissed off the mob and reaped the rewards. That killing was tenable, but a teen girl wasn't. The mob didn't often kill police, prosecutors, judges or women. It was an unwritten rule and something exceptional must have happened for someone to cross the line. It made sense that the murderer would have hid the body, repercussions for killing an innocent seventeen year-old would be severe.

Barclay stirred slightly when Curtis got up to pull the file off the printer. Curtis gave him a scratch behind the ears and sat down, settling in to have a go at it, line by line. Three minutes later he sat bolt upright, eyes wide. He read on for a minute, then grabbed his cell phone and dialed a familiar number.

"Curtis, this is a nice surprise." His mother's voice was smooth and calming.

"Hey, are you home for a while?"

"Your dad and I are both here."

"Can I stop by? I'd like to have a chat."

"Of course," she said. "When are you coming?"

"Leaving now."

"Wonderful. See you soon."

Curtis ended the call, tucked the file under his arm and headed out to his car with Barclay in tow. The twenty minute drive to Brookline took him to another world, filled with lush trees, quiet winding streets, and massive homes. Landscaping crews were at work, trimming the expansive lawns and grooming shrubs. Curtis pulled into his parents' driveway and hopped out. Richard and Janis Westcott were in the garden behind the house, sitting on the patio reading the newspaper. They both perked up when he came around the edge of the house and Barclay bounded over to meet them.

"Good morning." Janis smiled and scratched Barclay behind his ears.

"Hey, Mom." He gave her shoulder an affectionate squeeze. "Dad."

Curtis dropped into one of the padded chairs. He enjoyed the visits, especially in the summer when the yard was in bloom. It stirred good memories of his youth, when his friends would drop in and they'd spend hours playing football on the grass. He asked his mom and dad how they were doing, what was new, and caught up on things. Then he angled his chair so he was facing his mother.

"Got a few minutes?" he asked. "I have an interesting file on my desk."

Her curiosity was immediately piqued. "Of course."

"Alexi Volkov. Name ring a bell?"

She gave Barclay a last rub, then sat back in her chair and took a deep breath. "You know it does."

"You were the presiding judge for his trial on racketeering charges," Curtis said. His mother had been on the bench at Suffolk County Superior Court for almost thirty years, her career focused on criminal cases from the Boston, Winthrop and Chelsea areas of Massachusetts.

"Racketeering, perjury and obstruction of justice," she corrected him. "He was a piece of work."

It didn't surprise Curtis that his mother remembered the case. "And then he was murdered. Halfway through the trial. *That* doesn't happen every day."

Richard Westcott peered over his glasses, suddenly interested in the conversation, then removed them and settled in to listen.

"No, it doesn't," Janis said. "The DA was building a solid case against him on racketeering charges. Volkov had mob connections, but he wasn't what I would call an inside guy. He was on the outside looking in, hoping to be accepted."

"By whom?" Curtis asked.

Janis shrugged. "As I recall he'd made some inroads with the Irish and the Russians, but the Italians kept him at arm's length. Volkov was working the field and trying to get something to stick. He wanted to be a player but was having trouble breaking in."

"He was Russian, right?" Curtis asked, then continued when his mother nodded. "So why didn't the Russians want him?"

"Volkov had a way of alienating people. He was pushing too hard to make an impression and some of the stuff he did made the decision-makers nervous."

"What sort of stuff?" Curtis asked.

"Oh, like beating people up for no reason. One guy owed him money, paid up, and Volkov put him in the hospital for "being late"." She used her fingers as quotation marks.

"So he was sabotaging his own success."

"Pretty much." She picked up her cup and took a sip of coffee, then said, "You're likely wondering who killed him."

"I am."

"Well, that's a good question," she said. "It certainly looks like one of the crime syndicates took him out. BPD assigned two homicide detectives and they requisitioned the trial transcripts. I spoke with them numerous times." She glanced up and her eyes narrowed. "Tony DeMarco was one, I can't remember the other man's name."

"Bill Nyson," Curtis said.

"That's right. They seemed competent and I got the feeling they were trying hard to work out who killed him. Honestly, I think there just were too many variables and not enough cooperating witnesses for them to get there. They told me every time they approached any of the organized crimes guys they got shut down. No one would talk."

"Typical," Curtis said. It was always a problem on homicides that were linked to the mob.

"Why is this one on your radar?" Janis asked.

"His daughter, the one who disappeared a few months after he was killed. They found her body a couple of days ago, stuffed inside a wall in a building in Jamaica Plain."

"I remember that," Richard piped up. "It was all over the newspapers back then."

"Really," Janis sighed, disgusted by the killer's callousness. She'd seen enough crime photos while on the bench to envision how awful it was. "You think they're linked."

Curtis shrugged. "Aislinn is working the daughter's murder and I thought I'd take another look at Alexi's file."

"Christ, Curtis," his father snorted disapprovingly. "This job of yours."

Curtis took a deep breath. "They don't kill cops, Dad. Besides, I'm poking around on a twenty-year-old case. I'm no threat to them."

"Still," Richard mumbled.

"I could use some of that coffee," Curtis said, pointing at his mom's cup and heading for the patio doors. He returned and visited a bit more with his parents, this time catching up on all the latest neighborhood gossip. Michelle was having an affair and Tom caught them by the pool, Mandy was accepted to a nice college, Leroy crashed his car into a tree, Jacquie and Mark were thinking about selling and moving into a condo. And on, and on.

He listened, interested but detached. The leafy, affluent streets of Brookline were from his past, now his days were spent in a spartan office where the pictures on the wall were crime scene photos. He didn't miss the trappings of his youth and considered himself lucky that he'd found something he loved doing and was good at. Police work – especially murder – was gritty and unsettling, but cutting through the chaff and getting to the truth that was often deeply buried was enough for him. He thrived on the methodical, precise approach to solving the crime. He liked being a cop.

When his mother was finished updating him on the latest news, Curtis gave her a hug and nodded to his dad, then followed Barclay back to his car. He drove slowly along the street and couldn't help but shake his head when he drove by Michelle and Tom's house, wondering if it would be going up for sale soon. Tom and Michelle were more his age than his parents' and he'd spent plenty of time by their pool. It wasn't hard to paint a mental picture of the whole thing.

He checked the time and gave Brandy a quick call on her cell. She was content to spend another hour at the mall, so he headed for the office to reopen Alexi Volkov's investigation. They had a few active murders on the books, but the workload was manageable. Taking on two cold cases wasn't going to affect things much.

"Twenty years," he whispered to himself. "This should be interesting."

CHAPTER SIX

Curtis figured Aislinn would be in the office and she didn't disappoint. Easy to spot, her bright orange shirt was a dab of color in the humdrum beige and brown of the bullpen. Hunched over a sheet of paper with a list of names on it, she looked up when he rounded the corner.

"LT," she said, dropping her pen on the paper and leaning over to give Barclay a rub. He was over the moon to see Aislinn and his tail thumped loudly against her desk. "Didn't expect to see you today."

He held up Alexi Volkov's file. "I have something to work on."

She laughed, Westcott never sat on his hands. "New case?"

"Old one. Alexi Volkov."

She straightened up a bit and smiled. She'd called it. "Thought you might work that one."

Curtis perched on the desk next to Aislinn's. "Two murders, same family, six months apart. It reeks of collusion."

"That's what I'm thinking," Aislinn said. Barclay was poking her with his nose and she got back to petting him.

"Maybe you can help me a bit here," Curtis said. "You were good friends with Darina. How well did you know her parents?"

"Not very, she was the one who always went to other kids' houses, nobody went to hers. At least, not very often. I remember talking with her mom a few times and she seemed okay, but a bit disinterested. Like she was just putting in time talking with you until she could get back to watching television. I hardly ever saw her dad, he was always out."

"What was he like?"

"He spoke with a heavy Russian accent. Kind of scared me to be honest. He had these dark eyes and he stared without blinking. It was creepy."

"Darina's mother – Tania Volkov – when are you going to see her?" Curtis asked. "I don't want to overlap."

"I already stopped by to let her know we found Darina's body. She was in no condition to talk and I told her I'd drop by later. I'll get what I can from the other witnesses who saw Darina on prom day then pay Tania another visit."

Curtis nodded his approval. "I imagine that back in the day you knew about Darina's dad being up on racketeering charges."

"Yeah, of course," Aislinn said. "Darina was embarrassed by the whole thing so we didn't talk about it much. But we both knew what was going on."

"Makes sense."

"It was a regular topic at the dinner table, Dad telling me to be careful."

"Hanging around with Darina?" Curtis asked.

"Right, but it wasn't a problem. Darina was excitable and a bit of a diva, but she studied hard and had her head screwed on."

"You want something weird?" he asked and she nodded. "My mother was the judge on Volkov's trial."

"Holy crap. Really?"

"Serious."

"Did she have any thoughts on who shot him?"

Curtis shook his head. "No one specifically, but she figures it was a mob hit. Alexi was mixed up with the Russians and the Irish but he was sort of persona non grata. She suspects he pissed someone off and they took him out."

"Sounds about right," Aislinn said.

Curtis smiled at her. "Well, now you get to figure out how this extends to Darina." He pointed at the printout on her desk. "What's that?"

"I got a list of everyone attending my twenty-year high school reunion. I'm checking to see if the four people who saw her on prom day are coming."

"Are they?" Curtis asked.

"Yup." She held up a note pad with a few names. "Three of them are attending. The fourth is Kayla Walsh, she's not going but she still lives in Jamaica Plain."

"That's handy." Curtis held up Alexi's file. "Let's run the investigations independently and share information." He gathered up Barclay and started to leave, then asked, "All signed up for the reunion?"

She grimaced. Attending a few events would get her access to the list of attendees without having to flash the badge and a chance to speak with Cody, Shane, and Kristin without bringing them into the precinct.

"Looking forward to it?" He grinned, knowing she wasn't.

"Yeah, can't wait." Sarcasm dripped.

Curtis glanced at his watch. "Brandy's shopping at Copley Square. I'm on borrowed time before I have to pick her up."

"*Go*," Aislinn said.

"Just need to check on a couple of things."

Aislinn gave him a chastising head-shake. "She's not here every weekend."

"I know," came the response from the hall.

Aislinn touched her keyboard and her screen lit up. She signed into the city planning department using a special app available to the Boston Police and entered the address where Darina Volkov's body was found. There was a building permit from 2001 and she opened it. Shiba Contracting had pulled the necessary construction permits and she scrolled down until she found the company representative who had filled out the forms. Bert Collier. She tried the number listed next to his name but it was disconnected. No surprise there. A quick

Google search found a construction company named Shiba Contracting based in South Boston, but the link to their website was a dead end. She switched back to the city portal and searched for a business license. The last one issued was in 2008 – nothing since. The company had likely been dissolved.

Social media was next, and she typed Bert Collier into Facebook. Six profiles popped up on her screen and she glanced through them. One fit nicely – a man in his sixties with numerous posts on fixing things around the house. His residence was listed as Charleston, South Carolina and after a couple of minutes on the national police database she had his address and phone number. She dialed and a man answered.

"Is this Bert Collier?" she asked.

"Yes, who's calling?" His voice sounded weak and he seemed out of breath.

"This is Detective Aislinn Byrne with Boston Homicide. Were you involved with Shiba Contracting back in the early 2000's?"

There was a noticeable pause, then he said, "Yes, I owned it. Had to sell because of health concerns. What's this about?"

Aislinn wondered what sort of nasty lung condition the man had developed from ripping apart all those old buildings. "I need some information on a job you did back in 2001. It was an office on the third floor of a building at Center Street and Seaverns Avenue in Jamaica Plain. Do you remember it?"

Another long pause, then he asked, "When was this?"

"June of 2001."

"Oh, yeah, that was for a dot-com. They wanted an open concept with..." He started coughing and it took almost a minute before he was ready to keep talking. "Sorry about that."

"No problem."

"They wanted everything open, no offices. Lots of Internet connections and power stations. Heavy duty routers, that sort of stuff."

"Any reason you remember it so well?" she asked.

"Yeah, one of my subcontractors, the HVAC guy, was pissed off at the architect because she didn't leave enough room in the chases for him to run his ducts. He was a real piece of work – set fire to her blueprints. That triggered the sprinklers and we had the cops and fire guys all over us. It caused a ton of damage and the place was a goddamn crime scene for three days while they sorted things out." A long coughing bout followed.

"So a lot of people would have known there was construction work going on."

"Everyone in the neighborhood. I'm telling you, it was a real mess."

"Do you remember if the drywall contractor had finished when all this happened?" she asked.

"Um, let me think." A few seconds passed, then he said, "The drywall was up but probably not taped or mudded. I'm pretty sure because that was when the HVAC guy realized the chases were too small."

"How did you fix it?"

"We found him some extra room on a different wall."

"Not in the center of the room?"

"No, definitely not. There was a small electrical chase running next to a metal structural column in the middle of the floor, but the rest of the room was wide open."

"And was the electrical chase at the same stage of drywall as the rest of the room?"

There were a few long, deep breaths, then he said, "It must have been. The drywall guys like to do all their mudding and taping at the same time. They were moving quick, trying to get finished, so they would have got the first coat of mud on the day after installing the drywall."

Aislinn made a note of that. If the drywall had gone up on the day of the prom and the crew had sealed it with mud the next day, then Darina's body was put in on prom night.

"You're sure of that," she said, wanting confirmation.

"Absolutely. The guys worked the weekend to get it ready for priming and painting."

She put an exclamation mark next to her scrawl. That narrowed down the time of Darina's death to sometime on Friday night. Bert Collier was proving to be a good resource.

"How about access to the site while the work was ongoing?" she asked. "Did you have a master key or a lockbox?"

"Lockbox with a combination. A bunch of guys had the combo, probably twenty or more."

"Can you get me a copy of the permits for the job, plus a list of the guys who had access to the combination?" That would give her the full scope of workers coming in and out of the construction site. She recited her phone number and email address for him.

"I'll have the permits tucked away in a file, but I'll be guessing at names if they aren't on the permits."

"Okay, Bert, let me know when you're sending that over," Aislinn said. "Thanks, you've been really helpful."

"What's going on?" he asked.

Aislinn considered not telling him, but the story was going to hit the news at some point and he'd been a hell of a good source of information. "The space is being renovated and they found a body in the electrical chase."

"Oh, shit," he said. "Oh, shit, that's awful."

"Yeah, sure is. Thanks again, and take care of yourself and that cough."

"Will do."

Aislinn tapped her pen on the desk and looked at her notes. It would have been better if only a few people had known about the construction. She could identify and interview them and see if there were any connections to the Volkov family. But with the entire neighborhood aware of the renovation it made the list impossibly long. Plus, there was no way anyone else was going to remember the details like Bert Collier, whose company had been caught in the dispute between the HVAC guy and the architect. There was no doubt that anyone tied in with organized crime in Jamaica Plain would have known exactly what was going on the moment the crime scene tape went up. Chasing witnesses along that line was going to be a long and arduous process, but one that could produce tangible results. She'd get a couple of juniors from the bullpen to work that angle when Bert's list came in.

Aislinn checked her email and found a welcome message from the organizing committee for The English School's Twenty-Year Extravaganza. It was signed by Becky Oliver and Aislinn wracked her brain trying to picture her. Eventually a face emerged from the haze – a bubbly, talkative girl whose clothes never seemed to fit quite right. Aislinn vaguely remembered Becky as liking to volunteer for things and chairing the committee for the yearly river cleanup. It made sense she would be helping to organize the reunion.

The schedule of events was included and Aislinn printed it. She had little desire, none actually, to attend any of the events. Aislinn tucked the schedule in her file and pulled out the page with the four friends who had seen Darina on the day she went missing. Kayla Walsh, Cody Hall, Shane Collins and Kristin Sanders. She scanned the list, stopping at Kayla's number, then dialed, her foot tapping out a steady rhythm on the worn carpet as the call connected.

CHAPTER SEVEN

Saturday be damned, Curtis needed to talk with Stan Lamers. He dialed Stan's number and when the big man answered he sounded hungover. Stan strongly suggested a half hour to wake up, get some coffee, and check his phone for any info that might have come through on Bill Nyson.

"Fifteen minutes," Curtis replied. "I need to pick up Brandy at Copley." Promptly on the quarter hour, Curtis called back.

"Jesus, LT," his detective said. His words were clear now and he sounded awake. "I'm still drip drying."

Curtis shook his head, trying to dislodge the fleeting image that had snuck through.

"Hang on." A few seconds passed as Stan slipped into a bathrobe, then, "Okay, heading for the kitchen and that coffee."

"How did things go last night," Curtis asked. "You were having fun."

"Hey, open bar at an Irish pub." Stan laughed. "Even talked with Aislinn's dad for a while. He's a nice guy."

"He is." Curtis had gotten to know Cian fairly well over the years through Aislinn. He shifted to the reason for the call. "Did you get anything on Bill Nyson?"

"I did. Oh shit, hang on again." There was a thump, like the phone had hit the floor, then Stan's voice bellowing from across the room. "Whoa, no metal in the microwave." This was followed by some distant mumbling, then Stan again, "It *is* metal. You're old enough to know better." More mumbling, footsteps and Stan was back. "Sorry about that. Kids. He was about to reheat a take-away container in the microwave."

"Yeah, not a good idea," Curtis said.

"Sometimes I wonder how there are any boys left in the world. They're walking accidents."

"Right. About Nyson..."

"Nyson died in 2015, natural causes, and his partner at the time of the Volkov investigation was Tony DeMarco, who was shot in 2003 responding to a burglary in progress."

"Do you have the particulars on DeMarco's death?" Curtis asked

There was a slight rustling of paper, then, "It was a break-in at an electronic shop in JP and DeMarco was the closest guy to the action." There was a tinge of disbelief in Stan's voice as he continued. "So DeMarco heads over and goes in without backup or a vest. Took two 9 mm slugs to the chest and died at the scene."

That set Curtis back in his chair. Everything about DeMarco's response to the break-in was wrong. "Brutal."

"Yeah, no kidding. A lot of shit hit the fan over that, cop getting killed and all."

"I can imagine," Curtis said. "Send me everything you have on it."

"Will do."

"One more thing," Curtis said. "If I wanted to talk to a couple of wise guys who were in the know back in 2001 – one Russian and one Irish – who would they be?"

There was a long pause, then Stan said, "I have some thoughts on that but let me check with Vice first and get back to you. Want to make sure I give you the right names."

"Yeah, that's a good idea."

"Anything else?" Stan asked.

"That's it for now. Go ahead and finish drying."

Curtis set his phone on the desk and stared out the window, Barclay watching him with one eye open, one eye closed. The sun was climbing and people were out and about enjoying the warm weather. He got up and walked over to Aislinn's desk with Barclay in tow. She was on the phone and he waited, listening in on the tail end of the conversation.

"Tomorrow then," Aislinn said. "George Howell at two-thirty."

She hung up and dropped the phone. "Not looking forward to that one."

"Do you have your interviews lined up?"

She nodded. "Everyone who saw Darina on the day she disappeared. That was Kristin Sanders."

"You're meeting her at George Howell, just around the corner?"

"Her choice – she's in from New York and staying at the Godfrey, so it's an elevator ride for her."

"You'll get more out of her than was in the original file," Curtis said.

"Exactly, maybe Darina said something that didn't seem important at the time. The usual stuff." She pointed at her notes. "Found out from the owner of the construction company that the site was a crime scene for a couple of days and pretty much everyone knew the offices were under renovation." She explained about the angry tradesman setting fire to the architectural drawings.

Curtis raised an eyebrow at the story. "Now that doesn't happen every day."

"Nope." Aislinn snapped her notebook shut. "And...he was adamant that the drywallers sealed the wall on Saturday, which means Darina went in on Friday night."

"He's sure?" Curtis asked.

"Absolutely – the exact word he used."

"Well that nails down her time of death to the night of the prom. Good work."

Aislinn pointed at her watch and gave him a disapproving look. "You're going to be late."

"C'mon, Barclay, let's go get Brandy." Curtis snapped on his leash and hustled to the elevator. He angled across the parking lot to his car and Barclay jumped into the back seat as Curtis pulled out onto the street and rang Brandy's cell.

Brandy was surrounded by clothes in the change room when she answered his call. "I need about twenty minutes," she said. "You're welcome to let me know what you think of what I'm trying on."

Not a chance, Curtis thought. *Much too easy to make a foot-in-mouth comment.*

"Hey, there's one more thing I'd like to do and it'll take about half an hour. Call you when I'm done?"

"Oh, perfect," Brandy said. "We can grab some lunch."

"I'm all for that," Curtis said, killing the call and pulling a U-turn.

Traffic was light and it was a painless drive to the house where Alexi Volkov had been shot. Curtis glided up in front of a faded blue two-story set back from the street and partially hidden by two massive, gnarled willows. A gutter was broken and hanging by a lone screw and a sea of dandelions poked through the uncut grass.

Curtis walked up the driveway, crime scene photos in hand. It was hemmed in between the hedge on one side and the house on the other, and with no windows on the side it was possible Volkov's daughter could have seen his killer leaving the scene without knowing the car was there. An occasional vehicle drifted down the street, but mostly the road was quiet. The further Curtis walked up the drive the more secluded it felt. The hedge was so thick that Curtis figured even twenty years ago, in the depths of winter, it would have obscured the end of the driveway from the street. He held up a photo and moved a bit so he was in the exact place where Volkov had been found, lying face down on the asphalt. The road was completely hidden.

It had been a set up. Volkov's killer was waiting in the shadows for Volkov with every intention of killing him. What the killer hadn't expected was for Volkov's daughter to show up at the exact moment he walked out onto the sidewalk. *An eyewitness that had to be removed six months later?* Curtis wondered.

The back door opened and a woman stood on the porch looking at him. "What do you want?" Her voice carried a distinct Russian accent.

Curtis held up his badge. "Boston Homicide. Are you Tania Volkov?"

"Yes." Volkov's widow leaned on the railing, scowling. "First Aislinn, now you. All these years, *now* you show up."

He stood his ground without responding, knowing from experience that her initial surge of anger would dissipate.

"Why are you here?" Tania asked.

"We're looking into your husband's murder," Curtis said.

"All of this because someone found my daughter's body?"

"They could be linked," Curtis said. "We're not sure at this point."

Tania slipped a pack of cigarettes from her pocket and lit one. The smoke curled around her dark-rimmed eyes. "You couldn't find his killer twenty years ago, how will you now?" Her voice was biting and accusatory.

Curtis wanted to tell her that twenty years ago he had been a law student with no intent to join the murder squad, but instead said, "Sometimes new evidence comes to light, Mrs. Volkov." He waited a minute, then asked, "The night Alexi was killed, you didn't hear or see anything?"

She shook her head. "Nothing."

"Your husband's car was in the driveway for a couple of hours before you found him."

"It was winter. The doors and windows were closed. It's very private along the side of the house."

"Yes it is," Curtis said, looking about. "What about Darina? She told the detectives that someone had come out from behind the hedge as she approached the house. Can you tell me about that?"

"He startled her, all dressed in black with his face covered – she wasn't sure where he had come from. Darina came in through the front door and didn't think any more about it until we found Alexi's body."

"She said this person had a chrome wristwatch and a silver pendant on a chain."

Tania shrugged. "And..."

"Do you have anything to add?"

She shook her head.

"How was it that you found Alexi?" Curtis asked.

"I went outside," she started, her voice now cracking with emotion. A minute passed, then she tried again. "I went outside with the trash and saw him lying in the snow."

"Where were you prior to going outside?"

"In the living room, watching television." She dropped the cigarette on the deck and ground it out with her heel. "If that's everything..."

"One more thing," Curtis said. "Your husband had connections to organized crime. What can you tell me about that?"

Her face took on a distinct shade of red. "Alexi was a good man. I know nothing about that." She turned and walked into the house, letting the screen door slam shut behind her.

Curtis was halfway down the driveway when his phone buzzed. He checked the caller ID, it was Stan Lamers. "Hey, what's up?"

"Got some names for you," Stan said.

"Nice work. Who are they?"

"If you want to find out what the Russian gangs were up to back in the day, talk to Dimitri Kalatonov. He's running a strip club, still in things up to his elbows."

"I know Kalatonov," Curtis said. "Who's the Irish connection?"

"Patrick O'Reilly. He's almost seventy now and retired. Good source though, according to Vice. He'll talk to you, but there are lines he won't cross."

"Of course. Probably why he's still alive."

"Yeah," Stan laughed. "A seventy year-old gangster. That should be fun."

"Oh, they never change." Curtis took a last look around the driveway. "Set up the interviews, Stan. And let's do it on their turf, not at the station."

"You got it, LT."

"Thanks, Stan. Good work."

"What about the Italians? You gonna talk to them?"

"I am," Curtis said as he walked back to his car. Barclay's head was hanging out the half-open window and he let out a short, excited bark when he saw Curtis. "I'll call Giuseppe Salvatore myself. We've met."

"Salvatore. Nasty piece of work. Lucky you."

"Yeah, lucky me." He killed the call.

Curtis slipped his phone into his back pocket. A murdered wanna-be Russian gangster. A dead cop who worked the file. The gangster's daughter killed and wrapped in poly and crammed into the wall of a construction site that had been a crime scene.

Nothing ordinary about this one, he thought as he started the car and headed for Copley Square.

CHAPTER EIGHT

Judging from the avalanche of shopping bags, Curtis figured Brandy had emptied at least one store in Copley Square.

"You've had some success," he said, jumping out of the car and taking a good portion of the bags from her.

"Immeasurable." She grinned and her eyes sparkled. There was no denying her enjoyment in finding clothes worth taking home. "I'll model for you...if you want."

"Oh, I do," Curtis said, then quickly added, "Thanks for being so understanding about me going in on Saturday. I wanted to stay out of the office but this new case of Aislinn's is going to take some serious work."

"Her friend," Brandy said. "Murdered and crammed in a wall. It's like something out of a horror movie."

His mind was alive with the nuances of the new mystery facing them. Why was Darina murdered, and why did her killer risk putting her in the wall rather than simply taking her to some field and dumping her in a shallow grave? And why prom night? There would be a reason – there always was.

"Yeah," he said after a short break. "One of the scary movies you wished you'd never watched."

"You promised lunch," Brandy said.

"And I have just the place in mind."

After a relaxing stint on the patio of Curtis's favorite restaurant they returned home and he opened a bottle of Chardonnay. He sat on the couch in his sunny living room as Brandy paraded in and out with her new clothes. She had an off-the-rack figure for a five-seven woman and everything fit. He had his favorites and made sure she knew which ones they were. As did Barclay, wagging his tail with great abandon at every new offering. When the fashion show was over, Brandy joined him on the couch with a glass of wine.

"Question," she said, then continued when he nodded. "Are you just going to leave that check stuck to the side of your fridge?" She sipped her wine and snuggled in closer to her.

"Ahh, that," Curtis said.

"It's a hell of a bribe. Your dad really wants you at his law firm."

Curtis smiled. "Well put, and he does. He sees it as a signing bonus of sorts."

"Right, your law degree."

Curtis toyed with the handle on his mug. Law school had never been his idea, he'd gone because he didn't *have* a plan.

Curtis let out a long sigh. "It's tempting, Brandy. I'm not rich, and that's a lot of money, but I just can't do it. Some days I wish I could."

"I don't think the Renee Charlesbois case would have ended the way it did if you were working at a law firm. No one else could have deciphered those clues in time to save her."

"I suppose." A long, cold chill ran down his spine. She was right and they both knew it.

"Let's do something fun today," Brandy said.

"Like what?" he asked.

She pulled back a bit and gave him a warm smile. "Boston is *your* city, I'll handle the fun things when we're in Napa. This is on you."

Curtis thought about that, then said, "I have an idea. Oh, God, I have a great idea."

* * *

AISLINN HAD BEEN antsy all day.

The upcoming interview with Kristin Sanders had her stomach in knots, something that was foreign to her these days. When she conducted an interview she had control. Witnesses and suspects couldn't throw her off her game, but this was different. The school reunion was dredging up some long forgotten feelings. Kristin Sanders, Aislinn thought, was giving her a touch of teenage angst.

Kristin was more than just the ice queen. She was beautiful, intelligent, and brimming with confidence. Aislinn had logged onto Kristin's Facebook page, secretly hoping that her hips and ass had ballooned out like a puffer fish, but the opposite was true. Kristin was almost unchanged and her profile indicated she was a New York CEO with an MBA from Brown University.

"Damn," Aislinn muttered.

Aislinn was seated next to a bank of windows in the trendy George Howell coffee shop when Kristin Sanders entered. She spotted Aislinn and headed across the room, no change to the expression on her face. No smile as she sat down, just a nod.

"You're looking well," Kristin said, motioning to the server. "Coffee, please."

"Kristin," Aislinn acknowledged.

"How is it you're still in Jamaica Plain?" Kristin let the last two words tail off.

Aislinn ignored the comment. "Thanks for coming."

Kristin laughed – it sounded shrill, condescending even. "I got the feeling I didn't have a choice."

Aislinn gave her the tiniest of shrugs. "Yeah, there is that."

The server stopped by with coffee and Aislinn watched closely as Sanders added a packet of stevia and stirred. There were tiny lines at the edges of her eyes and the flawless skin had a thin layer of skillfully applied foundation. Her lips were slightly enhanced, barely enough to notice, but it said *Botox* in quiet whispers. Aislinn wondered what Kristin looked like without her paint.

"So you're a detective," Kristin said after sampling the coffee.

"I am. Homicide."

"The real thing." Kristin sat back with her cup cradled in her hands.

Yeah, Aislinn thought, *I'm the one who breaks people who lie to me.* "This is about Darina Volkov."

"Yes, you mentioned that when we spoke," Kristin said. "What about that?"

"We found her body the other day." Nothing more, just that.

"Oh, I didn't know." A flash of something passed across her face, then the mask was back. "What happened to her?"

"She was murdered."

A long silence settled over the table. Finally, Kristin said, "I don't imagine you're going to tell me how. I know you cops are very guarded about things like that."

"Are we?"

Kristin laughed. "Well, on television at least."

"Yeah," Aislinn said, her anxiety ebbing. "But this isn't television." She waited a bit, then said, "I want to talk with you about the night Darina went missing."

"Okay, what do you need to know?"

"Anything you can think of. What did you two talk about when she came to the house? How long did she stay? Who did she call? What frame of mind was she in?"

Kristin took a small sip of coffee and set the cup on the table. "She was in a flap when she arrived. Shaking and totally distracted, but she didn't seem to want to talk about it. I got the feeling she was about to flip out." She dabbed her lips with a napkin. "But then that was Darina, wasn't it?"

Yeah, that was our drama queen, Aislinn thought, a tinge of guilt creeping back through the cracks as she thought of how unbothered they all were by Darina's absence the night of the prom.

"She sat on the couch for a few minutes," Kristin continued, "then said she needed to make a phone call. *Private,* she insisted, and I showed her the phone in the den. She shut the door and I went off to get dressed. When she came out she was really upset."

"Did she say why?" Aislinn asked.

"No, she headed straight for the front door and said she had to leave. I watched her run across the street in her dress. She actually smoked the tires when she drove off."

"What was she driving?" Aislinn asked.

"Her red Mazda," Kristin said. "What ever happened to it?"

"Don't know." There was an entire section in the file on the hunt for the car. No trace of it had ever turned up. "Did she say *anything* that would give you a clue who she called or what was on her mind?" Aislinn asked.

"No, nothing."

"Did she make the call on a landline?"

"Yes, the home phone."

"Do your parents still have the same number?"

Kristin smiled. "Of course. Why would they give it up when they both have cell phones?"

Aislinn felt herself relax even more as Kristin warmed up to her. Jesus, how could this woman still have so much control over her, even after all these years. "My parents too. What's with their generation?"

Kristin laughed and glanced at her watch. "I have a meeting in twenty minutes."

"I'll need your cell number." Aislinn made a note in her book as Kristin recited.

"Lastly, fill me in on your movements once Darina left your house," Aislinn said, pen still poised over paper.

Kristin didn't say *So I'm a suspect,* but it was written all over her face. "I waited at home, alone, for about an hour until Shane and Eddie, my date, arrived. I told them about Darina leaving in a huff and we weren't sure what to do. We sat around for a while, maybe half an hour, then left for the dance. We went to an after party until about 1:00, then Eddie drove me home."

"What about Shane? Did he go to the after party with you?"

"No, he left the dance early. He was *not* happy."

Aislinn stopped writing and gave Kristin a confused look. "You took Eddie's car from your place, is that right?"

"Yes."

"So Shane didn't have wheels," Aislinn said.

"Actually, he did. Eddie and Shane drove to the school and dropped Shane's car in the parking lot before coming to my place. That way he and Darina wouldn't be relying on us for a ride after."

"Okay." She started to close her notebook, then said, "Were your parents at home when you got in from the after party?"

"They were."

"And they can verify that?"

Kristin looked full-on irritated at that. "Yes," she answered tersely. "I suppose you'll need their contact information as well."

Aislinn nodded. "I have their landline but I need their cell numbers."

"Yes, of course you do."

"Good, that's it for now." Aislinn jotted down the numbers and tucked her notebook in her blazer pocket.

"Are you going to any of the events?" Kristin asked, regaining her composure.

"Maybe, not sure. I'll see what my schedule is like. How about you?"

"Oh, all of them. Especially the big dance on Saturday night. Wouldn't miss it."

"So you're staying for a few days," Aislinn said.

"Flying out on Sunday." Kristin stood and smoothed her silk blouse so it fell just right over her slightly ripped jeans. "Nice seeing you, Aislinn."

"Likewise."

Aislinn didn't move for a bit, replaying the conversation, pulling out the parts with meaning. There had been a momentary reaction when she told Kristin they had found Darina's body, but that was to be expected. It had been twenty years and any news of that sort would be a shock. Still...

Then there was Kristin's attempt to stereotype detectives as secretive, like the ones on television. Was Kristin up to her old tricks and trying to trivialize the job or was there more to it? Aislinn wasn't sure if she was reading something into nothing. Kristin's version of things was consistent with her witness statement so nothing new there, but Aislinn had gleaned a couple of new things from the interview. First, if it checked out, Kristin had an alibi. Second, there was a gap in Shane Collins' timeline for the night – an unexplained break that would have given him enough time to kill Darina and hide the body.

She glanced about. The café was getting busy with customers filtering in from the hotel and Aislinn left some cash for the coffees and headed out. She caught her reflection in a wall mirror near the door and slowed as she passed. No makeup, no silk blouse, no pumped up lips or highlighted hair. Just a youthful face where freckles had once lived. *Time,* it occurred to her, *was treating her well.*

There was a lightness to her step as Aislinn walked to her car. Kristin Sanders had been the dreaded one, the girl with the upper hand who made those around her feel small and insignificant. That hadn't happened, despite some underlying insecurities she had held her own. She still wasn't happy about attending the upcoming reunion, but felt she was ready to meet the others who had seen Darina on that fateful day – and find out what sort of adults they had grown into.

CHAPTER NINE

"Remind me again how we got here," Brandy said as they approached the security gate for the Boston Yacht Haven.

"I called Chloe Harrah looking for theatre tickets," Curtis said. "Sure as hell didn't expect this."

Ahead of them yachts bobbed in the gentle sway of harbor waters and the lights of East Boston reflected off the bay. The sun had set and all around them the city was glowing, its sidewalks filled with couples strolling hand-in-hand and friends out for dinner and drinks.

They reached the gate where a woman dressed in a crisp white uniform greeted them. "Curtis Westcott for Chloe Harrah."

She checked a printed sheet on a clipboard and stopped at his name. "Do you have identification with you?"

"Of course." Curtis provided a driver's license which was studied closely and returned.

"Ms. Harrah's boat is on Dock B, slip 11." She pointed. "That way."

"Thanks."

Slip 11 was at the far end of the dock where the big boats lived. The deck lights sparkled and a handful of guests were mingling on the upper deck, drinks in hand. Curtis estimated the yacht at eighty feet, give or take. Not a super-yacht, but capable of ocean travel. He knew from talking with Chloe at one of her infamous house parties that she used it mostly to cruise up and down the Eastern Seaboard, stopping in at The Hamptons, New York and West Palm Beach. *I like to be within swimming distance of the shore,* she had told him with a smirk, *just in case.*

"Are you sure I got all the tags?" Brandy asked as they reached the gangplank.

"Relax," Curtis said, giving her new outfit a last look over. "You look incredible."

A smiling young man checked his iPad for their names and welcomed them aboard. Curtis felt Brandy's grip on his hand tighten as they strolled across the crowded aft deck to a bar, tucked under the overhang from the upper level. They both left with a Stella Artois, sweat beading on the cold glass in the warm, humid air. Brandy poured hers into a mug and Curtis opted to drink from the bottle.

Brandy leaned against the railing as the boat pulled away from the wharf, watching the eclectic crowd with an appreciative eye. "How do you know Chloe?"

Curtis thought about that. "Not sure, really. I think the first time I met her was through my parents, and then she started inviting me to her parties. She collects people and keeps them in her orbit, which is substantial."

Brandy's eyes locked onto a well-known celebrity. "No kidding. Is that who I think it is?"

Curtis took a quick look. "Absolutely."

She glanced at him. "So if you're in Chloe's orbit, then you're an interesting person."

"Trust me, I'm on the bottom rung of that ladder. Chloe gets some kind of perverse enjoyment out of having a homicide detective around."

A slim, birdlike woman in her seventies came down the stairs to the main level and spotted Curtis. She smiled and headed for him. "And there she is," Curtis said.

"Curtis, who is this exotic creature?" Chloe asked.

"Brandy Eagleson, Chloe Harrah."

"My dear," Chloe said, grasping Brandy's hand. "You have the *most* beautiful eyes."

Any trepidation in Brandy melted away as the two women launched into a conversation. Others joined in and soon they were a rowdy group of eight with opinions and laughs flying back and forth. One of the women asked Brandy where she was from.

"Napa. I work at Frog's Leap," she said.

"Oh, I love your slogan." The woman snapped her fingers. "Got it. Time's fun when you're having flies."

Brandy grinned and sipped her beer, leaving a trace of lipstick on the glass. She glanced at Curtis – the pride in his eyes said it all.

"This one," a man perched by the bar said, holding up a wine bottle. "Laughing Stock Vineyards – Blind Trust Red. What are your thoughts on it?"

"Ahh," Brandy said. She launched into the story of the Wall Street couple who retired and bought a Canadian winery, then gave their head winemaker absolute discretion over the blend, like the executors running a blind trust in the financial world. She paused, then added, "Full bodied, robust taste. Absolutely lovely."

That started a conversation about wine with Brandy in her element. Chloe slipped in beside Curtis, took him by the elbow and maneuvered him away as her yacht drifted past the glittering waterfront. They moved through the crowd easily until she sidled up to a mid-fifties man with black hair, greying at the temples, and serious eyes. More formally dressed than the others, he was the only one wearing a tie and looked a bit out of his element.

"Curtis Westcott, this is Elian Perez, your soon-to-be Police Commissioner."

Curtis nodded. "Good to meet you."

The commissioner turned to face him. "You as well."

Chloe looked quite pleased with herself and headed off to mingle with her other guests.

Perez was new to town and Curtis steered the conversation to Los Angeles, where Perez had been on the police commission for almost two decades until being poached by Boston. Eventually, Perez set his empty glass on the table and looked Curtis in the eyes.

"I understand you're a bit unconventional," he said. "I'd like to know what that means."

Curtis considered his options. Perez was coming on board in less than a week, which meant every department at BPD would report to him. Curtis could play it safe or be brutally honest and let Perez know that to him, politically correct wasn't always the best route. There really wasn't an option.

"It means I'll go after the truth, whatever it is."

Perez wasn't sure how to respond, then it sunk in. "Some things are sensitive, detective. They need to be handled carefully."

"Agreed," Curtis said. "But never at the expense of the truth."

"That's a line in the sand?" Perez asked quietly.

Curtis finished his beer and set the bottle next to Perez's glass. "Money, influence, power – all that fades during a murder investigation."

Perez's eyes were guarded. "All right, good to know where you stand." He looked around. "I should find my wife."

Curtis smiled. "Sure, nice meeting you."

Curtis found Brandy in the same conversation pod as Chloe's movie star friend and she seemed to be more than okay with that. The evening slipped by and when Curtis checked his watch it was after one in the morning. They caught up with Chloe, thanked her for the invite and slipped off the boat, which had docked an hour earlier. They walked back to the car, Brandy excited about the one-on-one conversations she'd had, and making the drive to Back Bay animated and fun. Curtis steered onto his street, deserted at the late hour, and slowed to a crawl.

"You were wonderful tonight," he said.

"I had fun," she replied. "I really like Chloe."

He broke into a wide grin at that. "Yeah, she's pretty special. I called her once to get some information on a case and she sounded hopeful that she might be a suspect."

Brandy burst out laughing. 'Oh, God."

Curtis touched the opener and the garage door started up. "There's something I have to do tomorrow morning."

She shook her head. "Do your thing. I'm sleeping."

Curtis pulled the car into the garage and the door closed. Even in the darkness, tiny bits of light caught and reflected in her deep teal eyes. He reached out and took her hand, not wanting her ever to leave.

CHAPTER TEN

Sunday morning dawned with a dreary mist hovering in the cool air and Curtis turned on his windshield wipers for the drive into South Boston. He didn't need Google Maps, every longstanding Bostonian who worked out knew where Peter Welch's Gym was. A lot of Tier One boxers had trained in the ring with the giant shamrock on the canvas. He pulled into the parking lot and locked his car. South Boston had gentrified over the years, but this section was still a bit gritty.

The gym was surprisingly busy – a sparring match between a couple of welterweights was underway in the main ring and it had attracted a handful of spectators. A few others were working the bags or skipping rope. Curtis stopped at the reception desk and asked for Patrick O'Reilly.

"Are you Curtis Westcott?" she asked, glancing up at him.

"I am."

"He's in the back, under the flag." She went back to her computer screen and resumed typing.

Curtis hugged the edge of the room, staying out of the way of the boxers and weightlifters. A mild sweaty odor tickled his nose and the constant sound of leather gloves hitting canvas bags followed him as he walked. He spotted three men sitting in the corner near a flag pinned to the wall – one was older with a thatch of thick silver hair and the other two looked like muscle. Patrick O'Reilly, the legendary gangster, was waiting for him.

Curtis angled over and said, "I'm Westcott."

O'Reilly gave him a hard look, then nodded to his bodyguards. They backed off a few feet, keeping their eyes on the newcomer. Curtis sat across from the aging mob boss with a good idea of whom he was facing. O'Reilly had come up the ranks in the Winter Hill Gang when Whitey Bulger was at the pinnacle of his power and the Irish controlled loansharking, extortion and bookmaking in Southie, as South Boston was commonly known back in the day. Under Bolger the gang expanded into arms and drug trafficking and truck hijacking, in all of which O'Reilly played a key role. To top things off, Vice suspected O'Reilly of complicity in at least twelve murders. There was little doubt he was still very dangerous.

"Boston Homicide," O'Reilly said. He scratched his heavily creased cheek with a shaky hand. "Not just any detective either. I get a visit from the head of homicide." He leaned forward a couple of inches, but even that felt menacing. "Am I in trouble?"

"Should you be?" Curtis asked.

O'Reilly's face was emotionless, not even a twitch.

Curtis could play it one of two ways – take control of the conversation and threaten O'Reilly with the wrath of the law or be a nice guy. It was an easy choice.

"I need some help on a cold case," Curtis said.

"How cold?" O'Reilly asked with a trace of an Irish accent even though he'd come over to America as a plucky eight year old.

"Twenty years. You probably had your ear to the ground a bit back then. You know, before the Big Dig, when Southie was still Southie."

The Big Dig had gentrified South Boston by connecting it to Logan International and the city's business district. Some liked the change, some hated it. Curtis had a pretty good idea which side of the fence O'Reilly was on.

O'Reilly settled back into his chair and smiled. "That fucking tunnel, nothing but a conveyor belt filled with rats in suits." He waved his hands in disgust. "Some asshole developer came in and converted the Collins mansion into condominiums. Fucking condominiums, can you believe it? Destroyed a landmark, they did."

"Hmmm," Curtis said.

O'Reilly, his rant over, stared at Curtis for a minute. "What do you want to know?"

"We're looking at Alexi Volkov's murder. He was shot in his driveway back in December of 2000. Know anything about that?"

"Volkov," he said. "Why would I know anything about some Russian guy?"

"He was trying to break in with Winter Hill or one of the Russian syndicates. Didn't have much luck from what I can see."

O'Reilly shook his head. "Don't think I knew him." He didn't sound very convincing.

"Somebody took him out halfway through his trial on racketeering and extortion charges. Then a cop working Volkov's murder got killed a couple of years later."

"Oh, fuck," O'Reilly said. "The Tony DeMarco thing."

Curtis was surprised to hear DeMarco's name on the tip of O'Reilly's tongue. "Yeah, that's the one. What do you know about it?"

"Just that you guys were all over us, like ants when someone steps on their nest. Shut down a lot of our...business interests...for a long time. Your guys at the top wanted answers and when they looked back at the cases DeMarco had worked they saw Volkov's name. That's when things got totally out of hand."

Curtis had figured O'Reilly knew Volkov and there was his confirmation. "Well, a cop getting killed and all."

"We don't do that," O'Reilly said. "Bad for business."

"Yeah, I know." Curtis steepled his fingers and asked, "Why do *you* think DeMarco was killed?"

O'Reilly shrugged. "No idea, all I know is that it wasn't us."

Body language, tone of voice, direct answer – everything said O'Reilly was telling the truth. Curtis shifted topics a bit and said,

"Okay, now that Volkov's top of mind, what can you tell me about him?"

O'Reilly motioned for one of his guys to come over and told him to get a couple of beers, then said, "It wasn't us."

"Who then?" Curtis asked.

"Hell, Volkov was Russian, maybe *they* got pissed off at him being such a fucking irritant."

It was obvious O'Reilly knew exactly who Volkov was and remembered the two murders much better than Curtis could have hoped. "Okay, say I was going to have a sit-down with one of them, someone from back in the day. Who would that be?"

The beers arrived and O'Reilly took a long drink from one and set the other in front of Curtis. "Sergei Ivanov probably." He lit a cigarette and blew the smoke under the table. No one said a word. "Or Dimitri Kalatonov."

The last thing Curtis wanted at ten in the morning was a beer, but he picked it up and took a drink. Insulting a top-of-the-heap Irish crime boss wasn't on his to-do list. "There's something else."

"What?" O'Reilly asked, frowning.

O'Reilly was losing patience and Curtis's welcome was wearing out. "Volkov's seventeen year-old daughter, Darina. We found her body a couple of days ago, stuffed in a wall in Jamaica Plain. Someone took her out about six months after her dad."

"Not cool," O'Reilly said sharply. "We would never touch a woman, or a kid." He leaned forward again, this time a lot closer to Curtis. "Never."

"I only want what you know," Curtis said quietly. The bodyguards had both moved in a bit. "Not looking at you for it."

A long pause, with O'Reilly staring directly into Curtis's eyes. "Someone killing a kid is despicable. Makes me angry."

Curtis finished his beer. "Right." He dropped a business card on the table. "My cell number. If you remember anything it stays between you and me."

O'Reilly picked up the card and slid it into his pocket. "Kids shouldn't get whacked."

"No, they shouldn't." Curtis stood up and gave him a nod. "Thanks for the beer," Curtis said, then looked down at the man and asked, "You ever meet Whitey?"

O'Reilly let out a low snort. "Yeah, lots of times." A few seconds passed, then he said, "He was an asshole. No, worse than that. He was a rat. A fucking rat."

Curtis turned and headed back through the gym, his pulse racing. What was it with gangsters that they never got any less intimidating? He passed the main ring where two boxers were going at each other. One of them caught the other with a devastating uppercut and the man went down in a heap. Trainers jumped into the ring and Curtis overheard someone watching say, *Man, that was powerful.*

The real power in here today, Curtis thought as he pushed the door open, *is the seventy year-old sitting in the back nursing a beer.*

CHAPTER ELEVEN

Aislinn poked her head into the house and yelled, "Mom? Dad?"

Silence greeted her and she slipped off her shoes and padded through the living room to the back of the house. They'd renovated a few years ago and paid an interior designer to pick out the colors, furniture and artwork. It had been a huge success and they followed up with the kitchen and the bathrooms. Now, the hundred and forty year-old house sparkled and looked almost new.

She found her mother in the kitchen chopping vegetables for a salad, and the aroma wafting from the stove was heaven. While Fiona was a marvel in the kitchen, these days she mostly talked Cian into going out for dinner. Apparently, that wasn't happening tonight.

"Trapped in the kitchen, are you?" Aislinn said.

"I am, but tomorrow – *night off*."

"Well done."

"How are things?" Fiona asked.

"With Bruce?" Aislinn was well aware of what Fiona meant. "No, Mom, we broke it off a month ago. I told you."

She looked disappointed. "Oh, that's too bad. I liked him."

Aislinn shrugged it off. Her mother never said it out loud, but every time she dated a guy long enough to bring him to Jamaica Street and introduce him, her mother got her hopes up for a son-in-law. So far, the job had prevailed and all potential husbands had slid off the road into the ditch, either by their hand or hers.

"What's Dad up to," she said.

"He's in the backyard."

Her father was wedged under the low branches of a tree, pulling weeds. He was more than ready for a reprieve from yardwork and brightened when she came banging out through the screen door.

"A," her father said, on his knees and looking spent. "I didn't expect you."

She plopped down in a bright red Adirondack chair near the top of the heavily sloped yard. "That was a great party, the guys went all out for you," she said.

"Drunken sots, all of them," Cian said with a grin as he got to his feet.

"Including you," Aislinn said, smiling. Of course her father had put back a few too many, it was his party.

"What's up?" Cian asked, easing into the chair beside her. "You didn't call to let us know you were coming."

"Actually, I wanted to talk with you about the case I'm working on."

Her father raised an eyebrow. "Well, you know I'm retired now. Maybe I can go on the clock and send you an invoice. Private eye sort of thing."

She laughed out loud at that. "No budget for that. This is going to be strictly pro bono."

He got serious. "What can I help you with?"

Aislinn shifted a bit in her chair so she was facing her father. "You were patrolling the streets when Alexi Volkov was killed and Darina went missing. Maybe you can give me the lay of the land back then."

Cian nodded. "What do you need?"

"It's likely that Darina's murder is tied in with the hit on her dad, which has us looking at organized crime. Who was calling the shots? How dangerous was it if you were in a gang? What sort of stuff were they into?" She shrugged. "Anything that might give me a starting point. I mean, I was a teenager when this went down so I don't have a clue how things worked twenty years ago."

"Yeah, yeah, I get it," he said, figuring she needed to start thinking like them.

Cian wiped a few drops of sweat from his brow. "Well, the Irish guys were in the Winter Hill Gang. They were on top for a lot of years and Whitey Bulger was the boss until '94 when he made a run for it. After that Kevin Weeks took over, but things fell apart in late 1999 or 2000 when he got arrested and turned informant. They weren't much of a factor after that, mostly into illegal gambling, extortion and loansharking. Weeks was killed around Christmas '99, so he was still around when Alexi Volkov was taken out." He thought about that for a minute, then added. "It's possible he could have been involved."

"If the Winter Hill gang was coming apart, who controlled Jamaica Plain?" Aislinn asked.

"The Russians, the Italians – they'd always had their toes in the water. With Bulger and Weeks gone they moved in and things got ugly."

"How so?"

Cian launched into the details, grateful that the gangsters had stopped killing each other on a regular basis and that his daughter didn't have a lot of dealings with organized crime.

"First off, you have to understand how the Italians and the Russians run things. The Italians have a vertical structure." Cian held up his right hand. "This is the boss, or the Don as he's often referred to, and right under him is the underboss. Then the captains, or capos, and under them are the soldiers." He kept moving his hand down as he spoke. "All those guys have to be full-blooded Italians and they are *made men*."

"Untouchable," Aislinn said.

"Right. If someone takes out any of those guys there is going to be some pretty severe retaliation."

"Walking dead man."

"Yeah, that's about it," Cian said, nodding. "Under the soldiers are the associates. They don't have to be Italian, and they can never be made men."

"Expendable."

"Yeah," Cian said. "These are the guys who do the dirty work."

"Like kill people."

"Like that. But, and this is a big *but*, they don't kill cops or prosecutors, or women."

"Ever?" Aislinn asked.

"It would have to be pretty serious for them to whack a woman, or a girl."

"Got it, what about the Russians?"

Cian thought about that. "They're a bit different. They lack some of the top-down structure. It's more a collection of guys in loose networks that focus on crime as a business. That's what links them." He gave Aislinn a grim look. "Some of the gangs have a boss at the top, some don't. And there's more violence in the ranks."

"So they might kill a woman – or a seventeen year-old girl."

"Just like that." Cian snapped his fingers. "The threat of violence is always there. Those guys, *they* scare me."

Aislinn's heart was beating faster and she felt the blood pulsing through her veins.

Cian pushed himself out of his chair, walked to the edge of the patio and crossed his arms. He turned back and looked down at his daughter. "They like to use guns – automatic, semi-automatic, sometimes with silencers. A lot of it from close range."

"Like Alexi." She shuddered. "He was shot in the back of the head from a couple of feet away."

"That sort of thing," Cian said. "So, getting back to your question, none of them had total control, it was a catfight."

Aislinn sat back and took a deep breath to calm herself. She stared over the carefully tended beds, lush and in full bloom. Alexi Volkov was Russian, so it made sense he would be looking to the Russians if he was trying to break into a gang. They were violent, used guns and would kill women. Everything was pointing at them to have taken out Alexi – and if the two murders were related then it could be that the

Russians had grabbed Darina and killed her. It gave her one possible direction to move in with her investigation.

"Alexi and Darina," she pressed on. "What do you know about them?"

"There was talk in the precinct for sure. The detectives working the files didn't share a lot, and most of what we heard was secondhand."

"Like..."

"It was speculation – Alexi was a mob hit. He was already on our radar for a bunch of stuff like protection rackets, extortion, and collecting debts. Vice had him pegged as a low-level bagman for the Russians."

"So he had broken in with the Russian mob."

Cian shook his head. "Not really. From what I heard he was on the outs, trying to get in. The guys in Vice didn't think the Russians trusted him for anything other than collecting money and handing out beatings."

"But he was running rackets."

"Yeah."

"By himself? That doesn't add up. He wouldn't have enough clout for business owners to start forking over protection money."

"Don't know for sure. That's what I heard," Cian said.

"Okay." She checked her notepad, then asked, "Do you think it's possible Darina saw her dad's killer? In her witness statement she described a guy suddenly appearing on the sidewalk dressed in black with a balaclava over his face. She thinks he might have come out of their driveway."

"It's possible."

"The detectives thought Darina was a credible witness," Aislinn added. "She noticed things, like the guy's watch and that he was wearing a pendant."

"Yeah, I remember something about that."

"Any thoughts? Anything to chase down there? The watch is likely useless, but the pendant could be something."

Cian smiled and let out a low chuckle. "Yeah, the watch doesn't count, but I wouldn't pin much hope to the pendant either. Twenty years ago a lot of the guys were wearing something around their necks. Cops, gangsters – hell, I had one. All the Irish guys wore Celtic Knots on chains, and they were all different. My barber had a beauty. It was a great conversation piece."

"The one Darina saw was silver," Aislinn said. "Does that matter?"

"Well," Cian said slowly, "it might. The Italians and the Irish would wear anything, but the Russians were all about gold. Had to be gold. Looks more expensive." He snapped his fingers. "Maybe that takes the Russians out of the equation."

Aislinn shook her head. "Could have been white gold, it looks like silver."

"I suppose." Cian looked doubtful. "If the Russians were going to wear gold they'd make sure it *looked* like gold."

"Okay, what about Darina?"

Cian shrugged. "You knew her better than I did."

"No, not that. What can you tell me about her case? Stuff that might not be in the file."

"The press was all over the guys working the case and they kept it close to their chests, even more than usual." He took a deep breath and exhaled slowly. "It had a huge impact on people. Young, pretty girl goes missing on prom night. It made for a good story and her disappearance spilled over from Jamaica Plain into Boston, then across the state. It was big news."

She nodded, remembering all the fuss that had stemmed from Darina's disappearance, then said, "It was definitely a big deal."

"Goddamn tragedy," he said quietly. "Sorry I can't help more."

She glanced over at her father, who was staring at the garden with vacant eyes. This went back to his watch, when he was in his prime and working the streets. At the time, Darina's disappearance had hit her father hard – it could have been *his* daughter who was taken and killed. She shuddered – the reality was that if she had been with Darina they might both have ended up in the wall. It was an unnerving thought that her father must have had many times since.

He placed his hand on hers until Aislinn stood up and said, "Gonna check out my room. Haven't seen it for ages."

He smiled. "Feeling nostalgic?"

"Yeah, I think so."

Aislinn took the stairs two at time, like she had when she was a kid eager to get to her room for some unimportant reason. The door was closed and she hesitated, her hand on the knob, then she twisted, pushed it open and walked in. Her bed and dresser were gone, replaced by a sewing machine and a rack covered with spools of different colored thread. The drapes were open and the bushy linden tree that had blocked her view for so many years was in full canopy, like a blanket that protected her from the outside world. It still reassured her.

The only remnant of the eighteen years she had spent in the room was a Linkin Park poster still pinned to the wall. She sat down at the sewing machine and pulled out her iPhone, then searched for *In The End* by Linkin Park. Soft, staccato piano notes spilled out, then the bass line and drums kicked in. Then the lyrics. She mouthed the words, thinking of Darina and that moment, in this room, on the bed, giggling and gobbling down cold chicken salad.

The song ended and Aislinn slipped her phone back in her pocket, her anger welling up.

"I'll get the bastards who did this, Darina."

CHAPTER TWELVE

Curtis dropped Brandy at Logan early Monday morning, already missing her. "Come back soon," he said, breaking off a long hug.

"Or," she said with a tempting smile, "you could take a few vacation days and visit Napa."

He thought about that and nodded. "I could."

He watched her walk into the terminal. Relationships, especially long distance ones, were tough. They needed to be nurtured if they were to grow into something special. He took her offer as a good sign and considered whether he could take her up on it soon. When she had disappeared into the crowd he slipped back into his car and headed for work.

The weekly meeting in Curtis's office lasted the better part of an hour and when it broke up he motioned for Aislinn and Stan to hang back. After the rest of the detectives had filed out, Curtis pointed at the door. Stan gave it a kick with his size twelve and it slammed shut.

"Where are you with Darina Volkov's case?" he asked Aislinn.

She opened the file and one of the photos dropped onto the carpet. She picked it up and handed the small stack to Stan.

Stan thumbed through them and said, "You were just kids."

She took a deep breath. "Stars in our eyes."

Stan held up the photo of Darina posing in her dress. "This her?"

"It is. She looked so pretty."

"Yeah." He thumbed through the pictures and said, "You all did." He handed them back across the table.

Aislinn tucked the photos in the file and launched into her update. "We're waiting on the ME's office for toxicology and autopsy to determine cause of death. I interviewed Kristin Sanders, the last person to see her alive, and I'll use the school reunion to catch up with the other three who saw her the day she disappeared. Another angle I'm chasing is how the crime families fit into this."

Curtis nodded. "I can help you a bit with that. I met with Patrick O'Reilly yesterday. He was way up the totem pole in 2000 and remembers Alexi's murder and Darina's abduction. I got the feeling he especially remembers Tony DeMarco getting killed. He didn't say no when I asked him if DeMarco was set up."

"You think the Irish mob took out Tony?" Stan asked.

Curtis shook his head. "Not really sure, but the coincidences are stacking up – he was one of the detectives working Alexi Volkov's murder and he takes a bullet a couple of years later. It makes me think we should be looking at DeMarco in addition to Alexi and Darina."

"I have time," Stan interjected.

Curtis nodded. "Yeah, pull the file and have a look. Keep it on the QT. We're talking about a cop here and there's likely a lot of anger still simmering with the old-timers."

"I'm on it."

Aislinn turned to Curtis. "Got anything on the go with the Russians or the Italians?"

"You like the mob angle," Curtis responded.

"Sort of," she said slowly. Murder cops didn't set the agenda of an investigation, the facts and clues did that. Making a subjective decision early in the game that affected the direction things moved was a very bad idea and she knew it. "Keeping an open mind though."

Curtis nodded his approval. "I have an interview set up with

Dimitri Kalatonov." He checked his watch. "At eleven-thirty this morning."

"You need backup?" Stan asked. "Kalatonov is one mean son-of-a-bitch."

"You know him?" Curtis asked.

"Oh yeah," Stan said. "I interviewed him on the Prescott murder a couple of years ago. He scared the shit out of me."

Curtis started laughing. "Nobody scares you. You scare other people."

Aislinn was laughing now and Stan couldn't help grinning. "Not shittin' you, LT. He's a piece of work."

"I'll be okay," Curtis said, "but thanks for the offer. He's not going to whack me on his home turf when everyone at the precinct knows that I'm going there."

"Never said he was smart, just mean," Stan said. That started them all laughing again.

Curtis interjected, "Listen, this has the potential to get really ugly. If these murders are connected and the shooters are still out there, they're not going to be happy we're poking around. We all need to be careful."

The smile faded as Stan got to his feet. "Yeah, if someone set up DeMarco then we're looking at a cop killer."

If they'll do it once, they'll do it twice, was what they were all thinking.

Curtis waved a hand at them. "Get out of here, go do some work."

Curtis dug into the stack of active files for the eight squads that fell under his supervision, reviewing the notes for each case. By the time he was up to speed it was eleven o'clock and time to leave for his meeting with Dimitri Kalatonov. Aislinn's head popped up in her cubicle as he passed.

"The initial forensics report is ready on Darina Volkov. I'm heading over at one-thirty."

"Let me know what they found," Curtis said, and kept moving.

The drive to South Boston was mercifully short and he pulled up to the address on Jan Karski Way five minutes early. The street had a working class feel to it, with the Pipefitters Union building on one corner and his destination, the Second Channel Nightclub, across the road. He'd checked out the website for the club and wasn't impressed. It professed to be the reincarnation of the iconic Channel club that had seen bands like the Red Hot Chili Peppers, Iggy Pop and The J. Geils Band grace its stage back in the 80's and 90's. Problem was, those days were long gone.

There were already twenty or thirty cars parked in front of the long, single-story building, and a poster on a sandwich board had pictures of six women in lingerie posing on a stage with a pole. Apparently the place doubled as a strip joint over the lunch hour.

He walked in, leaving sunshine behind and stood at the front door until his eyes adjusted to the low light. A raised stage at the front overlooked a massive dance floor and Curtis figured the place could hold about eight hundred people when it was packed. A classic Rolling Stones tune thundered over the sound system and a mostly-naked girl writhed around on the stage. A few feet from the entrance a guy Stan's size stood looking at Curtis.

"Dimitri Kalatonov around?" Curtis yelled over the music.

"Who wants to know?"

"Curtis Westcott. He's expecting me." Curtis didn't bother pulling his badge.

The bouncer spoke into a mic on his collar, then pointed to a door near the back of the room. "He's in there."

Curtis ignored the stage show as he wove between the tables. He knew the damage that often went with young women using their bodies to earn a living and it saddened him. Broken families, sexual abuse, low self-esteem – it was a hard chasm to climb out of. Mixed in with all of that were the drugs and violence that so often crept in and took over. He was approaching the door when another bouncer opened it from the inside. *Cameras.* They were watching him. He passed into a short hallway that led to an office, where Dimitri Kalatonov sat waiting at his desk. Curtis stopped at the door.

"Come in," a thin man standing next to the Russian gangster said. He was in his late twenties or early thirties and had short blond hair.

Curtis stepped inside and glanced both ways. There were three others in the room, all of them thick with gym muscles and serious expressions. He gave each of them a look, then walked across the threadbare carpet to the desk and sat in a chair facing Kalatonov. The Russian took a long drag on the cigarette dangling from his fingers and blew the smoke into the stale air.

"I will translate for Mr. Kalatonov," the young man said. "You have five minutes."

"I have five minutes," Curtis repeated, staring at Kalatonov. He glanced at the man who had offered to translate. "What's the street address here?"

Kalatonov's hang-around looked confused. "20 Jan Karski Way."

Curtis pulled out his cell and dialed Stan's number. He touched *speaker* and set the phone on the edge of the desk.

Stan answered on the third ring. "Yeah, boss, what's up?"

"Got a minute?"

"I can make time. What do you need?"

"A search warrant for 20 Jan Karski Way and uniforms here to lock it down while we wait for the warrant."

"What are we looking for?" Stan asked.

"Warrant should be as open-ended as the judge will allow. See if you can get Sanderson, he'll give us what we want. We're looking for drugs, underage women working as strippers, undocumented staff, and code violations. Get forensics down here as well, I want them to look at some blood spatters."

There was a short pause, then, "Uniforms are on the way," Stan said. "Typing up the warrant now."

Kalatonov raised his hand and shook his head. "No need for that, Westcott."

"What was that?" Stan asked.

Curtis sat in the chair, glaring at Kalatonov. Finally, he said, "We good?" Kalatonov nodded and Curtis said, "Hold the warrant for now. Cancel the uniforms."

"Aw, shit, LT. They pulled four cars off patrol, dispatch is going to fucking freak."

"Cancel them, Stan."

"Okay."

Curtis reached over and touched the red button, killing the call. Stan, a master of playing along, was probably grinning ear to ear on the other end of the line. Every call that started with *got a minute* was a set up.

Curtis spoke directly to Kalatonov, who he knew spoke English. "I don't care about your nightclub or what you're up to right now. I'm here about something that happened twenty years ago."

Kalatonov ground out his cigarette and asked in a thick accent, "What do you want, Westcott?"

"Alexi Volkov. Took a bullet to the back of the head in December 2000. Remember him?"

"Vaguely."

"Was he one of your guys?" Curtis asked.

"What do you mean, one of *my* guys?"

Curtis leaned forward. "Don't play games or I get back on the phone and shut this place down for a week while we wait for forensics on the blood."

"You fucking guys," Kalatonov spat. "Always a problem."

A long silence followed, then the Russian said, "I remember Volkov."

Curtis waited, using the time to evaluate Kalatonov, the room and the hired muscle. Kalatonov was sturdy, built like a tree stump with short, thick branches for arms. Now in his fifties, Curtis figured he must have been a tough son-of-a-bitch to be so high up in the organization twenty years ago while a young man. Dark eyes stared out from under bushy eyebrows and little, if any, humanity emanated from them. Curtis looked away and scanned the dreary space with its dated carpets, embossed wallpaper, and the hired help looking appropriately menacing, their arms crossed over barrel chests.

Curtis tired of waiting for Kalatonov to continue and reached for his phone.

Kalatonov lit another cigarette. "Alexi was trouble."

Again, Curtis waited.

"He was too eager and he made mistakes." Kalatonov sucked on the cigarette. "He was out of control."

"Not a good thing," Curtis said.

"No."

Short, terse answers weren't going to help. Anything Kalatonov said could be used to incriminate him and Curtis needed to get him talking.

"Nothing we discuss today goes any further than this room unless it has a direct tie to Volkov's murder. Tell me he was your bagman and it gets left out of the report. Tell me you shot him, that goes in the report."

"Okay." Kalatonov shifted a bit, the first time he'd moved other than to light the cigarette. "Alexi was playing the field, trying to break in with anyone who would have him. We took him on to collect debts, move cash and drug shipments around, intimidate witnesses – that sort of thing."

"The charges he was on trial for, were they tied into your organization?"

Kalatonov shook his head. "The rackets were his thing, again, a problem. He was collecting protection money from a few businesses, nickel and dime stuff, and he got nailed for it. The obstruction charges were for beating up a witness."

"Perjury?" Curtis asked.

Kalatonov actually smiled. "I think he lied in court. Very bad person."

"How could he run a racket by himself? You need an organization, muscle behind you, to intimidate people into paying."

The Russian shrugged. "He was tied in with someone, but it wasn't us."

"The Irish?"

"Nyet, not the Irish. They tolerated him, but he had no standing with them."

"Italians?"

"Fuck no. They hated him." Kalatonov raised a bushy eyebrow. "Maybe someone was scared he was going to cut a deal with the DA."

Curtis nodded. "Yeah, that's what we're thinking."

Kalatonov seemed pleased that Westcott had given him something close to the chest.

"What about his daughter?" Curtis asked.

"What about her?" Kalatonov's eyes narrowed.

"Well, we found her a couple of days ago stuffed in a wall in Jamaica Plain."

"We don't kill little girls." His voice took on a threatening tone.

"*Someone* killed her," Curtis said. "And it's likely tied to Alexi's murder."

Kalatonov flicked the ash off his cigarette. "Not us."

"One more," Curtis said. "Tony DeMarco."

"Who?"

"Cop who was killed responding to a burglary about two years after Volkov's murder. He was one of the guys who worked the file."

Kalatonov's face took on color. "Don't go there, Westcott. Don't point a finger at us for killing a cop," he hissed.

It was the ultimate crime, murdering a police officer, and if there was even a hint of suspicion on an organization, it could mean the end. Constant pressure from street cops, detectives, prosecutors, and judges required a lot of resources from the police and the courts, but it could break even the most well-oiled criminal gang if the motivation was there to see it through. Killing a cop meant that sort of pressure.

"Maybe DeMarco was in the wrong place at the wrong time," Curtis said.

"Yeah, maybe."

Curtis had what he wanted. He dropped a business card on the desk, then stood up and gave Kalatonov a slight nod. "Call me if you want to talk. You know, if you find out who was involved."

"Those other guys," the Russian said.

"Them," Curtis said.

He turned and left, back through the cavernous room with the young women and their broken dreams. The sun felt good on his skin when he stepped onto the sidewalk and as he walked to his car he began slotting the pieces together to form an image of Alexi Volkov. Wanna-be gangster or not, Volkov had somehow managed to get a protection racket off the ground, which meant he had partners. Was Volkov the muscle on the street or was he the one pulling the strings? Either way, it was a protection racket with money on the table, and money can get you killed. Volkov was proof of that.

CHAPTER THIRTEEN

The Office of the Chief Medical Examiner for Boston was in a nondescript three-story brick and granite building on Albany Street. Aislinn parked in the adjacent lot and took the stairs to the basement. The receptionist buzzed her in and she asked for Rebecca Carlisle, then leaned against the wall and checked her email.

Rebecca, decked out in her lab clothes, showed up with a CSI technician in tow and motioned for Aislinn to follow them. They walked side-by-side down a long, sterile corridor to a windowless door which Carlisle opened with her security pass. Inside was a metal-clad wall housing rows of doors, each with a small whiteboard and heavy-duty handle. She strode over to one where *Volkov* was scrawled and pulled. The door dropped down and a gurney slid out from the wall. What was left of Darina Volkov lay on the slab.

"Lenore Sutherland." The CSI tech introduced herself to Aislinn.

"Detective Aislinn Byrne." They all focused on the body.

"She's essentially mummified," Carlisle said. "The electrical chase had a conduit running through it that exited at the roof so there was cool air flowing next to her. The polyethylene was sealed, but not airtight, so the moisture inside would have slowly depleted until there was nothing left but shriveled skin and bones."

"What about the odor?" Aislinn asked.

"Essentially, none. The release of air from inside the poly probably took years and it vented up the chase and directly outside." She shook her head. "Honestly, I've never seen a body this desiccated. It's bizarre."

Darina's flesh resembled leather that had folded in on itself like pages in a book and her fingers were curled into claws. Aislinn's legs felt weak and for a moment she thought she might collapse in a heap. She fought it as the room began to spin, locking her knees and gripping the cold steel of the gurney so hard it left marks on her skin. She felt Rebecca's hand on her shoulder, then an arm around her waist, and didn't move. Seconds passed and she was still on her feet. Then a minute, then two. Her equilibrium gained a foothold and Rebecca slowly released her grip and walked back to the other side of the gurney.

"Darina was your friend," Rebecca said quietly.

"Yes," Aislinn managed, staring at Darina's desiccated body. "She was."

It was Lenore's turn and the CSI tech said, "I didn't get anything off the poly – no fingerprints or DNA traces. Same with the dress, nothing worthwhile."

Aislinn nodded, still not trusting her voice.

Carlisle started in with the cause of death. "It appears she was hit from behind with a blunt object. Her skull is partially caved in..." Carlisle pointed at a spot behind the left ear, "...here, but that didn't kill her."

"What did?" Aislinn asked in a croaky voice.

"She was strangled. Something extremely thin, like piano wire or a garotte. Sliced right through her trachea."

"Professional job?"

Carlisle shrugged. "Could be. Whoever did this must have worn gloves, and not everyone carries thin pieces of wire around with them."

"Any other injuries?"

"No broken or cracked bones. Nothing that would indicate she had been abused or tortured prior to being knocked out and strangled."

"Well, that's something." Somehow it didn't feel very reassuring. Dead was dead.

"I've taken tissue samples for a toxicology scan, but it will be a couple of days before I have anything for you."

Aislinn took one last look at her friend and said, "Thanks, Rebecca." She nodded to the CSI tech.

"I'll call you when I get the tox scan," Rebecca said.

Aislinn couldn't get out of the medical examiner's building fast enough. She burst through the front doors and stood on the street corner feeling sick and broken, asking herself why she had chosen homicide for a career. It had come at a monumental cost to her personal life but that wasn't a shock, her dad was a cop and she had been acutely aware of what she was getting into from the start. All the violence and death, it was wearing on her psyche, slowly eroding her empathy and goodwill. She was constantly forcing herself to remain objective and to stay at a distance with her emotions in check. Objectivity solved cases, subjectivity led down rabbit holes.

This was different. Twenty years had slid past, but her emotions were welling up as strong as the dark days after Darina went missing. Aislinn started down the sidewalk, teetering on the edge of whether to hand back the case. She would have to shake off anything that might distract her, stay completely focused if eventually she was to stand face-to-face with Darina's killer. She took some strength from envisioning that moment and decided to wait until after she'd interviewed the friends who had spent time with Darina on prom day before making that decision. Dealing with them would be as good a test as any. Two of the three, Cody Hall and Shane Collins, were registered for the reunion and she would track them down at one of the events. Best if they didn't know she was going to be looking for them, no chance to rethink or alter a story.

Kayla Walsh was another matter, she still lived in Jamaica Plain but Aislinn hadn't seen her in years. Funny, Aislinn thought, she saw more of Kayla's dad these days now that he was a regular at her parents' house for cards. Kayla wasn't going to the reunion, which didn't really surprise Aislinn. Kayla had always been the pretty one who used her looks to get what she wanted, and when that didn't work was quick to lie and manipulate others. She had burned a lot of bridges over the years. Aislinn checked her watch. She had a couple of hours before Kayla's interview and she needed that time to sit down, have a coffee and try to get her head back together.

* * *

STAN LAMERS RUBBED his massive mitts over his shaved head as he waited for the file on Tony DeMarco. Jamaica Plain wasn't his stomping grounds and he seldom, if ever, ventured into District E-13. He didn't know the guy working the records desk and had to wait in the queue. All it took at A-1 was a quick call and things were waiting for him when he showed up.

The old-timer on the desk shuffled back and glanced up at Stan over his reading glasses. "You can get this stuff online." He heaved an armful of thick folders and a sign-out sheet onto the counter.

"I like the real thing. Can spread it out and see more than one page at a time." Stan looked around. "Got a pen?"

The man dug around in the drawer until he found one and Stan signed out the file, then lugged it back to his car and headed home where a comfortable chair was waiting for him. Curtis wouldn't care where he worked and a year after Covid he still preferred his house over the bullpen. His wife was working this week and the kids were finishing off their school year, which meant the place was all his.

He spread out on the dining room table and got started with the initial report from the crime scene. A call had come in at 8:27 – burglary in progress at an electronic shop on Center Street in Jamaica Plain. Tony DeMarco was close by, only two blocks away, and radioed in that he was on it. Dispatch recommended he wait for backup, but the detective went in alone, parking in the back alley and entering through a door that looked like it had been forced. The attending officers speculated that he had drawn his weapon because it was found on the floor next to his body. Forensics found two 9 mm slugs in his chest and ran ballistics – no match to any guns used in other crimes. DeMarco had been driving home from the precinct at the end of his shift and wasn't wearing a vest. He left a wife and three kids.

The staff who worked at the store were fingerprinted for elimination purposes and their prints compared to the ones taken off the door. Aside from a few unusable smudges any with decent ridges belonged to the staff. Whoever pried open the door likely wore gloves. They had also taken their crowbar away with them and the alley was asphalt, so no footprints or tire tracks. CCTV was pulled from the existing cameras on buildings within a kilometer, but the coverage in 2003 was sporadic at best. What footage they had was scrutinized extensively – cars, trucks and vans were tracked between cameras and a rudimentary nexus established and put on a grid. Nothing came of it. None of the vehicles caught on-camera had stopped for long enough to break-in, start grabbing expensive electronics and then shoot DeMarco when he showed up.

Two hours in and Stan was impressed with the thoroughness and attention to detail by the detectives assigned to the case. All leads had been followed up and eventually run into the ground, every possible suspect or witness interviewed at least twice looking for inconsistencies in their stories. By all appearances it was a botched robbery and Tony DeMarco had been in the wrong place at the wrong time.

Stan shuffled through the crime scene photos – all angles of DeMarco laying on the ground were covered. His gun was a couple of feet from his shooting hand and the aisle where he was shot was neat and tidy except for a couple of boxes laying on the floor. Stan found a close-up of the boxes – a 35 mm camera and a game console – probably dropped by the thief. Things had changed in eighteen years, everything was Apple or Android phones and laptops now.

Stan stared at a photo of DeMarco's body, taken looking toward the front of the store, its aisles packed full of electronics. Something was bugging him but he wasn't sure what it was. *Why was he driving by at that time?* he wondered, and dug into the details about DeMarco and the cases he had worked. Halfway down one page he found a notation that indicated it was normal for DeMarco to start late and work until eight or nine o'clock, then take the same route home every night. Maybe that was something, and Stan flagged the page with a Post-it note.

The front door swung open and the kids bounded in like they were on a sugar high. Fourteen and twelve, Stan's kids were done with the books and itching for summer holidays to kick in. Stan piled the stack of paper back into his expandable file and snapped it shut. That was it for work today.

CHAPTER FOURTEEN

Aislinn was meeting with Kayla Walsh at her home in the Mildred C. Hailey Apartments, a red brick high-rise housing development near Jackson Square. After circling the block twice in search of a parking space she found a loading zone, pulled in and set her police permit on the dash. The couriers could double park.

Kayla's apartment was on the sixth floor and she took the stairs two at a time, arriving out of breath in a dimly lit hallway with fresh paint. Someone's dinner was cooking and an appealing smell, heavy with herbs and spices, made her stomach growl. The odor dissipated as she moved down the hall to unit 610, where she knocked and waited.

Aislinn barely recognized Kayla Walsh when she answered. Her thick, luscious blond hair was shorter and the flirtatious smile replaced by lips set in a thin, tight line. Only her eyes were the same, guarded and suspicious. A middle-aged man with a slight paunch, dressed in khakis and a golf shirt showed up and stood a few feet behind her.

"Aislinn," Kayla said, not moving from the doorway. "You wanted to see me."

"I did." Aislinn waited for about ten seconds, then said, "In your apartment."

Kayla reluctantly opened the door and backed off. "Aislinn, this is Mike."

"Hi," he said.

Aislinn followed them into the living room, a sunny space with new furniture and a large, flatscreen television mounted on the wall. The view was panoramic, looking out over the tennis court at Jackson Square Park and the heavily forested community of Fort Hill. Mike and Kayla took the sofa and Aislinn sat in a chair beside the window.

Kayla turned to Mike. "Aislinn's from my high school, we used to hang out. She's with the police these days." There was no disguising the anxiety in her voice.

"Homicide," Aislinn said to Mike. "I don't work other crimes." Aislinn wondered if Kayla still had her fingers in some things she shouldn't.

"Homicide?" Mike asked. He shot Kayla a quick look, then said, "Why are you here?"

"Concerning an ongoing investigation." She waited a moment, then added, "Why are *you* here?"

That flustered him and he didn't know how to answer. Kayla cut in, "We're engaged."

"Congratulations," Aislinn said with zero emotion. "I'd like to speak with Kayla. Alone. No offense."

"Oh, none taken." He leaned over, kissed her on the cheek. "I need to get to work."

"See you later," she muttered, glancing at her phone when it buzzed. "Sorry, my sister is pregnant and expecting any day. I'm waiting for a text."

"It's okay," Aislinn said.

The door closed behind Mike as he left and Kayla said, "What's this about, Aislinn?"

"Darina Volkov."

"Darina?" Kayla's eyes shot open for a moment. "Why Darina?"

"We found her body a couple of days ago. I'm going back through the file and speaking with everyone who saw her the day she disappeared."

Kayla's shoulders sagged a touch as she relaxed.

"Mike seems nice," Aislinn said, running her finger along the arm of the new chair. If she could get Kayla more at ease the interview would go better. "Reliable sort of guy."

"I had my share of bad ones," Kayla said. "Mike's good with the kids."

Aislinn smiled. "So it's time for you to settle down."

She nodded. "He's an accountant. Bookkeeper actually, but he makes good money." She brightened. "We've bought a house and we're moving there in a couple of months."

Aislinn was aware Kayla had moved into Bromley Heath years ago, back when it had been a dangerous place, rampant with crime and drugs. That was until a strong-minded woman, Mildred Hailey, had almost single-handedly changed everything. It was still a bit rough around the edges and nearby Jackson Square wasn't the best place to hang around at night, but the housing development was much safer now.

Kayla smiled again and this time it came easier. "The new place should be better."

So the cute girl, the one who could wrap the boys around her finger and get whatever she wanted, had finally settled. Aislinn wasn't sure if she felt vindicated or glad for her, so she settled on being happy that Kayla and her kids would likely have a decent home life.

"I'm sure it will," Aislinn said reassuringly. "And Arnie, he's quite the proud granddad."

Kayla cocked her head slightly. "You see my dad?"

"Sure, over at my parents' house playing cards. Apparently, Arnie's going to get Dad out golfing now that he's retired."

Kayla managed a short laugh. "That should be good, your dad golfing."

"Yeah, no kidding." Aislinn let the conversation die off until the silence was becoming awkward.

"Darina was murdered," Aislinn said, shifting to the reason she had come.

Kayla looked down at the carpet for a moment, then back up at Aislinn. "I guessed as much, you being with homicide and all."

"What can you tell me about the day of the prom?"

"I gave the police a statement," Kayla said.

"I read it." Aislinn shifted slightly and her blazer slipped off her hip revealing her gun. She tucked it away – she didn't want Kayla focusing on it and tensing up. "Tell me what you and Darina did that day. What you talked about. Her frame of mind. That sort of thing."

"Not sure. Can't remember."

"I'm not here for anything but Darina's murder," Aislinn said. "Providing you didn't kill her, you have nothing to worry about." She managed a hint of a smile.

"Okay, let me think." A full minute slid past, then she said, "Darina was excited about the prom, but Shane Collins wasn't her first choice. She really liked Cody Hall, but he had asked a different girl."

"Right, good old Cody. Heart of the party." Aislinn leaned back, giving Kayla more space, keeping her at ease. "What else can you think of?"

"You probably remember a bunch of this. We hung around my house for a while then went to get our hair done." She snapped her fingers. "Oh, right, the hairdresser only had two chairs and Darina and I went first, you and Sofia had to wait."

Aislinn nodded. "Tiny place, it was."

"Yeah, then Darina and I went next door for lunch. We had burgers, I think, and she was still really wound up about her dad. She got pretty vocal about it when we were eating. That some fucker had murdered him and the police couldn't figure it out. A bunch of people were staring at us."

"Anyone you knew or that you can remember?"

"What do you mean?" Kayla asked.

"Maybe the wrong person overheard Darina," Aislinn said. "Try and put yourself back in the restaurant and recreate the scene. Picture the faces staring at you."

Kayla chewed on her lower lip as she struggled to recall the details. "There were a couple of guys with black hair and sort of tanned skin, I think they were Italian or something."

Aislinn sat quietly and waited.

She started nodding emphatically. "Yeah, pretty sure it was Italian. I used to date an Italian guy and he spoke it to his parents when we were at their house. And, these two guys, they were really watching us."

"Anything else?"

Kayla shook her head. "No, that's it."

"All right, then what?"

"We all piled into Darina's car and went back to my house." She stopped and shook her head. "Of course you would know that, you were in the car with us."

"No, it's good for you to tell me everything. Don't leave out bits because I was there. You might remember things I don't."

"Oh, okay." She sat up a bit straighter and said, "Darina only stayed at the house for a few minutes, then she headed over to Cody's place."

Aislinn nodded, reassuring Kayla she was doing well. "I think you were right that she liked Cody."

"Yeah, they were good friends."

Aislinn sat forward, keeping her blazer closed so it covered her gun. "Darina returned to the house a while later – around 4:30," Aislinn said. "Do you know why?"

Kayla's face took on color. "No, no idea."

"I remember you and Darina – out by the pool – talking. She looked upset." The short breaks between the words were inserted for impact.

Kayla swallowed hard and shook her head. "I...I don't remember that."

Aislinn knew she was lying and could either push now or wait until she'd interviewed Cody and Shane, then come back to it. Patience, she figured, was the best option.

"Fair enough," Aislinn said. "I didn't see your name on the list of people attending the reunion."

Kayla stared at Aislinn with hard eyes. "I'm not going."

Aislinn waited a few seconds, then stood and said, "We'll talk again."

Aislinn left her card and took the stairs to the main floor, wondering where she would fit in at the reunion. By the time she was walking through the building lobby she realized it wasn't all that important. She had set her goal to make detective and had been successful – that's all that mattered.

She reached her car and leaned on the quarter panel, staring up at what had been Bromley Heath when she had been a kid in JP. One woman had changed all that and Aislinn shook her head at her tenacity. She couldn't begin to imagine what Mildred Hailey had gone through to pull it off.

"Now that's success," she whispered to herself.

Aislinn slid into her car and texted Curtis what she'd got out of the interview with Kayla Walsh. *Hours before she disappeared a couple of Italian guys were interested in Darina ranting about her dad getting killed. Call if you need details.*

Her phone buzzed ten seconds later. "That was quick."

"I'm on my way to meet with Giuseppe Salvatore," he said. "Fill me in."

Aislinn gave Curtis the story and paused, "Might be nothing."

"Good to know, though," he said. "Talk to you later."

She pulled out from the curb, thinking about Kayla's haughty response to the reunion. The woman didn't have a lot to show for twenty years. But then aside from the Mildred Hailey's of the world, Aislinn wondered who did.

CHAPTER FIFTEEN

The last leg of Curtis's organized crime trifecta was a meeting with Giuseppe "the big fish" Salvatore. A legend in so many ways it was difficult to find a transgression where he wasn't the top of the heap. Alleged murders, kidnappings, racketeering, drug trafficking, loansharking – but he was most notorious for his absurdly low conviction rate. The courts had come down on him once, and for that he served two years. Even Curtis was amazed someone could be that slippery.

Their meeting was at Mamma Maria, an upscale Italian restaurant in the North End. The soft green and yellow façade, with its large, black-framed windows, was the most pleasing retail front on a beautiful street. Curtis pulled up nearby and climbed the short staircase to the door, contemplating how many illegal deals had been brokered inside the restaurant's walls.

Giuseppe was sitting at a deuce by the window and Curtis stopped and waited until the Italian kingpin motioned for him to sit down. They'd met a couple of times before on homicide cases and Curtis knew no one – absolutely no one – set the agenda with the Italian don.

"Thanks for seeing me," he said, a tiny shiver running up his spine.

He couldn't see the muscle but was damn sure they were close by, watching his every move.

Salvatore adjusted the napkin tucked in his collar. "What the fuck do you want, Westcott?" he asked without looking up from his linguini.

"Info on a cold case," Curtis said casually. He wasn't going to get sucked into a pissing match with the gangster.

"Alexi Volkov."

"Yeah, how did you know?" Curtis said, taken aback.

"One of my guys says they dug his daughter out of a wall in Jamaica Plain. Who else would you be asking about."

Christ, do these guys know everything that goes on in the city?

"Okay." Curtis shifted slightly, uncomfortable with the level of knowledge the Italian had. "Not sure where you got that." They still hadn't released their discovery of the body to the press and Curtis was wondering if they had a leak inside the department. If so, it was big trouble.

Salvatore burst into a robust laugh and finally looked up from his dinner. "Police secrets. Fuck, please."

"Did you know him?" Curtis asked.

"Total piece of dogshit," Salvatore said, attacking his pasta with his fork. A few chews followed by a drink of wine, then, "He was trying to be a big man. Couldn't get it through his head that it wasn't going to happen."

"Wanted to be a made man? Curtis asked, knowing only trusted Italians could ever be accepted into the family.

"Fucking Russian."

"Were you the one dealing with him?"

Salvatore nodded, his double chin wobbling with the motion. "Yeah, lucky me. I met with him at least five times, every time telling him to back off. He had some Mickey Mouse protection racket on the go and I had to..." Salvatore leaned forward a few inches, "...*finally* step in and let him know that we didn't appreciate it."

"By killing him?"

Salvatore found that funny and snorted out another spurt of

laughter. "You'd be the last fucking person to know." His voice trailed off. "But nah, we never killed him."

"Who did?" Curtis asked.

Salvatore didn't smile at that. He dug into his pasta and finished it before answering. "You're homicide, Westcott. Whoever whacked this guy is on you."

Jesus, Curtis thought, *you know who pulled the trigger.* He fought to keep the disdain from creeping over his face – he was sitting across the table from the arrogant son of a bitch who could give him the shooter, and probably a lot more. But that wasn't happening and pressing the Italian for it would only incense him.

Curtis backed off and asked, "These rackets Volkov was running, who was he leaning on for protection money?"

Salvatore gave that some thought, then decided to take the safe route. "Not sure about that."

"Did he take any business from you?"

Salvatore smiled coldly. "If he had, that would have changed my answer to your previous question."

Curtis looked out the window to the manicured street. Boston at its absolute finest. "I don't really care about Volkov. I want who killed his daughter."

Salvatore sat back with his wine in hand. "Then why isn't your Irish bitch here talking to me?"

Curtis leaned in, every word deliberate, threatening. "Careful, Giuseppe."

Curtis caught a motion on the far side of the room in his peripheral vision. He didn't look – his eyes stayed locked on Salvatore's. He wasn't going to give the gangster any sort of win on this one.

"All right," Salvatore finally conceded. "Why isn't *Detective* Byrne here?"

"She may be at some point," Curtis said quietly. He leaned back and added, "I don't give a damn what you did twenty years ago, and I don't care what you're up to now, providing it doesn't end up with a body. All I want is who did this. Darina Volkov was seventeen. She was a kid."

"I would *never* kill a kid." The raw edge in his tone resonated loudly – anyone who *did* kill a kid would answer to him.

"Yeah, I know."

Curtis got up and carefully set his card on the table. Dropping it was disrespectful and that would be a mistake with consequences.

"Call me if you think of anything."

"Sure, I'll put you on speed dial."

Curtis let himself out and sucked in a few deep breaths of fresh air. *Christ,* he thought, *sitting across from these thugs was going to take a year off his life. Maybe forty if he said something wrong.*

Salvatore was formidable and had every reason to hate the authorities – from the cops to the courts and the federal jail where his only son, Vincenzo, had been set up and brutally murdered a few years ago. To date, no one had paid the price for the killing and Salvatore was still seething over it, a wild card ready to snap.

Curtis slid into his car and tried to relax – it didn't work. If Giuseppe Salvatore knew who killed Alexi Volkov, then he likely knew who murdered Darina. What *that* meant, was the organized crime angle had legs, which was the *last* place any cop wanted to be working the clues and connecting the dots.

CHAPTER SIXTEEN

Tuesday morning at District A-1 was slow, which is a good thing for a homicide department. The detectives at the top of the rotation were helping organize files while they waited for a call and Curtis made time for coffee with them before settling into his office. Stan showed up five minutes later with a folder tucked under his arm and plopped his large frame into a chair on the opposite side of the desk.

"What have you got?" Curtis asked, rubbing his temples. He hadn't slept a wink all night.

"Nothing yet, I spent a few hours going over the notes in DeMarco's file."

"Anything there?"

Stan flipped the folder open and pulled out a crime scene photo of Tony DeMarco lying on the floor of the electronics store. He handed it to Curtis. "DeMarco surprises the burglar, has his gun out but doesn't get off a shot before the other guy pumps two bullets in his chest. That make sense to you?"

Curtis studied the photo. DeMarco's body was halfway down a long aisle, and a few boxes were lying nearby. "Not really," Curtis said slowly. "What do you get from this?"

"He's midway down the aisle. The perp had to show up at the far end, level his gun and fire from about twenty-five or thirty feet. Damn good shooting to hit such a tight pattern from that distance. Then there's the boxes on the floor." Stan leaned over and pointed at them. "If the thief had those boxes in his hands, that meant he was already halfway down the aisle."

"Right, and how did he get off two shots if his hands were full."

"Exactly," Stan said.

Curtis kept looking at the photo. "DeMarco's gun, it's only a foot or two from his body."

Stan took another look. "Too close. If he's raising his arm to fire and gets hit, the gun goes flying. It's not going to land right beside him."

"Yeah," Curtis said. "Looks like this was staged."

Stan thumbed through the file to a Post-It note. "Says here that DeMarco often worked late and that he drove the same route home every night."

"So if someone wanted to take him out and make it look like a break-in gone wrong, they could wait for him to leave work, then make the call. Burglary in progress, DeMarco is the closest and goes in alone."

"That takes more than one person and surveillance beforehand."

Curtis nodded. "One watching the precinct, the other already in the store."

There was a sharp knock and Aislinn poked her head in. Curtis waved at her and she slipped into the seat next to Stan.

"You look like shit, LT," she said. "No sleep last night?"

"Well, you know," Curtis said. "We were just talking about DeMarco and thinking it might have been a setup." He took a minute to rub his hands over his bloodshot eyes, then brought her up to speed while Stan fed her the crime scene photos.

"Tied into the Volkov hit?" Aislinn asked, staring at DeMarco lying on the floor.

Stan shrugged. "First the old man, then his daughter, then the detective working the file. Lot of coincidences there."

"Too many," Aislinn said. She handed the photos back to Stan. "Anything come out of your meeting with Salvatore?"

"He's adamant they didn't kill Volkov." Curtis smiled grimly. "The same as the Irish and the Russians."

"So nobody killed Alexi Volkov," Stan said. "He shot himself in the back of the head in his driveway and then got rid of the gun."

"Yeah, there's got to be something to this organized crime angle," Aislinn said. "Alexi was pissing off almost everyone with his racketeering business."

"Well, the old guard know we like one of them for it," Curtis said. "If we keep poking we might get a push in the right direction." Curtis opened Volkov's file and pulled out the contact info for the three gangsters he'd met. He turned to Aislinn. "Salvatore won't be upset if you show up. You can surprise the other two."

"Good cop, bad cop," she said, snapping a picture of the page with her phone.

"I was thinking just bad cop, if you're comfortable with going in alone." Curtis knew Aislinn could take care of herself but wanted to be sure. When she nodded, he continued. "What else have we got?" The last thing they wanted was to head down the wrong rabbit hole.

"DeMarco could have simply been in the wrong place at the wrong time," Stan said.

"You believe that?" Aislinn asked.

"No."

"Say it's a setup," Aislinn postulated. "That means someone who knows his schedule, his route home, and…" she thought for a moment, "…that he wasn't wearing a vest."

"Not sure I get how the shooter knows he doesn't have a vest," Curtis said.

Aislinn reached over and picked up the photo. "He's halfway down the aisle, it's dark and he has a gun in his hand, so the perp probably has him for a cop. Cops wear vests, but the shooter aimed at his chest."

"Good point," Curtis said. "Stan, what do you think?"

Stan shook his head. "You're throwing out everything except a setup if you go there. If it's a burglary and the shooter comes around the corner and spots DeMarco, maybe he just aims and fires. Reflex, without thinking about a vest."

"That's possible," Curtis said. "So we're not sure."

Both detectives nodded, but not convincingly. All three of them were thinking someone had set out to kill a cop. A long, awkward silence followed.

"And the interviews with the friends who saw Darina just before she was killed?" Curtis asked Aislinn.

"Two down, two to go," she said. "I've done Kayla Walsh and had a quick chat with Sofia Morales – the one who moved to Europe with her family right after she was finished school. That didn't go anywhere, so nothing much yet. I'll have it wrapped up by tomorrow night." Sensing Curtis wanted more, she added, "The first reunion event is tomorrow and Cody Hall and Shane Collins are both registered to attend. I'll track them down and chat with them after they've had a couple of drinks."

"Not very private," Curtis said.

"It'll be okay, lots of places to pull them aside. Busy tonight, dinner at the parents'."

"Ahh," Curtis said thoughtfully. "You'll be seeing Cian."

"Of course, and dad's retired buddies from the force will be there as well. They're playing cards after." She caught the look in Curtis's eyes and said, "Are we thinking the same thing, that these guys could be a resource?"

Curtis nodded. "Giuseppe Salvatore said Volkov was running a protection racket. Grocery and electronics stores, a dry cleaner, a funeral home – maybe your dad, or one of the guys, would have an idea which businesses they targeted. If we can narrow it down, we can talk with whoever was in charge of paying Volkov the protection money. Maybe his partner was collecting it."

"That could be *very* helpful," Stan agreed.

"If I remember right, Larry and Ken were officers and Arnie was a sergeant," Curtis said, turning to his computer. "Let's see if there's anything sketchy on their records before we involve them."

Aislinn and Stan sat quietly while Curtis accessed their profiles.

"Ken Smith." Curtis paused to scroll through the file. "He was stationed at Dorchester and his record is spotless." A minute later, "Larry Toews spent most of his career on the streets in Roxbury. Zip on him too."

"I've seen dinosaurs type faster," Stan said as Curtis tapped on his keyboard.

Curtis threw him a look, then said, "Arnie Walsh was a staff sergeant. Got himself written up for getting a bit rough with a drunk in a remand cell, but nothing ever came of it. Retired in 2016."

"Arnie was always a bit excitable," Aislinn said. "Kayla knew how to push his buttons."

"What kid doesn't," Stan said, and there was little doubt it was coming from personal experience.

"Ahh, Cian Byrne." Curtis raised an eyebrow. "Now here's trouble." He grinned at the modicum of shock on Aislinn's face. "They all look okay."

Curtis cleared his throat and said emphatically, "Make sure they know everything you talk about is confidential."

"Of course."

"Okay, if they're agreeable I don't see any downside."

She laughed. "I'm pretty sure they'll be up for it. Back in the game and all that. Dad said he was going to bill us for his time."

Curtis grinned. "Good luck with that."

CHAPTER SEVENTEEN

The Rat Pack were in fine form as Aislinn started up the walk to the house, all laughing at some joke, then settling back into a wash of dull murmurs as they spotted her approaching. Four pairs of eyes were focused as she stopped part way up the sidewalk, leaned over and plucked a weed from the flower bed with a solitary, deliberate motion. She held it up like a trophy.

"You missed one," she said to her father. That started a cacophony of hoots from the crowd.

"Sneaky little bastards they are," Cian proclaimed loudly over the din.

Ken chimed in. "And they never stop. Christ, the old ticker could give out."

Larry grinned, his teeth just crooked enough to make his smile unique and, somehow, pleasing. Tanned and lean from non-stop golf and triathlons, he hardly looked seventy-two. "Condo living, baby, that's where it's at."

"I wish." Arnie's smooth Dean-Martin voice quieted the throng. "That damn swimming pool is more work than it's worth. Skim it, clean the filter, test the pH, top up the water level – it's never-ending."

Aislinn smiled. "Yeah, but it was the best when we were kids. Everyone loved going to Kayla's house."

"And you kids ate all my food," Arnie crooned with a smile and a whiskey in hand. That elicited a fresh wave of laughs, especially from Aislinn. Arnie's good looks had passed straight through to Kayla and it was little wonder she was the gorgeous one in the group. "Almost had to work two jobs for God's sake."

"Well, look at you now. All retired and happy." Aislinn grabbed a beer from the cooler, sat in a chair beside her dad and turned to face the line of ex-cops. "Mind if I pick your brains a bit?" she asked the group.

The crew brightened at the prospect of getting their toes back in the water. They were all ears.

"Absolutely." Cian spoke for the bunch. "Is this about your latest case?"

"It is." She settled in, getting comfortable. "Anything we talk about is confidential. You guys okay with that?" They all nodded and she continued. "Westcott gave me the okay to discuss things with you and get your input. You were on the streets back in 2000 and we're thinking it might be good to tap into all that first-hand experience."

"How can we help?" Arnie asked, leaning forward.

"We're thinking Alexi and Darina's murders may be linked. Considering she probably ran into the guy who killed her dad, we're looking at who might have wanted Alexi Volkov dead, and that got us focused on his racketeering business."

"So he *was* running rackets," Cian said, and Aislinn nodded. "Who was the muscle behind him?"

She shrugged. "No idea. Curtis talked to some of the mob bigwigs – Irish, Russian, Italian – guys from back in 2000, but none of them have admitted to working with Volkov."

Larry shook his head. "You can't run a racket without some sort of organization. Not a chance."

Aislinn nodded in his direction. "That's the thing. One of them must be lying."

"Okay," Cian said. "So you're wanting help with which businesses might have paid Volkov protection money and thought we might have some ideas."

Ken sipped his beer. "Aislinn, you should be talking to the guys over in Vice."

Aislinn gave him a slow nod and a hint of a smile. "Maybe, but I don't get invited to their place for dinner. Thought I'd start with you four dinosaurs." Her smile disappeared. "You were on the street. You saw which businesses were vulnerable, who was protected and who wasn't. You probably know more than you think."

Ken was nodding now, slowly at first, then a bit faster. "You're right. Between the four of us we could make a pretty good list. Might take a day or two."

"Anything else?" Larry asked.

"Nah, that's it for now," she said. "Unless you think of something that might be relevant. Don't be shy."

"Where are you in the case?" Arnie asked.

"I'm talking with everyone who saw Darina the day she disappeared, but nothing concrete so far."

"Right, the girls who were at our house before the prom," Arnie said.

"And some others," Aislinn said. When none of the group said anything, she added, "Kristin Sanders, Cody Hall and Shane Collins – they were all part of things on the day."

"Didn't they give witness statements at the time?" Arnie asked.

"They did, but I want to speak with them again."

"Man, I remember that night," Cian said. "Arnie and I were both on shift."

"Me too, stuck in a patrol car with a rookie," Ken said. "That weekend hasn't faded much over the years."

"You offered to drive the kids home if they drank too much," Cian said to Arnie.

Arnie shook his head "None of them took me up on it. I think most of the little buggers stayed out all night." That got a few muted chuckles.

Ken said to Aislinn, "You must have filled out a witness statement."

"I did."

"Did you get a chance to read it?" Larry asked.

"Yup," she said. "That was strange, reading what I told the police when I was a teenager."

"But you were a good witness." Cian stated it as a fact.

Aislinn laughed. "Sort of. They called me *credible*. Kristin Sanders was probably the best – said that Darina made a phone call from her place before taking off in her car."

"Who did she call?" Arnie asked.

"No idea. There was a note in the file that they were unable to trace it."

Aislinn's mother pushed open the screen door. "Aislinn, sweety, are these...people..." She scanned the entire group. "...bothering you?"

"Just talking with the boys." Aislinn smiled.

"Dinner isn't going to cook itself." Fiona gave Cian an admonishing look. "Someone needs to get on the barbeque."

"Pushy," Cian said with a wink as he hauled himself out of his chair.

The group padded around to the back yard, leaving Aislinn alone on the verandah. She curled up in the chair and scrolled through her emails, then pulled up the agenda for the English School's twenty-year reunion – Wednesday night was the first event. It was an icebreaker in the gym, or in other words, a full-frontal assault by hundreds of kids with whom she had spent the most stressful years of her life. She cringed at the thought. Nevertheless, it would be interesting to see if the cool kids were still on top. She had her doubts.

Her phone rang and she checked the caller ID – it was CSI.

"Byrne," she said.

"Aislinn, it's Lenore Sutherland with Forensics. I might have something for you on Darina Volkov."

"What?" Aislinn asked, her heartbeat picking up.

"Rebecca Carlisle peeled away what was left of the skin covering the impact point on her skull and I put it under some serious magnification. It looks to me like it was made by a pistol butt with an identifiable pattern. Not positive, but it looks like a Heckler & Koch P2000 – that's my best guess at this time."

"So whoever killed her had a gun, but they knocked her out and strangled her," Aislinn said.

"I think so."

"So why not just shoot her?" Aislinn said.

"Too noisy, probably."

"Makes sense." Aislinn waited for more, but Lenore was quiet. "Anything else?"

"Not right now. Rebecca mentioned that she should have your tox scan soon. FYI."

"Good, and thanks."

The aroma of burgers wafted around the side of the house and Aislinn shut down her phone and joined the gang for dinner. They were a rowdy bunch, bantering back and forth about pretty much anything, and Fiona joined them and got in her two-cents worth a few times, not an easy thing to do in such an opinionated crowd. Eventually the conversation returned to Aislinn's case.

"How well did you know Tony DeMarco?" Aislinn asked her dad.

"Tony and I were tight," Cian responded as the others quieted. "Yeah, he was a good guy."

Fiona cut in. "I really liked Tony. Polite, always took a minute to ask me how I was doing."

Her mother knew most of the guys from the precinct. They had been stopping by for years to play poker or darts and drink beer, and Cian's was the place to let off steam. Aislinn remembered those days vividly as well – the men in the basement with the dart board, their howls of agony or joy at missing or making a shot still fresh in her head.

"And Tony running into that building when it was on fire, saving those two people," Larry said.

Aislinn cocked her head slightly. "I don't know that one."

"Shit, he was only nineteen, got a medal for bravery," Larry said. "That's what led him into the force."

"What's the story?" Aislinn asked, her curiosity piqued. All the guys looked at Cian, the storyteller in the group.

"Tony was walking down the alley behind this three-story on Center Street," Cian said. "A woman was hanging out the window on the top floor with a toddler, screaming. The building was on fire and Tony was on the scene before the fire department arrived. Crazy bastard ran into the place, got to the top floor and carried both of them out. The whole thing went up like a matchstick. Another minute and that woman and her kid would have died in the fire."

"Wow," Aislinn shuddered. "That's impressive."

"Yeah, it sure was," Larry said. "That was Tony, always willing to take a risk."

"Anything else you can tell me about him?" Aislinn figured she had hit gold with the gang, they would know things that never made it into a personnel file.

Cian reflected on it, then said, "Very thorough, took his job seriously. He could be the toughest son-of-a-bitch in the precinct when he had to."

"Remember that young guy who got run over," Ken said. "That really shook Tony up."

"Oh, yeah," Cian said. "There was this hit and run where a guy died. Ken was first on the scene, I got there a couple of minutes after, and then Tony arrived. The young fella, he was all smashed up and the paramedics did everything they could but it was awful. I looked over at Tony and there were tears. The real thing. It shook him up bad."

Aislinn thought about how she would have reacted and knew there would be no tears. The job was already tough enough without people seeing your emotions.

"Did you hear anything about how Tony died?" she asked.

The guys all looked at each other, then Cian shook his head. "No more than anyone else on the force. He stopped in on a burglary in progress and was shot. Fucking tragedy. No reason for it."

"Well, maybe there was," Aislinn said.

That caused a few heads to jerk about. "What? What are you saying?" Cian asked.

She instantly regretted how she'd blurted it out, but these were guys who had known Tony and they might give her something that wasn't in the police records. "Stan Lamers has reopened Tony's file. We're looking at it as potentially tied to the Volkov murders." She held up a finger to her lips. "Confidential, guys. Let's keep this between us."

Five pairs of dumbfounded eyes stared back at her.

"Yeah, of course." Arnie swallowed hard. "Jesus…Tony."

"Sorry to bring this up," Aislinn said.

"You thinking that Tony was getting close on the Volkov file and someone took him out?" Larry asked.

"We're not leaning one way or the other right now," Aislinn said. "Just keeping an open mind on Tony's death is all."

"I thought these mob types don't kill cops," Fiona said.

"They don't…usually," Cian replied.

Aislinn stood. "Well, anything you can think of that might help."

"Got it," Arnie said for the crew.

She left it at that and set her empty on the table. "Later, all." She could hear the anger in the men's voices as she headed down the sidewalk for home. *Time,* she thought, *doesn't heal all wounds.*

She started her car but didn't put it in gear. Her hands were shaking slightly and she felt a touch queasy. The idea of someone deliberately killing a cop for doing their job was something they all had to live with. What if it was Curtis or Stan – or her for that matter? She couldn't begin to imagine the shit that would hit the fan – there would be hell to pay. That was probably the motivation behind making Tony DeMarco's death look like a bungled robbery rather than a planned assassination.

Night was settling in and the street darkened. Aislinn locked the car doors, uncomfortable with the feeling they were dealing with a well-organized, sadistic killer or worse, killers.

CHAPTER EIGHTEEN

Stan Lamers plopped into his chair on Wednesday morning and opened the email from Tony DeMarco's bank. It was five years of bank records from 1997 to his death in 2002. He clicked on the encrypted file, entered the password he had received earlier from the bank and started scrolling through the statements.

It didn't take a forensic accountant to expose the anomalies. DeMarco's account had seen a series of deposits over the years that were out of sync with the rest of his banking history. It was only a few thousand here and there, but enough to raise red flags. Stan opened the file from the 2002 investigation and went through it, line by line.

There was no mention of any anomalies in Tony's banking records.

He leaned back in his chair and stared at the screen. There was no way the detectives working the file would have missed that. Unless they purposely left it out. Which meant they were thinking DeMarco was taking money from someone and they kept it under wraps in order to protect his reputation. It was the only explanation. He printed ten pages of statements – enough to establish a pattern – and hoofed it down the hall to Westcott's office.

"Got a minute?" Stan asked.

"Sure." Curtis rolled his chair sideways a couple of feet so he didn't have to look over his screen. "What's up?"

"I think DeMarco was on the take." He handed over the printouts and waited while Curtis looked through them. "Hard to miss," Stan said when Curtis was done.

"Yeah, very hard." Curtis set the thin stack of paper on his desk. "Are you thinking the detectives working DeMarco's case ignored it?"

"What else? It's impossible that they didn't see it." Stan flipped back to the first page in the case file. "Whitney and Brooks were the guys assigned. They've both retired."

"Oh shit," Curtis groaned. A hot potato had just dropped in their laps.

"Oh shit, what?" Aislinn appeared at the door and Curtis waved her in. Stan gave her the lowdown on what he'd discovered and her already pale face went whiter.

"So we've got a dirty cop who has been dead almost twenty years and *we* get to deal with it," she said.

Curtis rubbed his hand over the stubble on his chin, his lips set in a thin line. "Let's think this through." He motioned for Aislinn or Stan to close the door. "DeMarco is a respected cop killed in the line of duty and that's something we don't want to mess with unless we have to. Agreed?"

"Yeah," Aislinn said.

"Abso-fucking-lutely," Stan said.

"Okay then, what we have so far is mounting evidence that DeMarco was set up. We think – and I emphasize the word *think* – that his murder was planned and somehow tied to Alexi Volkov's."

"And Darina's," Aislinn added.

"Right," Curtis said. "Everything is pointing to organized crime having a hand in this. Whether it's the Italians, the Russians or the Irish, if the mob is involved it's entirely possible that DeMarco was on the take for either some sort of service or his silence."

"Probably for keeping his mouth shut," Stan said. "He might have uncovered something when he was working the Volkov case."

"When did the payments start?" Aislinn asked.

Stan reached over and picked up the bank statements. He scowled and dropped them back on the desk. "At least a year before Alexi Volkov was killed. I didn't print everything the bank sent so not exactly sure."

"Figure out when the payments started," Curtis said. "If DeMarco was taking money prior to Volkov's murder, then how he got the case is suspect. Was he in the rotation or did he worm his way in on it."

"Fuck, this just keeps getting better," Stan said. "If DeMarco talked another detective into giving him the case, then he likely threw the investigation as well."

"And..." Curtis said, "...we have Whitney and Brooks closing ranks and ignoring the payments to DeMarco. If this gets out they could end up on charges and lose their pensions."

Curtis got up and walked over to the window. Twenty years old or not, this had all the markings of a front page story. Worse, his team would be the ones crapping all over the reputation of a decorated, respected cop shot on the job. The two detectives who worked the file managed to leave DeMarco's reputation intact, but now Aislinn and Stan were painted into a corner. Sullying DeMarco's name had the potential to crater both their careers on the spot – after that they'd be ostracized and no one would work with them. As for himself, his own job would be unworkable if he lost the trust of his detectives and they shunned him.

If they got caught keeping it under wraps and ended up in front of Internal Affairs, the three of them could lose their jobs, their pensions and their reputations. Elian Perez was new to the job of Police Commissioner, and from their brief meeting on Chloe's boat Curtis suspected the man would be furious at the scandal. It was doubtful Perez would charge them with obstruction, but no matter how things went they were in a terrible situation.

He turned around and said, "We need to be cognizant of Perez on this one. He's going to see shades of Rampart in it."

"The police corruption thing in LA." Aislinn rolled her eyes. "Great."

They all knew Rampart, it was the notorious division of the LA police that had been assigned the newly-formed CRASH unit – Community Resources Against Street Hoodlums – back in the late '90's. It hadn't gone well.

"Perez was being considered for the LA police commissioner position before everything hit the fan."

"But this is nothing compared to that," Stan said. "The whole precinct was corrupt, something like seventy officers."

Curtis nodded. "They were planting evidence, gunning down gang members without any provocation, dealing drugs and then perjuring themselves in court. They even robbed a bank – got something like three-quarters of a million dollars."

Aislinn shook her head. "Hard to believe."

"Well," Curtis said with resignation. "It gutted the reputation of the LA police department for decades and Perez will view this through the same lens."

Curtis turned and stared out the window, painfully aware of the crosshairs that would be focused on all three of them. He kicked around their options for a minute, then faced Aislinn and Stan.

"Not a word of this gets out," Curtis said. "Stan, once you've established when the payments started, encrypt the bank file and lock it away somewhere no one will find it. Shred those printouts. Stay away from Whitney and Brooks, we run the investigation on our own. No good can come from bringing in the guys who let a dead officer off the hook eighteen years ago."

Relief was painted all over Stan's face. "Got it."

"Aislinn, have a chat with your dad, get a feel for whether there were any rumors back then."

"Tony's name came up last night at dinner with Dad and his buddies," Aislinn shot back.

Curtis waited, then said, "And where did that go?"

"They all knew him, Dad especially, said they were really tight. Kind of guy who was highly regarded. Mom thought he was a bit of a hero."

"You remember him?" Curtis asked Aislinn.

"I do. Tony was one of the quiet ones, at least when I was around. He seemed nice, but I didn't get to know him much. I was Cian's kid, that's all." Aislinn's pulse picked up, this was hitting close to home. "Dad never mentioned anything about anyone taking cash."

"He wouldn't have, even if he suspected." Curtis returned to his desk and sat down, worry lines creasing his forehead. "Cian's a good resource, Aislinn. My guess is that he may know more than he's letting on."

Aislinn bit her lower lip. "I don't think I can just come out and ask him. He's pretty old school that way. It's going to take some coaxing, especially if he thinks we're looking to out a dead cop for being dirty."

"Well, we have time," Curtis said. "These cases aren't going anywhere."

"I asked Dad and his friends to make a list of businesses that might have been paying for protection. Maybe I can segue in from that."

"It's a stretch," Stan shook his head.

They both looked at Curtis, who said, "If we're going to keep this tight to the chest then we can't start asking *anyone* questions about whether DeMarco was clean or not. The shit would hit the fan in no time. I think our only resource right now is Cian Byrne, and that's only because his daughter is in the crosshairs."

"Agreed," Aislinn said. "But I need time."

"Want me to pull Nyson's bank records?" Stan asked.

Curtis shook his head. "No, I don't think so. It'll light a fuse if someone notices you're pulling bank statements on two different cops. Nyson died a couple of years ago of natural causes so we can look into him down the road if the mob connection to DeMarco has legs."

"Yeah, yeah. Right."

Curtis gave both his detectives a long look. "If these murders are linked and we start uncovering stuff that threatens the killer, they're coming after us. Twenty years down the road or not."

Neither of them said a word.

"All right, let's keep pushing ahead on all three files. Everything offline, that way no one in the department can see what we're looking at. We share everything we find, in this office, in person, nothing by email or text."

"Ugly," Stan said, looking grim.

"Beyond ugly." Aislinn's pale skin was white as snow. "*Way beyond.*"

CHAPTER NINETEEN

Aislinn psyched herself up for the awkward moment of walking into the school and being surrounded by people who were now mostly strangers. After twenty years the feelings of uncertainty she'd lived with during her high school years had washed away, as had most of her childhood friendships. It was normal for high school friends to drift apart and not see each other for years, or maybe never again, and not surprisingly that was exactly how it had played out for her.

She had lost track of Cody Hall immediately after graduation and had only a vague idea of what he'd been up to for the past two decades. She knew Shane Collins had joined the marines and shipped off overseas, but that was about it. Truth was, she hadn't put any effort into staying in touch with anyone, and now the opportunity to talk with Cody and Shane was her main reason for attending the icebreaker. Both had been decent guys and it might actually be nice to catch up with them.

Aislinn found a parking space in the crowded lot and walked toward the school, an imposing, low slung brick building with impressive sporting fields. The English School, as every kid who ever attended knew, was the first high school in America. It was a badge of honor every alumnus wore, and to this day a chill went up her spine when she thought of the history they were part of.

Aislinn rubbed her hands over her jeans, tight to her hips, and touched her gun to make sure it was far enough back on her belt to be out of sight under her blazer. Her blue crewneck tee was snug and she drew a few looks as she strode under the welcome banner into the cavernous lobby.

The place was bustling without being packed and the anonymity of being a face in the crowd felt good. Numerous smiling alumni were manning a long reception table and she joined the queue for the letters A-C. The well-dressed, slightly balding man in line ahead of her turned and said, "Rob Coutts."

She smiled. "Aislinn Byrne."

The look on his face said he didn't remember her. "This is really something. Becky's knocked it out of the park."

She smiled. "Becky was always good at organizing."

A bit more small talk as they waited, then it was his turn at the table. He collected his package, wished her a good time at the event and disappeared into the crowd. Aislinn stepped up, gave her name then waited as the man flipped through the envelopes. She noticed Shane Collins' package was still in the box and she decided it would be best to hang around the lobby and wait for him to check in.

After going through the entire box without finding hers, the man checked a list sitting off to the side. "Oh, it looks like you just signed up. We don't have a package for you, but here's a program and a blank name tag. Just write your name on it with felt pen. There's some at the end of the table."

"Thanks."

She moved off to the side and slipped the name tag in her pocket, then leaned against the wall and watched the constant stream of people filing in through the entrance. She recognized an occasional face, but twenty years after sharing the halls she was drawing a lot of blanks. Two men ambled into the lobby and Aislinn breathed a bit easier. Cody and Shane had arrived together, Cody limping and using a cane. They split up and got into their lines, and when Cody got through first she sidled over.

"Hi," she said.

"Aislinn." Cody broke into an easy smile. "Oh, shit, you look good girl."

The long, thick dreadlocks were gone, replaced by kinky hair, tight to his head and a well-groomed beard that suited him to a T. What hadn't changed were those unmistakable fun-loving eyes, still brimming over with peace and compassion.

"What's with the cane?" Aislinn asked.

"Never heard about the accident?" he asked and she shook her head. "I hit a five ton truck head-on when I was visiting friends in Connecticut."

Shane had spotted them but was still a good way from the front of his line. Cody grinned and waved at him, pointed at Aislinn and mouthed her name. Shane gave them a wave back.

"So you still hang out with Shane," she said.

"Yeah, we stayed in touch. He's had a rough go of it."

Quintessential Cody – the one who had almost died in a car crash – thinking Shane was the guy who had it rough.

She focused on Cody. "Looking good yourself." She backed up a couple of steps and gave him a head-to-toe look over. "No, better than good – great."

He just laughed at that.

Aislinn felt a sudden interest in what Cody was up to. "So, where did life take you?"

He beamed at that. "I'm a software developer."

She raised an eyebrow. "Nice. What sort of software?"

"Games. You know, like Grand Theft Auto and Assassin's Creed."

"Seriously?" she said. When he nodded she added, "That's big business."

"It is, it's huge."

"I'm still back in the Super Mario days."

He burst out laughing. "Video dinosaur," he teased her. "I don't know, I always liked gaming and thought up different ways the game could have gone to make it better. Now I get to design the flow."

"Sort of like a game architect," she said.

"Yeah, yeah, nicely put. I like that." His eyes were sparkling now.

"I hope they pay you well."

He just grinned.

They shuffled toward the wall as a large, noisy group went past, then he said, "I heard you're a cop now."

"I am."

"Where's your beat?"

"Mostly Central Boston and JP, but I move around," she said. The look on his face said he wanted more. "I'm a homicide detective."

He let out a low, appreciative whistle as Shane Collins came toward them, lanyard already around his neck. He still had the same long gait and rigid posture, but other than that she barely recognized him. He'd aged, his cheeks gaunt and covered with two days stubble. His eyes were dark and sunken, but he wore a wide smile as he approached.

"Aislinn Byrne," Shane said when he reached them. "Still got the red hair, but where are the freckles?"

"Wore off," she said, smiling.

They moved into the gym and lined up at one of the bars. Drinks in hand they found a quiet space to talk and got at the task of catching up. Shane had deployed to Iraq in 2003 in an armored division and was promoted to tank commander two years later. She asked him what it was like overseas but couldn't get through his protective shell. Aislinn let it drop, his demeanor was telling her everything she needed to know – Shane was struggling with PTSD. She'd seen it numerous times when interviewing veterans during homicide investigations. Shane excused himself from the group after a while, leaving Aislinn alone with Cody.

"I wanted to talk with you," Aislinn said over the crowd. "Can we go somewhere quieter?"

"Sure."

Aislinn set a reasonable pace so Cody could keep up, him favoring his leg that had been shattered in the crash. They settled into a nook just off the main lobby and she got right to the issue at hand.

"Remember Darina Volkov?"

"Of course," Cody said, massaging his thigh.

"Well, we found her," Aislinn said, watching his face closely.

His expression turned serious. "Oh, oh. This doesn't sound good."

She shook her head. "It's confidential for now. We haven't released anything to the media yet." He nodded that he understood and she filled him in on their gruesome discovery, then said, "I wanted to talk with you about the day she went missing."

"Oh – my – God." Cody took a deep breath. "Unbelievable." He closed his eyes and sat rock-still for a minute. When he finally opened his eyes, he said, "How can I help?"

Aislinn pulled out her notebook. "Darina stopped by your place after she had lunch with Kayla Walsh. About what time was that and what did you two talk about?"

He took a minute to get the memory straight, then said, "She came over around 1:00 or 1:30 and we cracked a beer on the patio in the back yard. My parents were working so no one was home and I remember that it was sunny and warm. A really nice day."

Until someone grabbed Darina and killed her, Aislinn thought.

"She was uptight about going to the prom with Shane, told me he wasn't her first choice."

Aislinn studied his face, looking for any sign that Cody knew he was the one Darina had wanted. She didn't see any telltale signs. "Anything else?"

"Well," he hesitated. "She probably shouldn't have been carrying that much money around with her."

Aislinn's head jerked around. "What sort of money are you talking here?"

He shrugged. "It was a lot of bills, in the thousands for sure."

Aislinn leaned in, wanting more. "Tell me exactly what happened – how you saw the money, where she kept it, everything you can think of."

Cody rubbed at his beard, focusing hard. "She had it in that bag she always carried around with her. She was digging for her keys and I saw it. She gave me this *You never saw that* look, then turned her back to me, pulled out one of the rolls and thumbed through it. Then she freaked out."

"Freaked out? How so?"

"She was all upset and mumbled something like *Fucking Kayla* or *Fuck you Kayla,* then she stuffed it back in her bag."

"How thick was this roll of bills?"

"There were five or six rolls, each with an elastic." He held out a hand, his finger and thumb nowhere near touching each other. "All of them, except one, about that same thickness."

"What denominations?"

"Hundreds."

"You sure?"

"Oh, yeah. It was nuts." He stopped for a moment while a couple of attendees walked by. "I always half wondered if she made a run for it." He stared up at the ceiling. "All that cash, then she just vanishes."

"I can see why you'd think that." Aislinn flipped back in her notebook and put a star beside the note she had made earlier about following up on the college cash. The investigating detective's entry in Darina's file about her having some *college money* certainly didn't paint the same picture as what Cody had just told her, and it was now looking like a possible motive.

"You didn't know?" Cody sounded a bit rattled.

"Not really," Aislinn said. "Why didn't you tell the police?"

There was a long break, then he said, "I didn't want them to think I took the money. That I had any sort of motivation in her disappearance. And," he paused again, "if she *had* wanted to disappear, why make it harder for her."

Aislinn weighed his response, keeping in mind that Cody was in his teens at the time. Fear of getting pinched by the cops was a very real thing, especially twenty years ago when he was a black teenager and money was missing. His reasoning was entirely believable. *Sadly,* she thought, *not much had changed in two decades.*

"Did she talk about her father's death at all?" Aislinn asked.

He nodded. "Sort of. After a couple of beers the emotions started to flow. She was still really upset about what happened to her dad. Who wouldn't be?"

Aislinn prodded him for another ten minutes, but there was nothing else of interest, just talk about what was going on at school at the time and the upcoming prom. Finally Aislinn said, "I'm going to find Shane and have a chat with him. Darina went to his place after she left yours."

They walked together into the gym where Janet Jackson was on the sound system and groups of alumni were standing about talking. She gave him a smile and scanned the room for Shane Collins. The layers were starting to peel back like they always did as the investigation heated up. The truth coming closer all the time.

CHAPTER TWENTY

Curtis parked his car near the front door of Murphy's Law, where Patrick O'Reilly was waiting for him. *The danger,* Curtis thought, *wasn't immediate.* That wasn't how it worked with gangs and gangsters. They were like wild animals – the ones with incredible patience – able to assess their prey and then wait for the right moment to pounce. Every interaction with them was a cat and mouse game where pushing too far could set off their simmering resentment, unleashing a cascade of violence down the road. Not now, but always later, when it wasn't expected. *That,* Curtis knew, *was the danger.*

The Southie pub was quiet when he entered. A few guys were at the bar watching sports, and *Whisky in the Jar* played on the stereo just loud enough not to be a bother. He walked through to the back where Patrick O'Reilly was sitting at a table with two of his guys. They got up when Curtis arrived and O'Reilly pointed at one of the chairs. Curtis checked out the room noting where the muscle had settled in, then he sat facing O'Reilly.

"Our second meeting in one week. People are going to talk." The Irish gangster seemed in better spirts than when they'd met at the gym, probably owing to the wide array of empty beer mugs on the table.

"I doubt they'll think we're dating," Curtis said, politely waving off the server's offer of a pint.

"What is it this time?"

"Today is entirely off the record," Curtis said, then doled out the familiar spiel. "Nothing we talk about goes any further than this table. It doesn't go in my file and you don't say a word to anyone. You okay with that?"

O'Reilly's interest was piqued and he managed a tight smile. "Okay, off the record."

"Tony DeMarco, was he dirty?"

A brief look of surprise registered on O'Reilly's face. "That's an interesting question."

"It's meant to be," Curtis said. "Was he taking money from someone?"

O'Reilly motioned to the server and she sauntered off to the bar and returned with a frothing beer. He took a drink and wiped the foam from his upper lip.

"Why ask that?

Curtis knew what he wanted from the meeting and he wasn't going to get there by doing any sort of dance or letting O'Reilly ask the questions. And the Irishman was smart enough to know that even off the record he could incriminate himself on other criminal activity. Straightforward was the best way.

"We dug into DeMarco's bank records," Curtis said. "It looks like he was on someone's payroll, we're just not sure whose."

O'Reilly's bushy eyebrows went up at that. "And that got him killed."

"Something like that," Curtis said.

"Serious shit you're talking – premeditated murder of a cop." O'Reilly dug into the beer with a renewed vigor, draining most of it in one draught. "There was talk. DeMarco's name came up a few times."

"Was he in with you?"

"Not a fucking chance," O'Reilly spat.

"Then who?" Curtis asked.

O'Reilly hunkered down. "Like I said, word was out on the street. Not sure where it all led to."

Curtis was pretty sure O'Reilly knew *exactly* where *it* led to, but pushing any more wouldn't be productive, or smart. There were other ways to find out.

"Think DeMarco's death is tied in with Volkov and his daughter?" Curtis asked.

"Still off the record?" O'Reilly asked.

Curtis was careful answering – if O'Reilly admitted to involvement he couldn't look the other way. "If there's a link between you and the murders we'll chase it down."

"Then *no comment*."

"Fair enough." Curtis had the answer he needed. "Unless you have something else to add."

"That's what I live for, helping the cops."

Curtis sat without moving for a half minute, eyes locked on O'Reilly. "This was helpful and I won't forget. I'm not coming after you unless you give me a reason."

O'Reilly grinned. "Like I'd fucking do that."

Curtis stood and walked out without looking back. He had what he'd come for. Validation that the discovery of Darina's body had dumped an absolute shitstorm on him and his detectives. Nothing was worse than overturning a rock and finding a cop on the take. Except, maybe, when that cop had died in the line of duty without a shred of scandal to his name. *Yeah,* Curtis thought, *this is a fucking doozie.*

* * *

AISLINN CAUGHT Shane's eye as he mingled with a group of ex-jocks and gave him a shrug of her head. He nodded, broke off from the group and joined her against the back wall of the gym. *You Rock my World* by Invincible came blasting out from the bank of speakers and the dance floor was instantly crowded.

Aislinn leaned in and yelled over the music, "Need to talk."

Shane pointed at the exit and she nodded. They escaped the noise and walked down the hallway, lined on both sides with lockers, until Shane stopped near a water fountain and leaned on the wall.

"Takes you back, all this," he said. "My locker was along here."

Aislinn was fascinated by his eyes, how they flickered, taking in every detail around him. "Sure, because you were one of the cool guys."

He laughed. "So were you."

"Freckly, skinny little thing, I was," she said. "Never cool."

His eyes seemed to settle for a moment, then they were moving again. *No peace of mind,* she thought, still wondering what had happened over there. Being a tank commander couldn't have been easy.

A couple of heavy drinkers came jostling down the hall loudly. They made a stupid comment about Aislinn's jeans being just the right amount of tight on her ass and Shane tensed up. Aislinn gripped his arm, he was waiting for them to say something else.

"I have a gun," she said quietly. "In case they diss off some other body part."

He started to laugh. "Got it. No problem here."

Aislinn waited until the sots were gone, then said, "Maybe you can help me with Darina Volkov."

There was a blank look for a moment, then he said, "*How*?"

"We found her body a few days ago."

"Jesus, Aislinn." He sucked in a deep breath and peered down at her with shattered eyes. "You okay?" When she nodded, he said, "That whole idea that she just took off never made a lick of sense to me." His voice sounded agitated.

"Why not?" Aislinn asked.

"She was done high school, had her college money. She was out of here anyway, why would she put her mom through that, especially after what happened to her dad."

"You knew about the money?" Aislinn said.

Another group of guys with drinks in hand rounded the corner before Shane could answer and headed back down the hallway. They slowed as they approached Aislinn and Shane, then stopped.

"Hey, I think I remember you," one of them said to Aislinn. "Cute redhead – Byrne somebody."

Aislinn slipped out her badge and held it up. "Go back to the party."

Shane watched them tuck in their tails and get moving. "Handy thing, that."

"Yeah, it is. About the money?"

"Darina told me her mom had given her enough cash for a good part of her upcoming time at college. Tuition, rent, food – I got the feeling it was in the thousands of dollars. She seemed pissed, said some of it was missing."

"Did you see the cash?" Aislinn asked.

That caught him off guard and he looked confused. "No. Why?"

"Just wondering. Did she give any indication how much was missing or who might have taken it?"

"She said something about Kayla Walsh being a bitch, but I don't know if that's related. I mean, those two were always at each other." He hesitated, then added, "Kayla was always a bit sketchy."

"Did she say anything about going to see Kayla?"

He shook his head. "No, she came over to talk about prom night and what *not* to expect."

"A relationship," Aislinn said.

"Yeah, she was setting the ground rules. That was fair, at least I knew where I stood."

Aislinn nodded, then asked, "Did she talk about her dad? About what happened to him?"

Shane churned it over for a few seconds. "She mentioned how tough things were for her mom, but nothing specific about him."

Aislinn propped herself against a locker, wondering how Darina's mom had suddenly come up with a fistful of money for college. Husband dead, no pension, single woman with a kid and a mortgage. She'd stopped in quickly to see Tania Volkov and tell her about her daughter, but had wanted to get a clearer picture of the day Darina went missing before interviewing Tania. Aislinn decided now was the time for that visit.

Shane interjected on her thoughts. "She was going to the bank when she left my place. Freaked out totally when she looked at her watch and saw the time. Said she had to get there before it closed."

"What time did she leave?"

He struggled to remember, then said, "About ten to four, I think. Not sure exactly."

"What about your movements that night?"

He gave her a sardonic smile. "My alibi?"

"Everyone's a suspect, don't feel special."

He looked at the worn tile floor, thinking back twenty years and filling in the gaps. "I went to the dance with Kristin and her date, hung around for an hour or so, then left and went home. Mom and dad were having a hell of a fight so I took off and found an after party." He glanced up at Aislinn. "You were there."

"I was, and I remember you showing up," she said. "Is there anyone who can back up your story between leaving the dance and arriving at the party?"

He shook his head slowly. "No."

"All right. Anything else you can think of?" Aislinn asked.

Shane shook his head and they walked back toward the gym, past small groups of men and women talking about the good times they'd had as teenagers. That was best, Aislinn figured, simply remembering the moments of joy and excitement. They reached the gym doors and Aislinn begged off saying she'd see him at the wrap up party on Saturday night.

She wandered out to the parking lot, glad to be alone. A light rain was falling but she didn't hurry to her car, her mind filled with thoughts of her old friends – Kristin all wrapped up in her success. Kayla trying so hard to be someone different and attract a provider, Cody happy with the world despite the cane, and Shane a total head-case from his time in the army. Twenty years in the real world had shaped them all. Whoever said *you can't go back* was so right.

She slipped into the driver's seat and checked her email. Cian and his buddies hadn't wasted any time. There was a list of businesses that might have paid Alexi Volkov for protection and she replied with a *thank you* and a smiley face emoji. The info would be useful on the DeMarco file, and she forwarded it to Stan and Bryan Cheung, a young assistant tasked with helping on the case. She added a note for Cheung to check and see if they were still in business, and if not to pull the corporate registry and try to locate the old owners.

She was about to pull out of the parking lot when she stopped and texted to Bryan with another instruction. *Call Kayla Walsh – her cell number is in the Darina Volkov file – and have her come to A-1 tomorrow at 11:00 for an interview. She does NOT have the option of refusal.* Aislinn hit send and dropped her phone on the passenger seat. Kayla hadn't changed, she was still a grifter, just a bit longer in the tooth. And she definitely knew more about what happened that day – time to find out.

CHAPTER TWENTY-ONE

Stan Lamers didn't know any of the businesses on the list Aislinn's dad had sent. Most were defunct long ago, a testament to how much things had changed in Jamaica Plain over the last twenty years. Of sixteen only four now existed, most with different names and addresses changed to meet the wants of younger buyers.

"Hey, I know this one," Cheung said, handing Stan a printout. "All Seasons Landscaping, used to be Arnold's Greenhouse in 2001. It's a nursery close to the Arboretum and we bought a bunch of shrubs there last year. Owner is Jack Braun."

Stan took the sheet and added it to the pile with the other three active businesses. "You keep searching, I'm going to drive over and talk with the owners to see how they react when I ask if they were paying protection money."

"On it," Cheung said.

"And when you're done that, check the construction permits that were issued around the time when Darina's body was dumped and see who had access to the site."

"Already part way through them," Cheung replied. "I've been cross-correlating the permits through the corporate registry to get a business number, then tracking the sub-contractors. I'm starting to get a pretty good picture of who was authorized to be on the site."

Stan raised an eyebrow and nodded. Bryan Cheung was young, early thirties, and it was common knowledge he wanted a shot at being promoted to detective. Keen to be seen as someone who could dig deep, he was great at ferreting out information, especially the technical stuff.

"Let me know what you find," Stan said as he headed out.

Stan checked his watch as he took the elevator to the main floor. Nine-fifteen. Perfect time, smack dab between breakfast and lunch on a Thursday morning. The greenhouse would likely be only moderately busy as most gardeners had already bought their spring quota. He found the nursery easily enough, it covered half a city block and the large, glass greenhouses were visible from the street. He'd driven by it a hundred times but had never stopped in. Probably because he hated cutting grass and avoided yardwork at all costs.

Jack Braun turned out to be an affable seventy-something with thinning silver hair and a lopsided smile. He studied Stan's badge for a few seconds, then suggested they find a private place to sit and talk. Stan followed him through one of the greenhouses and into a shaded garden where a wrought iron table and two chairs were tucked in by a gurgling fountain. They settled in at the table and Stan set his notebook in front of him.

"I should get a fountain for my garden," Stan said, looking around at the lush vegetation and imagining himself sitting on the deck under a leafy canopy listening to the soft sounds of trickling water.

"Well, we have lots of fountains to choose from," Braun said. "They *do* take work to keep clean, I like to warn customers up front."

Stan's image of himself lounging with a beer in his own backyard amidst tropical plants faded to scrubbing an algae-encrusted chunk of rock and he abandoned the idea on the spot. "You owned the nursery back in 2000," he said.

"I did, since 1981 actually. It was Arnold's back then. I thought naming it after the Arboretum might generate some additional business, but it didn't really. I can't tell you how many people came in and asked for Arnold. So I changed the name to All Seasons a few years ago."

Stan nodded. "We're looking at something that happened in 2001 that may have ties to organized crime. I was wondering if anyone approached you back then as part of a protection racket."

Braun's easy going manner disappeared and he looked worried, bordering on scared. Stan picked up on the abrupt change in demeanor.

"It's a cold case, Mr. Braun," Stan said. "Unless you're still being pressured you have no reason not to speak with us."

Braun got up and walked around the small clearing, stopping at the far side with his back to the cop who was asking him to reopen a deep wound. Finally, he turned around and said, "It's stopped. If talking with you is going to get the mob after me, then I don't have a comment."

Stan shook his head. "No chance of that. This is strictly between you and me, it goes in the file and helps us to understand who was running protection rackets in 2001. Nothing gets out, nothing to ruffle any current-day feathers."

"Okay," Braun said, relaxing slightly.

"Were you paying for protection?" Stan asked.

Braun nodded. "I was."

"Who did you pay?"

"The damn Irish," he said. "No offense."

Stan couldn't help grinning. "Do I look Irish?"

Braun loosened up a bit at that. "It all started in the 80's with the Winter Hill Gang. Whitey Bulger and his crew showed up one day and demanded monthly payments. I told them to leave and not bother coming back. I had one greenhouse at that time and they smashed every window in it. I didn't have a choice."

"Bulger himself showed up," Stan said, raising an eyebrow.

"Well, he wasn't as famous back then as now."

"How long did you pay them?" Stan asked.

Braun threw up his hands. "Years. Decades." He thought for a minute, then said, "It stopped around 2000, give or take. One month they didn't show up. I kept the cash in the safe for the entire month but that was it. The gangs were worried about RICO."

Stan nodded. The Racketeer Influenced and Corrupt Organization Act had come along in the 70's, but it wasn't until a task force used it twenty years later to take down the Lucchese crime family that organized crime started to realize how powerful the law was and how vulnerable they were to it. A lot of illegal activity stopped because of RICO.

"Did anyone else approach you?"

"You mean another crime syndicate or gang?" Braun asked and when Stan nodded he said, "No, that was it. I haven't paid protection money since then."

"You never knew or met a Russian named Alexi Volkov?"

Braun shook his head. "Never heard of the guy."

"Can you think of any other business owners who were targeted back in 2000?"

"Oh, man, that's a tough question, it's so long ago. No one comes to mind off hand, but I could call you if I think of anyone."

"Sure, that would be great." Stan handed over a business card. "Thanks for your time today. Much appreciated."

Stan took the path back to the main building, walking slowly and enjoying the still, fragrant air. Flowers of every description were out in full bloom and the effect was soothing. He kicked around the idea of picking up a few plants and shrubs, then reality hit him. The only way his thumb was green was if he painted it. As much as he wanted it to be, this wasn't his world. He took a deep breath and headed back out to the street.

* * *

AISLINN WALKED into the interview room at 11:03. The positioning of the metal chairs facing the camera was purposeful – they were crowded behind a table that was a bit too close to the wall, essentially trapping the person being interviewed. The lighting was harsh and the room a uniform white, all of it making it a very undesirable space.

Kayla Walsh was already seated and next to her was a thin man in an ill-fitting suit with an unopened briefcase on the table in front of him. *Lawyered up already,* Aislinn thought. She sat in the chair opposite them and turned on the recorder.

"Aislinn Byrne, Senior Detective Homicide Division, beginning interview with Kayla Jane Walsh at 11:04 am on Thursday, June 17th, 2021. Present is Ms. Walsh's legal counsel. Please state your name for the record."

The man leaned forward slightly. "Travis Eagan."

"Your firm?" Aislinn asked.

"Eagan Professional Corporation," he said.

Aislinn pegged the man for an independent – they were usually cheaper and able to make appointments on short notice. "Kayla," she said, "I'm going to start with the meeting we had at your apartment on Monday. There appear to be some inconsistencies in your story and I need to get them sorted out. Okay?"

"Yes." Kayla could barely speak, her throat dry, the single word little more than a whisper.

"Is my client a suspect?" Eagan asked.

"Close enough," Aislinn said, and launched into reading Kayla her rights.

"Would you like some water?" Aislinn asked when she was finished with Miranda. When Kayla nodded, Aislinn made a drinking motion at the camera.

Eagan cut in. "Can you please state what case this concerns."

"Yes, of course," Aislinn said. "We're investigating the murder of Darina Volkov, who disappeared in June of 2001, and whose body was recently discovered in a building on Center Street in Jamaica Plain."

"Thank you."

Aislinn turned to face Kayla. "We've established that Darina, Sofia and I were at your house the morning of June 15th, then we all headed for the hairdresser together in Darina's car."

"That's right."

"You and Darina were first in the stylists' chairs, then the two of you went next door for lunch."

"Yes."

There was a sharp rap on the door and Bryan Cheung entered with a glass of water. He set it on the table in front of Kayla, spun on his heels and was gone as quickly as he had showed up.

"Who paid?" Aislinn asked when the door closed.

She took a sip of water and looked at her lawyer. When he nodded his approval she answered, "Darina."

"Cash?"

"Where is this going?" Eagan asked.

"We've determined Darina had a substantial amount of cash on her that day, and by mid-afternoon some of it was missing. It goes to motive." She glanced at Kayla. "Did you take the money?"

Again, the deferral to her lawyer and this time he shook his head. "No comment," she said.

Aislinn sat back and folded her arms across her chest. She stared at Kayla for the better part of a minute, then said, "Murders are committed with motive. It's very seldom someone just decides to kill another person for no reason. I'm damn sure there was a reason why Darina was killed and I aim to find out what it was. If you didn't kill her then you have nothing to worry about. If you took the money and tell me truthfully what happened, then I can decide, based on what you tell me, whether it's motive for murder. However, if you clam up or lie about what happened, then you're going to dig yourself in deeper. It's entirely up to you."

"I need to speak with my lawyer," she said.

Aislinn leaned over and said, "Interview temporarily terminated at 11:09 am." She touched the stop button, got up and opened the door. "Knock on the door when you're ready, the camera and microphone will be turned off."

Bryan Cheung was standing in the hall when Aislinn exited the interview room. "Stan and I have been chasing down the people on your dad's list," he said. "We checked in with Lieutenant Westcott and he wants to meet in his office at noon. He asked me to see if you could make it."

"Sure, I'll be there."

"Perfect," Bryan said as he hurried off.

Aislinn stood in the hallway, pretty sure that Kayla would be staring at the desk, feeling beat down with worry all over her face. Her lawyer talking, explaining things in detail, making sure she understood the ramifications of talking or keeping quiet. After a few minutes there was a knock on the door.

Aislinn entered the room, restarted the tape and said, "Okay, what have you got for me?"

"Kayla won't be charged for theft if she took some of the money," Eagan said.

"She will not be charged."

"Then she admits to taking two thousand dollars," he said.

Aislinn was taken aback by the amount. "Two thousand? That seems like quite a bit."

"Darina had a bunch of cash," Kayla said. "I saw it when she paid for lunch. She went to the bathroom as soon as we got back to the house and I went through her purse and took some. I was hoping she wouldn't notice."

"You thought she wouldn't notice two thousand dollars?" Aislinn asked incredulously. "She was a high school student. How could she not notice?"

"She had some serious money. What I took hardly dented it."

"Where did she get it?" Aislinn asked.

Kayla shrugged. "I don't know and I sure as hell wasn't going to ask her. Not after I took some. I was glad she decided to go to Cody's."

"The heated discussion by the pool, after Darina had been to Cody's and Shane's, was that about the money?"

Kayla swallowed and glanced at her lawyer, who nodded. "Yes, she'd noticed some was missing."

"What did you do?"

"Denied it," Kayla said, in tears now. "Told her I never took it."

"Then what?"

"You saw – she stormed out, yelling at me. Said we'd sort this out later. That I wasn't going to get away with it."

Aislinn leaned forward and spoke directly to Kayla. "This doesn't look good for you. You stole money from the deceased and didn't disclose it to the police back in 2001, or to me when I interviewed you earlier this week. The building where Darina's body was found is only a few blocks from your house and it was common knowledge the third floor was under construction. That gives you motive, opportunity, and means."

"I didn't kill her," she blurted out.

"Well, someone did." Aislinn leaned back in the chair. "I'll need a DNA sample."

"Do you have DNA from the crime scene?" Eagan asked.

"Sorry, that's privileged." Aislinn closed her notebook and stood up. "Don't leave town Kayla, and take my call if I phone you."

She left the door open behind her and made a beeline for the bullpen. After updating Darina's file with the latest information she called Tania Volkov and asked to meet later that afternoon. They agreed on two o'clock and she headed for Curtis's office.

CHAPTER TWENTY-TWO

Bryan Cheung was upbeat when Aislinn arrived, happy to be in on a meeting with two senior detectives and the chief of homicide. Cheung had earned his place in the room – tech-smart and meticulous when tasked with digging up information on an investigation, Aislinn knew Curtis was seriously considering him for detective. She sat next to him and gave him a smile.

Curtis finished a call and motioned for Stan to shut the door. "We need to be careful," he said. "Three cases could be linked but here's the thing, there's no concrete evidence they actually are. We do *not* want to get tunnel vision."

Tunnel vision was focusing on one avenue of investigation rather than leaving it open to other possibilities. It narrowed the scope and in extreme cases ended up with detectives forcing the evidence to fit their line of thinking. Innocent men and women were in prison because of this and Curtis constantly pushed his detectives to ask whether they had let the facts steer things after chasing down all the relevant leads.

"Stan, you and Bryan were following up on the list of businesses we got from Aislinn's dad. Anything there?"

Stan gave Bryan a quick nod and the young man checked his notes and said, "There were sixteen businesses on the list and we've managed to track down the people who owned eight of them. Four are still operating and four have folded, the owners retired or gone into another venture. Bottom line is, they all paid protection back in 2000 but none of them were involved with Alexi Volkov."

"Who were they paying?" Curtis asked.

"Depends – Irish or Italians mostly – one guy paid the Russians."

"RICO was pretty damn effective," Stan said. "The protection rackets were all shut down by about 2005."

"Yeah, that law had some teeth," Curtis agreed. "Any additional leads from talking with the owners?"

Bryan held up his notebook. "Two so far. A bowling alley and a seafood vendor. We're following up with them."

"Good work, keep on it." Cian's list had given them a start, and if they could build on it they'd have a better chance of finding someone who was paying Volkov. He looked at Aislinn. "What have you got for us?"

"I've talked with all the friends who saw Darina on the day she disappeared and there's a pattern emerging. Darina was in a good mood at the start of the day, flush with cash for college, and ready to have fun at the prom. Until she noticed some of her cash was missing."

"I saw the note about the money in her file. How much are we talking here?" Curtis asked.

"Don't know for sure, but it looks like some thousands at least. I'm sitting down with Darina's mom this afternoon so that might shed some light."

Curtis said, "That's an entirely new angle."

"It is, and Kayla Walsh has admitted taking two thousand dollars. Darina was really pissed and accused Kayla of stealing it."

"When was that?" Curtis asked.

"At Kayla's house when we were getting dressed for the prom. That was after she left Shane's but before she headed to Kristin's."

"The disagreement by the pool, she was accusing Kayla of stealing the money," Curtis said.

"Right." Aislinn was impressed with Westcott's knowledge of the specifics. "Then Darina heads for Kristin Sanders' house and gets on the phone. I want to know who she called." She turned to Bryan. "Contact the phone company and put in a production order to have them pull the records. I'll give you the time and number the call originated from."

Bryan nodded and made a note in his book.

"DeMarco and Nyson looked at that when the case was still active," Curtis said. "I think it came up untraceable."

"It did," Bryan said. "But maybe they didn't push hard enough."

"Think so?" Curtis asked.

"Technology wasn't what it is today, and searching for blocked numbers was difficult, but not impossible. It could have been there, buried, and if DeMarco and Nyson got the wrong technician on their request, they might have missed it. My feeling is, it's going to be archived somewhere."

Curtis gave Bryan a nod. "Chase it down. We need to know who she called from Kristin's house."

"On it," he said, looking pleased.

"Bryan and I checked Bill Nyson's bank records," Stan said. "There isn't a hint of anything untoward. No extra money coming in, no big expenses. Seems like he was clean."

"He might have stashed some cash," Curtis said. "Bypassed any sort of paper trail at the banks."

"Maybe," Bryan interjected, "but we checked his mortgage balance, car loans and other debts he'd have been tempted to pay down but there was nothing. He cleared the mortgage on his house three years before he died – twenty-five years of monthly installments."

"Still, how could DeMarco possibly run a rackets business without Nyson knowing?" Curtis rubbed at his temples.

"Yeah, it would be tough." Stan had a thought and added, "It's a well-known fact that DeMarco worked late, and if his partner booked off earlier in the day then DeMarco could have taken care of business after hours without his partner knowing."

Curtis gave the line of logic a nod. "But are we heading down the wrong rabbit hole, thinking DeMarco was dirty? Maybe there's more to Darina's missing cash than we're thinking."

Aislinn cut in. "I'll run it down, but there are details that don't sit right. First off, Kayla was a teenager, not a hardened criminal. Somehow she kills Darina, finds a roll of polyethylene, bags her up without leaving any fingerprints or DNA, drags her up to the third floor of a building she may or may not have known was under construction, takes the wall apart, stuffs her inside and replaces the drywall so that it goes unnoticed."

"Put that way," Stan said.

Curtis agreed. "Yeah, that one's a long shot."

Aislinn's phone buzzed and she glanced at the incoming text. It was from Rebecca Carlisle – *Darina Volkov's tox scan came up clean but I found some trace material under a fingernail and forwarded it to Lenore Sutherland in forensics. It's a tiny bit of blue material, unrecognizable at present. Will have Lenore follow up with you, but she's thinking the sample is so small it might be impossible.* Aislinn texted back *thank you.*

"Nothing on Darina Volkov's tox screen," she said, holding up her phone. "Carlisle found some trace evidence, but she's out on whether forensics can do anything with it. Sample might be too small."

"Well, it's something," Curtis said.

Stan cut in on a different tack. "You're still working the old-time gangsters angle. Anything more come from that?"

Curtis rolled his eyes. "I checked in with O'Reilly again and I'll forward you my notes. He did the squid."

"What's that?" Bryan asked.

"The squid." Stan held his hands out and wiggled them around. "Not me, didn't do it. Don't know what you're talking about."

"Got it."

"O'Reilly remembered the DeMarco thing really well, which makes sense," Curtis continued. "A cop getting killed would have made his life hell, lots of police crawling all over them. He insisted DeMarco wasn't in with them and I sort of believed him."

"Sort of?" Aislinn said.

"He may hate cops but this guy is old school about killing one. You just don't do it."

"What about The Big Fish?" Stan asked, going back to the interview with the Italian boss. He turned to Bryan as an aside and said, "Giuseppe Salvatore, it's his nickname. Claims he has a dick the size of a whale."

"Someone should tell him whales are mammals, not fish," Aislinn said after everyone stopped laughing. Which only caused more of the same.

"I think Salvatore knows who pulled the trigger on Alexi Volkov," Curtis said. "He told me it was my job to figure it out."

"Interesting," Aislinn said. "If he knows, he's kept it close to his chest for a long time."

Curtis nodded. "And, like I said before, he indicated Volkov was running small-time rackets."

"That's got to piss them off," Stan said. "Honing in on their business."

"Maybe, but why would he give me the impression he knows who the shooter is? That doesn't make sense if one of his guys did it." Curtis shook his head. "No, I've been thinking, if I had to pick one I'd say it was the Russians."

"Why?" Aislinn asked.

"They don't have the same code of ethics on cops and women as the Irish and the Italians. They'll take someone out if they have to. Thing is, I don't believe they had sufficient motivation to kill DeMarco. Alexi Volkov, maybe, but not Darina."

"So why kill one guy but not the other?" Aislinn asked.

"Exactly. It doesn't add up," Curtis said. "Kalatonov told me they used Alexi for some grunt work – collecting debts and moving drugs – but I don't think he was in tight with them. Kalatonov figured Alexi was working some sort of protection racket on the side but he didn't know with whom."

"You believe him?" Stan asked.

Curtis thought about that for a bit, then said, "Yeah, probably. The thing about all this is, it's twenty years ago and none of these guys have any interest in what happened back then. They're not going to create some web of lies to frame someone, but they're also not going to come right out and tell us who did what. So yeah, Stan, I kind of believe them."

The room was quiet for a minute, then Curtis checked his watch and said, "Good work, guys. We're moving ahead at a steady pace and keeping all our options open. No tunnel vision here." He looked at Bryan. "Let's find out who Darina Volkov called. It's important."

"Will do," Bryan said.

"That's it," Curtis opened his laptop. "Go figure out who the bad guys are."

CHAPTER TWENTY-THREE

The sight of the house always sent shivers down her spine. For twenty years she'd simply steered clear of the street, not wanting the memories. This was her second trip in the last few days and it didn't feel any easier than the first. There it was, a faded blue two-story overrun with trees and shrubs, tucked in amongst an unremarkable stretch of houses. Chances were that not one of her neighbors knew the agony Tania Volkov had suffered so long ago. Chances were, nobody cared.

Aislinn parked by the curb and took the sidewalk to the front door. She glanced over at the driveway where Alexi Volkov had been found, lying in the snow next to his car with a bullet in the back of his head. Then, six months later, the woman's daughter disappeared.

"Fucking nightmare," she whispered as she rang the doorbell.

Tania Volkov looked tired when she answered, but a tiny light flickered in her dead eyes as she saw Aislinn. Then she managed a smile.

"Aislinn," she said, opening the screen door. "Good to see you again."

"Hello, Mrs. Volkov."

"Please, come in."

Aislinn followed Darina's mother through the small foyer into the living room. The space was tidy, as it had always been, and furnished with the same dated sofa and loveseat. She sat where directed, her back straight, her hands folded in her lap.

"Thank you for coming by the other day to tell me about Darina," Tania said.

"I am really sorry, Mrs. Volkov. Darina was..." Aislinn let the words trail off, then added, "...wonderful."

"You are with the police now," Tania stated. "In what capacity?"

"Detective," Aislinn said, wondering how the woman's accent could still be so noticeable. "Homicide."

"Yes, homicide." She adjusted her skirt, then asked, "Would you like something to drink? Tea perhaps?"

"No, thank you."

Tania sat unmoving in the chair, her face a study of depression and angst. Her fingers curled into fists, bunching up her skirt as she relived the pain of losing her daughter. Aislinn looked around the bleak room, it was as if time had stood still, and she wondered if the woman's hurt had ever diminished.

"I'd like to ask you some questions if that's okay," Aislinn said.

"Yes, of course."

Aislinn started with easy things – what Darina had done before leaving the house that day, what she was wearing, whether she was excited about the prom, where she bought her dress. Then she got into the tough stuff.

"Darina had quite a bit of cash with her," Aislinn said. "What do you know about that?"

"Her college money," Tania said, tears welling up. "I should never have given it to her."

Guilt, Aislinn thought, *was a persevering emotion.* "We're not sure the money was the reason Darina was killed."

Tania Volkov pulled a handkerchief from her sleeve and wiped at her eyes. "Alexi gave me an envelope about two years before he was killed. It was for college after Darina finished high school. We hid it under a floorboard and it stayed there…" She hesitated. "…even after he was shot. I never took it out until the day of the prom."

"How much was there?"

The woman looked shattered. "Twenty thousand dollars. Alexi had split it into five rolls with elastics around them."

Aislinn struggled to keep her facial expression emotionless. Twenty thousand dollars in cash could get someone killed really fast and Darina's mother had made a grave error handing it to a teenager on prom day. The one day when she would likely be drinking. It was little wonder the woman was carrying around a massive burden of guilt on top of her grief.

"That's a lot of money."

"Darina was taking it to the bank," Tania explained, her face creased with emotion. "She promised me that she would have it there right after lunch."

"Did it ever get deposited to Darina's account?" Aislinn asked.

Tania wiped at the tears clumsily and shook her head. "No." She buried her face in her hands for the better part of minute. "I should never have given her that money."

"Well, Mrs. Volkov," Aislinn said softly. "We're not convinced that's why Darina was taken."

Silence settled in until Aislinn finally asked, "Do you know where your husband got the money?"

She shrugged, an inconsequential motion that belied the seriousness of the question. "From work, I suppose."

"What sort of work did he do?"

Another shrug, then, "Construction mostly. A lot of his customers paid cash, so he always put some aside for Darina."

Aislinn wasn't sure if Tania actually believed that. How was it possible to live with someone and not know he was a career criminal. "Can you give me the names of some of the other trades he worked with? Electricians, plumbers, drywallers, that sort of thing."

Tania shook her head. "I don't know these things. Alexi didn't talk a lot about work."

I'm sure he didn't, Aislinn thought. "Did Darina say anything out of the ordinary to you before leaving the house on the day of the prom?"

"No, she talked about the dance. She was so excited about her new dress."

"What was her reaction to getting the money?" Aislinn asked.

Tania smiled. "She knew we had been putting money aside for her but she was surprised with how much there was. She was very happy and thankful, hugged me, promised me – *she promised me* – she would go to the bank." The smile disappeared and her eyes teared up. "Then she left."

Aislinn wrapped up the interview around 3:00 and walked into the back yard to look at the section of driveway where Alexi Volkov was killed. It was well protected from the street, and a person could easily hide in the hedge. There was little doubt Volkov's murder had been planned and the timing – in the middle of his trial – was telling. Someone, perhaps more than one person, had been worried about Volkov exposing them. She walked slowly down the driveway, the same route the killer had taken before almost running into Darina as she arrived home. Talk about awful timing, if she had come along two minutes later she'd likely still be alive.

Aislinn leaned on the rear quarter panel of her car, taking long rhythmic breaths to calm herself after the interview. Sitting across from Darina's mom had taken a huge emotional toll on her, but allowing her personal feelings to creep in wasn't going to help anyone. Remaining objective, gathering evidence, following the clues – that was the way to solve this and give Tania Volkov the justice she deserved. After a few minutes her head cleared and she felt a coolness coursing through her veins again. She was back.

Aislinn pulled out her phone, called the Godfrey Hotel and asked for Kristin Sanders. She waited while it rang, thinking she might need to call Kristin's cell number instead. Then Kristin's voice was on the line.

"It's Aislinn," she said. "Do you have time for a quick meeting?"

"When?" Kristin sounded put off by the request.

"Now is good. I'm in Jamaica Plain, so about twenty minutes?"

There was a pause, then, "Okay, in George Howell. Twenty minutes."

"See you then."

Aislinn killed the call and got into her car, sitting with the ignition off. Something wasn't adding up here. Darina was looking forward to the dance and flush with a cash windfall, but by the time she arrived at Kristin's house she was angry enough to storm out after making the phone call and smoke her tires as she drove off. Something else had happened. Kayla stealing some of the money may have been enough to set Darina off, but Aislinn wasn't convinced. She was missing something, but right now it was all a fog. She started her car, Kristin Sanders would be waiting.

Aislinn pulled up in front of the Godfrey Hotel and put her police parking pass on the dash. Kristin was perched at a deuce near the front window with a coffee for herself and one waiting for Aislinn.

"It's a dark roast. Hope that's okay," Kristin said as Aislinn joined her.

"It is, thanks."

"So what's up? Are you going to any of the reunion events tonight?"

Aislinn shook her head and tried the coffee – it was excellent. "I wanted to go back over the phone call Darina made from your house that night. Tell me everything you can about it."

"Nothing to tell really. I showed her to the den and she called someone. I have no idea who."

"Did you overhear anything?"

Kristin shook her head. "Nothing. I was in the living room. I might have heard a mumble, but nothing I could make out."

"So she wasn't yelling?"

"No, just speaking in a normal tone or I would have heard her."

Aislinn jotted down four words in her notebook as Kristin was speaking. *Getting dressed* and *living room*. How to play this? Best to come straight at Kristin, she decided. "Now that's interesting."

"What?"

"Previously, you said you were getting dressed when Darina made the phone call, now you've indicated you were in the living room. Which is it?"

Kristin's jaw muscles twitched and her eyes flickered. It was only for a second but enough for Aislinn – Kristin Sanders had just been caught in a lie. "It was a long time ago," she said.

"If you know something, Kristin, now is the time to get it off your chest." Aislinn metered the words carefully, ensuring they were just the right amount of threatening.

"What could I possibly know, Aislinn?" she shot back. "Darina came to my house, made a phone call and left. Then she disappeared. What does that have to do with me?"

"Not sure." Aislinn said. "Yet."

Aislinn took a sip of coffee and waited, but Kristin wasn't about to say anything else. "The phone company has archives of every call, even from twenty years ago. We'll have the number she called in a day or two. And we have trace evidence off Darina's body. We're putting it together."

Another long silence. "Well, that's good."

"It's what we do. Tiny things that seem unimportant, we string them all together." She gave Kristin an emotionally cold smile. "We'll figure out what happened to Darina."

Kristin glanced at her watch and said, "It's late, I have to run."

"Thanks for meeting with me. Try and remember more about that phone call. It's really important."

"Okay." Kristin stood up, smoothed the wrinkles in her dress pants and walked away.

Aislinn stayed, sipping her coffee after Kristin was out of sight and going back over their conversation. The woman wasn't being truthful, and that was disconcerting in a lot of ways. Did she actually know something that came from listening to the call? If she did, was she somehow complicit in Darina's murder? That was so over-the-top implausible that Aislinn could barely wrap her head around it. Kristin had been a popular seventeen year-old with no apparent motivation to be involved in a murder. It didn't make sense, yet there it was.

She had been sort of honest with Kristin on their progress. There was a chance they might get the number from the phone company, albeit a slim one, and CSI had found trace evidence under one of Darina's fingernails, but it was so slight they might not be able to identify it. Still, letting Kristin know they were honing in on things might get her talking in a day or two.

"What could you possibly know?" Aislinn asked herself as she finished her coffee. "That's the question."

CHAPTER TWENTY-FOUR

Rush hour was well underway by the time Stan and Bryan pulled into the Century Bowl parking lot. As they started for the front entrance, Stan said, "Keep in mind I'm the big dog and you're the little dog. Little dog doesn't talk unless the big dog says it's okay."

"Got it. Big dog, little dog"

Stan grinned. "You'll go far."

Smoked glass doors closed behind them cutting off the warmth and light of the afternoon sun. Inside was a world of neon and glitz, with soft carpet underfoot and the sound of bowling balls hitting and rolling on hardwood. Video machines blinked and beckoned, and a long row of pool tables sat racked and ready to go.

Stan walked up to the rental counter where a young man with long hair was spraying and sorting shoes. "Can you let Andy know Stan Lamers and Bryan Cheung are here? He's expecting us."

"Sure, he mentioned that." A long, skinny arm stretched out and pointed to the far end of the building. "Through that door. His office is at the end of the hallway."

"Thanks."

The lanes were about half full with a wide range of bowlers, most of whom weren't very good. One woman lined up, threw a gutter ball and started laughing. Apparently, high scores were secondary to having fun.

"It's a good game," Bryan said. "Hard, takes a lot of know-how."

"What I want to know," Stan said, "is what sort of fungus is living in those rental shoes."

"Enough that I bought my own," Bryan said as he pushed the door open.

The corridor leading to Corruthers' office was in marked contrast to the Vegas-like glamor of the main hall. Harsh florescent lighting illuminated worn carpets and walls covered with gouges and chipped paint. They found the office easily enough and Stan knocked on the open door.

Corruthers looked up and waved them in. He was in his seventies and sported shoulder-length white hair and a goatee that suited his thin face. He took off his reading glasses and stood, offering his hand.

"You must be Stan Lamers."

"Guilty," Stan said, handing over a business card. "This is Bryan Cheung."

Corruthers said hello and motioned to the chairs facing his desk. "You wanted to talk about the protection rackets back in the 90's."

"Around 2000 or 2001 actually," Stan said. "You said you were paying someone back then."

Corruthers' face flushed red. "Yes, and it almost ruined me. I had no money left at the end of the day. They took all the profits. Those guys were real bastards."

"Seems like you're doing okay now," Stan said. "The place looks top notch. Makes me want to lace up."

"It took a long time," Corruthers said.

"You have a name for us?" Stan asked.

"Alexi someone. I never got more than that."

Bryan glanced at Stan, who nodded. "I have some photos, Mr. Corruthers," Bryan said. "Could you look at them and see if you recognize any of these men?"

"Sure." He leaned into his desk and set his reading glasses back on his nose. "That's him," he said when Bryan set the first photo on the worn desk. "That's the piece of crap."

"His name was Alexi Volkov," Stan said. "Someone killed him in 2001."

"Good, he deserved it," Corruthers said. "Guess that explains why he stopped coming by every month."

"Probably," Stan said.

"I kept the cash in the safe for the first six months, thinking at some point there'd be a knock on the door. That never happened again, so I used it to renovate and changed the name to Century Bowl. New millennium and all that. The young crowd liked the new look and it's been hopping ever since."

"I'm glad," Stan said. "Terrible you went through such a rough stretch." He pointed at the thin stack of photos in Bryan's hand. "Do you mind looking at a few more?"

"Not at all."

He passed on identifying Kalatonov, O'Reilly, Salvatore and some of their lieutenants. He tapped the last photo with his finger when Bryan set it on the table.

"I saw this guy twice. He was talking to Alexi."

Stan swallowed hard. "Are you sure?"

"Fucking positive," Corruthers said. "This guy hung around across the street. I'd turn the lights out in my office and watch them. I saw his face once in the light from the streetlamp when he got into his car. That's him."

"He never came in to collect?" Stan asked.

"No. The only other time I saw him was a few blocks down Center Street. It was mid-afternoon in January and really cold. There was hardly anybody on the sidewalk and I spotted Alexi. I stayed back and watched. They were having a meeting of some sort, and I'm damn sure that's him. They were tucked in a doorway and mostly out of sight, but I saw them."

"Okay, thanks. Is it okay to call or drop by if we need any more information?"

"Anytime."

They retraced their steps to the main entrance and called Curtis from the car.

"How did things go at the bowling alley?" Curtis asked.

"Really interesting," Stan said. "Bryan and I showed the owner a pile of photos – Russians, Italians and Irish – he recognized two of them."

"Let me guess," Curtis said. "Volkov."

"Yup. He was the one picking up the money every month."

"Bingo," Curtis said. "And Kalatonov?"

"Nope" Stan waited a few seconds, then said, "Tony DeMarco."

There was a very long silence, then Curtis said, "Was he sure?"

"One hundred percent, LT. He saw Volkov and DeMarco talking to each other on two separate occasions."

"Is Bryan with you?" Curtis asked.

"Yes."

"Bryan, you know how important it is to keep this under wraps. I'm going to update Aislinn, but only her for now."

"Got it," Bryan said.

"Oh, man," Curtis said. "This is getting real."

"Yeah, lucky us."

Stan hung up and slipped the phone into his pocket. He glanced over at the up-and-comer. "One word of this gets out and your chance of *ever* breaking into Homicide is over. Understand?"

"Yup, blab and I wreck my career forever," Bryan said.

Stan started the car. "Aptly put, little dog."

CHAPTER TWENTY-FIVE

Aislinn pulled over to the curb and answered her cell phone. "Hi, Mom. What's up?"

"I was wondering if you wanted to come by for dinner tonight," Fiona said. "The Rat Pack are coming over for potluck."

Aislinn laughed. "Again?"

"Sometimes I think they've forgotten where they live," her mother joked back. "But they do bring mountains of food."

Aislinn kicked it around for a few seconds. She was done with Kristin Sanders and wasn't going to the reunion event that night so why not.

"Okay, I'll head over."

"Wonderful." Fiona sounded happy with the decision. "See you soon."

She called Curtis on hands-free and caught him on the way home. "Hey, I'm heading over to the parents' house for dinner and the boys are going to be there – Ken, Arnie, and Larry. Should I dig for some info on DeMarco?"

There was a long silence, then, "They know it's highly confidential."

"They do."

"Remind them again," Curtis said slowly. "Try and get something without giving up too much."

"Okay. I'll fill you in after."

Aislinn pulled a U-turn and settled in with the late afternoon traffic streaming into Jamaica Plain. There was an accident on Tremont Street near the I-90 overpass and she considered briefly using her lights to get through the backed up traffic, then decided she didn't care how long the drive took.

Her mind drifted to Cody, the guy with the big smile and unshakable good nature. He was a bit broken from his accident, but the scars didn't seem to go a whole lot deeper. Perhaps it was just willpower that had kept him from getting hooked on prescription painkillers. She'd seen the damage painkillers could do over the years, and Cody was more than just keeping his head above water, he was thriving.

Her pulse quickened as Cody lingered in her head. It wasn't that he was particularly handsome, he had a natural confidence and his eyes were honest and compassionate. She'd seen enough sad eyes in her life to appreciate the happy ones that promised an upbeat, healthy mind lurking behind them. Aislinn definitely liked Cody Hall – maybe more than she should. She gave her head a shake and threw off the thought.

Shane was a different story – the kid with reprehensible parents who had to fend for himself from day one. She'd always been impressed with his ability to cope, but years in the army had pushed him to the edge and beyond. She didn't need to see a clinical analysis to know his PTSD was real and eating away at him every day. Although a stretch, it was possible either he or Cody could have been involved in Darina's murder. They both were still seated at the suspects' table.

Kayla, on the other hand, was the product of her own hubris. Approaching forty and a single mom, the magic touch was gone and she wasn't sure how to function without it. Her new boyfriend seemed nice, and Aislinn hoped that in time she would come to appreciate him. She gave that about a twenty percent chance – underneath, Kayla seemed to be as selfish now as twenty years ago.

Kristin was an enigma, she struck Aislinn as the same cold-hearted bully and perhaps the least changed of them all. And like Kayla, she had been caught in a lie. *Those two,* Aislinn thought, *definitely warranted more attention.*

Her old gang had all been altered by time, Aislinn thought, in one way or another. Even her – perhaps especially her. Her cross to bear was knowing the potential for evil in every person, and that was a very disruptive thing to live with. Every murder cop handled it in their own way. She internalized the violence and ugliness, and it was becoming more difficult as time progressed to connect with people outside the police, especially men.

Traffic picked up once she was past the accident and she arrived at her parents' a bit before six. Her mom was in the kitchen sipping chardonnay while Larry and Arnie busied themselves setting out the food.

"Did you make that?" Aislinn asked Larry, pointing at a lavish salad.

"Sure did," he beamed. "And it's full of good stuff."

She looked at a massive cardboard container filled with lasagna, then glanced at Arnie. "Not even going to ask," she said. "Where is he?"

Fiona pointed to the back door. "On the barbeque, where else?"

Aislinn poked her head outside and immediately saw a plume of smoke billowing from the barbeque. Cian had a spray bottle and was furiously dousing the flames, Ken at his side gesturing. She grinned and snuck up behind him. "What are you cremating?" she asked, poking him in the ribs.

"A," he said, jumping at the surprise. "Damn sausages, they're loaded with fat and it's impossible to cook them without a five alarm blaze."

"Try turning the heat down," she said. "Way down."

"Aww, that's for sissies." Cian worked the spray bottle hard with Ken encouraging until the flames subsided. They kept a close eye on the grill, Cian ready to spring back into action, but most of the grease had burned off and the smokies sizzled quietly on the rack.

"Okay, nice work you two."

She plopped down in one of the padded chairs and stared out over the yard. She had never really appreciated how manicured and peaceful it was when she lived at home, but now it felt soothing to just sit and enjoy the greenery. Maybe it was the job, maybe it was getting older – she didn't care, it was a simple pleasure and that was good enough.

"How's the reunion? Been to any of the events?" Cian dropped into the chair next to her, still eyeing the barbeque.

"One, and it was pretty much what I expected." She made a smushed up face and he laughed. "Saw a couple of old friends, which was nice."

The men came banging through the door, each carrying a tray loaded with food and condiments, Fiona on their heels. They started down the stairs to the picnic table and she wagged a finger at the barbeque.

"We need those," she said to Cian.

"Yes, dear," he replied, grinning and winking at Aislinn.

As usual, dinner was a raucous affair, with opinions about almost everything flying about like sparrows at a feeder. In the end, they all agreed on one thing – Cian had burned the sausages. Fiona retired to the house after the dishes were cleared and the four retired cops and Aislinn sat on the porch, sipping beer and chatting.

"What's with this?" Larry asked Arnie, pointing at his chin. "You run out of razors?"

Arnie laughed. "It's stylin' these days," he said, rubbing his hand across the stubble. "All the young guys are doing it." He winked. "I think Elspeth likes it."

"Well, at least there's *one* thing your wife likes about you," Ken fired back, which got the whole crew roaring.

Arnie's phone rang and he jumped to answer it. "Daphne is expecting." He said *okay* a few times, then hung up, a disappointed look on his face. "Not yet."

"How much younger is Daphne than Kayla?" Aislinn asked.

Arnie nodded. "Five years, she's our youngest."

"She must be close. When's she due?" Cian asked.

Arnie glanced at his watch and laughed. "Now."

All the guys gave him the usual *good luck* salutations, and the conversation inevitably drifted around to the case and whether Aislinn had anything new.

"The list of businesses was helpful," she said to the group.

"Did someone ID Alexi Volkov?" Cian asked.

She shook her head. "No one from your list, but we asked them for other businesses that might have been paying and we got a hit. Century Bowl. Stan's checking it out."

"Should have thought of that one," Arnie said. "They've been around forever but it had a different name. Can't remember it offhand."

"Not important," Aislinn said. "Can I ask you something?" She waited a few seconds, then added, "It's about the case and it's highly confidential. It goes no further."

All of them nodded.

"Tony DeMarco, did he ever spend big? You know, above his pay grade."

Eyes narrowed at that and Larry said, "What are you asking, Aislinn?"

"Could he have been taking money?"

Cian shook his head. "No way. Tony was straight up."

"Agreed," Arnie said, turning toward to Cian. "Never saw anything at the precinct."

"No, neither did I." Cian leaned forward slightly in his chair. "He liked to travel, that's about it."

"What sort of travel?" Aislinn asked.

Cian shrugged and looked at the rest of the crew. "He liked Europe, but that was affordable on his salary."

"He took his family on that African safari," Larry said. "Somewhere in Kenya."

"Glamping, he called it," Ken said. "High end camping."

"Might be a stretch for a cop," Aislinn said. She'd seen the prices for that sort of vacation while poking around online and they were prohibitive. "When did he take that one?"

"About a year before he was killed," Larry said after thinking about it. "Yeah, I remember thinking it was a good thing he'd done that, with everything that happened."

A long silence followed. Finally, Cian said, "Is this what you were talking about when you said Tony's murder might be more than a burglary gone wrong?"

Aislinn didn't answer and her father continued, "I'm just putting two and two together, Aislinn. You already said Tony's death might have been tied in with Volkov's murder."

Aislinn shook her head. "Can't talk about it."

"Sounds like you're looking at Tony's death as premeditated," Arnie said tersely.

All eyes were on Aislinn now. "We're not sure how it went down, so we're following up on all the possible angles. It's strictly conjecture at this point." She met their stares and said, "And something that it *not* to be repeated."

"Jesus," Larry said. "No fucking way."

"Like I said, strictly conjecture." Aislinn was already thinking about how to tell Curtis that her dad's friends knew more than they should. This wouldn't sit well with him. She decided to deflect the conversation away from Tony and minimize the damage.

"This investigation isn't about Tony, it's about who killed Darina Volkov. We have another angle where the motive is stronger. It's tied into some missing money and Tony doesn't figure in that scenario."

"That angle, that's your focus?" Cian was aware his daughter was taking the conversation in a different direction.

"It's part of what is driving the investigation at this point," Aislinn said. "It would have been a spur of the moment thing so there are a few inconsistencies that don't sit right. One thing's for sure, whoever killed her didn't leave much for us to work with."

Ken nodded. "Yeah, and the evidence is twenty years old."

"It is." Aislinn's phone buzzed and she checked the caller ID – it was Curtis. "Gotta take this."

She answered and asked him to wait while she walked around to the back yard. "Okay, boss, I'm good now."

"Where are you?" Curtis asked.

"At the folks' for dinner."

"Okay. I think Stan might have dug up something that points to Tony being involved with Alexi Volkov." He explained what Stan and Bryan had found out at the bowling alley. "He definitely identified DeMarco from a stack of photos."

"Shit," Aislinn said. "Not good. If Tony was in on this, then he probably knew who killed Volkov."

"Which made him dangerous to Volkov's shooter," Curtis said.

"So they took him out." Aislinn felt sick to her stomach. The worst possible explanation was getting some serious legs. "Did Stan show the guy at the bowling alley pictures of your gangsters?"

"He did. Nothing there."

"Are you going to pull them in?" Aislinn asked.

"Oh, yeah. Bryan is already setting up the interviews." A few seconds passed, then Curtis asked, "Can you check with Cian and see if he has any thoughts on who Tony was involved with back in the day."

"Good timing on that, he and his buddies are all still here. It'll mean bringing them up to date with where we are. You okay with that?" She held her breath as Curtis made up his mind – it could be her get out of jail free card.

Curtis was struggling with this one – it was chock-a-block full of risk. Which way to lean? The old-timers were a potential gold mine of information that wasn't in any books or digital files. They were the crew who had their boots on the ground when the gangsters were still running protection rackets, living history with first-hand knowledge. No hearsay. Countering that was the possibility of one of them speaking out of turn and blowing the whole thing open. That wouldn't endear him to the new police commissioner.

Ah, God hates a coward, he thought.

"Yeah, I think so," he said. "See what you can get from them, but be careful how much you give them on what happened to Tony. And Aislinn, they need to stay quiet."

"Yup, got it." Aislinn could feel the stress melting away. She had just dodged a nasty bullet.

"Come in tomorrow for the interviews," Curtis said.

"What time?"

"We're starting at ten."

"See you then," Aislinn said.

Aislinn returned to the porch, the conversation at a standstill as she sat down. "Again, I can't stress how confidential this is," she said.

There was a series of nods but no one spoke.

"We have a concrete ID linking Tony DeMarco and Alexi Volkov. They were seen together near the bowling alley."

There was an immediate cacophony of rebuttals, but Aislinn raised her hand and shook her head. "If you really want to help, think back to *any* signs that Tony might have been part of the protection racket Volkov was running. There's no turning this back now."

Cian slumped back in his chair. "Jesus, Tony." He stared out at nothing for a while, then asked, "What are you looking for?"

"Who did he favor – the Italians, the Russians, the Irish – that sort of thing. There might have been times when he leaned one way or the other. That could give us an idea of who they were working with and who the competition was."

Cian and the boys spent a good deal of time on the question, kicking it back and forth, and finally agreed on one thing. "Tony always seemed a bit harder on the Russians than anyone else," Cian said. "There was one case where he was all over this Russian, totally relentless, like a truffle-seeking pig. He eventually got the guy up on some drug charge."

"Was it a good collar?" Aislinn asked, thinking that if it was, then DeMarco had simply done his job well.

"It got thrown out in court. Tony was mad as a poked hornet. Said the judge was *fucking stupid* to let the guy walk."

"What did you think?"

Arnie chimed in first. "I remember that one. A lot of the guys were out on it at the time. The evidence was thin, but the prosecutors felt there was enough to run with it. Then the whole thing fell apart and there was egg on their faces. Personally, I think Tony's actions were justified."

"A lot of guys didn't agree with that," Cian said.

"So Tony might have been out to get this guy?" Aislinn asked.

"Maybe, Aislinn. Shit, I don't know," Cian said.

"Then it came back on him," Larry said, to which Aislinn just shrugged.

Cian looked up at his daughter with angry eyes. "So you think they killed him."

Aislinn gave him an imperceptibly slow nod. "Maybe. Think about it. DeMarco is linked in with Alexi Volkov as the muscle in his protection racket. Who better than a cop? Then Volkov gets charged, and when it looks like he's going to flip in court someone kills him. DeMarco knows everything, which puts him in the crosshairs. At some point they decide having DeMarco around is too risky."

"So we need to come up with something on who *they* are," Cian said angrily.

"Whatever you can think of," Aislinn said.

"How close are you?" Arnie asked. "Anything solid?"

"Not sure right now, but we're getting there." She gave all of them a serious look. "You can see why this is confidential."

"No shit," Ken said.

"If it gets out at the station all hell will break loose," Cian said.

"Yeah, so Curtis is keeping this tight to the team working it. You guys are in the loop because we need voices from the past."

Cian swallowed hard. "Remember what I told you at the start of all this?"

"That stuff would come out when I started digging."

"Well, there you go." Cian turned and stared out at his carefully tended garden.

"Give us some time, Aislinn," Arnie said. "We'll come up with something for you."

"Yeah, that would be appreciated." She stood up and pulled her blazer over her gun. "See you later."

CHAPTER TWENTY-SIX

The house on Washington Street, a cream-colored two-story, was quiet when Aislinn arrived home. The old girl, built in 1927, had been turned into a two-unit condo a few years back and she had jumped at the chance to buy the suite on the upper floor when it came on the market. An astute move, it was now worth almost double what she had paid for it. Howie Cardel, who occupied the main floor, was into classic rock and played his Fleetwood Mac and AC/DC albums a bit too loud sometimes. She didn't complain, she liked the music and could have had a far worse neighbor.

Her phone lit up and she gave it a glance, fully prepared to ignore it until Friday morning. It was Lenore Sutherland, and that changed her mind. She put the CSI tech on speaker so she could leave the phone on her lap. She was exhausted.

"Lenore, you're working late."

"Yup, can't seem to catch up."

"Do you have something for me?" Aislinn asked, a tinge of hope surging through her.

"I'm actually not sure what I have," Lenore said. "The trace evidence under Darina's fingernail is definitely some sort of fiber."

"Like material from cloth?" Aislinn asked.

"I think so," Lenore replied. "It's really small, almost invisible, but I can see some striations."

"Color?" Aislinn asked. "Still think it's blue?"

"Dark blue or black, yes."

"Do you think you'll get any more or is that it?"

"I think that's it," Sutherland said. "The sample is too small."

"Okay, thanks." Aislinn hit the button and closed her eyes. She drifted off in seconds.

The phone rang again and roused her. The evening sun was no longer streaming through the living room window and it took a few seconds to get her bearings. Her voice was groggy when she answered – Bryan Cheung was on the other end of the line.

"We traced the call Darina Volkov made from Kristin Sanders' house," he said. "It was there all along, the technicians back in 2001 did a crap job. They could have got it if they'd dug harder."

That woke her up. "Where to?"

"The main Jamaica Plain police station," he said. "Not sure what it was about. I reviewed the log for that night and there was no file opened under her name."

She slumped back into the couch. That was a letdown. "Did she make a second call?"

"No, that's it." Bryan said. "I checked and found out that back in 2001 the station still used a main switchboard to receive incoming calls."

"Who was working the switchboard that night?" she asked.

"Patricia Morriscey. She's retired now," Bryan said.

Aislinn shook her head to wake up a bit more. Chasing it down was likely a waste of time, Darina would have been calling to report the stolen money and then changed her mind. "See if you can talk with the Morriscey woman," Aislinn said.

"Already tried," Bryan replied. "She's on some sort of an eco-tour and the itinerary puts her in Haast, New Zealand."

"Haast? Where the hell is that?"

"It's a speck of a town on the southern island. It's in the middle of nowhere and you'll love this. They got the Internet in 2018. Coverage is awful and she's just started on a four day trek down the coast. Can't reach her until she returns."

Aislinn yawned. "That's okay. Keep trying and let me know when you get hold of her."

"Right."

"Good work."

"Thanks."

Aislinn got up and traipsed into the kitchen in search of food. There was one chicken pot pie left in the freezer and she turned on the oven. She leaned against the counter and stared out at the leafy backyard, thinking about the reunion. It was Thursday night and there had been a touch football game on the sports field that might have been fun, but she felt drained. Tomorrow was the sock hop in the gym, something she was definitely adverse to. Truth be known, the case was knocking the stuffing out of her and she just wanted to be left alone.

It was a bit after midnight when the pot pie was cooked and she ate it lying on the couch watching an episode of *Dead to Me*. It amused her that the producers could leave so many gaping plot holes without trying to plug them. Nonetheless, it was entertaining and she was amazed at her connection with the two women, both of whom were killers. God knows, she had sat across the table from enough real-life murderers to know who they were and how they thought. It wasn't pretty.

Tomorrow she would visit Kayla Walsh and rake her over the coals. Find out once and for all if there was anything to the missing college money angle. Kayla had definitely stolen some money and Darina had been furious when she noticed – angry enough to call the police, but not enough to follow through. Nothing had come of it. No investigation, no note in the file about the call, no resolution. It was a hanging thread and Aislinn hated those.

The chances of Kayla having killed Darina were remote at best. It would require a teenage girl in a heated moment to think like a professional. No fingerprints, no DNA, body wrapped tight enough to keep it from rotting and creating an odor, dragging the corpse up the stairs to the third floor and stuffing it in the wall. The odds were astronomical of that being the chain of events. Still, she had seen stranger things.

A phone call to Kristin Sanders was on tomorrow's to-do list as well. Now that she knew Darina had called the police, it was time to press Kristin again. She had the feeling Kristin knew more than she was letting on.

* * *

CURTIS PUSHED the front door open and Barclay made a run for it. The leash unspooled and snapped tight at exactly the same time as Barclay put on the brakes. There was no jerking of the head, no undue pressure on the neck – the dog was a master of leash length – he knew it to the inch. He waited until Curtis caught up then turned and headed east – *apparently,* Curtis thought, *we're going to the park.*

It was three in the morning and the streets were dark and deserted. He was dead tired but there was no chance of sleep, his mind was too full of Darina Volkov, aging gangsters, and Brandy Eagleson. He smiled as a vision of Brandy's face drifted through the mist enveloping the low, warm lights of Back Bay. Something about Brandy settled him and gave him hope that there was goodness in people's hearts. She'd risked her life a few months back helping with the Charlesbois case and they'd stayed in touch since.

He hadn't been sure if they could make a go of it – until he called and asked her if she wanted to fly out from Napa to visit him. Her response – *Yes, Curtis, I would love that* – told him everything he needed to know. Crazy as it seemed, it had worked, and now it was just a matter of time before one of them packed up and moved to be with the other. Curtis didn't assume it would be her clothes in the suitcase, he could always get a job with the San Francisco police. He wouldn't be the top dog in Homicide, but that didn't matter. He'd never gone looking to be in charge, it had found him.

Barclay discovered a new not-to-be-overlooked scent and spent an inordinate amount of time sniffing before moving on. They reached the edge of Boston Public Garden and headed across the lawn. The thick grass was soft underfoot, and ahead, gnarled branches reached up against a black sky punctuated by pinpricks of flickering light. The pair skirted the quiet water of the pond until Curtis found a bench and sat down, Barclay staring up at him. Curtis glanced around, not another person was in sight, and he unsnapped Barclay's leash.

"Do *not* chase squirrels," Curtis told him in his best *I'm-in-charge* voice.

Barclay meandered off, his all-powerful nose leading the way, and Curtis let his thoughts drift back to who killed Darina Volkov. That, really, was the question. Figure that and the rest would fall into place. He was unsure how Salvatore, O'Reilly, or Kalatonov fit into the puzzle, or if they even did. The Irish and Italian gangsters had rules, guidelines actually, that prevented them from killing cops and women, so they were looking less and less likely to be the ones. Still, given enough motivation, they were entirely capable.

The upcoming interviews with the mob bosses were crucial. He needed them to go on the record about DeMarco's involvement – that he was dirty and up to his neck in running the racket. That opened doors for them to chase the DeMarco angle without it looking like he and his detectives were the ones who threw a decorated cop under the bus. He was on a tightrope with this one, tilting one way then the other to keep the investigation balanced and moving ahead.

Barclay came back, checking in, and Curtis said, "No one is off the hook, Barclay. Right?" To which he got a definitive tail wag.

Curtis leashed his dog and started for Back Bay and home, mentally reviewing where they were on the case. Aislinn was working hard to find the link connecting Darina's murder to Alexi's, convinced something or someone from prom night was the key. Stan had uncovered witnesses that could link DeMarco to Volkov, and Bryan had traced the call Darina made just before she disappeared. And tomorrow the parade of gangsters was on the agenda.

"We'll get them, right boy?" Curtis said, but Barclay was too busy sniffing to worry about a twenty year old cold case.

CHAPTER TWENTY-SEVEN

Curtis assembled the team in his office on Friday morning prior to the interviews with the three crime bosses.

"Two key things for today's interviews," he said, shutting the door behind them. "First, and most important, is we need to get one of these guys on tape saying DeMarco was in on Volkov's protection racket. Once they say it, then it's out there and it didn't come from us. It's really important that this originates from one of them. Got it?"

All three heads were nodding.

Curtis gave each one of them a look, then said, "It all changes if they say it. Every cop in Boston, from the beat guys to the chief, will see Tony as bent. The pressure comes off us and he's open game."

No one said a word or moved.

"Second," Curtis continued. "We've been looking for businesses that were paying protection money to Volkov's crew. We're chasing that because it could expose Volkov's partners. Today we need to ask the direct question – who *exactly* was working with Volkov?"

More nodding.

"I'll handle the interviews with Aislinn in the room. Stan, you and Bryan can watch the camera feed." He gave all of them a long look, then said, "This is going to crack open soon and when it does all hell will break loose. The DeMarco thing will have the police chief and the commissioner on the phone non-stop. Anyone want out before it hits the fan?"

No one nodded.

Curtis clapped his hands. "All right. We need something substantial out of these guys."

The Irish were up first in the small room on the fourth floor of District A-1. Patrick O'Reilly sat cross-armed in a metal chair, bristling and flanked by two high-priced lawyers. In the monitoring room, Stan hit the *record* button for the audio and video as he and Bryan watched the screen.

"Thanks for coming in," Curtis said. "Let's get to it."

"My client is not prepared to make a statement at this time," one of the lawyers said.

Curtis pointed his finger at the woman. "I'm not asking you questions. I'm not talking to you. Unless you're going to speak directly to your client, keep your mouth shut." He ignored the angry look on her face, turned to O'Reilly and read him his rights.

"So now I'm a suspect," O'Reilly said with a tinge of humor. "You cops."

Curtis ignored the comment. "We're still working on Darina Volkov's murder."

O'Reilly shook his head. "I told you, Westcott, we had nothing to do with that."

"Yeah, I remember. I also remember you telling me that you were going to look around and see what you could find out." He waited, then said, "Well, what did you find?"

"Be careful, Mr. O'Reilly," the woman said, then stopped when O'Reilly gave her a wave off.

"Alexi Volkov had a partner," he said.

"Who?" Curtis asked.

"Not prepared to say at this time," O'Reilly said. He crossed his arms over his chest again.

Curtis opened his notebook and jotted down a name. He turned it so only O'Reilly could see. "This the guy?"

O'Reilly gave Curtis a surprised look. "Yeah, that's the guy."

"So here's the problem. Somebody killed Volkov's partner. But you know that, don't you."

"Told you, we don't do that," O'Reilly snapped.

Curtis leaned forward. "We're moving fast on this now and we're not stopping. The truth is going to come out. Where do you want to be on that?"

"Right where I am," O'Reilly said. "Innocent."

Curtis couldn't help the tiniest of smiles. "That's a bit of a stretch."

O'Reilly stared at Curtis with unblinking eyes. "This murder stuff just follows you, doesn't it."

The line set Curtis off balance momentarily. "Well, it's my job," he said when he had recovered.

"All these people," O'Reilly said lightly. "On the wrong side of murder."

That stopped Curtis in his tracks again for a few seconds. There was more truth to O'Reilly's callous words than the gangster could ever imagine. Murder *did* follow him, and far beyond the nine-to-five work day. It crept into the deepest recesses of his mind and gave him little respite, his unsolved files churning in his head, dragging him into the office on the weekends and affecting his relationships.

One thing was for certain, Curtis thought as he glared at the cold eyes across from him, *there was no right side to any of it.*

Curtis prodded him for another twenty minutes, pushing for anything that would connect Volkov and DeMarco with one of the crime families. O'Reilly wasn't budging and Curtis finally told him to leave. Bryan shut off the cameras and recording devices and the group of detectives met in the interview room and talked it over. There was a consensus that O'Reilly wasn't the guy.

"That was DeMarco's name you showed him," Stan said and Curtis nodded. "So he knew DeMarco was Volkov's partner, which means our next two guests likely know it too."

"Yeah, let's push harder and get one of them to say DeMarco's name on tape," Curtis said.

"Don't need it on tape, LT," Stan said. "In your notes is good enough."

"I know, but on tape is irrefutable, and we have them in the room being recorded. This is our chance."

"True," Stan concurred.

"As far as O'Reilly goes, I don't think he knows anything beyond DeMarco being in on it," Aislinn said.

"Agreed," Curtis responded. "He's still useful to us, but mostly as a general resource."

"Speaking of resources," Aislinn said. "Last night my dad told me about a case where DeMarco was pushing hard to take down a Russian guy, some thought too hard."

"What happened?" Curtis asked.

"It didn't have the legs to stick in court."

"So DeMarco was adversarial to the Russians," Curtis said, thinking it through. "Points the finger at him being in with the Italians or the Irish."

"Could do," Aislinn said. "And O'Reilly was emphatic it wasn't them who killed DeMarco."

"Well, we have Kalatonov up next," Stan said.

Curtis glanced at his watch. "Back in your room, you two."

Dimitri Kalatonov came in with no lawyer and ready for a fight. He refused to spell his name for the audio recording and told Westcott he was a total fucking asshole for dragging him into the precinct. That got absolutely no rise out of Curtis, who started in by reading the Russian his rights.

"So you think you shouldn't be here," Curtis continued after Miranda. "You admitted to knowing and working with Alexi Volkov before he was killed. You knew he was running a rackets business and that he beat up a witness. Of everyone on my list, you are at the top of people who should be here."

Kalatonov shifted on the uncomfortable chair. "What the fuck do you want, Westcott?"

"I want the guy who killed Alexi Volkov and his daughter, and I want the guy who killed Tony DeMarco."

"I fucking told you," Kalatonov exploded, "that I don't know nothing about the dead cop."

Curtis checked his notes. "No, you never said that. You told me not to go there." Curtis looked up and leaned forward, getting into the Russian's space. What Kalatonov *hadn't* said in that sentence was more interesting than what he *had*. "So you don't know who killed DeMarco, but maybe you *do* know who killed Volkov and his daughter. That's what I'm hearing."

"Oh, c'mon, I didn't say that." Kalatonov's face went scarlet and he balled his hands into fists. "I got no idea who killed those people."

"Top of the list, Dimitri. That's where you are." He let the words sink in, then said, "So if you're not our cop killer, who is?"

"No idea."

Curtis sat back. "I need a DNA sample."

Kalatonov scoffed. "Good luck with that."

"We have trace evidence and you're a suspect in a murder. The judge will draw the line between the points. We'll get the warrant." Curtis leaned back and waited. If they got his DNA it would be on file forever, and that was the last thing Kalatonov would want.

"I should have brought my lawyer."

"Well, you didn't, so it's just us." Curtis ran the nib of his pen across a page in his notebook. Time to bait the gangster. "You said the Italians hated Volkov. That's not what we're seeing. Maybe you could be wrong."

"Nah, they despised him. Salvatore got stuck dealing with Volkov but he had no use for him. I told you, Volkov was a loose cannon and that's why he got busted. Beating up a witness, what a dumb ass."

Curtis scratched a quick line in his book. Kalatonov hadn't bit – it would have been so easy to slide the blame onto Salvatore's crew but he hadn't done it. That bought the Russian some credibility.

"Tell you what, you give me something I can use and I'll forget about the DNA – for now."

Kalatonov got up and paced the small room, a thick, hairy bundle of muscle. Aislinn looked at Curtis but he wasn't going to tell the

Russian to sit down. Finally, Kalatonov dropped heavily into his chair and let out a long sigh.

"DeMarco," he said. "He was dirty."

"Really. Tony DeMarco." Curtis kept a straight face. They had what they wanted – one of the crime bosses on the record exposing DeMarco. The pressure was off the team. "How?"

"He was Volkov's muscle."

Curtis shook his head. "Tony DeMarco wasn't a big guy. I don't buy that."

"Not that way. Volkov shook his marks down in person. DeMarco used the law to shut down businesses that didn't pay up."

"No, I don't think so. Someone would have noticed."

Kalatonov laughed, dark and threatening. "You're just as thick as the cops back then. You think you know what's going on." He pointed across the table, finger out, thumb like a cocked gun. "You're fucking clueless."

"Who else were they working with?" Curtis asked, not taking the bait. "I'm not going away, Dimitri. None of this is going away."

"Like I care."

Curtis turned to Aislinn. "Set up a joint operation with Vice. Dig into every business Kalatonov has a stake in and tear it apart. Tie in with the IRS and the tax court and get forensic audits on the books. Anything that crosses a state line goes to the FBI. We share everything. Got it?"

"Got it," Aislinn said, writing furiously in her notebook.

Curtis turned back to Kalatonov. "Care now?"

The Russian shot them a menacing look, the threat directed squarely at Curtis.

Curtis didn't stop. "Give me what you know – names – guys who were involved with DeMarco and Volkov."

Kalatonov sat, staring at Curtis and weighing his options. A long silence settled in, then Kalatonov decided holding back was a bad idea. "There were a couple of guys hanging around. Aaron somebody and..." his face screwed up as he struggled to remember the other name. "Danny Zebiak. Yeah, that's them."

"Aaron somebody and Danny Zebiak?" Curtis repeated.

Kalatonov gave Curtis a nod. "Yeah, those two."

"You still haven't convinced me it wasn't you," Curtis said.

Kalatonov shrugged. "Whatever."

Curtis shifted over to asking him for the names of businesses Volkov's crew had been extorting and got a couple of leads before the Russian decided he'd had enough and dried up. Eventually, Curtis closed the file and he walked out with Aislinn on his heels. They joined Stan and Bryan in the monitoring room.

"Got him on tape saying DeMarco was dirty," Stan said. "Nicely done."

"Saves our asses," Aislinn said. The relief among the entire crew was palpable.

"And...we have a couple of names," Curtis said. "One of them could be the guy running the show."

Aislinn cut in. "It's good having a couple of new leads, but I'm not counting Kalatonov out. He's pretty slick, moved things around on us a bit there. You caught him on denying killing DeMarco but not Volkov."

"Could have been nothing," Curtis said. "But I agree he's not off the radar." He ripped a page out of his notebook and handed it to Bryan. "Chase down these businesses after we're finished with the interviews, find out if Volkov was threatening them."

Bryan took the list and tucked it in his pocket.

"Got yourself a full time job here, LD," Stan said. "Well done."

"LD?" Aislinn asked, confused.

Stan tapped himself on the chest. "Big dog." Then he pointed at Bryan. "Little dog."

Curtis couldn't help laughing, that image was definitely going to stick. He checked his watch. "Time to have a chat with Giuseppe Salvatore."

"Creepy old bastard," Aislinn said. "Always stares at me."

"Ahh," Stan said. "He likes you."

Aislinn gave him the finger.

The recording devices in the interview room were turned back on and the crime boss was led in with a lawyer on his sleeve. Curtis read Salvatore his rights and gave the gangster's counsel the same warning as the lawyer who had accompanied Patrick O'Reilly. *Talk directly to your client or keep your mouth shut.* They settled in, with the Italian don taking his time to get comfortable. Which suited Curtis just fine, as he was still deciding how to approach Salvatore.

"Detective Byrne," Salvatore said pleasantly, staring at Aislinn from under his thick eyebrows. "How nice to see you again."

"You as well," Aislinn said with every bit of insincerity she could muster.

"We know who pulled the trigger on Alexi Volkov." Curtis opened strong – the last time they had met he was convinced Salvatore knew who'd killed Volkov. "But that still leaves his daughter Darina."

Salvatore smoothed the lapel on his suit. "Then arrest whoever killed Volkov and see if they did the daughter as well."

"Can't arrest a dead man," Curtis said, watching for Salvatore's reaction. For a brief second Curtis was sure Salvatore thought they had the wrong guy. Which meant if the shooter was still alive, it wasn't DeMarco. "I'm through dicking around. I want some answers."

Salvatore was eyeing Aislinn. "Then ask some questions, detective."

"Who killed Tony DeMarco?" Curtis said.

"Who?" Salvatore asked.

"A detective who got shot back in 2003."

Salvatore's lawyer started in but the old man shook his head and refocused on Curtis. "What the fuck, Westcott. Now this is about some cop who got shot. You're all over the fucking map."

"They're linked, and your name keeps coming up. This isn't about a Russian thug who got himself murdered anymore, it's about nailing a cop killer."

"Oh, you're so fucking wrong," Salvatore bellowed. "You got nothing on me."

"We now know that DeMarco was working with Volkov. Volkov was pushing hard to get on the inside track with the Italians who were running things in Boston. You were the liaison between Volkov and the family. Volkov and DeMarco both get killed. You tell me why we're not looking at you for this."

"Because you have no evidence."

"Really?" Curtis said.

"We need disclosure," the lawyer said. "Whatever you have."

"I told you to shut up," Curtis snapped. "Darina Volkov was seventeen, Tony DeMarco was a respected detective. I start pointing the finger at you and things are going to crumble pretty fast. The rats are going to jump ship and you'll be there all by yourself."

Salvatore sat back and chewed on his lower lip for a long time. "All right," he finally said. "DeMarco was working with Volkov."

"We know that, I just said it. Give me something new."

"Like what?"

"I need two sets of names." Curtis was careful, he had the fish on the line. "First, if DeMarco and Volkov were partners, someone at one of the businesses they were extorting is going to know something. Give us a list of shops that were paying them."

Salvatore raised an eyebrow. "You're like a ferret, Westcott. Dig, dig, dig."

"That's what we do," Curtis said. "Names."

"There was an auto body shop on Brookley Road. I think it's still there."

Aislinn was jotting down notes and she said, "R & D Auto Body."

"That's it," Salvatore said, turning his attention back to Aislinn. "A woman who knows her cars. I like that."

She glanced up at him. "Guy got his brains blown out there in the parking lot three years ago." They stared at each other for a few seconds, then she said, "I don't like cars, they're like men – expensive and break down a lot when they get old."

Salvatore grinned at that. "Feisty."

"I need the guys working with DeMarco and Volkov." Curtis waited, then added, "Since it wasn't you."

Salvatore's eyes narrowed and his lips clamped shut.

"Fine," Curtis said. He glanced over at Aislinn. "Make up a list of all known associates of Mr. Salvatore. Start digging into all unsolved crimes from the last twelve months and see if any of these associates could be linked to them. Bring them in for interviews. All of them."

"That is entirely inappropriate," the lawyer said. "You're forcing things to fit your agenda.

"Do it, Aislinn," Curtis said.

"All right, all right." Salvatore let out a deep breath. "But this didn't come from me."

"We're a black hole," Curtis said. "Stuff goes in, nothing comes out."

"There was this guy – Aaron Brock. He had his fingers in it."

"Aaron Brock. Who is he?" Curtis asked.

Salvatore shrugged. "Nasty piece of work who couldn't play nice. Same as Volkov, stuck on the outside."

"Where is he now?"

"How the fuck would I know?" Salvatore snapped.

"What about Danny Zebiak?" Curtis asked.

Salvatore looked confused for a few seconds, then he recognized the name. "Oh yeah, Danny. He was pretty low level. Don't really know much about him. Might have been involved, can't say for sure."

Curtis poked a bit more, got nothing in return and let the Italian leave. Stan and Bryan joined them and Stan was smiling like the cat that got into the sardine tin.

"Salvatore's going to swipe right on you," he said to Aislinn.

"Jesus, Stan." She rolled her eyes.

Stan got serious. "We have a confirmation on Aaron Brock from two sources."

"Right," Curtis said. "He's our best bet right now. Aislinn, since these are all tied together let's have you chase down Aaron Brock. Find out how he fits into all this."

"Done," Aislinn said.

"Stan, you and Bryan locate Danny Zebiak. No confirmation like we have on Brock, but he's still a good lead."

"He is," Stan agreed.

"Did you catch the look on his face when I said you can't arrest a dead man?" Curtis asked and they all nodded.

Stan chimed in. "Yeah, he was a bit shocked. Like you had it wrong."

"That's what I'm thinking," Curtis said.

"So if the guy who took out Alexi Volkov is still alive, it's not DeMarco," Aislinn said.

"Which confirms yet again that Volkov and DeMarco were definitely working with at least one other person, probably more," Stan said.

"Do you think Salvatore knows who pulled the trigger?" Aislinn asked.

Curtis gave that some serious thought, then said, "I think he knows it wasn't DeMarco but I wouldn't go as far as saying he knows who it was. And I don't think we're going to get much more out of him. These old timers have a code, and it involves not talking too much."

Aislinn smiled. "Oh, I don't know, they were Chatty Kathy's today. Nicely done, boss."

Curtis grinned. "Okay, guys, you all know what to do. Let's make sure we pick up any overlap between the three cases. Super important, the last thing we want is to get a lead on one case then fail to connect the dots."

Aislinn headed down the hall. Finding Aaron Brock was now at the top of her agenda and she was pretty sure that Stan was thinking the same thing about Danny Zebiak. They had exactly what they'd been looking for – confirmation on DeMarco from an outside source, and two more names attached to the protection racket DeMarco and Volkov had been running.

The gears were moving now, each revolution bringing them closer to the truth.

CHAPTER TWENTY-EIGHT

Stan Lamers located Danny Zebiak easily enough. He was incarcerated at the Pondville Correctional Center in Norfolk, a minimum security facility about forty miles southwest of Boston. One of the admin staff at the center pulled his file and told Stan that Zebiak was in a pre-release program and at work until noon on Fridays. Stan set an appointment to talk with him at one o'clock and looked into Bryan's cubicle.

"Want to go for a ride?" Stan asked. "I'm heading down to see Danny Zebiak."

"Sure do."

"What's in his file?"

"He was in for grand larceny," Bryan said. "Spent a few years at a medium security jail before being transferred to Pondville. Behaved himself and is due for full release in September."

"Arrest history prior to that?" Stan asked.

"Assault in 2002, did four years. Carrying a concealed weapon when prohibited in 2009, two years. Then the larceny conviction in 2015." Bryan looked up. "The guy doesn't seem to learn."

"More common than you'd think," Stan said. "What kind of weapon was he carrying?"

Bryan scanned the sheet for the particulars. It took a minute to find the details on that arrest. "Glock G17."

"Worth a try. Forensics in Darina Volkov's file says she was hit from behind with a Heckler & Koch P2000 before she was strangled."

"Still could be him," Bryan said.

"Bad guys like to use a certain kind of handgun, but even if he had a P2000 on him that doesn't tie him to the murder. Let's not force the evidence." He gave the rookie a smile. "I'm not telling you anything you don't already know."

"Good to have a reminder."

Stan leaned on the divider between the cubicles. "You like this stuff? Homicide?"

Bryan wasn't sure what the right answer was. "Yeah, I guess."

"Why?" Stan asked.

"It's the ultimate crime, murder. Taking someone's life. Catching the person who did it, that's important."

Stan nodded. "Yeah, that's true. It's like solving a puzzle. All the pieces are there and you need to connect them." He raised his index finger and said, "Here's some advice. Don't rush things or move too quickly – you'll run by the evidence like a kid on an Easter egg hunt. Miss an egg and later, when the clues start to finger-joint, not everything jibes."

"Don't rush," Bryan repeated.

"And don't arrest the bad guy too fast."

Bryan looked skeptical. "Well, if you're sure they did it."

"Hey, the moment you arrest someone, their friends suddenly don't want to talk. They know what they say is going to end up in court. Much better to let the perp dangle while you chat with his or her accomplices. Plus, you can only hold someone for twenty-four hours without some really solid evidence."

"Good to know," Bryan said.

"It is." Stan stood up and grabbed a mug off his desk. "Coffee time, little dog."

* * *

Aislinn leaned back in her chair and put her feet on the desk. She had spent a good deal of time looking for Aaron Brock and had little to show for it. Brock was keeping his head down, which meant he was likely still into something illegal. No registered address, no car tags or insurance, no social media presence and no bank accounts or credit cards. That was off-the-scale strange. People left digital trails, like slugs crawling along a sidewalk, and that trail was extremely hard to disguise. Either Aaron Brock was very good at masking his trail, had changed his name, or he was dead. She had feelers out and would know soon enough. Right now it was time to report back to Westcott.

"What a bag of dirt." Aislinn walked into Curtis's office and dropped Aaron Brock's file on his desk. "And now he's disappeared."

Curtis opened the file and scanned Brock's priors. "He's been a busy guy."

"Breaking the law, yeah," Aislinn said. "There's a lot of stuff from 2000 to 2005, most of it involving violence." She leaned over and pointed at one line among many. "Laid a beating on someone for not paying up and got charged with attempted murder."

"Must have been quite the beating," Curtis said, looking over the remainder of Brock's arrest record. "And he's missing."

"Yeah, he's fallen off the edge of the world. I'm looking to see if he changed his name and running a check through VICAP in case he's on the books in a different state."

They often used the FBI's Violent Criminal Apprehension Program, or VICAP as it was commonly known, to track potential suspects who might have fled Massachusetts and set up somewhere else in the US. Linkage breaks between different states was a major obstacle in tracking serial offenders and the criminals often exploited it. They knew if by moving around they could keep their name out of VICAP, it would be difficult for one jurisdiction to see that they were wanted in another.

"This charge of attempted murder for beating the guy, it's the kind of thing he'd be doing if he was involved with a protection racket," Curtis said.

"*Exactly* the kind of thing," Aislinn agreed.

"Maybe this one has some legs."

"Could." She scooped up the file. "What are you up to?"

"Gonna let the chief know what we heard in the Kalatonov interview.

"That Tony DeMarco was on the take?" Aislinn asked.

"Yeah, that."

"Lucky you," she said.

After Aislinn left Curtis picked up the phone and dialed Ted Dawson, Chief of Police for Boston and ultimately, his superior officer. It went through to voice mail and he left a message for Dawson to call him back, then got up and stood by the window, watching the passing clouds for a few minutes to clear his head. Stan and Bryan were heading for Pondville to talk with Danny Zebiak and Aislinn was working on unearthing Aaron Brock. It was highly possible that something would gel from talking to one or both of these guys. He felt strongly that the key to solving all three murders was to reassemble the team that was working with Volkov and DeMarco and then wear them down until one of them either admitted guilt or pointed the finger at someone else.

Aislinn wasn't giving up on the possibility that the stolen college money was motive enough to kill Darina, but that didn't explain why the girl's father or Tony DeMarco had been murdered. Perhaps Alexi was treading on some big toes and one of the crime families got pissed off enough to put a bullet in his head. Maybe DeMarco had simply been shot while checking out a botched burglary. Maybe. Perhaps. He didn't like those odds, and he didn't like coincidences.

"These are linked," he said quietly as his cell phone buzzed.

"Chief," he said. "Thanks for returning my call."

"No problem, Curtis," Dawson said. "What's this about?"

"Tony DeMarco," Curtis said. "He was on the job back in 2003 and was killed responding to a call for a burglary in progress."

"I remember it. Damn tragedy, and they never found the perp."

"Well, we've had additional information come out of some leads on a different cold case."

Curtis filled him in with everything they had, including the independent corroboration from three sources that DeMarco was working with Alexi Volkov. He finished with, "DeMarco's death might have been premeditated." Then he waited.

"How sure are you DeMarco was involved with this Volkov character?"

"Ninety-nine percent," Curtis said.

"And that someone set him up in the electronics store?" Dawson asked.

"Fifty-fifty, could go either way at this point."

"All right, since you're rock-solid on DeMarco being on the take, we'll admit it's possible if we're asked. The other thing, that DeMarco's death might be tied into this, we hold that tight to the chest right now. Deny anything that comes at you, if it does."

"Yes, sir."

"Jesus," Dawson said. "What a mess."

"It's that alright," Curtis said. "I'll be in touch the moment we know more."

"Okay, and I'll pass this along to the commish, then if he thinks it's appropriate, the mayor."

"Thanks."

There was a moment of dead air, then Dawson said, "I hear you had a chat with Elian Perez at one of Chloe Harrah's parties."

"I did." The memory of his brief conversation with the new police commissioner on Chloe's boat was fresh in his mind. "He seems okay."

"Well, they probably do things differently out in LA, so be ready for some changes."

"Sounds good." Curtis had no intention of telling Dawson his first impression of Perez wasn't great. "Anything else?"

"No, that's it."

Curtis waited for the chief to hang up, then set his phone on the desk. Eighteen years had passed since DeMarco was killed, but memories ran deep and the department was in the unenviable position of having to admit that back in the day one of its own was shaking down businesses for protection money. To say that the media was in for a feast was an understatement.

CHAPTER TWENTY-NINE

Stan had Bryan Cheung drive to Pondville and spent most of the time staring out the window at the lush countryside. He was almost always behind the wheel and the break was refreshing. When they arrived at the minimum-security facility he felt relaxed and even a bit sleepy. That disappeared fast when they got to the main counter in the admin office.

"Check your guns here," the guard said.

"Rather not," Stan responded, knowing the protocol but not liking it.

"Not a request," the uniformed officer said.

Stan mumbled under his breath as he trailed the guard to an unloading station, popped out the magazine and put his gun in the tray the guard had provided. Bryan followed suit and they inserted the trays into secure slots in the wall, much like safe deposit boxes at the bank. Stan and Bryan locked their respective boxes and pocketed the keys.

"Meeting room's this way," the guard said. "Or there's a secure table outside."

"Outside would be better," Stan said, thinking Danny might open up easier in a less regimented setting.

"We're not going to see him in his cell?" Bryan asked.

Stan shook his head. "The other inmates see two cops walking into his space and he immediately gets labeled a snitch."

The inmates' block was close by and it only took a few minutes to gather up Danny Zebiak and deliver him to the freshly-painted table set in a small, sunny clearing ringed with thick shrubs.

"Who are you guys?" Danny asked, sweeping his shoulder-length sandy blond hair back from his thin face.

Stan and Bryan held up their badges and the inmate had a close look at them.

"Homicide?" he said after studying Stan's. He sat down opposite them, a worried look on his face.

"Nice place," Stan said, looking around. Danny didn't respond and he said, "You're out of here soon."

"Done my sentence." A good length of time passed and signs of nervousness started to show. "What do you guys want?"

"Answers," Stan said, then elaborated. "Correct answers."

Bryan set his notebook on the table and clicked open a pen. He sat with his hand poised over the paper. The only noise was a fluttering of tiny wings at a busy birdbath on the far side of the grassy area.

"Fuck this up, Danny, and you can forget getting out of here." Stan opened a text on his phone that he'd sent to himself and read it out loud. "Assault, concealed carry, theft under – that's three felony charges. Not sure why you're at this country club."

"I did my time. Never caused any trouble." He was visibly shaking now.

"Sure, but ghosts from the past, they can trip you up."

"What ghosts?" he asked.

"Alexi Volkov."

Danny's eyes widened. "Ahh, man, that's twenty years ago. You got nothing on me there."

"Except three unsolved murders." Stan's eyes narrowed. "And you're on the radar. The big blip right in the middle of the screen."

"What the fuck," Danny said. "No way you're pinning Volkov on me."

"Volkov, his daughter, and *a cop*." Stan leaned in, using his size to intimidate the smaller man. "You the guy, Danny?"

Danny leapt up from the table and backed off a dozen feet. He stood on the grass shaking his head. "None of that was me. None of it."

Stan relaxed and pointed to the bench. Eventually, Danny returned and sat down. "Now that's interesting," Stan said. "You never asked me *which cop*."

Danny just sat and stared at the table.

"Volkov and his protection racket. Tell us about it. Who was involved, what your role was, who took out Volkov."

A bird landed on the far end of the table and hopped over to Danny. He dug in his pocket, found a couple of crumbs and dropped them on the wood. "I feed them." They all watched the bird peck at the crumbs. "They trust me."

"Volkov," Stan said.

"I picked up the cash," Danny said. "Aaron was the muscle."

"Aaron Brock?" Stan asked.

Danny's eyes widened slightly as he realized the cops already had a line on things. "Yeah, Aaron Brock. He was a crazy fucker, that guy. All excited when someone didn't pay and he got to use his baseball bat."

"Why would Aaron kill Alexi Volkov?" Stan asked.

"Never said he did." Danny found some more crumbs and two new birds showed up.

"Any bent cops on the roster?" Stan's tone of voice made it sound more like a statement than a question.

"Maybe." Danny fished around in his pocket but came up empty. The birds hung around for a minute, then left. "You know about Tony?"

Stan nodded. "Sure do."

Danny squirmed about and shivered. "I never liked being in business with a cop. Didn't seem right."

"Who was running things?" Stan asked.

Danny shrugged. “Must have been Tony. Everything stopped when he got killed.”

“Two guys who are in business together get whacked,” Stan said. “That suggests their murders are linked. Then one of those guys’ daughter goes missing and shows up dead a few days ago. I think she’s linked too. What do you think, Danny?”

“Could be.”

“Alexi got himself killed halfway through his trial. Did DeMarco take him out because he was worried Volkov would cut a deal with the DA?”

“I don’t know if it was Tony. Might have been Aaron.”

“Who killed DeMarco?” Stan asked.

“Could have been Aaron. I don’t know.”

Stan shook his head. “That doesn’t make sense. Aaron’s got a good thing going and he kills the golden goose.”

Danny gave Stan a furtive glance. “You don’t know Aaron. He’s fucked up.”

Stan looked over at Bryan. “What do you think? This guy telling the truth?”

Bryan closed his notebook, set his pen on the table and gave Danny a long, hard look. “Yeah, I think he is.”

Stan nodded. “Me too.” Stan stood up and stared down at Danny. “Lucky you.”

They collected their weapons and headed back for Boston, Stan texting Aislinn and Curtis with the bare bones of the interview with Danny Zebiak as Bryan drove. He finished with *More to follow* and hit send. He and Bryan took the time to talk over the different ways things might have played out, and no matter which way they looked at it, Tony DeMarco came out as the guy running things with Aaron Brock as the triggerman. Locating Brock had just moved up big time on the priority list.

CHAPTER THIRTY

Aislinn had found Aaron Brock.

Brock was now Brendan Moore. He'd changed his name in 2006 and cut all visible ties to his former life. What he hadn't quit was his criminal lifestyle. Brock had settled into Charlestown, across the river from Boston, and carved out a niche moving stolen goods from the dock area to sketchy retailers along the Eastern Seaboard. The cops knew him, but either weren't aware of his previous life, which was unlikely, or they didn't care, which was probably more like it. Brock had learned to keep his head down and was an irritant more than a threat, so they left him alone.

He was far more than an irritant to Aislinn and she was *not* going to leave him be, especially since one of his arrest records involved carrying an unlicensed Heckler & Koch pistol.

Brock lived in a flat that backed onto the John Harvard Mall, a historic park under a canopy of mature shrubs and trees. Downtown Boston to Charlestown was a short drive, and given his past propensity for violence Aislinn had a couple of uniforms follow her in their squad car. They waited at the curb while she knocked on Brock's door. It was mid-afternoon on Friday and Aislinn didn't really expect him to be home. She was pleasantly surprised when he answered.

"What?" Brock said, his eyes first on Aislinn, then settling on the cops waiting by the curb.

Aislinn flashed her badge. "Boston Homicide. Are you Aaron Brock?"

Brock smiled, coldly. He was mid-forties but looked older, with age lines etched into his skin and bags under his dark eyes. His thick, blond hair was disheveled, like he had just got out of bed. Aislinn figured him for a gym rat – wide shoulders and a thin waist with biceps straining against his T-shirt.

"Not anymore," he said.

"Yeah, I saw the name change. We need to talk."

"About what?"

"Alexi Volkov," Aislinn said.

Brock shifted back a bit and Aislinn thought for a moment that he was going to slam the door on her. She tensed up, ready to throw her weight into it, but instead he motioned for her to come in. She gave a quick hand signal to the uniforms and one of them hustled up the short walk to the front door and came in behind her.

Inside, the drapes were closed and it was dark, but from what she could see the furnishings were carefully chosen and expensive. She followed him into a large living room, her hand close to her gun, then relaxed a bit when he pulled the curtains open, flooding the room with light. He pointed to a couch and sat down in an armchair facing her.

"What do you want?" he said.

"You and Alexi Volkov were involved in a business venture about twenty years ago," she said. "I'm interested in anything you can tell me about that."

He shook his head in a slow and deliberate motion. "Why are you here? Something has triggered this."

"Fair enough," Aislinn said. "We found Darina Volkov's body in Jamaica Plain a few days ago. We're looking into how she got there."

"So what's that got to do with Alexi...and me?"

It was Aislinn's turn to smile. "You want to play games, we go downtown to finish this conversation." She crossed her legs and said,

"We know quite a bit about what was going on back then and I need you to fill in some of the blanks."

"All right," he said, sitting back, the look on his face saying it wasn't. "Ask away."

"Volkov had a protection racket on the go. Who were his partners?"

He mulled that over for a minute, then said, "Danny Zebiak."

She shook her head. "Not the grunts, his partners."

"There was a cop. Tony DeMarco. Got himself killed a few years later."

"That's better," Aislinn said. "Who else?"

Brock shrugged. "That was it. Me, Alexi, Tony and Danny. We didn't need anyone else."

"Well, that leaves you in a precarious situation. Alexi is dead. Tony is dead. And Danny, from what my colleague tells me, was just a gopher. That leaves you as the only one who could have pulled the trigger."

"What the fuck," Brock said, jerking forward. "You're thinking I killed Alexi and Tony? Are you fucking crazy?"

"And Darina," Aislinn said.

He stared at her in disbelief. "Holy shit, you come walking in here and accuse me of three murders? You have absolutely no proof, and I know because I didn't kill them."

"You owned an unlicensed Heckler & Koch back around that time."

"So what," he said. "I got a fine and I paid it."

"Darina Volkov was smashed over the head with the butt of an H & K."

Aislinn let that sink in, stopping short of giving him anything about Darina being strangled with a garotte. That information was part of their holdback and not being released to anyone. Even giving Brock the tidbit about the H & K was risky, it could come back to bite her in the ass later. But right now, she needed to use anything she had to connect him to the crime and get him talking.

"This is bullshit," Brock said.

"You're a professional criminal, Aaron," Aislinn said. "And the last man standing."

"Listen, I didn't kill them. Tony was freaking out during Alexi's trial, thinking that he was going to start coughing up names to cut a deal with the DA. But he never came to me, never asked me to kill him. I always thought it was Tony."

"Was he capable? He was running a racket, but a cop murdering people, that's a stretch."

"Oh, he was capable," Brock said. "Tony was a mean bastard under all that nice-guy exterior."

"Okay, but Tony didn't shoot himself in the chest. So who did?"

"Maybe it was just a burglary."

"You think so?" Aislinn asked.

Brock didn't answer.

"Aaron, this isn't going to go well for you," Aislinn said. "Like I said, last man standing."

"I don't know what else to tell you. Tony was the guy behind the racket, Alexi was the front man and Danny and I were the muscle. You already know everything."

Aislinn shook her head. "I'm not convinced Tony DeMarco killed Volkov and his daughter. And then there's the whole thing with Tony getting murdered. What I'm missing is the shooter. I'm homicide – I don't care about the racket except how it plays into the murders. I want the person who pulled the trigger."

"Can't help you with that," Brock said.

Aislinn stood. "We'll see." She started to leave, then said, "Don't even think about legging it."

Outside the sun was warm on her skin and she sat alone on a wood bench across the street from Brock's place. She chewed on a fingernail and considered whether she believed him or not. His reaction when she accused him of being the guy who cleaned things up by killing people was immediate and vehement. *You have absolutely no proof, and I know because I didn't kill them.* That was a definitive statement, not just some generic *I didn't do it* line. Career criminals were good at the standard lines professing innocence, but this was different and Aislinn was leaning toward believing him.

Sort of, but not completely.

Something else was eating away at her. Darina had somehow gotten sucked into this mess, but not until six months after her father's murder. Why the time delay? If Darina had unwittingly passed Alexi's killer on the sidewalk in front of the house, why not just kill her on the spot? Why wait? There was something off with that and it was constantly churning in the back of her mind.

A text came in from Curtis and she read it. *Debrief at the office at 3:00.*

She pushed herself off the bench and got in her car. A visit with Kayla Walsh was next on her list. The pieces were starting to fall into place. This was going to come together.

CHAPTER THIRTY-ONE

Bryan Cheung was already seated with his notebook out when Aislinn entered Curtis's office. She gave him a wide smile. "You're becoming a regular."

He grinned. "Yeah, can't get rid of me."

"Good thing." Aislinn felt he'd done some serious digging to ferret out the phone number Darina had called from Kristin's place, and that was earning him a place on the team.

Curtis motioned for her to close the door and said, "Three murders – Alexi Volkov, Tony DeMarco, and Darina Volkov – and they're connected."

"Yup," Stan said.

"Absolutely," Aislinn chimed in.

Curtis looked at Bryan and he nodded. "Okay," Curtis said. "I agree. Question is, do we have one killer, or more than one."

Aislinn shrugged. "Tony may have killed Alexi Volkov to keep him from talking during his trial, and he may have taken out Darina as well, but he didn't kill himself. Could be two shooters."

"Or Tony didn't take out Alexi," Stan said. "Maybe one person killed them all."

"Bryan?" Curtis asked.

Bryan was nervous at being in the spotlight but had an opinion. "I like the idea of one shooter, but I don't think we've seen him yet. None of the crime bosses we pulled in had sufficient motivation and Danny Zebiak isn't the kind of guy to kill three people in cold blood."

Curtis raised an eyebrow. "You don't like Dimitri Kalatonov?"

"Not sure. He's the most likely of the three, but it doesn't seem right."

Curtis glanced at Stan. "Do you agree with Bryan on Danny Zebiak?"

"Yeah, he strikes me as being scared he's going to get dragged into something he had very little, if anything, to do with. I think he was a small cog in the wheel when the racket was up and running. He was good for some info – confirmed Tony DeMarco was in on it and that Aaron Brock was a key player. Other than that, he's off the radar."

Curtis looked at Aislinn. "Aaron Brock, what about him?"

Aislinn wasn't entirely sure how she felt about Brock and while she didn't want to come across as waffling, she wasn't about to go on the record with something she didn't entirely believe.

"He's a career criminal," she said. "Very slick in how he presents himself and doesn't let you get a true picture of who he is. I think he's dangerous and can probably become violent easily enough. It's possible he's a sociopath, and if he is, his lack of empathy lets him come across as unrepentant, which can be interpreted as innocence."

"*Sociopath*," Stan said, imitating Aislinn's voice. "Look at the big brain on you."

"He's tough to read," Curtis said, throwing Stan a *stop-fooling-around* look.

"Very," Aislinn agreed, grinning at Stan. "I think he was a major player in the racket and more than capable of pulling the trigger, but I'm not sure he did it."

"Danny Zebiak told us Brock was fucked up," Stan said. "That he liked using his baseball bat on guys who didn't pay."

"And Brock owned a Heckler & Koch pistol," Aislinn added.

"Darina Volkov was hit over the head with an H & K P2000 before she was strangled."

"Any chance of getting our hands on Brock's gun?" Curtis asked.

"No, I checked and it was destroyed years ago."

Curtis nodded. "Fair enough. We'll keep Aaron Brock high on our list." He scanned the page on his desk. "The businesses that were paying protection money to Volkov and DeMarco were a help, but I don't think we need to find any more. We have a good idea of who was involved, so let's back off on that, aside from following up with any you already have."

"Yeah," Stan agreed. "We keep coming up with the same guys. We have two left and then we'll shut it down."

"Where are you on Darina's file?" Curtis asked Aislinn.

"I just came from a meeting with Kayla Walsh," she said, then reminded them Kayla was the one who had stolen some of Darina's college money. "She's sticking to her original story, that Darina threatened her by the swimming pool and demanded the money back."

"But Kayla never admitted to Darina that she stole the money," Stan said.

"No, she didn't," Aislinn confirmed.

"Do you believe her?" Curtis asked.

"I do," Aislinn said, "but I still have questions."

"Like what?"

"Darina starts the day happy, but by the time evening rolls around she's angry and upset. I'm not sure it was just the money, but that's speculative. What isn't speculation is her call to the police station from Kristin's house. She's ready to tell the police that Kayla stole the money, yet there's no file opened or charges. It simply becomes a black hole."

"Maybe she made the call then decided to back off," Curtis said.

"Entirely possible," Aislinn agreed.

Curtis pointed at Bryan. "You were following up on…" He checked his notes. "…Patricia Morriscey, the woman on the switchboard that night."

"Still out of reach in New Zealand," Bryan said. "She's due back in Haast in a couple of days."

"Okay, stay on top of it." Curtis motioned for Aislinn to continue.

"Darina disappears six months after Alexi is killed. Why the delay? If Darina saw her dad's killer, why didn't he take her out sooner?"

"That's a good point," Curtis said. "Any ideas on it?"

Aislinn shook her head. "None. It's not making any sense, unless something triggered it. I can't get a handle on what that might be."

"Anything else?" Curtis asked.

"Kristin Sanders," Aislinn replied. "I have a gut feeling that she knows more than she's telling me."

"About the phone call from her house?" Stan asked.

Aislinn shrugged. "Not sure, it could be more than that. I have a ticket to the dance tomorrow night for the reunion. I'm going to show up and have a chat with Kristin."

Stan couldn't help himself. "You're going to a dance? You bought a ticket to a dance? Who are you and what did you do with Aislinn?"

She gave him the snarkiest sideways glance she could muster. "It was included with the registration."

Bryan looked confused and Stan couldn't help grinning as he gestured at Aislinn. "Retirement party for one of the detectives, her moves got tagged as *doing the donkey*. It's still top of mind for lots of the guys."

Bryan wanted to laugh, but looking at Aislinn told him not to. Curtis couldn't help letting out a low chuckle.

"Going forward," Curtis said after a moment. "We have three gangsters and their cronies that are still on our radar. There could be a link between Volkov and them that we haven't seen yet, and I have a small team pulling all the criminal cases, complaints and dismissed charges on their records. If there's anything, we'll find it."

Curtis stood up and stretched. "Bryan, I've arranged for you to stay with Stan through to the end of this case."

"Excellent," Bryan said.

Curtis gave him a hint of a smile. "You're earning it."

"Sort of," Stan snorted at the new recruit.

"Wonderful," Aislinn threw in, grinning.

Then they were gone, leaving the newcomer to follow them into the hall.

CHAPTER THIRTY-TWO

Aislinn took Saturday off and went shopping. She found a couple of colorful short-sleeve tops and texted an image of them to Stan with the caption – *Darn, couldn't find these in camo* – and got back a laughing-face emoji.

She tried on some jeans at American Eagle and liked the look. Snug but not tight. Aislinn stood in front of the mirror staring at her reflection. With her striking red hair and thin figure, she turned heads and she knew it. What was missing, she thought, was turning the right head – the guy who understood her and made her smile. He was out there and patience was the key. It wasn't her strong suit and she grinned as she thought of an old-time poster with two buzzards sitting on a withered branch with the words – *Patience be damned, I'm going to kill something.*

The early afternoon sun was glorious as she walked along the waterfront back to her car. Boston was alive with early-summer fever and she was glad her shopping bag had clothes with tangerines and yellows. An attractive man about her age smiled as he passed and she smiled back. She risked a quick glance and he was still looking. She almost stopped and waved – maybe he was the one – but she didn't. She kept walking and he was gone.

How to meet the right person to share her life with was really hard, and she was becoming more aware of her age every year now. Thirty-eight wasn't a spring chicken. She thought about Cody. Now there was a big heart, and it didn't hurt that time had been kind to him.

Her car was waiting, hot from sitting in the sun, and she rolled the windows down rather than turn on the air-conditioning. She headed for home and on a whim decided to cruise by and see her parents. The drive was painless, traffic light and the Eagles on her radio. She arrived in good spirits and found Fiona at the kitchen table reading the newspaper.

"Aislinn," she beamed.

"I was driving by and thought I'd stop in," Aislinn said. "Did some shopping today," she added as she dropped into an empty chair with her booty. "Where's Dad?"

"Golfing with his buddies. So, what did you buy?" Fiona asked, closing the paper.

"I'll show you," Aislinn said. Fiona had great fashion sense and Aislinn was glad to have her all to herself for a while. It took half an hour for to Aislinn try on the clothes for her mom, who gave the new additions her stamp of approval. One thing they both agreed on was that summer was the best season, and it was about time Aislinn introduced some bright colors into her wardrobe.

The door banged open and Cian trudged in with his golf clubs draped over his shoulder. He dropped them on the floor and wiped his brow. "Well, my two favorite women."

"Were you golfing or running a marathon?" Aislinn laughed. His hair was a mess, like he'd been sweating and hadn't bothered brushing it after.

He pulled a score card out of his back pocket and proceeded with a play by play summary of the game as Aislinn surveyed the penciled-in numbers.

"A hundred and four," she said. "Is that good?"

"Completely blew up," he complained, looking utterly dejected.

She read the rest of the scores. "Larry got 82 – of course he did – and Ken got 94. Arnie only scored on the first two holes."

"Oh, yeah." Cian brightened at that. "He got a call on the third tee. His daughter was finally in labor." Cian started laughing. "Arnie grabbed his clubs off the cart and went jogging back to the clubhouse. Funniest thing *ever,* him running with golf clubs." His laughter was so infectious they all started.

"Any word yet?" Fiona said, struggling to stop.

"Yup, she had a little boy – both mother and son healthy."

"Ah, that's great," she said.

"It is," Aislinn said. She texted Curtis with the news, just in case any of the old-timers at the precinct wanted to put together a basket for the newborn and his mom, then she held up the score card. "Going out again this week?"

"Sure am," he said with all the conviction he could muster.

Cian went to the fridge and fished out two cold beers. He handed one to Aislinn. "Did those business names we gave you help?"

She twisted off the cap and nodded. "They led to some others that were paying money to Volkov." She took a deep breath. "We're still looking at Tony as the guy behind it. He *was* Volkov's partner."

Cian's mouth drew taut and he sat staring at the floor.

"And now we have corroboration from both Patrick O'Reilly and Dimitri Kalatonov," she said. "They knew, but those guys, they keep things close to their chest. Word's going to leak onto the street eventually though."

"Pandora's Box," Cian said, his brow creased with worry.

"Oh yeah, it's going to hit the fan."

He shook his head in disgust. "Fuck, what was Tony thinking? Cops didn't get paid all that well back in the day, but he didn't need to get involved in that."

"Bad choices," Aislinn said.

"Yeah, that's an understatement." He scratched at the label on the bottle for a minute. "Tony. Damn it all to hell."

"Question for you," she said. "Darina Volkov called the precinct the evening she disappeared. She had noticed some of her college money missing and was likely going to make a complaint. But that call doesn't show up in the nightly log. Any ideas?"

"Who took the call?"

"Patricia Morriscey was on the switchboard so we're assuming it was her."

"Who'd she put it through to?" he asked.

Aislinn shrugged. "No idea. She's in New Zealand right now and out of touch on some eco-tour."

"Well, she would have connected it to a someone in the back."

"Who was on that night?" Aislinn asked.

"No idea." He took a sip of cold beer and said, "I can't remember what I did last week."

"Yeah, right."

"Is the call important?" he asked.

She thought about that, then said, "I'm not sure. It's a loose end more than anything else. We're focused mostly on Aaron Brock and Danny Zebiak."

Cian squinted at her. "Who are they?"

"A couple of guys who were working the protection racket with Volkov and DeMarco. Both low level, but Brock might be capable of pulling the trigger. I just can't figure the motivation."

"You'll get there," Cian said. "It's pretty amazing how you dig up all this stuff."

"Thanks, Dad." She got up and smoothed her shirt. "Well, I'm off. It's the windup dance at the reunion tonight."

He started to laugh but caught the look on her face and stopped. "Not saying a word."

CHAPTER THIRTY-THREE

Aislinn arrived at the school an hour after the event started and trawled the entire lot for a parking spot. Nothing was open and she pulled up in front of the main doors and stuck her police pass on the dash.

"Screw it."

She jumped out, circled the car, and took the stairs two at a time, the beat of *Bootylicious* booming through the warm June air. Inside, the sound bounced off the walls of the empty foyer and Aislinn strode over to the dark auditorium. She stood just inside the doors, scanning the room, peering into a sea of pulsating strobe lights.

Kristin was here somewhere, she would never miss a chance to shine in front of so many former classmates. Finding her was another story. It was difficult to make out faces in the low light and Aislinn didn't move for five minutes until she spotted a figure walking through the crowd with a cane. Cody Hall. She moved quickly before he could disappear and caught up to him midway across the cavernous room.

"Hey," she said.

"Hi." Cody gave her a warm smile. "Haven't seen you at any of the events."

"Busy," she replied, feeling a tinge of guilt at not telling Cody that the reunion wasn't really her thing. "Couldn't make it."

"Ahh, that's too bad. I saw a lot of the old crew. You missed a good time."

The white lie grew inside her and she couldn't let it go. She needed to be honest with him. "The reunion," she said, scrunching up her face. "I'm not all that comfortable."

His eyes widened and he looked a bit shocked. "A, you dissolve into this crowd like sugar in water."

That set her back a step. She hadn't seen it that way. "You think?"

"Yeah, yeah, of course." Every part of his face was smiling. "I can't believe you'd think otherwise."

Aislinn looked away and thought about the skinny kid she had once been, with the freckles and the shy smile. "That's so kind, Cody," she said.

"It's just the truth," he said, eyes soft and without an ounce of malice. "Wanna dance?" he asked, then held up his cane. "A slow one."

She grinned and put her hand on his arm. "Also not my thing." She let her hand linger on his arm, her eyes locked on his. She slipped her hand from his and asked, "Have you seen Kristin tonight?"

He shook his head. "No, and I was looking for her. There's someone I wanted her to meet."

"That's not like her to miss a party," Aislinn said.

"Totally out of character," he agreed.

"Gotta find her. Catch up with you later."

"Okay."

Aislinn gave him a smile and made a slow rotation around the room, watching for Kristin and thinking about what he had said. *You dissolve into this crowd like sugar in water.* After one full sweep of the room – a few minutes at least – it had soaked in that he was right. She shuffled her emotions off to the side and focused on finding Kristin Sanders. Twenty minutes of searching was the limit to her patience and she approached the DJ while he was queuing up the next song.

She flashed her badge. "Could you page someone for me?"

He studied the badge and said, "Sure – who?"

"Kristin Sanders. Ask her to come to the auditorium doors. Don't say why."

"Right, got it."

"Thanks."

Aislinn walked the length of the room, hugging the wall before ducking out into the foyer and leaning against the wall. Kristin Sanders knew something. Aislinn was kicking herself now for not pushing harder when she had Kristin sitting across the table from her. Tracking her down and getting the truth out of her was going to be tougher now that Kristin had decided to keep her head down and stay off the radar. What was she hiding? What *could* she be hiding? The only thing that came to mind was the phone call, but that brought the theft of the college money back into play and she didn't think that was the motive.

"Teen girls don't kill other teen girls and stuff their bodies in walls," she said to herself. Just hearing the words reassured her she was on the right path.

Five minutes passed, then ten. She whispered *fuck, fuck, fuck* under her breath as the truth sunk in – she had blown it with Kristin. Her foot was tapping impatiently on the linoleum and she pulled out her phone and called the Godfrey Hotel. The receptionist answered and Aislinn asked for Kristin Sanders. There was a short wait, then the man said that they didn't have a guest by that name.

"You should," Aislinn said. "Please check again."

"We don't have anyone by that name registered with us," he repeated.

"Okay, thanks." Aislinn killed the call and paced slowly up and down the hallway. There were numerous possible scenarios here, the most obvious that Kristin had been called back to New York on business. Or that she had simply tired of the reunion and decided to fly out a day early. Both explanations were logical and ones that Aislinn would gravitate toward if Kristin hadn't been elusive about things. But she had, and that was stuck in the back of Aislinn's mind. Perhaps Kristin had returned to New York so she didn't have to face another round of questioning over Darina's murder.

That thought ratcheted Aislinn's heartrate up a few notches. She had felt from the get-go that Kristin knew more than she was letting on, and now she was missing in action. Maybe, just maybe, she could still catch Kristin before she left. The hotel would know what time she had checked out and Aislinn kicked around whether finding out was a worthwhile exercise or not. Her other option was to head back into the gym where the dance was in full swing.

"Not a dancer," she said, heading for the door.

She strode to her car, frustrated at herself for not getting what she needed out of Kristin when she was sitting across the table from her. The short drive into Boston did nothing to calm her angst, and when she arrived at the hotel she flashed her badge and asked for the manager.

A woman stepped out of an office behind the desk and said, "Dawnell Browne, I'm the night manager. How can I help?"

"You had a guest, Kristin Sanders, and I need to know if she's still registered or has checked out."

"I'll have a look," Browne said. She tapped on the keyboard, then hit the print button. A single page rolled off the printer and she handed it to Aislinn. "Ms. Sanders checked out earlier today."

Aislinn read the sheet, taking it in line by line, then asked the manager, "Did she check out in person or electronically?"

Browne leaned in and looked at the code. "Electronically. We billed the credit card we had on file."

Aislinn didn't want to overreact, but something about this wasn't sitting right with her. "So no one saw her leave."

Browne looked a bit confused, then said, "I don't know. I'd have to find out from the day staff."

"That would be very helpful," Aislinn said, then added, "Is the room still vacant?"

"I'll see." She checked the computer, pulled the room number up on the screen and said, "Yes."

Aislinn's gut instincts were starting to take over. She had no evidence that anything was wrong, but those instincts had been crucial to solving crimes in the past. "Can you take it out of inventory?"

"For how long?" Browne asked, concern creeping onto her face.

"Not sure," Aislinn replied. "A few hours perhaps."

"I can do that." She keyed a few commands into the computer. "It's locked out."

Aislinn glanced around the lobby. There were cameras behind the desk and at least two more covering the lobby entrance. The quickest way to determine when Kristin Sanders had left the hotel was to view the footage.

"You have CCTV," Aislinn said. "Is it stored on the cloud?"

"Yes."

"Is it possible to look at the footage for an hour or so after Ms. Sanders checked out?"

Browne was in uncertain territory now, and said, "We may need a warrant for that, I'm not sure."

"What if I showed you a picture of Kristin and you looked at the feed?" Aislinn said. "You could freeze it on a frame when she's leaving the hotel."

Browne was completely out of her element – this sort of thing had never happened to her. "I suppose that would be okay, Detective Byrne."

"Excellent." Aislinn left Browne with the immediate task of tracking down the camera footage, then walked over to a quiet corner of the lobby and called Curtis.

"Want your opinion on something," she said when he answered.

"What's that?" Curtis asked.

"Kristin Sanders checked out of her hotel a day early. I'm getting a strange feeling about it."

"She's the one you felt knew more than she was letting on," Curtis said.

"That's right."

"She might have headed home early. It could be nothing."

"Could be, but Kristin is the kind of person reunions were made for. She was having a good time showing off her success, and it's completely out of character for her not to be at the dance."

"So what are the other options?" Curtis asked.

"Not sure, but we're stirring up a lot of muck on Darina and Alexi's files and if she *did* know something..." Aislinn let the sentence trail off.

"You're worried about her?" Curtis asked.

"Maybe." Aislinn tried not to sound too committed, but that was *exactly* what she was thinking.

"What's the plan?" Curtis asked.

"The hotel manager is reviewing the CCTV footage for the hour after Kristin checked out. I'm going to call the airlines and find out if she moved up her flight. If all that pans out then things are good."

"And if that's not the case?"

"I may need Bryan to go over the hotel CCTV."

"Call Stan and have him shift Bryan over to work on this. Did she have a rental car?" Curtis asked.

"I think so. The hotel will have the license plate on file."

"So you're thinking that maybe our killer is still around," Curtis said.

"Could be. Might be panicking."

"I know it's a long shot, but go with your hunch on this. It could play out."

"Thanks, LT." She hung up as Dawnell Browne rounded the corner and headed straight for her.

"None of our cameras caught Ms. Sanders in the hour after she checked out," Browne said.

"Including the one in the underground parkade?" Aislinn asked.

"Yes." Concern was written all over the manager's face.

"Could you see if you can get authorization for us to view the CCTV without a warrant? I'm going to start things on my end to get another detective here to view it."

"Okay." Browne spun around and made a beeline for her office.

Aislinn called Bryan's cell. There was music and voices in the background when she reached him. Saturday night, young guy, likely at a party.

"Hey, it's Aislinn," she said. "You busy?"

"Not anymore. Hang on a second," he said, the background noise dying off as he found a quiet spot to talk. "What's up?"

"I'm at the Godfrey Hotel. I need you down here to look at some CCTV footage. Kristin Sanders could be missing."

"See you in twenty."

She headed back to the reception desk where Dawnell Browne gave her some good news. "I've managed to get approval for you to look at the CCTV," Browne said, gesturing to a door set into a wood-panel feature wall. "You can watch it on the monitor in my office."

"Excellent," Aislinn said. "Bryan Cheung will be here in twenty minutes and he can go over the footage. Can you look and see whether Kristin had a rental car registered?"

Browne went to the open computer and keyed in a command. She nodded and hit print, then retrieved a sheet of paper with the plate number and handed it to Aislinn. "I talked with the cleaning woman who works that floor and she didn't see Ms. Sanders this morning. The day clerk on the front desk was sure that she didn't see her leave the hotel."

"What time did she check out?" Aislinn asked.

"Eleven-ten this morning," Browne said without checking.

Aislinn called the plate number into dispatch and asked for the owner – Avis. Gut churning, she called the main number and was promptly put through to admin. The car had not been returned – the best they could do was flag the file with a message to call Boston Homicide the moment the vehicle came back.

Cheung came bounding through the front doors, sharply dressed, having likely given up a fun night to sit and look at a television screen.

"Thanks for coming," Aislinn said.

They marched together into the manager's office where Dawnell showed Bryan how to queue up specific times on each of the cameras.

Aislinn texted a headshot of Kristin to Bryan's phone and he opened it and said, "Good to have a photo."

"Right."

He propped the phone up on the monitor and started the footage, using the fast forward button to move through periods when there was no activity. Aislinn left him to it and returned to the quiet part of the lobby where she phoned in an APB on the rental car. Then she called Curtis to update him.

"I still need to check with the airlines to see if she moved her flight up by a day," Aislinn said as they wrapped up.

"You got onto this fast," Curtis said. "Might make a difference if it's a problem."

"Let's hope it's nothing," Aislinn said firmly, pushing her emotions off to the side.

She checked in on Bryan, then headed up to look at Kristin's room. If Kristin had legged it or been taken, something had triggered it. Stan and Bryan's trip down to see Danny Zebiak? Or that the police were onto Aaron Brock? Maybe Curtis's interviews with the crime families? There were still too many variables, too many suspects, and they weren't eliminating many, if any of them. She felt frustrated at that, and it was kicking around in the back of her mind that all this digging may have resulted in Kristin being injured or killed.

CHAPTER THIRTY-FOUR

The evidence was sparse, but by ten o'clock on Sunday morning Aislinn was getting more suspicious by the hour that Kristin Sanders was missing.

CCTV footage had shown her taking the elevator to the parkade at 9:13 on Saturday morning and the camera covering the exit from the garage had her car on tape at 9:20. Bryan Cheung had canvased any local businesses with cameras and tracked her heading south along Tremont Street on the east side of Boston Common. Cheung was given two assistants and they were rapidly pulling together information from the cameras to determine where she had gone.

Curtis trusted Aislinn's gut instinct and shifted Stan onto the Sanders' case as well. He was working on securing her cell phone logs and tracking the GPS on her cell phone, accessing her banking statements, and dredging up close contacts for potential interviews.

Kristin's hotel room was designated a possible crime scene and CSI brought in. Despite her having no luggage when she entered the parking garage under the hotel, there were no suitcases in her room. They pulled the CCTV footage from every camera inside the hotel but there were massive gaps in the coverage, including the stairwells and upper-floor hallways. It should have been impossible for anyone to enter the hotel through the back and use the fire stairs to access her room, but a prep cook admitted to sticking a wedge in the kitchen fire door so he could go out and have a cigarette without it closing behind him.

Curtis stood in the dimly lit hallway leading from the back door to the stairs. "Was that the one he propped open?" he asked.

Aislinn nodded. "Once our perp was inside there was nothing to stop them from accessing the stairwell."

"And no cameras anywhere back here," Curtis said.

"No reason for cameras," Aislinn said. "Providing that the fire door was firmly closed. This is a staff-only part of the hotel."

"Yeah, providing the door was closed," Curtis repeated sarcastically.

Curtis walked to the staircase and started up, Aislinn falling in behind him. They reached the seventh floor and found Kristin's room easily enough – it was the one with CSI techs in booties. Curtis stood in the foyer of the small suite and looked about. The bed was made, the room clean and ready for the next guest. The cleaning staff had done a good job, unfortunately.

"So no luggage," Curtis said. "She didn't have it with her when she left the hotel."

"She did not," Aislinn confirmed.

"All right, let's assume someone grabbed her," Curtis said slowly, percolating things in his head as he spoke. "Does the missing luggage back it up?"

"Well, someone must have been up to the room," Aislinn said. "And they could have checked out through the app on the television, then took her luggage."

Curtis nodded as he looked around. Hotel rooms were petri dishes for DNA, fingerprints, and trace evidence. Scary even, under ultraviolet lighting.

"I'm not confident we're going to get anything useful here," Aislinn said.

"Probably not." Curtis leaned against the wall. "Assuming, of course, that Kristin Sanders is involved somehow, it appears she's reacting to our investigation. Or the killer is, and something we did has them running scared."

"Agreed." Aislinn checked her phone as a text came in. She read it, then said, "They've picked up her car traveling west on the I-90, near Fenway."

"That's the Turnpike and it's a toll road. Tell Bryan they can use the tolls to track her."

"He's on it," she said, holding up the text.

Curtis glanced at it and said, "He's a keeper."

"Yeah."

Curtis's phone rang and he spoke for a minute, then hung up. "Stan found her plane reservation – American Airlines to JFK leaving today at 9:14. She didn't change the flight and she wasn't on it."

"Someone took her or she's legging it," Aislinn said.

"Someone took her," Curtis said, his instincts in overdrive.

"I agree," Aislinn said.

They checked in with the crime scene team and got exactly what they expected – lots of trace evidence but nothing definitive. They needed a DNA profile to run in the national DNA database and for that they needed a suspect, which they didn't have at this point.

"The interviews with Aaron Brock and Danny Zebiak were promising," Curtis said as they took the elevator to the main floor. "Let's bring them back in and follow up with an in-depth chat."

In other words, Aislinn thought, *grill the shit out of them.*

"Will do," she said.

"I'll get word out to the media on this," Curtis said. "Vehicle description and a recent photo of Kristin for the nightly news, see if we get any hits from the public."

"Good thinking," Aislinn said, glancing at her phone.

Bryan Cheung was calling and she put it on speakerphone so Curtis could hear. "What's up," she said as they tucked into a quiet corner of the lobby.

"The timing between when Kristin's car left the parking garage at the Godfrey and passed the camera near Fenway isn't right," Bryan said. "It looks like she might have stopped somewhere. I'm sending one of the guys to do some door knocking at every business with a camera to see if we can pick up where."

"Good work," Aislinn said. "Keep us up to date when you have something."

"Of course."

She slid the phone in her back pocket and said to Curtis. "Definitely time to talk with Brock and Zebiak."

He nodded. "Oh yeah."

CHAPTER THIRTY-FIVE

Aaron Brock was so pissed when they brought him in that he kicked one of the uniforms who picked him up. That got the pressure on his handcuffs ratcheted up a couple of notches, and they weren't overly careful when they dumped him into the interview room and slammed the door. By the time Aislinn and Curtis arrived he was in a frenzy.

"What the fuck am I doing here," he screamed when they arrived.

Curtis turned around and walked out, Aislinn on his heels. Just before the door closed he said, "We'll be back when you've calmed down."

They hung around the monitoring room, watching him on the camera feed and discussing the case for half an hour. Stan showed up around the time Brock was getting the message that no one was coming until he settled. Stan looked tired, his face drawn and his eyes bloodshot, the long hours and lack of sleep getting the better of him. He clutched a steaming coffee like it was a winning lottery ticket.

"Just got back from driving down to pick up Danny Zebiak," he said.

"Right, well, he can wait," Curtis said. "Mr. Brock's up first."

"Good, that should ripen Zebiak up a bit. He was pretty nervous when we grabbed him," Stan said, settling into a chair to watch the interview.

Curtis and Aislinn let themselves back into the room and took their seats across from Brock. They stated the day and time and identified themselves, then advised that the conversation was being recorded. Curtis read Brock his rights, then set his notebook on the table and clicked open his pen.

"You're here because we think you abducted Kristin Sanders," Curtis said.

"Who?" Brock asked. "Who the hell is Kristin Sanders?"

Curtis ignored the question. "Where were you yesterday between eight in the morning and two in the afternoon?"

"At home sleeping."

"That seems like an odd time of the day to be sleeping," Curtis said. "Why?"

"I was tired," Brock said.

Curtis set his pen on the notepad. "This could go very badly for you, Mr. Brock. I highly recommend you cooperate with us."

"I told you, I was at home sleeping. I had a late night on Friday and was catching up."

Curtis gave Aislinn a glance and nod and she said, "We don't care if you were moving stolen goods on Friday night. The time that's important to us is Saturday between eight and two. Can anyone confirm you were at home then?"

"No, I was alone." He was sweating now. "What's this all about?"

"Three murders and a missing woman," Aislinn said. "Do you have cameras on your house?"

"Yes, but they're turned off when I'm home to save the batteries. I had the GPS on my phone turned on. Check it."

"That doesn't tell us anything, you could have left your cell phone at home." Aislinn leaned forward. "I stop by your house and ask you about a murder Kristin Sanders may have witnessed, and less than twenty-four hours later she's missing. That all but implicates you."

"No fucking way. It's a coincidence."

"We don't like coincidences." Aislinn leaned back. "We're liking you for this unless you come up with something to get us looking in another direction."

"Look at Danny, man. He's probably the one who took out that guy with his car."

"What guy?" Aislinn asked.

Brock shook his head and crossed his arms over his chest. "Some stupid fucker who pissed off Tony."

"Elaborate," Aislinn said.

"That's all I know. Danny's capable of bad shit, that's all I'm saying."

"When did this happen?" she asked.

"Fuck, I don't know. A couple or three years before Tony got offed in that burglary. I'm not a fucking memory stick, how am I supposed to remember."

"What was this guy's name?"

"Joe, or something like that."

"Okay."

Aislinn knew that in the monitoring room Stan would be all over that angle – leverage on Danny Zebiak. Still, she suspected there was a lot Aaron Brock wasn't saying.

"Even if Danny killed a guy with his car back in 2000, give or take, that still doesn't get you out from under Kristin's disappearance."

Brock's face went flaming red. "I'm telling you, I don't know who that person is."

"Fair enough," Aislinn said, standing. "We're looking at some CCTV footage right now. You can stay here until we get back to you."

"You can't keep me," Brock said.

"You're not moving until we're convinced you didn't take her."

Aislinn led the way out of the room with Curtis in tow. She leaned against the doorframe and said, "He's not out of the woods."

"Agreed," Curtis said, glancing over as Stan came down the hall. "Find anything on the guy Zebiak supposedly took out with his car?"

"Nothing yet."

Aislinn snapped her fingers. "Hey, my dad said something about

Tony being all choked up when some young guy died in a hit-and-run. Maybe that's him."

She whipped out her cell phone and dialed Cian. When he came on the line she said, "Do you remember telling me about Tony DeMarco getting all teary about some guy who got killed in a hit-and-run?"

"Yeah, of course."

"When did it happen?"

The line was silent for a few seconds, then Cian said, "I'm pretty sure it was '99. It was warm out, so likely summertime."

"You remember the kid's name?" Aislinn asked.

"No, sorry," he said. "What's going on? Why do you need that?"

"Just following up on a lead. Thanks, Dad."

"Summer of '99 he figures," Aislinn said after hanging up. "That might help narrow it down a bit."

"Got it," Stan replied and sent a quick text. "There, the guys are working on it."

Curtis cut in. "Stan, you work the Zebiak interview, Aislinn and I will take notes from the monitoring room."

Stan grinned. "Nice, I get to work the barbeque."

Aislinn gave him a *what-the-fuck* look, then shook her head.

He smiled. "Yup, gonna grill me up a suspect."

CHAPTER THIRTY-SIX

Danny Zebiak was a changed man from when Stan and Bryan had talked with him. His eyes were dark and hostile, his mouth set in a determined line and his arms crossed over his chest. He stared at Stan when he entered the dismal space, pretty much a carbon copy of the room where Aaron Brock had just been raked over the coals.

"Danny," Stan said cheerfully. "Your turn."

Those two words were intentional and unnerving. They told Danny Zebiak that his story would be measured against what others were saying and any lies more easily uncovered. Stan hit the *record* button and rattled through the preamble to the interview – who was present, the time and who they were interviewing. Then he took his time to read Danny his rights, emphasizing words like *in court* and *against you*. Setting the tone for what was coming.

"Where were you yesterday between eight in the morning and two in the afternoon?" Stan asked.

"Working."

Stan waited for more, but Danny kept his mouth shut. "If we have to pry every word out of you it's going to make me really angry," Stan said. "Where were you working and how did you get there?"

"I have a job at a tree farm about ten miles from Pondville," Danny said. "I drove there."

"Pondville – they give you a car?" Stan asked.

"Nah, it's not them." Danny squirmed in the seat. "The nursery provides the truck."

"Who were you working with?" Stan asked.

"No one. I was by myself in the south field watering the trees."

"Why would you do that?" Stan asked. "It rained the other day."

Danny shook his head. "It doesn't work like that. We keep on a schedule even if it rains. That way none of the trees get missed."

"So you're out in some field watering trees for the whole day and no one can vouch for that."

"Yeah, that's right."

Stan shifted midstream. "When did you meet Kristin Sanders?"

That took Danny by surprise and his eyes widened. "Who?"

"You heard me."

"I don't know that name."

Stan slipped a headshot of Kristin from his file and set it on the table. "Sure you do, Danny."

He leaned forward, took a look and shook his head. "No, never seen her before."

"She's missing, Danny. Disappeared about the time you were watering trees."

He swallowed hard. "Don't know her."

"Do you have a cell phone?" Stan asked.

"No, they won't let us have phones."

Stan picked up the photo of Kristin and slid it back into the file. "Summer of '99. What was the guy's name?"

"What guy?" Danny asked.

Stan smiled. "C'mon, Danny, the guy you ran over. The hit-and-run you pulled."

"What the fuck," Danny said. "First it's this woman I never heard of and now you're asking me about something from twenty-two years ago. What is with you guys?"

"What's his name and why did you kill him?" Stan asked.

Danny's hands were shaking now. He slipped them under the table and grabbed his knees. "Wasn't me."

"No statute of limitations on murder, Danny," Stan said. "If you didn't take this guy out, who did?"

"Don't know." Danny's voice was just a whisper.

Stan's phone buzzed and he checked the text. He set the phone on the table and said, "Now that's interesting."

Danny waited a full minute for Stan to continue, but the detective didn't say another word. "What's interesting?" he asked finally.

"I just got a name on my phone." He gave it a long break before saying, "Joe Napier."

Danny stared at the table.

"Joe Napier," Stan repeated. He picked up the phone and read from the text. "Run down on Rockview Street in broad daylight on Tuesday, July 13th, 1999. No tire marks to indicate the driver tried to stop. No witnesses. Napier was known to the police, possible connections to organized crime."

Danny continued to stare at the table.

"This isn't going away, Danny. You're either part of the solution or you're part of the problem. Providing you didn't run this guy down, you can walk out of Pondville on time." Stan paused for effect. "Or you can rot in a federal penitentiary. You'd better think really hard about this before you answer."

"I was watering trees," Danny said.

"Sure," Stan said. "What about Joe Napier?"

"Wasn't me."

"Then who?" Stan asked softly.

There was a long stretch of silence. "It was Tony, man. It was Tony."

Stan leaned back and sucked in a long, deep breath. Having Tony DeMarco as a confirmed criminal was bad enough, but now with fingers pointing to him being a murderer, the media was going to be like buzzards on a fresh carcass.

"How do you know it was Tony?" Stan asked.

"He got us all together and said something like, *Bad shit happens to people when they cross me*. We found out later that Joe had been killed."

"But you didn't see him do it. You have no definitive proof."

"No."

"So it could have been someone else," Stan said.

Danny just shrugged.

"Let's review who was involved in this little rackets business you guys had on the go. There was you and Aaron Brock, Tony, and Alexi Volkov. Anyone else?"

"Not that I know of."

"And how did it wrap up? When did it stop?"

"When Tony died. That was the end of things."

"So that brings us back to who killed Tony," Stan said. "Any new thoughts?"

"None."

Stan picked up the file and stood. "We're going to check out your story, Danny. Chances are the nursery has some sort of GPS tracking device on their truck, so we can see where it went yesterday."

"Went from Pondville to the nursery," Danny said. "If it's got GPS then you'll know." He looked a bit hopeful.

"We're keeping you here until we sort this out."

"I have to get back. I'll be in violation."

Stan gave Danny the slightest hint of a smile. "Oh, I don't think they'll care if you stay with us for a few nights." The door click closed behind him.

They stood in a group at one end of the hall – Aislinn, Stan, and Curtis – and went back over the interview in hushed tones. None of them were counting Danny Zebiak out, but his uptick at the prospect that his truck might have a tracking device pointed to him not being involved in Kristin's abduction. The conversation eventually ended on Tony's role in Joe Napier's death.

"If he killed Napier it's going to make us look pretty bad," Stan said.

"Yeah, it will," Curtis sighed, rubbing the back of his neck. "I'll call Dawson and bring him up to speed."

"My dad warned me," Aislinn shook her head.

"About what?" Stan asked.

"At his retirement, he said that a lot of stuff was going to come out when I started digging."

"Betcha didn't expect this."

CHAPTER THIRTY-SEVEN

Ted Dawson's executive assistant was working Sunday when Curtis arrived and he ushered the head of Boston Homicide into Dawson's office. Curtis shut the door and sat across from Boston's chief of police, an elegant man in his late fifties with a military bearing. Dawson was a native of the city, had a family history in America that went back over two hundred years, to when his ancestors had been brought over on slave ships. Known as a fair and ethical man, he expected no less from his officers.

Curtis nodded to Elian Perez, who was perched on the edge of the desk. He got a curt nod in response.

"I take it this is about Tony DeMarco," Dawson said once the commissioner was seated.

"It is, and it's getting worse," Curtis responded. "We have corroboration from six people now that Tony was running a rackets scheme in Jamaica Plain around 2000. We're not sure when it started but we suspect it ended with Tony's death."

"So he was at the top of the food chain?" Dawson asked.

"We're not sure about that. If he was, then the question is, who killed him."

"Maybe it *was* a burglary gone wrong." Dawson didn't sound sure about that.

Curtis shook his head. "Doubtful, and there's been a new development. Looks like Tony might have been involved in a fatal hit-and-run in the summer of '99. We have one of his business associates on tape saying he thinks Tony ran over a guy named Joe Napier."

Perez sat bolt upright. "Tony DeMarco was a detective out of Jamaica Plain."

"Yes," Curtis said.

"And he murdered someone?" Perez was livid. There was no doubt the Rampart mess was churning around in his head.

"It's looking that way."

Dawson stood and paced over to the window. "Who knows about this?"

"Aislinn Byrne, Stan Lamers, Bryan Cheung, and me. We were all sitting in on the interview."

"They know not to say anything?"

"Of course," Curtis said. "One more thing."

"What's that?" Dawson asked, his jaw clenched so tight Curtis could hear his teeth grinding.

"We have a missing woman – Kristin Sanders from New York. She was in town for a high school reunion and Aislinn's been looking at her as a possible witness to Darina Volkov's murder. Her disappearance is likely tied to the cold cases we reopened a few days ago, the one that got us focused on DeMarco."

"Jesus," Perez said. "So it's possible our perp is still out there."

"I would say it's *probable*," Curtis replied.

"Any suspects?"

"We have two guys who worked with DeMarco and Volkov – Danny Zebiak and Aaron Brock – neither of them have alibis, but they're not all that convincing as suspects. Then there's the organized crime angle – we've looked at Giuseppe Salvatore, Dimitri Kalatonov, and Patrick O'Reilly."

"Organized crime. Anything there?" Dawson asked.

"Nothing concrete. Not yet at least." Curtis hesitated, then said, "I think Salvatore knows who we're looking for, but he's not saying and there's no getting it out of him until he's good and ready. Whenever that is."

"Pressure him, make him give you a name," Perez interjected.

Curtis shook his head ever so slightly. "It doesn't work that way. Not with him or the other guys at the top of the crime families. Code of silence, like the LA gangs you dealt with."

"You must have something on them, some sort of leverage." Perez was looking for a quick fix, one that would cut things off at the knees before officially landing on his desk.

"Nothing that would get him talking," Curtis said. "In fact, if I go after him too hard he'll never talk."

Dawson cut in. "You need to find this guy, and fast, before he kills this Kristin Sanders woman. God Almighty, Curtis, the press is going to have a field day with this."

"They certainly would," Curtis agreed, the meeting over. "We'll stay on it and report back." He glanced over at Perez. "Good seeing you again, sir."

Curtis headed back down the elevator to Homicide. It looked a bit shabby after the executive floor, but there were a lot of caveats that went with the soft carpets and wood paneling. Like dealing with the press when a cop was suspected of killing someone. He ducked into his office before anyone could latch onto him and checked his email – the first two were from Bryan Cheung.

Cheung had been right about the time discrepancy between when Kristin left the Godfrey and was first sighted on the I-90 near Fenway. A CCTV camera at Eliot Norton Park had picked her up stopping to use a pay phone on Shawmut Avenue, and Cheung was working on the phone company to cough up the number she had dialed. The second email was in regard to tracking her car on the I-90. She had exited northbound onto Blue Sky Memorial Highway, which was not a toll road, making it more difficult to monitor her progress.

Curtis closed Cheung's email and scrolled down to one from the

CSI team. They were finished with Kristin's room at the Godfrey – *Nothing of apparent value* was the summary. There was trace evidence to follow up on, but without a suspect to compare it against they were shadow boxing in the dark.

Another message rolled in, this one from Stan. The New York phone provider had been expeditious in giving him access to Kristin's cell phone logs and he'd grabbed a couple of juniors from the pool to go over them. Her bank had promised access to her records before the end of the day. Curtis texted back – *Well done. Anything back on tracking her cell phone?*

Aislinn stuck her head in the open doorway and said, "Do you have a minute?"

"Sure, c'mon in," Curtis said, checking his phone as Stan texted back. *Nothing yet.*

"Aaron Brock's lawyer is here, wants him out of our holding cells," she said, plopping into one of the empty chairs.

"Threaten him with a warrant to search Brock's house for stolen goods. Tell his lawyer if he pushes for Brock's release we'll execute the warrant and use what we find to charge him. That'll keep him here for a day or two."

"Right. I spoke with the admin guys over at Pondville, and Danny Zebiak has a day job at Sunnyside Nursery, a few miles from the facility. He's been there for a year and they let him drive one of their trucks. So that much of his story checks out."

"Did they confirm that he was watering trees and whether the truck has a GPS locator?"

"Working on that," Aislinn said. "I talked with the receptionist but she didn't know. The owner is going to call me back."

Curtis gave her a slow nod. "Kristin Sanders, we still don't know if she's connected to this."

"Oh, I think we know she is," Aislinn said. "It all goes back to that phone call."

"Does it?" Curtis asked. He let the words trail off and Aislinn waited for him to continue. "We only have her word that it was

Darina who made the phone call to the precinct. We can't ask Darina if she made it, so that leaves us taking Kristin at her word. We've been basing a lot of our speculation on that phone call being an important cog in the wheel."

"And you're saying it might not even *be* a cog," Aislinn said.

"Raising the possibility."

"What else could there be?" Aislinn asked.

"Go back over the day of the prom," Curtis said, leaning back and cupping his hands behind his head.

"Okay." Aislinn pulled out her notebook. "Darina's day starts well – her mother hands her a whack of cash for college with the condition that she put it in the bank."

"So Darina's in a good mood," Curtis said.

"Right, then she picks me up and we head to Kayla Walsh's house."

"So there are four of you now – Kayla, you, Darina, and Sofia."

Aislinn nodded. "Then it's off to get our hair done. Darina and Kayla go first then head next door for burgers. Some Italians overhear Darina mouthing off about her dad getting killed."

"And we have no idea who these guys are," Curtis said.

"Nope."

"That would implicate the Italians and I'm not convinced they're involved. I'm almost at the point of striking Salvatore off the list. I don't think any low-level Italian wise guys would have done an end run around him back then."

"So there's nothing to the Italian men in the restaurant?" Aislinn asked.

"Very low possibility."

"Okay." Aislinn waited for a second, then continued. "It's pretty common knowledge that Darina likes Cody Hall and she heads over to his place. They have a beer and talk, and Darina pulls out the rolls of cash and notices that one of them is smaller than it should be. She's furious when she leaves for Shane Collins' house."

"Let's slow down a bit," Curtis said. "At this point we only have Cody's word that Darina noticed the missing money."

Aislinn got a sickening feeling in her stomach. "That's right."

"So Cody might be leading us."

"He could be," Aislinn said. "But I doubt it."

"Why?" Curtis asked, watching her closely.

Stay objective, she thought. *Stick to the facts.*

"When Darina got back to Kayla's she dragged Kayla out to the pool and was all over her. There's little doubt it was about the money. Kayla told us that she stole two thousand dollars, but never admitted to Darina that it was her. That points to Kayla and leaves Cody without a motive."

"What about Shane Collins?" Curtis asked. "Darina went to his place from Cody's."

"Shane is similar to Cody, he had little motive to kill her. The timing really doesn't work either – neither Cody nor Shane had enough time to strangle her, put her body into the electrical chase and get to the dance."

"Tight, but it might be doable," Curtis pointed out.

"It's broad daylight at that time," Aislinn fired back. "How do they get a body into a building on Center Street when it's still light out?"

"The back way, through the alley."

"Yeah, maybe, but incredibly risky," Aislinn countered.

Curtis gave her a sardonic smile. "Well, murder's usually risky."

"Good point," she said. A cool chill ran down her spine as she realized Curtis was right – either Shane or Cody could have done it. She was blurring the lines between friends and suspects, and that had to stop.

"All right," Curtis said. "Let's skip to after Darina visited Cody and Shane, and up to the moment when the two girls were out by the pool. Kayla denied taking the money and that sent Darina into a rage."

"Yeah, she was really mad. There's no speculation in that – I was an eyewitness."

"Right," Curtis said. "Handy you were there. What about her state of mind. Aside from the obvious anger about the money, when did she get spooked?"

"Spooked?"

"From what I've heard and read in the file, it seems Darina was pissed off but she came back in from the pool and dressed for the dance. So it appears she's managed to calm down. But you and the other girls all said she left the house suddenly and in a huff. It sounds to me like something happened at Kayla's house that spooked her."

Aislinn settled back into her chair and closed her eyes, digging deep to dredge up the details. After a minute she opened her eyes and said, "We had our hair and nails done and were all excited about getting into our dresses. Kayla's room wasn't big enough for all of us to change so Darina and I went to her parents' bedroom. There's a view of the pool through some sliding glass doors and she was facing toward the doors and a short section of wall with a bureau. She had her dress on already and was putting on her shoes. We were just chatting, then Kayla walked in and said something about Cody taking another girl to the prom. Darina started to snipe back at Kayla, then she stopped and got this look on her face, like she remembered something."

"But she didn't say anything."

Aislinn shook her head. "Not a word."

"Then she just got up, walked out of the house and drove to Kristin Sanders' place."

"Yes."

"Did she?" Curtis asked. "Drive to Kristin's?"

Aislinn's eyes narrowed as she took herself back to the moment. "Not sure," she finally said.

"Exactly," Curtis said. "We're relying on Kristin's account of things and we have no corroboration of anything she's told us. Now she's missing."

Aislinn was starting to get where Curtis was going with this line of thinking. "Kristin?"

Curtis got up and walked about the office for a minute, then sat on the edge of the desk. "Kristin is a cold fish, emotionally unattached. She uses people. She's a strong personality who knows what she wants and how to get it. Maybe she borders on being a bit of a narcissist or a sociopath. And she's the last person to see Darina alive."

"But there's the professional feel to the murder," Aislinn countered, testing Westcott's line of reasoning, trying to poke holes in it. "The Heckler & Koch imprint on Darina's skull. Kristin didn't have a pistol."

"How sure are you that Kristin's parents didn't have a gun in the house?"

"Point made, but how did she drag Darina's body up three flights of stairs, stuff her in the electrical chase, repair the drywall, then get to the prom on time."

"It's tight," Curtis agreed.

"And why did she kill her? What's the motivation?"

"The college money," Curtis said. "It never showed up. Someone took it."

Aislinn's heart was beating faster now as she realized this new line of thinking was entirely possible. "Twenty thousand dollars is a lot of money," she said. "Still, I'm not sure I buy it."

"Well," Curtis said, pushing himself off the edge of desk and returning to his chair. "Either someone grabbed Kristin or she's running. It's one or the other."

"Agreed." Aislinn pulled herself together and checked her watch. "Gotta go. We need that search warrant for Aaron Brock's place."

"We do," Curtis said, tucking into his endless string of emails.

Curtis had put another possible scenario on the table, and Aislinn kicked it around as she walked back to her cubicle. Was Kristin capable of killing Darina? Surprisingly, it wasn't a question she could answer easily either way. Curtis was right in his evaluation of her character – it was entirely possible that Kristin was a sociopath, and one thing they were good at was deceiving others, even those close to them. Kristin had opportunity and motive, and was likely strong enough to haul Darina's body up the stairs. It was possible, but Aislinn wasn't leaning that direction.

What this line of thinking unveiled though, was that Kristin's character was sufficiently amoral for her to be involved in Darina's death. Why else would she have disappeared? By the time Aislinn reached her desk she was firmly convinced that Kristin Sanders had a finger in this somehow.

She signed into her computer and started on the paperwork for the warrant.

CHAPTER THIRTY-EIGHT

Bryan Cheung's endorphins were on overdrive. He had helped with files before but never actually been an integral part of a team working a case, especially one that included the head of Homicide. Westcott was well respected – a hands-on kind of leader, and Bryan was seeing why all the lieutenant's detectives were so solidly behind him. And, he was vividly aware that this was his chance to break in. He was pushing with everything he had.

After spending part of his day driving up and down the streets that intersected Blue Sky Memorial Highway, he hit paydirt at Solomon Pond Shopping Mall. He'd stopped in and got the security staff to check the lone CCTV camera covering the entrance to the parking garage. Kristin Sanders' rental car had driven into the covered lot at 10:47, and a quick search located the car on P3. Now he was standing next to it, calling Westcott's personal cell.

"We found her car," Bryan said when Curtis answered.

"Is she in it?"

"No, there's no sign of her."

"Where is it?" Curtis asked.

"Solomon Pond Shopping Mall, P3 level. I'll stay with it until the uniforms get here."

"Excellent work. Have you called for a CSI unit?"

"Not yet."

"You stay with the car, I'll have Aislinn or Stan call it in. Don't let anyone near it."

"Right."

Curtis hung up and headed for Aislinn's desk. She was on the phone and he made a motion for her to wrap it up, then said, "Kristin's car is in the parking lot at Solomon Pond Mall. No sign of her. We need a crime scene unit."

"Got it. What level?"

"P3 – Bryan found it."

"I like that guy," Aislinn said as she picked up the phone. "Oh, we've submitted the warrant application for Brock's house. It's iffy whether we'll get it or not."

"Right, let's coddle the bad guys," Curtis said while they waited for her call to go through to CSI. "I'll deal with Brock's lawyer if we get the warrant, you should head up to Solomon Pond."

Aislinn nodded and got on with talking to dispatch about the crime scene unit.

Curtis spun and started back for his office, convinced that nothing good had happened to Kristin. His gut feel was that if she *was* running, it was from their killer, not the police. She had somehow stuck her toe into this whole mess and was now paying the price. His cell buzzed and he read the text from Bryan Cheung – *the telecom got back and the call from the pay phone went to an untraceable burner cell.* Curtis responded *thanks* and kept moving toward his office.

He left his door open and leaned against the window jamb, staring out at the clear blue sky. What had started with a dried up body falling out of a wall had morphed into four murders that were likely tied together by a single killer. Now, with Kristin Sanders' disappearance, it could be five.

That was bad enough, but throw in a dead cop who might have been a killer and it became a nightmare. Curtis felt a tightening in his gut – he knew Ted Dawson and Elian Perez were watching their progress closely and this would send both of them into batten-down-the-hatches mode. Dawson he could handle – the chief of police would react in a reasonable manner and not throw anyone under the bus. Perez he wasn't so sure about.

He retooled his thoughts, back to Kristin Sanders. From reading the file he knew she was some sort of CEO from New York and that would add even more fuel to the fire. He was beginning to wonder how much collateral damage this investigation would cause. Reputations on all sides were on the line, possibly even careers depending where the evidence led.

One of the admin staff stopped at his door and said, "Marc Abrams is here to see you." When Curtis shrugged, she added, "He's Aaron Brock's lawyer."

Curtis took a deep breath. "Send him in."

* * *

Aislinn pulled into the Solomon Pond parking garage at a crawl, looking for cameras. As far as she could tell there was only one, and it was positioned at the main entrance. It was pointed into the garage to catch the rear end of the incoming traffic and she cursed under her breath – there would be no images of the drivers faces as they entered.

The lot was busy with Sunday shoppers but P3 was off limits and only those already parked on that level were being allowed in to retrieve their vehicles. Aislinn showed her badge and the uniform working the scene lifted the tape. She drove under it and cruised slowly through the space. It wasn't well lit and there were all kinds of spots that were obscured behind support pillars.

She had a bad feeling in her gut as she pulled up beside the CSI van. Bryan Cheung was watching over the scene and he gave Aislinn a tip of his hand as she traded her car for the pervasive odor of concrete and gas hanging in the cold air.

"No sign of her?" Aislinn shivered at the change in temperature.

"Nope."

The vehicle had been backed into a dark, secluded nook by the service elevator and Aislinn stood a few feet back, taking it all in. The car doors and trunk were open and two techs in white suits were dabbing and swabbing, looking for traces of blood. There were definitely no CCTV cameras, and there was no line of sight to the main elevators that shoppers used.

"This looks like a setup," Aislinn said to Bryan.

"Yup."

"Any cameras on the exit?" she asked.

"No, just the one at the entrance."

"And it's facing the wrong way," Aislinn said.

Bryan didn't speak, just continued to watch everyone as they moved about.

"How did you figure this out?" she asked.

"I drove up Blue Sky and spotted the mall. It occurred to me that if someone had wanted to meet with her they would have picked a place where no one could see them. What better spot than a mall parking lot before it opens on a Saturday."

Aislinn nodded. "It's not crowded when he grabs her, and an hour later it's packed with shoppers going in and out. No one would take a second look at him."

"That's what I was thinking."

She nodded her approval at his reasoning and watched the CSI crew at work. She was getting a very bad feeling about this.

"I have something else as well," Bryan said. "Kristin Sanders' call from the pay phone was to a burner cell."

"Who knows?" Aislinn asked.

"Lieutenant Westcott. I phoned him when I found out."

"Okay," she said as one of the crime scene techs approached.

"There are definitely traces of blood in the car," the tech said, slipping off her mask. "I'll have the type later today, tomorrow at the latest."

"Thanks," Aislinn said as they exchanged contact info. "Can you text or call when you have that?"

"Sure."

Aislinn let out a huge sigh and turned back to Bryan. "Looks like we were right. Something's happened to Kristin." Her emotions were all over the map, relieved that she hadn't wasted department resources, but far more worried about Kristin. She remembered something Curtis had told her early in her career – *Sometimes during the course of an investigation there can be collateral damage.* It had sounded so callous at the time, but now she knew it was simply the truth.

"Apparently," Bryan agreed.

Aislinn glanced around the parkade – concrete underfoot and overhead, with thick pillars every few yards – a truly awful place. "Have a look around the neighborhood for cameras and get the footage from ten minutes after Kristin drove into the parkade to about three hours later. Compare the vehicles to the ones that entered the parking lot sometime last night or this morning. Our guy had to get his vehicle in and out."

"Already on it," Bryan said. "Lieutenant Westcott gave me a couple of helpers and one is driving the area, the other is making a list of license plates that entered since the mall closed last night."

Aislinn raised a thin eyebrow. "Nice."

Her phone rang and she checked the caller ID – *Sunnyside Nursery.* "Detective Byrne," she said, walking slowly to the railing and looking out over the surface parking lot and the mall.

"This is Raylene Thompson from Sunnyside. You wanted to know if the vehicle Danny Zebiak drives has a GPS tracker on it."

"Yes, I did."

"I'm afraid it doesn't."

"Do you log the mileage for his trips?" Aislinn asked.

"No," she said. "Should we?"

"That's entirely up to you," Aislinn said. "Do you have any other way of knowing where Danny was on Saturday morning? Cameras on the road in and out of the tree farm? A gas receipt? Someone who can testify they saw him watering the trees? Dust on the truck when it should be clean or vice versa?"

"No, nothing like that. What's this about? Is Danny in some sort of trouble?"

"We're just checking some details on a file. Thanks for getting back to me." Aislinn slipped the phone into her back pocket and walked back to where Bryan was waiting. "Well, that's nice. Sunnyside Nursery hires ex-cons, give them trucks without GPS chips and doesn't bother checking on them."

"Not good for us," Bryan said. "Or for him."

Aislinn's phone went off and it was Curtis. When she answered he got straight to the point. "We need to know if Kayla, Shane, and Cody have alibis for Saturday morning."

When Kristin went missing, Aislinn thought. "Of course. On it."

"Tomorrow morning at the meeting is fine," he said and hung up.

Aislinn stood staring at the car. Did Kirstin set all this up? Was she running, throwing them off balance at every curve? Was she really that vicious and that intelligent? Would she really throw away everything she'd worked for over the last twenty years, or was she dead and crammed into the trunk of some nondescript vehicle motoring down the highway?

She shuddered and gave Bryan Cheung a look. "You're nuts if you want this. It's crazy shit."

CHAPTER THIRTY-NINE

Aaron Brock was a free man.

Curtis was steaming mad as his staff filed in on Monday morning. The judge had called their application for a search warrant a *fishing expedition* and deemed it *an end run to circumvent Mr. Brock's right to privacy*. It was entirely accurate, but that didn't ease the sting of being forced to release the suspect who was at the top of their list for at least four murders. Adding to his frustration was the lack of manpower he had at his fingertips to put 24/7 surveillance on Brock.

Once Aislinn, Stan, and Bryan were seated he said, "You know by now that we had to release Brock. Let's keep an eye on him as best we can so we can pull him back in when we get something to hold him on."

"I'll try and get a couple of juniors on it," Stan said, aware of the manpower shortage. "Probably a few hours a day at best."

Curtis couldn't hide his anger at that and balled his fists. "Get what you can."

Curtis shifted to Bryan. "What do you have on the car that might have been used to take Kristin Sanders from the mall?" He was leaning heavily toward Aislinn's theory that Kristin had been taken rather than making a run for it.

"I have a distinct possibility." He handed out a page with a color photo of a Toyota Camry and a blow up of the license plate. "This one entered the parking garage twenty minutes before Sanders' rental car and left ten minutes after. The owners live in Roxbury and when I called, the husband said he had reported it stolen late Friday, around ten at night. I checked on the system and confirmed his story."

"So, assuming this was an abduction, it was premeditated," Curtis said. "Were you able to track the car after it left the mall parking lot?"

Bryan shook his head. "We worked all night going over CCTV footage from every camera in the area and it's not on any of them."

"This guy probably knew where the cameras were and took a route that bypassed them," Curtis said.

"Could have," Bryan said.

"Then we have no idea where Kristin Sanders is," Curtis said. He looked over at Aislinn. "Danny Zebiak – any way of tracking his movements on Saturday?"

"No, the truck he drives doesn't have a GPS tracker and the nursery doesn't keep mileage logs for their vehicles."

"So Zebiak is still in the running," Curtis said. "Let's keep him here for now. Aislinn, inform Pondville of that."

"Right."

"Aislinn, you were going to check what your school buddies were up to when Kristin Sanders went missing."

She slipped out her notebook. "Kayla was shopping with a girlfriend in downtown Boston, Mike was watching the kids. I checked with the friend and it's solid. Shane Collins was hiking by himself on Blue Heron Trail in Cutler Park."

"Where's that?" Curtis asked.

"Oak Hill, across the river from Millennium Park."

"So on the west side of the city. Easy access to Solomon Pond."

"Sort of, it's a ways south. Certainly not a five minute drive," Aislinn said.

"If he was even there," Curtis said. "No one with him, I presume no cameras on the trail, and he likely didn't meet anyone he knew."

"Right, right, and right. There's no proof he was there unless we can get a triangulation fix on his phone, and that will take time."

Curtis nodded, aware a triangulation could take days or weeks. "And Cody Hall?" he asked.

Aislinn stiffened slightly. "At home working. I haven't checked with his company yet to confirm if he was online and signed into the system."

"Find out if they monitored his keystrokes or if the company uses a time screen to lock inactive computers," Curtis said. "If they don't use either, he could sign in then walk out the door."

"Got it," she said, her stomach beginning to knot up.

"Stan, where are we with Kristin's cell phone logs and her banking records?"

"Doing really well there, LT. The phone provider has promised to send over her call and text logs by noon today."

"That's fast," Curtis said.

"Yeah, and her bank in New York is moving just as quickly. We'll have something later today."

"Good work." He stood and walked over to the whiteboard and wrote eight names. Dimitri Kalatonov, Giuseppe Salvatore, Patrick O'Reilly, Aaron Brock, Danny Zebiak, Kristin Sanders, Shane Collins and Cody Hall. "Who likes Brock for a contender for the guy behind all this?" he asked.

Bryan and Stan raised their hands, but Aislinn kept hers down. Curtis put three check marks beside Brock, a sign that he was on side for keeping Brock simmering on the grill.

"Okay, who's on the top of your list?" Curtis asked Aislinn.

"I'm not sure I like any of them for it," Aislinn said.

Curtis walked back to his desk and sat down. He waited.

"I'm not counting out any of the crime bosses," Aislinn said. "It's entirely possible that they were connected to DeMarco and had their fingers in the rackets. However, and I see this as a major stumbling block, they all balked at Darina's murder. Kalatonov, Salvatore, and O'Reilly were all adamant they don't kill women or kids. And Darina was only seventeen. We should drag their asses back in here and rake them over the coals about Kristin, but I'm not sure it's going to get us anywhere."

"Sanders, Collins, and Hall?" Curtis asked.

Aislinn shook her head, albeit very slowly. "Well, they weren't much more than kids at the time. I'll stick with my gut feeling that we're dealing with a professional." She paused, then asked Curtis. "Did you fill Stan and Bryan in on what we talked about yesterday?"

He shook his head. "Haven't had time."

"What's up, A?" Stan asked.

"Curtis made a case for Kristin to be more of a player in this than we thought. We only have her word that Darina made that phone call. Maybe Kristin called the precinct, maybe not – Darina's not around to confirm that. Then there's the missing college money. It goes to possible motive."

"Kristin Sanders?" Stan asked. "You've got to be kidding."

Aislinn shrugged. "It's a stretch, but we've seen stranger things."

"I'm not leaning that way as much today, but at the very least Kristin knows more than she told us," Curtis said.

"I'll agree with that," Stan said. "But I'm with Aislinn, this looks professional."

"Okay, some good points. What about Brock and Zebiak?" Curtis asked.

"Unless Danny Zebiak is one hell of an actor, he's not a leader," Aislinn said. He's a guy who takes orders and does bad stuff, but I don't see him as a cold-blooded killer. I agree that Aaron Brock is the closest we have to checking off all the boxes, but my problem with him is, why did he kill Tony? He's part of a racket that is paying well and then he kills the golden goose. That doesn't make sense."

"That's where I end up as well," Curtis said.

Bryan's cell buzzed and he ignored it. They all looked at him and Curtis motioned to the phone. "Unless it's your wife asking you to bring home milk..."

He signed in and broke into a wide grin. "It looks like they might have found the car."

Curtis nodded. "And that's why we check our text messages. Where is it and how the hell did you find it?"

Cheung set the phone on his lap. "We tied into all the tolls and cameras for the major routes leading from Solomon Pond Mall, then concentrated on the side roads, with the ones that led to lakes or ponds at the top of the list."

"Lakes or ponds," Stan said. "In case they wanted to dump the car…or a body."

"Right. Boulder Way was in the top five because it went halfway around Rocky Pond then petered out. I told the guys to look for recent tire marks in the mud or grass and…" He checked his phone again, then continued, "…apparently, they found a set in a clearing at the north end of the pond. They've called in a scuba team to have a look."

"Do you think it's there?" Curtis asked.

Bryan nodded. "It's close by, the water is deep and there's a lot of heavy brush. One rainfall and the tracks would be gone."

"Nicely done," Curtis said and addressed Aislinn. "Get over to Aaron Brock's place and see if he's still around. Take a car with a couple of uniforms, and if he's home have them set up outside and keep an eye on him. I don't want to lose that guy."

"Brock was in custody when Kristin went missing," Aislinn said.

"Which means he has a partner," Curtis said. "I still like him for being involved."

"On it," she said.

"Stan, stay on top of Kristin's bank and phone records. Go over them one line at a time. If she's in on this, something will pop out."

"Ah, really?" Stan let out a heavy sigh. "Why does Aislinn get to have all the fun?"

Curtis gave him a sideways look. "Bryan, the car is all yours. Once you're certain it's in the pond order a CSI unit so they're on site when the car gets pulled out."

"Yes, sir."

"And don't call me sir," Curtis said.

They all stood and headed for the door. Curtis gave Bryan a slight wave. "Hold back for a minute." When Aislinn and Stan were gone, he said, "I'm putting your name in for promotion to detective. I want you on the rotation in my division."

Cheung could barely talk. "Thank you, sir. Oh, shit. Sorry."

"No problem," Curtis said, smiling. "You've earned this opportunity. It's out of my hands now, and it'll take some time for the request to work its way through the system, but the gears are in motion."

Curtis watched him leave, his feet barely touching the carpet. The job would knock that out of him eventually, but for now he could enjoy the upside of the promotion. Curtis had been keeping a close eye on Cheung for a while, looking for overconfidence, arrogance, or laziness, three traits that could cause a detective to miss clues or unknowingly twist the evidence to fit their perception of where the investigation should go. Instead, he'd seen the young man systematically put together a case built on solid groundwork. Bryan Cheung would be a very worthwhile addition to Boston Homicide.

A message popped up from one of the assistants in the bullpen – *Joe Napier connections* was the subject. He opened it and read through a three page rehash of the case from twenty years ago. Most of the information had no relevance to their current file, but not all. One line jumped out at him and he let out a low whistle.

"Okay," he said under his breath. "That's why you got yourself killed."

Curtis dialed Giuseppe Salvatore's cell number and waited. They needed to have a chat.

CHAPTER FORTY

Aislinn pulled up outside Aaron Brock's house, patrol car in tow. She made a beeline for the front door and knocked heavily. No one answered and she knocked again. Still nothing.

"Fuck." She walked briskly around the building and put her face to the glass, cupping her hands around her eyes so she could see through the window into the living room. It was dark and quiet. "Pulled a runner?"

After leaving a quick message for Curtis that Brooks wasn't at home, she hoofed it back to where the patrol car was waiting by the curb and told them to stay put. Aislinn leaned against the building across the street and scanned Brock's file on her phone. His regular haunts were in there, but if he was on the move he wasn't going to be near any of them. Buried on the second page was something interesting – Brock liked to sail.

Aislinn called the precinct and connected with the bullpen team. She asked them to call all the sailing and yacht clubs in or around Boston and see if Aaron Brock, using the name Brendan Moore, had a boat on their register.

* * *

Curtis walked into the butcher's shop and stood in the queue at the counter. The place was bright and appealing with afternoon sunlight glinting off the stainless steel display cases. Inside were rows of veal, pork, and chicken, the price per pound displayed on tiny signs anchored by toothpicks. The odor of freshly cut meat was strong and the cool air tickled his throat, making him want to sneeze. When it was his turn he showed his badge to the counter clerk and said, "Giuseppe Salvatore please."

The woman asked him to wait and returned with a man who's biceps were thicker than a man's legs. Curtis followed him past a row of slicers and grinders into the back room where meat was stacked up on an impeccably clean metal counter, ready for packaging.

Giuseppe Salvatore came out of an office in the corner and caught Curtis staring at a meat grinder. "Wondering if I ground up someone in that thing?" Salvatore said dryly.

Curtis tried not to smile but it was impossible. "Did you?"

Salvatore shook his head and shrugged. "Nah." He motioned for Curtis to join him in his office.

The windowless room was expensively furnished with one wall dedicated to a few pieces of original art by Rolling Stones guitarist Ronnie Wood. Curtis gave them an appreciative look, which seemed to please the aging gangster. Curtis sat in a soft chair facing Salvatore's desk, wondering how many illegal deals and murder contracts had been discussed in the room.

"What now, detective?" Salvatore asked.

"We're still trying to figure out this Alexi Volkov thing," Curtis said.

"How's that going?" The Italian's eyes narrowed just a touch.

"Pretty good, actually. We're this close." Curtis held his thumb and forefinger a fraction of an inch apart. "I need your help on a couple of things."

"What things?"

"Back when we had our chat at the precinct I intimated that Tony DeMarco killed Volkov. But I got the impression that you felt Volkov's killer is still alive. That's been bothering me."

"So?" Salvatore shrugged.

"Then there's DeMarco. We took a good look at that shooting and it's not adding up. We don't think it was a burglary gone wrong."

"I told you, Westcott, we don't touch cops." Salvatore said, losing his cool.

"But I think you know who did," Curtis said, his eyes cold and accusatory.

Salvatore stared back, unflinching.

"All right," Curtis said, "let's forget about that for a minute and talk about Joe Napier."

"Who?"

"Don't insult me," Curtis said. "Joe was your guy. You put him in the middle of Volkov and DeMarco's racket to keep an eye on things. They found out and killed him, ran him down like a stray dog in the street. That must have pissed you off."

Salvatore may as well have been a rock, sitting there, across the desk, unmoving.

"Joe's arrest record from '96 has Gino Perlotti on the signatory line as the guy who put up his bail. Gino Perlotti was one of your guys. It wasn't that hard to connect the dots."

Salvatore took his time deciding whether to deny being the one who put up the bail. Finally, he said, "So I knew Joey. It means nothing."

"Sure it does and we both know it," Curtis said. "It ties you and your organization into this mess. It gives you motive to kill Tony DeMarco. It gives me the justification to rip your life and your business apart to find out what you know." He waited a few seconds, then said, "Unless you tell me."

Salvatore let out a heavy sigh. "Dig, dig, dig."

"Yeah, like a ferret I think you said."

"Volkov and DeMarco were getting too confident," the gangster said after a long silence. "They needed to be shown what was acceptable."

"That's where Joey Napier came in," Curtis said.

"They took him on as an enforcer and that gave us a good look at who they had on their books. Once we knew who was paying them for protection we had Joey scale up the beatings on the clients who were late paying. Not enough to kill anyone, but perhaps more than was necessary. That made our phone ring."

"The business owners, they wanted the lesser of two evils," Curtis said.

"I don't consider myself an *evil*."

That's exactly what you are, Curtis thought. "So Joey laid such a beating on those guys that they came running to you."

Salvatore nodded. "And we were ready to accommodate."

"But the wheels came off when DeMarco and his crew figured it out and killed Joey."

"Like you said, ran him down like a stray dog."

Curtis had suspected it went down like that, but there was still something he didn't understand. "They killed your man and you let them walk. Why didn't you retaliate?"

"DeMarco was in a position to bring the weight of the entire police department down on us. We didn't need to hassle."

"That brings us back to who killed DeMarco."

"How many times do I have to tell you, Westcott, I'm not doing your job. You want the shooter, you figure it out."

"It stays between us, where I got this information," Curtis said. "No mention anywhere on the file."

Salvatore considered the offer. It would keep him from taking any heat on the streets for helping the cops and get Boston Homicide off his back. "Take a week and see if you can figure it out. Maybe I'll help a bit if you can't. Maybe, no guarantees."

Curtis shook his head. "We don't have a week. A woman is missing and it looks like whoever killed Alexi, Darina, Joey and Tony took her."

"That's entirely possible," Salvatore said.

"Tell me what you know, Giuseppe," Curtis said. "It could save her life."

"If she's gone, she's dead."

Salvatore touched a button on his desk and his muscle was at the door in seconds. Curtis got up and walked out, nothing he could say would change the man's mind. One thing was certain, if they were still treading water in a week he would be back.

CHAPTER FORTY-ONE

Bryan Cheung stood on the shore of Rocky Pond watching a winch truck pull the Camry out of the water, while two scuba divers bobbed on the surface, making sure the metal cable attached to the car's frame was holding. Slowly, the wheels rolled up onto solid ground and water dripped from cracks in the doors. Cheung waited until the divers had exited the water and the cable was detached, then walked over to the car and looked in. Remarkably, most of the interior of the car was still dry, the seals around the windows and doors had kept the water from flooding the space.

Kristin Sanders was lying on the floor, her body contorted in ways he had never seen. There was a tinge of blue to her skin and her eyes bugged out of her face. He looked away, gagging, horrified at the sight. After a few seconds he swallowed hard and forced himself back on task.

This is what you'll deal with. This is the reality of the job.

He stared at her body, looking for signs of trauma. There was a circular red mark on her forehead, like she had been hit hard with a round object and he could see a thin red line around her neck that cut deeply into the skin. *Hit and then strangled,* he thought. CSI and the coroner were both on site and setting up around the car. They would have preliminary findings soon.

He walked over to where the divers were slipping out of their suits and asked, "How deep was it?"

"Sixty feet," one of them said. "How'd you know it was in there?"

"Saw some tire tracks in the grass," Bryan said. "We were looking for a car and put two and two together."

"The car would have sunk into the mud," the other diver said. "It was already almost impossible to see even from ten or twenty feet. Once it settled into the silt it would have been all but gone."

"You guys did a good job." Bryan glanced around the scene. "So peaceful here, what a way to ruin it."

"Ain't that the truth."

Bryan sat on a nearby log and called Curtis as he watched the crime scene team take an initial look at the car. Most of their work processing the vehicle would be back at the forensics building after it dried out completely. When his boss answered Bryan said, "The divers just brought the car up."

"Is she in it?" Curtis asked.

"Yes."

"Ah, shit." There was a long silence, then Curtis said, "CSI on scene?"

"There was an air pocket in the cab and parts of the interior are dry. They're having an initial look at it now. I'm going to wait for a preliminary if that's okay."

"Yeah, do that." Curtis let the line go quiet for a moment, then said, "Fine work, Bryan."

* * *

Stan Lamers thanked the woman on the other end of the line and dug into his email, looking for the file she had just sent. He opened and printed it. Twelve pages of Kristin Sanders' bank records rolled off and he scooped them up.

These were the condensed version, showing monthly balances without giving the particulars of her daily banking. That was in another file, and he figured it would be possible to narrow down what he needed by having a closer look at the summaries first.

Sanders was well paid, with substantial sums coming in every two weeks. There was a six month break in 2016, then they started again. During the downtime her account balances depleted quickly and she started drawing on what little savings she had. Stan opened the more detailed file and studied her expenses for the three months before she stopped working, then through the six month drought, and for another three after. A pattern emerged quickly.

Kristin was paying her mortgage and utilities with no problem while her income was steady, but she was also taking out small amounts at ATMs – a hundred here, five hundred there, on a shocking scale. The ATM codes were often the same, indicating she was drawing most of the small amounts from one machine. Stan had seen that pattern many times before and knew exactly what it was.

Kristin Sanders had a gambling problem.

He headed down the hall with the printouts in hand and found Curtis at his desk talking on the phone. His boss waved for him to come in and take a seat until he'd finished the call.

"That was Dawson," Curtis said, setting his cell on the desk. "No surprise the chief isn't happy – we just found Kristin Sanders at the bottom of a pond."

"So she was in the car," Stan said.

"Yeah, I was going to tell you and Aislinn once I was off the phone with Dawson. Bryan did a hell of a job tracking that car."

"Sure did," Stan agreed.

"What's that?" Curtis asked.

"Sanders' bank records. She had a good income, but there was a six month break back in 2016. Looks like she really struggled between jobs. And, she was making regular withdrawals from the same ATM. Likely at some casino. I'll confirm it, but my guess is she was addicted to the machines."

"Check that out for sure," Curtis said. "And find out why she left a good-paying job and had no income for half a year. That's got to hurt if she had a gambling problem."

"Right."

Curtis leaned back and said, "What do you think? She knew something about Darina's murder and kept the killer on the hook all these years?"

"Could be."

"Well, we just pulled her out of a car at the bottom of a pond so that tells us a lot."

"I'm still waiting on her phone logs," Stan said.

"Don't tell Kristin's telecom provider that we found her. It might slow them down. Right now they think we're looking for a missing woman."

"Not saying a word."

"Stay on it," Curtis said. "Aislinn left me a voice mail, said that Aaron Brock might be legging it."

"No surprise there. I can't believe the judge wouldn't issue the warrant. Christ, we had him sitting in a cell."

"What do you think about him?"

Stan mulled it around for a minute. "He's a sack of shit who moves a lot of stolen property and manages to keep his ass out of jail. I doubt he's done an honest day's work in his life, but I don't see him as the brains behind the racket they were running."

"Still, even if he wasn't running the show twenty years ago, he might be the guy we're looking for."

"Maybe," Stan said slowly. "Do *you* think he is?"

Curtis shrugged. "Not really, but I'm not counting him out."

"Convoluted one, this." The big man stood up and headed for the door. "But what the hell, most of them are."

"You got that right," Curtis said.

His office was quiet for once, and Curtis turned on some soothing music and closed his eyes. He had no doubt that Kristin Sanders had seen or heard something on the night of the prom that had led to her murder two decades later. She had known the identity of the killer all this time and had likely parlayed it into a source of income, but her luck had finally run out. If Darina Volkov's body hadn't fallen out of the wall, Kristin would likely still be alive. The dominos were falling, and right now where and when they would land was anyone's guess.

CHAPTER FORTY-TWO

The bullpen team got a hit on Aaron Brock's boat when they called the South Boston Yacht Club. He kept a 26 foot Contessa under Brendan Moore, his new name, in one of the berths. Aislinn called, and after she identified herself the receptionist took a quick look on her computer to see if it was docked.

"Mr. Moore swiped his card this morning and he hasn't checked out. Let me see if his boat is still moored." The woman came back on the line a minute later short of breath. "His boat is there."

"I'll be there in fifteen minutes," Aislinn said and hung up.

Aislinn jumped into her car and pulled out into the evening traffic. It had started to rain and she switched on her wipers as her cell phone rang. It was Curtis and she took the call on hands-free.

"They found Kristin Sanders' body." He went on to relay the information from his conversation with Bryan Cheung. "Another one of your schoolmates." He hesitated a moment. "Sorry, Aislinn."

"We weren't close," Aislinn replied in a matter of fact tone. "How's Stan doing with her bank and phone records?"

"The bank got back to him."

"Anything there?"

Curtis explained the withdrawals from the ATM machines along with Kristin's lack of savings. "Probably gambling," he summarized.

"Yeah, what about her cash flow after high school? Student loan?"

"Let me check with Stan," Curtis said and the phone went quiet for a minute. When he came back on he said, "Cash flow looks normal, no student loans of any sort on her profile."

"No student loans, that can't be right," Aislinn said. "None of our parents had that kind of money, at least as far as I know."

Aislinn eased to a stop at a red light. Carrying a student loan after college was normal and getting through without one was unusual, unless she had a secondary source of money. Like blackmail.

"Her tuition had to come from somewhere," Aislinn said as the light changed. "Maybe she was holding someone over the coals for Darina's murder."

"Very possible," Curtis said. "She saw or heard something. Did you ever talk with Kristin's parents and check her alibi?"

"I did and it's solid. Pretty sure this goes back to the phone call Darina made from Kristin's house."

"She called the police station," Curtis said. "Could be the missing money or that she was scared."

"Scared makes more sense," Aislinn said. "Maybe she mentioned the killer by name and Kristin heard her."

"The woman who took the call at the precinct would have made note of that."

"Patricia Morriscey," Aislinn said. "Has Bryan managed to get hold of her yet?"

"No, she's still on that trek in New Zealand. Another day or two and she'll be back."

Aislinn pulled into the parking lot nearest the South Boston Yacht Club and killed the engine. The call went from hands-free to her phone and she hoofed it toward the entrance doors, cell to her ear.

"I think she was blackmailing our perp," Aislinn said. "Darina's body showing up set things in motion and got her killed."

"Could be right," Curtis agreed. "That's a solid line of thinking."

"And Cody Hall," she said confidently. "I've confirmed that he was on his computer working at the time Kristin went missing. The company logs keystrokes, so that strikes him off the list."

"It does. Good work." Curtis was pretty sure Aislinn was breathing a bit easier with that development.

"Gotta go, LT," Aislinn said. "Aaron Brock keeps a boat and I'm at the club where it's moored."

"I'll call in some uniforms. I don't trust that guy."

"Thanks. I'll text you the address. Have them come to the main entrance."

"Will do." Curtis hung up.

Aislinn sent the text then pushed through the door and took out her badge. She flashed it at the receptionist and said, "Detective Byrne. I called you about Brendan Moore's boat."

The woman pointed down the dock. "It's in berth 18." Then in a quieter tone, "Security has confirmed that he's on the boat."

"Thanks," Aislinn said and pocketed her badge. She checked the gun on her hip and hurried down the rain-soaked dock to where a sleek-looking sailboat with a navy blue hull and white upper deck was moored. The cover was still on the main sail and she stopped and yelled, "Aaron Brock, it's Detective Byrne. Come out with your hands where I can see them."

Brock's head appeared in the opening that led to the lower berths and he raised his hands as he came up onto the deck. He was wearing jeans and a windbreaker.

"Are you armed?" she asked.

He shook his head. "No." He lifted his jacket and slowly turned around so she could see the waistband of his pants.

"Get off the boat, please."

He stepped onto the dock. His lips were firmly locked together in a tight line, but his eyes gave him away. He looked worried, frightened even.

"You can't hold me," Brock said, breathing deep and fast.

He was close enough to come at her and Aislinn was wound tight as a spring. "I just want to talk to you."

"About?"

"Don't get cute," Aislinn snapped. "Kristin Sanders is dead and you know who killed her."

He shook his head, water flying off his hair. "I told you, I don't know who it is. All I know is that Tony was scared of him. *Really... fucking... scared.*"

"How do you know? What did he say?"

"I don't know, just something about the guy being a ruthless motherfucker."

"He said *the guy*. Anything else that could point to who this guy is?"

Brock thought hard, going back over the distant memory. "No, nothing like that."

"He never mentioned Kalatonov, O'Reilly or Salvatore?"

"I heard those names all the time. We all knew we were on their radar, but he never said anything about one of them being his business partner."

"You never saw Tony with anyone and thought, *hey that could be him*?"

"No, never."

Aislinn wiped the rain from her face. "So you're running."

"Not from you." His voice cracked. "Trust me, if I knew who this guy was I'd give him up."

Aislinn was soaked to the bone. She let the drops bead and roll down her face, staring at a thief and con man who was so scared he was dropping everything because of something that had happened twenty years ago. It almost made her feel sorry for him. But not quite.

"Between you and me," she said, "where are you going? Nothing goes on the record and I won't contact you unless I need to."

"My uncle has a place up the coast a ways, in Bar Harbor. I'm going to lay low with him."

"Do you have a GPS tracker on your boat?"

"Yeah. SPOT Trace."

She pointed to his phone. "Add my number to your app so I can see your boat's location." She held out a business card. "Text me your uncle's name, address, and a number where I can reach you."

He shielded his phone from the rain as best he could as he entered the information then hit send. A moment later Aislinn's cell phone pinged. She checked the message.

"Better get going," she said.

"Yeah." He stepped onto the boat, then turned and said, "Thanks."

Aislinn jogged back to reception and advised them that she had cleared Moore to leave, then ducked into the restroom and dried herself as best she could with the paper towels from the dispenser. The uniformed officers Curtis had sent were at the reception desk when she returned, and she thanked and dismissed them. There was a quiet place by a massive bank of windows overlooking the water and she settled into a comfortable chair with a view of Thompson Island looming in the distance through the mist and fog. She dialed Curtis, her hands shaking from the wet and cold.

"I take it you're okay," he said in lieu of hello.

"Fine," Aislinn answered. "Brock is legging it. The guy's terrified of whoever killed Kristin and he's staying with his uncle up the coast. I have his contact info in case we need it."

"You don't think he's our guy," Curtis said.

"If he is, he deserves an Oscar for best performance." She paused, then said, "I asked him if he had any idea of who it could be but he was adamant he didn't know."

"The silent partner," Curtis said.

"Brock called him a ruthless motherfucker."

"No argument there," Curtis said. "This guy has killed five people."

"Anything from Kristin's phone logs yet?" Aislinn asked.

"Nope, it'll probably be tomorrow before Stan gets anything back on that." There was a break, then Curtis said, "Go home. We'll meet in the morning."

"Okay," she said, hauling herself out of the chair.

Aislinn hung up and stood staring out over the dark bay, too spent and cold to move. It felt like summer was in retreat. The rain hammered down incessantly and the water was churning and unsettled. Maybe, she thought as she leaned against the window, we're on the wrong track – or – missing something important. Certain facts were now cast in stone and they were the foundation they needed to keep working from. Tony DeMarco had been in business with Alexi Volkov and had likely either killed Volkov or had him killed. Joey Napier had infiltrated DeMarco's racket and had paid the price. That much was pretty solid.

Speculation kicked in when they assumed Darina was murdered because she had seen or knew something. Aislinn was almost positive on that, but the door had to be left open a crack because of the missing college money. Still, that angle was pretty much moot now that Kristin was dead. Which brought them back to Darina having witnessed something that tied the killer to her father's death. But why wait six months?

Then there was the phone call to the police station from Kristin's house. Was it even relevant? It probably had to do with the stolen money, which meant it wasn't the motivation for Darina being murdered on prom night.

And why kill Kristin Sanders? The only logical explanation was that she had blackmailed the killer, and the discovery of Darina's body had sparked a crisis that ended in Kristin's removal. The lack of student loans supported the blackmail angle – someone had funded her tuition and living expenses at an expensive college.

"So why wait? Why not just kill Kristin twenty years ago?" Aislinn said out loud.

The moment she said the words she had the obvious answer. Kristin had squirreled something away that would come to light if anything happened to her. A note in a safe deposit box, a sealed letter left with her parents or a lawyer, a file on her computer, there were many ways of revealing the killer's identity. He had lived with that hanging over his head for twenty years. But now, something had changed and he had lashed out.

Dimitri Kalatonov, or one of his toadies, were at the top of her list. The Russian played by different rules than the rest of the organized crime boys. Kalatonov was the one who might cross the line and kill a woman – and two were dead.

Patrick O'Reilly wasn't completely out of the running either. The Irish gangster was ruthless and given the right circumstances might be capable of murdering a teenager. As with the other crime families, it meant there needed to be a connection back to the racket DeMarco and Volkov were running. The question was, did the protection racket matter enough to one of the crime families to warrant a killing spree? Probably not, but they could have been making an example. Cut in on our territory and this is what happens.

Curtis had some sort of tête-à-tête going with Giuseppe Salvatore, and was trying to pry a name out of the old Italian. Aislinn wasn't going to bank on that, and didn't think Curtis was either. But if Salvatore knew who had killed Volkov and DeMarco, then it wasn't him. Or, he might be lying to deflect the investigation – Joey Napier had been Salvatore's man and DeMarco had killed him, which must have angered the Italian. Bottom line was, none of the organized crime bosses could be completely ruled out.

A sailboat pulled away from the dock, struggling in the choppy water, bound for Bar Harbor. Brock was a survivor, a criminal who had managed to outsmart the authorities and other crooks for twenty-five years. Now here he was, running for his life. That spoke volumes. Aislinn watched until the boat was a distant speck then headed back to her car. One more marathon of a day gone, and not much closer to discovering the answer.

CHAPTER FORTY-THREE

Tuesday morning started off poorly for Boston's head of homicide. The *Boston Globe* led with *A Dirty Cop and a Pile of Bodies* as their headline, and it was selling a lot of newspapers. Curtis had purchased a print copy and it was sitting front and center on his desk when his detectives piled in for their eight o'clock meeting.

"Nice," Stan said sarcastically. "Thought she was your buddy."

Angela Burton was the *Globe's* writer, and Curtis had an ongoing, unwritten arrangement with her. He slipped her exclusives on occasion in exchange for her discretion on when to release time-sensitive stories that might spook a suspect. It was a smooth relationship at times, contentious at others. This one looked like it might fall into the latter category.

"Angela warned me it was coming," he said in her defense. "Her editor wrote the headline. She's just doing her job." Curtis tapped the paper with his finger. "When you think about it, most of her story happened twenty years ago."

"Sure, except for the Kristin Sanders murder," Stan said.

"Well, an attractive female CEO from New York visits Boston and gets murdered," Curtis replied. "It's news and there's no keeping it under wraps."

"Sure doesn't make Tony DeMarco look good," Bryan said.

"Well," Curtis didn't look happy to say it, "he wasn't. At least Angela hasn't put it together that Tony might have taken out Joey Napier."

"Not yet," Aislinn said. "She'll get there."

"Yeah, I know." He looked over at Stan. "Anything from Kristin Sanders' phone records?"

"We're going over them line by line and so far there's nothing out of the ordinary. Mostly calls to numbers that we can identify in her contact list. There were, however, two other calls to the burner cell from the pay phone on Shawmut Avenue near Eliot Norton Park."

"The same one she used the morning she was abducted."

"Yup, she was in touch with our perp at least three times since arriving in Boston," Stan said. "She wanted something."

"Likely money," Curtis said. "If she still had a gambling problem money would be an issue. What's her current financial status look like – mortgage, bank balances, loans, that sort of thing?"

"Grim," Stan said. "She's in overdraft on her checking account and her savings only has a bit over two thousand dollars. She's up to date on her mortgage, but it's about eighty percent of the value of her condo. Car is a leased high-end Mercedes, so no equity there. Basically, she's living paycheck to paycheck."

"Okay, that gives her a hell of a motive to meet with the guy she was blackmailing." Curtis glanced at Bryan Cheung. "Anything from forensics on the Sanders' murder?"

"Just in," Bryan said. "The coroner suspects the round end of a baseball bat for the mark on her forehead. There were maple wood fragments in the dent, consistent with something like a Louisville Slugger. Hit her hard, for sure. There's no broken glass so if she was sitting in the car she likely had the window rolled down."

"So she knew whoever was walking toward her," Curtis said.

"He could have had the bat at his side and out of sight. Then bring it up and pop her in the head." Stan raised his hands and thrust them forward quickly. "Bang, right to the forehead. She'd be out cold the moment the thing hit her."

Curtis nodded. "Then throw her in the Camry and get moving. Straight to Rocky Pond – no CCTV cameras on the route. Strangle her, dump the car in the lake and hoof it out. That was close, she almost disappeared forever."

"What about footprints?" Curtis asked.

"Some," Stan said. "CSI is working on getting a cast."

"Well, he made a mistake not cracking a window to let water in. Dry air inside the car means possible DNA samples." Curtis threw Bryan a quick look. He'd pulled a rabbit out of a hat finding the car that fast.

"Aislinn," Curtis said, shifting to a new thread. "Fill us in on Aaron Brock."

"Caught up to him last night as he was leaving the harbor on his sailboat," she said. "Absolute crap weather, nobody would be taking a small boat out on a day like that unless they had a damn good reason."

"Like someone coming to kill them," Stan said.

"Yeah, like that. He was ready to swear on a stack of bibles that he didn't know our guy's name. Said even Tony DeMarco was scared of him."

"Where is Brock now?" Stan asked.

"He was heading up the coast for Bar Harbor to stay at his uncle's place. He added me to his GPS tracking app so I can check. He'll take our call if we need to talk with him."

"Did he say anything about the Russians or the Irish being involved?" Stan asked.

"Nope."

"Fuck, this guy. Our killer." Stan gave his shaved head a hard rub with both palms. "He's a ghost."

"We'll get him," Curtis said quietly. "Bryan, stay on top of what CSI comes up with on the Camry and get that information out to the team immediately."

"Right," Cheung said.

"Get ready for a backlash from the *Globe* article." Curtis tapped the newspaper sitting on his desk.

"What if they start pointing the finger at DeMarco for Darina's murder?" Aislinn asked.

Curtis took a deep breath. "Well, that was the gist of my phone calls with Dawson and Perez this morning. We're ready to deflect as much heat as we can, but if DeMarco *did* kill someone, *especially* Darina Volkov, the shit is going to hit the fan even harder than it already has." Curtis didn't bother mentioning exactly how furious the new police commissioner was at the direction the investigation was taking. "Stan, keep digging into Kristin Sanders' life and see if there is *anything* that would tie her back to Boston after she moved to New York. Have another chat with Danny Zebiak. I don't like him for it but maybe he knows more than he thinks he does."

"Like he saw something and it didn't register at the time," Stan said.

Curtis nodded. "Bryan, contact Kristin Sanders' college and find out how she paid her tuition and whether or not she stayed in residence and how she paid for that as well."

"Okay."

"Aislinn, do you still think this goes back to the night of the prom?" Curtis asked.

She put her hands in the air, palms out. "It might."

"Stay on that. Go back and talk with your old schoolmates, the ones who spent time with Sanders at some of the reunion events."

Aislinn jotted it down in her notebook. "Right, that should help us track her movements over the last day or two before she was killed."

"Darina Volkov's murder always seems to be the linchpin," Curtis said. "It keeps rearing its head."

"Yeah, but chasing it back to the origin is the problem," Aislinn replied. "I can't seem to figure it out."

"You know how these things work," Curtis said. "If it's there you'll get to it."

Curtis's phone rang and he grimaced at the call display. "It's the mayor, gotta take it."

His detectives scattered from the office faster than rats off a sinking ship.

CHAPTER FORTY-FOUR

Aislinn set up a meeting with Cody and Shane together, not something she would usually do. While she was still looking for cracks in their stories, she thought putting them together so they could listen to each other's answers to her questions might trigger a new train of thought on the case. That, and she wanted to monitor each of the men's reaction to the *Globe* story on Kristin's murder. She wanted them in a relaxed setting, not in an interview room, and they agreed on Caffé Nero on Center Street in Jamaica Plain. There was ample parking and Aislinn pulled at the front door of the squat brick building ten minutes early. Inside, the air was thick with the aroma of freshly roasted beans, and soft music played on the sound system.

Cody and Shane arrived a couple of minutes apart, and she gave them a wave from her table on the upper level as they stood in line together. Aislinn sipped her coffee and watched them closely as they ordered drinks. Cody picked a pastry from the display case, but Shane shook his head at that. Both men wore serious expressions and their smiles looked forced.

"I love this place," Cody said as they joined Aislinn. His tone belied the upbeat words and his eyes looked sad.

"Me too," Aislinn agreed, knowing he was trying to lighten the mood.

Shane was sitting back in his chair, coffee in hand. "This has got to be about Kristin."

"It is," she said.

Both men were staring, and Aislinn got the feeling they were genuinely concerned for her. *So much for the small talk,* she thought.

"That was quite the article in *The Globe*." Cody shook his head. "Angela Burton sure unleashed on the police department."

"Sometimes it's deserved," Aislinn said. "Tony DeMarco was a crooked cop."

"That was almost twenty years ago," Shane said. "Old news."

Aislinn looked down at the table in resignation. "The public pays attention to stories about bent cops. It's big news no matter how long ago it was."

"You holding out okay?" Shane asked, studying her.

"I'm okay." Aislinn sucked in a deep breath and forced herself to focus. "Let's talk about Kristin. I'm trying to get a feel for what was going on before someone grabbed her."

"The article said they found her in a car at the bottom of a pond just outside the city." Cody was wide-eyed and waited for Aislinn to respond.

Aislinn looked from one man to the other, gauging the emotional impact of Kristin's murder. Shane was detached, like he had compartmentalized the awfulness of a friend getting killed, but Cody was suffering. His eyes held bits of guilt, and she wondered if somewhere inside he felt there might have been something he could have done to change the outcome.

"I can't talk about that part of the case." She took a sip of coffee and pressed on. "When was the last time you saw her?"

"Friday night, at the sock hop," Cody said. "She was in a really good mood."

"Yeah, we spent about an hour talking to her," Shane said. "Cody's right, she was happy and well primed. Probably put away two or three drinks while we were with her."

Cody nodded. "She was feeling it, kinda drunk actually, staggering a bit when she walked."

"What was she talking about?" Aislinn asked.

"What a dump Jamaica Plain was and how glad she was to be in New York," Shane said. "We both thought that was pretty ignorant."

"She was a real bitch to some people." Cody poked Shane on the shoulder. "Remember what she said to Melissa Turner?"

"Something about her jewelry," Shane snapped his fingers. "She dissed it off."

"Yeah, she actually grabbed her necklace and said something like *Nice fucking pendant.* It was weird. Melissa stormed off."

Aislinn cocked her head. "You're sure about that? Those words?"

"I think so." Cody looked over at Shane. "Does that sound right?"

"Yup, I'm pretty sure that was *exactly* it. Really bizarre. She was always a bit like that though."

"Okay," Aislinn said. "Did she mention anything about the cost of living in New York, trying to make things work on one salary, anything like that?"

"Oh, yeah." Cody took a small bite of cake. "She said her mortgage was a millstone and she should give up her car. Nobody in New York drives anyway so why bother with the expense."

"Actually, she went on about money a fair amount," Shane said.

"Like what?" Aislinn asked.

"She raved on about how much tax she paid and that there was never anything left for her. Fucking government, wasting it all. That sort of thing." Shane shook his head. "She even went off on how much the military cost until it hit her that there was a veteran standing there listening to her. Then she tried to give me a hug and laugh it off."

Aislinn shifted direction. "Did she say where she was going on Saturday?"

"Nope," Cody answered. "The only thing she said about the weekend was that she was looking forward to flying out on Sunday."

"Sunday, not Saturday," Aislinn said.

"Definitely." He finished the last of his cake and set the fork on his plate. "Sweet baby Jesus that was good."

Aislinn grinned. Cody was treading on the edge of being a possible suspect on a murder file and he could still make her smile.

She kept pushing for more info – did Kristin call anyone, did she leave the gymnasium for any length of time, did she seem worried – then closed her notebook and let things take a more personal slant. An hour later they broke it off and Aislinn drove back to the office, glad to have spent some time with her old friends. She had their numbers and wondered if she'd ever call. Probably not.

Curtis was in his office and she leaned on the door jamb. "How did things go with the mayor?"

He snorted. "Exactly as you can imagine they did."

Aislinn came in and sat down. "Perks of being the boss."

He leaned back and put his feet on his desk. "It's like all of this is somehow our fault – that the entire department is responsible because Tony DeMarco was a bad guy. And he wants an arrest on the Sanders file. Angela Burton has been pestering him – and me – all day for an update."

"Well, can you blame her? It's quite the story and she's a good reporter."

"Too good sometimes," he said. "How did things go with your old school buddies? Anything there?"

"Maybe," she said slowly. "Kristin was drunk, and happy, on Friday night at the sock hop, but apparently she got a bit bitchy with a few people. Cody and Shane both remember her grabbing another woman's necklace and saying *Nice fucking pendant*."

"That's pretty rude," Curtis said.

"It's not that, it's the word – *pendant*. Why not just call it a necklace?"

"What's so special about pendant?" Curtis asked.

"If you go right back to the start of this whole mess, Darina Volkov saw two identifiable items on the guy who likely killed her dad. The wristwatch and the pendant."

Curtis pulled his feet off the desk and sat up straight. "Is that the exact word Darina used in her report?"

Aislinn nodded. "Pendant."

"Pretty specific," Curtis said. "So where does this get us?" He stood up and walked over to the window. "She's drunk, in a good mood, and uses what could be a key word from Darina's murder. The next day she's dead." Another pause, then, "Follow up with the woman who was wearing the pendant at the reunion. Probably nothing there, but it wouldn't hurt."

Aislinn made a note in her book, then said, "It's possible Kristin talked to our killer and made some sort of a deal – so she was celebrating. That would explain her mood and the excessive drinking, and then she uses pendant instead of necklace because it's top of mind."

"Maybe," Curtis said. "It's a stretch, Aislinn. We don't have any connecting dots."

Aislinn ran a hand through her short, red hair. "Darina could have confided in Kristin, told her something about the pendant, and Kristin exploited it after Darina was killed."

"Risky business," Curtis said.

"Obviously, given she's dead. But why *that* night? Why did everything blow up on prom night?"

"Neither of them is going to tell us," Curtis said, stating the obvious. "Not now. We missed our chance with Kristin."

There was a sharp rap on the door and Bryan Cheung hovered in the hallway. Curtis waved him in and he held up a sheet of paper.

"Kristin Sanders paid her tuition at Brown University with bank drafts – on time and in full. The same with her on-campus residence and meal program."

"So a struggling student has the financial resources to pay her tuition at a prestigious university without any loans," Curtis said.

"Blackmail," Aislinn said. "She was blackmailing our killer."

Curtis rubbed his hand across the stubble on his chin. "He sends her a bundle of cash and she buys a bank draft. No paper trail leading back to him. She definitely had something on him."

"Yeah," Aislinn said. "It took twenty years, but whatever it was, it got her killed."

CHAPTER FORTY-FIVE

Aislinn woke early on Wednesday, June 23rd. It was almost two weeks since the construction crew had uncovered Darina's body and they were closer to a solve, but not there yet. Forensics on the Camry would be coming soon and that might give them something to work with. The killer couldn't have envisioned them discovering the vehicle so fast, and had been sloppy not opening a window. The car with Kristin's body had been under sixty feet of water, but because of a trapped air pocket Aislinn was holding out hope there might be trace evidence.

She lay in bed thinking about Kristin Sanders, the girl with everything. Attractive, smart, decisive, well educated – yet her life was in shambles. Built on deceit and manipulation, once the façade was ripped off there was little of value left. In retrospect, from the moment she made her deal with the devil, Kristin was a ticking timebomb waiting to detonate.

She rolled out of bed and showered, then rubbed the towel over her hair and stared at her reflection in the mirror – twenty years had passed since she'd walked out of The English School, and so many times she had questioned her choice to follow her father's career choice. She was a cop, simple as that, but as she thought back to the school gym, filled with classmates who now had two more decades under their belts, she realized that the road she had taken was one with merit. She'd made her time count.

She dried her lean body and slipped into her jeans and a T-shirt, then snapped her gun onto her belt. Blazer over her arm, she locked the door and smiled at her downstairs neighbor who was already outside and working on the garden.

"Hey, Howie," she said on the way to her car.

"Whoa." He stared at the gun, resting on her hip. "Don't shoot anyone with that thing."

She forced a frown as she walked past. "Damn, I was *so* looking forward to it."

The sun had reappeared and she rolled her window down and turned the radio on to a classic rock station. *Howie and his music,* she thought with a grin, *he's flipping me over to the oldies.* The drive to BPD was short and she had a hint of a smile when she pushed the door to Homicide open.

"What's with you?" Stan asked when she sat down at her desk with a fresh coffee in hand.

"Nothing."

"You look happy."

"Hey, I'm allowed to be happy," she said, sipping and making a face. "Oh, God, how is it possible that *our* machine makes the worst coffee in the world?"

"Seriously, why so chipper?" Stan asked.

Aislinn knew exactly why. "It's like..." She waited until she could find the right words. "Getting promoted to detective is a tough gig, you know that."

"I do."

"The job is hard on us."

"Whaaaat?" Stan smiled. "All that crap food and no sleep when you're on a case?"

"So true. And there are moments when I feel that I should have done something else. Not sure what, just something different. Do you ever feel that?"

He nodded. "Oh yeah, I know exactly what you're saying."

Aislinn brightened. "Well, today, I do *not* feel like that. I'm actually feeling pretty good about being a detective."

"Ahh," Stan said. "The reunion."

She cocked her head slightly.

"I get it," Stan continued. "They can make you crazy or they can be calming. You either question what you've done with your life, or come around to the realization you're okay with who you are. Trust me, I know, I've been to a few of them."

"You're a brilliant man, Mr. Lamers."

Curtis poked his head around the corner and waved at them to join him. He, on the other hand, did *not* look happy.

"Where's Bryan?" Curtis asked.

"Helping me with the phone logs," Stan said. "I'll fill him in later."

"Okay," Curtis said. "The mayor has laid down the gauntlet. He wants an arrest on the Sanders file."

"That's shit," Stan said. "He can't just snap his fingers."

"No, he can't," Curtis agreed. "We'll get there when it's right."

Aislinn perched on the arm of a chair. They were getting close. They'd identified most of the players and linked the murders. "Well," she said, "forensics on the Camry could put us over the top."

"If it's someone with a profile," Curtis countered. "Finding DNA or fingerprints that aren't in our database doesn't help much in the short term."

"It could eventually," Aislinn said. "We need to keep focused on the long game."

"We do," Curtis said. "It's off-putting, first Perez and now the mayor breathing down my neck." He took a deep breath. "What do you have that's new?"

Stan opened a file he'd brought in with him. "Kristin Sanders' calls from the payphone look like a dead end. The last two she made from it on Thursday are both to the same number and it's untraceable."

"It tells us that Kristin was pushing our guy as early as Thursday," Aislinn said. "She probably wanted money."

"See if we can get a wiretap on her phone – just in case," Curtis said.

"Right." Stan jotted that down in his notebook.

Curtis shifted to a new angle. "I had a heart-to-heart with Dimitri Kalatonov and Patrick O'Reilly about that last night. Threatened them with a full-blown assault on their operations."

"And…?" Stan said.

"Nothing." Curtis tapped his pen on the thick file sitting on his desk. "Maybe it's someone inside one of these crime families other than the guys we've been talking to."

"Unlikely," Aislinn said. "They know what's going on inside their own houses."

"Right," Curtis said, "but this goes back a long time. It could be one of the old-timers who went rogue and no one knew."

"That brings the Italians back into the picture," Stan said.

Curtis shook his head. "I don't think so. Salvatore says he knows who our guy is. If our killer was inside the Italian crime family, Salvatore would never have admitted he knew who it was, and would have already dealt with it."

"If Salvatore knows who killed all these people, bring him in and grill him," Stan said. "Take his business apart piece by piece until he talks."

Curtis sighed. "C'mon, Stan, you know exactly where that gets us. He clams up and never gives us anything."

His computer dinged and Curtis checked the new email. "Forensics is in on the Camry." Stan and Aislinn's phones pinged with the same file and they all sat studying the results. "Ahh, we have some DNA that may have come from our perp. Thank God for that air bubble."

"Yeah, but no match in the database," Aislinn said, skipping over the first page.

"At least when we find the son-of-a-bitch, we can match him to the DNA in the car," Curtis said. "That would give us definitive proof."

"The long game," Stan said. "Explaining *that* to the mayor will be fun."

"Do you want us to start looking at other guys in the Russian and Irish gangs?" Aislinn asked.

"I think so," Curtis answered. "Shouldn't be a long list, it has to be someone who was around in the late '90s."

"I'll get on it after I have my chat with Danny Zebiak." Stan stood and stretched.

"Think I'll sit in on that one if it's okay," Aislinn said.

"Yeah, yeah, of course."

"Let me know how that goes." Curtis turned toward his computer screen. The meeting was over.

CHAPTER FORTY-SIX

Danny Zebiak was a mess. He'd taken a beating while in custody and both eyes were swollen almost shut. His cheek was split open and needed stitches.

Stan took the chair across the table from him and Aislinn settled in off to the side. Stan gave the interview preamble while Danny sat hunched over, staring at the table.

"What happened to you?" Stan asked.

Danny looked up. "You guys happened to me."

Stan glanced over at Aislinn. "Did you do this to him? I didn't."

"You know what I mean," Danny said.

Stan knew *exactly* what he meant. Danny had been chilling out at a minimum security prison with a day job, and only a few months left to freedom. Then they had come along and thrown him in with the general prison population and forgot about him for a couple of days. If Danny was thinking they were assholes, he was right.

"Want some coffee?" Aislinn asked.

He nodded. "Yeah."

Aislinn motioned to Bryan, who was watching in the monitoring room. "Anything else?"

"Something to eat. Some big motherfucker took my lunch."

Aislinn nodded at the camera, then looked at Stan. "Let's see if we can get him out of here."

Stan chewed the end of his pen. "We need something, Danny. We can't let you walk without telling us what you know."

Danny let out a heavy sigh and leaned back in his chair. "I admitted I was involved. I told you Tony DeMarco was the guy. I told you he killed Joey Napier. What the fuck else do you want?"

"The other person who was part of the crew," Stan said.

"There was no one else. I already told you that."

"Shit, Danny, getting out of here today's not looking good for you," Stan said. "Give us something concrete."

The door opened and Bryan walked in with a ciabatta bun loaded with meat and a steaming cup of coffee. He stayed in the room and leaned against the back wall. They all watched as Danny dug into the sandwich.

"Where the hell did you get that?" Stan asked. "It sure didn't come out of the cafeteria."

"Bought it at a deli on the way in this morning," Bryan said.

Danny glanced up at the cop who had handed over his lunch. "Thanks, man."

"Danny," Aislinn said when he was finished eating. "This is going to go one of two ways today. You tell us what you know and you're back on track for release. Or you hold out and we play hardball. You stay here, we write up a report that ruins your chances of getting out on time, and you end up back in medium security. Bars on the cell, no day job, no watering trees, and more big motherfuckers stealing your lunch."

Danny took a sip of coffee and stared back at her.

"We want this to end well for you," Aislinn said. "There's no upside to anyone if you head back to lockup."

A few minutes passed, then he set the coffee on the table and said, "There was one more guy. He was Irish but I never heard his name."

All three homicide cops stiffened slightly, and Stan said, "How do you know he was Irish."

"From things Tony said."

"Like what?" Stan asked.

"Tony joked a few times that we never did bad shit on St. Patty's day 'cause of this guy."

"Why did you hold this back?" Aislinn asked.

"Because he'll kill me," Danny said in a matter of fact voice.

"He's not going to find out," Aislinn said.

Danny snorted. "Bet that's what the Sanders woman thought."

Stan leaned in. "This information, it's really going to help us. We'll get him."

"Yeah," Danny said, finishing his coffee, his hands visibly shaking. "Do that before he gets me."

Aislinn looked over at Bryan. "Release him to Pondville and give him a lift. Oh, and stop somewhere on the way and get his cheek stitched up." She stood and looked down at him. "Stay straight, Danny. You're an okay guy."

She and Stan left the room together and walked to Curtis's office. He was looking haggard and motioned for them to come in.

"Rough day?" Stan asked.

"Don't ask."

"We just got out of the interview with Danny Zebiak," Stan said. "He told us there was another person in the crew and that he's Irish."

"You believe him?" Curtis asked.

"I'd give it a ninety percent," Stan answered and Aislinn nodded.

"Irish," Curtis said, brightening a bit. "So O'Reilly's been lying to us."

"This is Boston, LT," Aislinn said. "There are Irish guys everywhere."

Curtis kicked that around for a minute, then said, "True, but this isn't some hack off the street. He's connected, professional, and ruthless. He's smart enough to scout out meeting places to make sure there are no CCTV cameras and connects through an untraceable burner cell. He had Kristin Sanders call from a pay phone that wasn't in range of any cameras. He killed her and dumped her body where we would never have found it if Bryan hadn't cottoned on. If he's Irish, my bet is that he was one of O'Reilly's men back in the day. Could still be."

"Maybe O'Reilly's not lying to us and didn't know the killer was playing around on the side," Stan ventured. "No one other than Tony DeMarco seems to be in on who this guy is. He kept his head down."

Curtis nodded. "Stan, dig into who was part of O'Reilly's crew around the time all this went down. Make a list of guys who are still around and you think are capable of pulling something like this off."

"You bet," Stan said.

"Aislinn, what's on your plate?"

She shifted in her seat and said, "We're missing something. I want to go back over everything we have and see if I can find it."

"You don't think it's one of O'Reilly's men?" Curtis asked.

She squinted and chewed her lip. "Not sure. It's just a gut feel I have. Something's not right here."

"Okay," Curtis said. "Run with it."

"Thanks, LT."

"Get out of here you two. Angela Burton is on her way up."

"You're giving *The Globe* an interview?" Stan asked, wide-eyed.

"If I talk to her I get some degree of control over what people are reading."

"Yeah, good luck with that," Aislinn said as she stood. "Cat's kinda out of the bag already."

CHAPTER FORTY-SEVEN

On her way home Wednesday after work Aislinn stopped by the house where Darina Volkov had grown up and parked across the street. To the passing traffic it was just a blue two-story in need of paint and yard work. To Darina's mother, it was the genesis of a twenty year nightmare.

Darina had been killed because of what she saw, Aislinn was firmly convinced of that. She got out of the car and leaned against the front fender. The sun felt warm on her skin and she closed her eyes, remembering her friend with the long dark hair and deep brown eyes that sparkled when she smiled. Someone special had been taken the day Darina disappeared – one life stolen, others forever changed.

Aislinn opened her eyes and focused on the house, envisioning Darina on her way home, walking up the street as the killer came down the driveway, the hedge shielding them from each other. They had met right where the bushes ended at the sidewalk and almost bumped into each other. Darina had been close enough to see his wristwatch and a silver pendant. She must have looked right into his eyes, and Aislinn wondered if the killer had been surprised.

Then nothing for six months.

"Why the break?" Aislinn asked herself. "Why prom night?"

The key to solving this had to be right there, staring back at her, but she couldn't see it. Danny Zebiak was positive their killer was Irish, and that narrowed things down, but Aislinn wasn't convinced he was part of O'Reilly's crew. The gangsters ran a tight ship, always had, and it was unlikely someone with the moxie to run a successful protection racket outside the crime family would have gone unnoticed. Which meant it was an outsider, someone savvy and connected enough to link up with a Boston Police detective and stay off the radar. Then there was Kristin's comment at the reunion.

...nice fucking pendant.

She had followed up with the woman wearing the jewelry and come up empty. There was no connection to their case, it was simply a matter of Kristin seeing the pendant after she'd had too much to drink and making a rude remark. Still, she had a feeling the thing with the pendant was part of the answer. She just wasn't sure how.

Something was lurking in the back of her mind and she pushed hard to retrieve it. Then it clicked – her dad had made some comment about Celtic Knots at his retirement party. Something about a lot of the Irish guys wearing them on chains twenty years ago. She Googled *Celtic Knot* on her phone and scrolled through the endless string of images. There was little doubt any one of them could be mistaken for a pendant. Maybe she had something.

"What else did he say," she whispered to herself, fast forwarding to a couple of days later when she visited him at home. Then she remembered, and her shoulders slumped slightly. *All the Irish guys had them and they were all different,* or something like that. "Damn," she muttered. "Doesn't narrow it down at all if everyone was wearing them."

Still, it was possible it gave the perp a reason to kill Darina. What if she had seen the pendant and figured it out? But again, why the delay? The other possibility was that Darina had bumped into her dad's killer on the day of the prom and been close enough to recognize his eyes. That made some degree of sense – Darina would likely never have forgotten those eyes. But where would she have seen them? They had gone back over her day numerous times and it was mostly spent one-on-one with school friends at their houses. The exception was when Darina and Kayla had gone out for lunch and Darina had got vocal about some piece of crap killing her father. Kayla said the whole restaurant was staring at them. She remembered the two Italian guys, but Curtis had never leaned toward the Italians being behind the murders, and Danny Zebiak's latest information pointed to an Irish connection.

Maybe someone in the restaurant was their guy. But how to find out? It was two decades ago and the only surviving witness she had was Kayla Walsh. There was nothing else there, the juice had been squeezed out of that orange.

Aislinn slipped into her car and drove away, taking one last look at Darina's old house. *Damn it all to hell,* she thought, *what am I missing?*

* * *

CURTIS HAD SAT across from Angela Burton enough times to know how intelligent and resourceful the reporter was. Short changing her was out of the question. Influencing what she wrote and when she submitted it for publication were the only items on the table.

"How close are you to an arrest?" she asked.

Curtis smiled. It was usually him asking the questions. "Let's go off the record for a minute, then I'll give you what we have."

She thought about that, then said, "You know I can't hold back information if it puts the public at risk. You just pulled a dead woman out of a car someone dumped in a lake. He's out there, Curtis."

"Agreed," he said. "Off the record for a minute?"

"Okay." She set her iPad on the edge of his desk and leaned back.

"We're almost positive this all goes back to Alexi Volkov getting himself offed in 2000, followed by his daughter's murder six months later."

"I've already reported on that," she said.

"There was one murder prior – Joey Napier in July of '99. It's starting to look like Tony DeMarco might have been involved."

She jerked forward in her chair. "A BPD detective killing people?"

"Maybe," Curtis said slowly in a calm tone, trying to keep the conversation under control.

"Jesus, Curtis, if DeMarco killed someone you're going to have people in the streets with pitchforks."

"Part of that depends on how you write the story," Curtis said. "Temper it by reminding everyone it was twenty years ago. You can help set the tone."

"Softens the story," she countered.

"Not really. Play the progress angle, bring up Rampart and the progress we've all made since then."

"That was LA," she said. "This is Boston."

"There was change because of it," Curtis said.

She gave him a slightly sarcastic grin. "So you're the good guys."

"We're supposed to be. It's not a bad angle."

"Back on the record?" she asked and he nodded. "What's going on with Kristin Sanders' murder and how are they connected?"

"Who said they were connected?" he asked.

"Oh, come on, Curtis. Darina Volkov murdered on prom night and Kristin Sanders flies in for the twenty year reunion. Then she's killed and dumped in a lake. Doesn't take a rocket scientist to figure it out."

"We're close," Curtis said. "We know all the players who were involved in the protection racket that got Alexi Volkov killed. We've interviewed them and have a concrete lead. I have three detectives working on it right now."

"Do you have a name?" she asked.

He shook his head. "If we had a name we would have him in custody."

"How long until you get this guy?"

"Not sure."

"Does he pose a threat to the public?" she asked.

"We feel Sanders was killed because she knew something about what happened twenty years ago."

"So he's only killing people who could identify him."

"Something like that."

"Anything else?" she asked and slipped her iPad back into her bag when he shook his head. "The DeMarco connection to Napier's death is safe, for now, but if it's the truth it has to come out."

"I understand, it's the timing we need to manage."

"Okay," she said.

"Thanks, Angela."

Curtis sat without moving for a minute after the reporter left, thinking about the repercussions of having a cop fingered for a murder, even if it was two decades ago. No matter which way he looked at it, things were going to get ugly.

* * *

BRYAN CHEUNG TURNED into the driveway leading to Pondville Correction Center and glanced over at Danny Zebiak sitting quietly in the passenger's seat. He looked content to be back.

"Detective Byrne," Danny said. "What's she like?"

"Tough as nails," Bryan replied. "Has to be."

"Yeah, I suppose. Probably makes it harder, her being a looker and all."

Bryan pulled into a parking spot. "Might be." He motioned to the door. "Let's go."

They started for the admin building and Bryan asked, "How are those stitches doing?"

"Good, yeah. Thanks for taking me to the clinic."

"No problem. You don't need a scar, what with being out soon."

Danny stopped short of the door. "Tony told me he was scared of this guy. That he had two sides to him. He could be nice or he could put a bullet in your head. Didn't care which."

"Sounds like a dangerous guy."

"You gotta find him, man. He'll kill me in a second for what I told you."

Bryan saw the fear in the man's eyes. Even the best actors couldn't fake that. "We'll get him."

They checked in and Danny headed off to his room while Bryan filled out the paperwork. There were going to be a lot of lessons learned over the next while, but here was one he knew he'd never forget. Not all the bad guys are rotten to the core. That, he figured, was important.

* * *

STAN CHECKED HIS WATCH – it was already after six and his son's baseball game started at 6:30. He packed up and hustled out to his car.

The drive gave him some time to think, and he ran through the list of Irish gangsters who were around twenty years ago. It was short, six names at best. Three of them were probably non-starters, having been street-level grunts when Volkov was killed. Not the kind of guys who would have the connections and pedigree to attract a police detective as a business partner. The remaining three weren't much better.

Two of them were so old now it was almost impossible to think they'd have the energy or technical savvy to pull off the hit on Kristin Sanders. Whoever had killed Kristin had accessed her hotel room, then used the in-suite checkout app and removed her luggage. The obvious reason was to buy some time until anyone noticed she was missing. But that would require jogging up and down seven flights of stairs to evade the CCTV cameras, which pretty much eliminated the next two, who were in their late seventies.

The final candidate was one of Patrick O'Reilly's most trusted men. He was well known to the police and had never shown the slightest desire to deviate from the family's business. Stan had pretty much ruled him out.

Which meant they were no further ahead now than they were before Danny Zebiak had given them the tip. Curtis was going to be disappointed, but there was no sugar coating the truth. They were dead in the water.

He pulled into the parking lot adjacent to the ball diamond and saw his son waving. He smiled and waved back, though he didn't feel like smiling in the least.

CHAPTER FORTY-EIGHT

Aislinn couldn't sleep and rolled out of bed at 3:45, having finally given up. It was pitch black when she walked up her street in sweats and a hoodie. The air was crisp and it was silent except for the rubber soles of her running shoes on the sidewalk. Every now and then she stopped and listened to the silence, rare moments in a busy city.

She started to run, slowly at first, easing her body into the rhythm, then faster until her legs were stretching full out with every stride. Shrubs and trees flew past and she kept up the pace for thirty minutes, then slowed to a walk and headed home, her mind cleared of everything except the murder of Darina Volkov.

"Why wait?" she whispered to herself. "Why did he wait six months?"

Did something happen on prom night that triggered a chain of events that led to Darina's murder? Right now she was trying to force the pieces into place and that never worked. They had to line up, and she felt that without knowing why the killer waited she was not going to solve Darina's murder.

She strode up the sidewalk to her front door, let herself in and headed for the shower. After spending a few minutes just standing still, letting the water course over her body, she got out and rubbed off with a towel, then slipped into her jeans and grabbed the car keys. The drive to Darina's house only took a few minutes on the quiet streets and she parked across the road as the sun crested the horizon. She slipped out of her car, staring at the house, thinking back over Darina's final day and distilling it down to bullet points.

Darina had picked her and Sofia up at their houses early in the day, with, unbeknownst to anyone, rolls of cash tucked in her bag. They went straight to Kayla Walsh's, then to the hair salon, with Darina and Kayla cutting out for lunch after their appointment. Kayla's description of what had happened in the restaurant was unambiguous. Darina had lost it, started yelling about her dad getting killed and the police not solving it. People were staring and listening – maybe the wrong people. And…it was there that Kayla had spotted the cash.

"Something there?" she whispered to herself. She pushed hard but couldn't make it work.

Next, Darina dropped everyone at Kayla's and left abruptly for Cody Hall's. They drank beer and when Darina pulled out the cash she got angry. Cody was positive that she felt some of it was missing. He didn't mention it in his police report so they wouldn't think he took it, which impaired the investigation.

Darina stopped at Shane Collins' place to lay out the ground rules for prom night, headed back to Kayla's house and dragged her out by the pool. She demanded the cash back but Kayla refused to admit stealing it. Aislinn had the rare advantage of actually being an eyewitness, having seen the girls argue by the pool. Darina finally settled down and they all changed into their dresses, Kayla and Sofia using Kayla's room, she and Darina in the master bedroom.

Then the meltdown. Out of nowhere Darina ran out the front door and tore off down the street, straight to Kristin's where she made the phone call. Somehow, that call had to be the trigger. The missing money, phoning the police station, running out of Kristin's house and tearing off in her car. Never to be seen again. Aislinn backed up and slowly replayed the entire scenario again. This time she stopped part way through.

"Oh, my God," she whispered. Her knees buckled and she almost fell.

It was like a game of Tetris and she had just found the key to the puzzle. With it in place all the other pieces started falling into their slots. Piece after piece, every one of them fitting perfectly. There was no doubt in her mind. She knew who it was.

She grabbed the car and held on, sucking air as the street wavered and threatened to go sideways. A passing jogger veered off the sidewalk and headed for her, asking if she was okay.

Aislinn waved her off and the woman continued on down the street, throwing an occasional glance back.

Aislinn slid behind the steering wheel and leaned over, opened the glove compartment and took out her personal crime scene kit. She removed the magnifying glass from under the elastic loop. Then she picked up the file folder from the passenger's seat and took out one of the photos from the day of the prom. With the interior light directly overhead she held the magnifying glass as steady as she could with trembling hands, searching for what she knew had to be there. She found it and her heart started pounding as she moved the magnifier closer, squinting to bring it into focus. Then all the stress in her shoulders melted away. Confirmation. There was no doubt.

Giuseppe Salvatore's phone number was in the file and she dialed it on her cell. She was surprised when he answered, given the early hour. "Mr. Salvatore, it's Detective Byrne."

"Detective Byrne," he said in a pleasant voice. "How can I help?"

"Can I stop by and see you?"

There was a long pause, then, "I'm at the shop all morning."

"Thanks." She hung up and sat without moving for five minutes.

When she finally pulled out from the curb she was back – focused and calculating. She made a quick stop at District A-1, where she sent a picture to the printer, then headed for Salvatore's butcher shop. The woman at the counter waved Aislinn through to the back office where she found the Italian sitting behind his desk. He motioned to a chair and she sat.

"This is a pleasant surprise," Giuseppe said. He pointed to the folded paper in her hand. "Is that what I think it is?"

"Probably," she said, leaning over and handing him the photo.

He didn't open it for a few seconds, just stared at her, gauging where she was with things. Finally, he flipped it open, took a quick look and closed it again. He handed it back to her.

"Is that him?" she asked.

"It is."

They sat in silence for a minute, then Salvatore said, "What now, Detective Byrne?"

"I arrest his ass," she said.

"Well now, that should be interesting." When she didn't move or speak, he added, "He's slippery."

She stood and gave him a slight nod. "Yeah, I know." Then she walked out.

Giuseppe watched her leave, his hands shaking with rage from the sight of the face on page. He'd wanted to settle the score with the monster personally for years, to rip him to shreds for his lies and complicity, but had been overruled by the new, younger members of the family. They were adamant that nothing good could come from exacting revenge. So he had sat, and waited, for this moment to arrive. The day when someone showed up and put a target on the son-of-a-bitch.

"Finally, Vincenzo," he told himself through clenched teeth. "Finally."

CHAPTER FORTY-NINE

Curtis had a copy of the *Boston Globe* on his desk when Aislinn strode in Thursday morning. It was open to the announcements page. She looked at the one he had circled.

"You figured it too," she said.

"Not entirely," Curtis said, "but I have my suspicions. Your text said Arnie Walsh's grandson was born on Saturday morning." He tapped the newspaper. "This announcement says it was Friday."

"Well, Walsh lied," Aislinn said. "He needed to be elsewhere."

"Like at the Godfrey Hotel." Curtis stared at the paper, then said, "You have it all pieced together?" When she nodded, he said, "Get Stan and Bryan. Let's see if everything sticks."

"Okay." She hustled out the door and was back in a couple of minutes with the other two in tow.

Curtis shut the door behind them and waited until they were all seated. "Floor is all yours, Aislinn," Curtis said.

She took a long, deep breath. "Well guys, our perp is Arnie Walsh."

"Walsh?" Stan's face was awash with disbelief. "No, seriously?"

Aislinn wondered if the expression on her face looked anything like Stan's. Inside, under the tough-cop exterior, she felt torn apart.

And not just because the killer was another cop – it was someone she had trusted and looked up to.

"One hundred percent." Aislinn's tone was matter of fact and belied the churn going on in her head and her gut.

"Shit," Bryan said, his mind racing ahead. "So if Walsh is our guy and DeMarco was set up…"

Curtis cut in. "Yeah, we have a cop killing another cop." He motioned for Aislinn to continue.

Aislinn took a long, deep breath and pushed aside her emotions. This had been her case from the start and she had ploughed through layer after layer of muck to get here.

"Right from the start," she began, "I felt the link between Alexi and Darina Volkov's murders went back to the day of the prom. I couldn't figure out why Alexi's killer waited six months to kill Darina or why it happened on prom night, but there had to be a reason."

She picked up Darina's file and pulled out the photo of Darina standing in the master bedroom of the Walsh house, smiling in her prom dress, nails bright red, shoes to match. The sight of her friend, completely unaware it was the last day of her life, set her pulse on a wild ride. She handed the photo to Stan.

"Look behind her, at the bureau," Aislinn said. "There's a pendant hanging on the edge of the mirror."

Stan plucked Curtis's magnifying glass from the pencil holder on his desk and positioned it over the photo. "Celtic Knot," he said. "Triangular."

Aislinn nodded. "Easily recognizable, and one she had seen before."

Stan handed the photo on to Bryan. "Yeah, on the guy's neck who killed her father."

"Exactly," Aislinn said as Bryan studied the picture. "That's why she got such a shocked look on her face and went tearing off to Kristin's. All these years I thought it was Kayla's comments about Cody's date being so gorgeous, but that had nothing to do with it. When I took the photo that day, the bureau and the pendant were behind Darina, in the picture. When she turned around to face Kayla, it was in her line of vision."

"So she saw the pendant – knew Kayla's dad was the guy," Stan said.

Bryan set the photo and magnifying glass on the desk and Curtis picked them up and had a look. He set them down and said. "What else do you have?"

Aislinn pulled out her notebook. "A lot. Once I knew it was him, everything fit. We have a mountain of evidence.

"I'll start at the beginning," she said and Curtis nodded. "Arnie Walsh and Tony DeMarco had a protection racket on the go. They kept it small because they couldn't afford for anyone to know two cops were running things. Tony was the most visible, he was the one Joey Napier, Aaron Brock and Danny Zebiak reported to. He handed out the assignments – when to collect the money, who to beat up for non-payment. Arnie stayed in the shadows – he was the leader, the guy who had put it all together.

"With two cops running things, they could bring the law down on anyone who messed with them. The crime families backed off and let them do their thing, providing they didn't try to expand. Giuseppe Salvatore was the only gangster who knew Walsh was involved, likely because he spotted Walsh and DeMarco together somewhere and figured it out.

"Then Walsh figured out Joey Napier was one of Salvatore's guys. Walsh was some pissed off and ran him down. That's why Tony DeMarco was in tears at the crime scene. Joey was one of the crew and when Walsh murdered him, Tony realized he was in business with a psychopath. Tony was in it for the money, he wasn't a killer."

"So Joey Napier was the first guy Walsh killed," Curtis said. "Back in '99."

"Yes." Aislinn was in a groove now, the words coming a bit easier. "Then Alexi Volkov got himself caught doing some stupid shit and was ready to broker a deal with the DA, so Walsh took *him* out as well. Walsh waited for Alexi to get home then shot him in the back of the head. It was nothing more than bad luck, him running into Darina as she came around the hedge. He knew from the police report that she'd seen his pendant, but he never figured Darina would see it hanging on the bureau in his bedroom. It was unique and easy to recognize, but none of the kids ever went in their bedroom. Then on prom night, we were getting dressed and that's exactly what happened."

"Bad luck for Darina," Stan said.

"There's our trigger," Curtis said. "The start of all this."

"A Celtic Knot on a chain," Aislinn said, shaking her head.

"Sometimes it's the smallest things," Curtis said.

"Often times," Stan added.

Aislinn waited a minute for it to sink in, then said, "Prom night was six months after Walsh had killed Alexi, and that was the reason for the gap between the murders. When Darina saw the pendant she made a beeline for Kristin Sanders' house and called the precinct. I know Arnie was working, because he told us that he could leave work to drive us if we'd been drinking. Everyone thought he was a great guy. All of us, saying that Kayla's dad was the best."

The anger had been building inside her like a simmering volcano, and it was getting hard to control. She bit her lip, trying desperately to erase from her memory any kind words she had ever said to the bastard. She was aware Curtis was watching her closely, looking to get a sense of how badly the case had scarred her.

"Yeah," Stan snorted in disgust. "Total fuck wad is more like it."

Stan's hatred for Walsh helped settle her. This wasn't all on her. "Darina went into the den for privacy," Aislinn continued, "but Kristin overheard the conversation. Darina wasn't calling to report Kayla Walsh stealing her college cash, she was calling to tell Arnie Walsh what she knew."

"If there was ever a bad fucking idea, that's it," Stan said, shaking his head.

Aislinn hadn't really thought of it that way. Stan was right, it had been a monumental error in judgement. "She likely asked for him by name, which is why Kristin knew Walsh was the killer."

"Are we still waiting to hear back from the person working the switchboard that night?" Curtis asked.

"We are," Aislinn replied. "Patricia Morriscey will be back in cell phone range later today or tomorrow, and I'm betting she'll confirm Darina asked for Walsh."

"But hang on, that would have gone in the daily log report for the precinct," Curtis said.

Aislinn shook her head. "Not if Walsh told Patricia that he had offered to drive the kids because it was prom night and that's why Darina called. He could have been reprimanded or even lost his job, so she kept quiet."

Curtis considered that possibility, then nodded. "Yeah, okay. What happened after she made the call?"

Aislinn sucked some air deep into her lungs. "It's a bit of a black hole and I don't think we'll ever know for sure, but Darina had been drinking and smoking pot. She wasn't thinking clearly and made some bad choices. As Stan pointed out, calling Walsh at the precinct was the first one. Putting herself in a vulnerable position where he could get at her was the second. Once Walsh caught up with Darina, he strangled her."

She couldn't push back a vivid image of Walsh with wild eyes, pulling hard on the thin wire cutting through Darina's windpipe, her body convulsing as she gasped for air, then collapsing into a heap at his feet. It shot through her brain like a runaway truck.

"You okay?" Curtis asked.

Clearly, she wasn't. After a minute she said, "Yeah, I think so." She had a drink of water as her colleagues waited, then she pushed on. "It must have been a hell of a surprise, Walsh finding out she was hauling twenty thousand dollars around in her backpack. That was a windfall for him – now there was a motive for someone else to kill her."

"The missing money got us looking in a different direction," Curtis said.

Aislinn leaned back slightly in her chair, water in hand. "Cops like Heckler & Koch pistols. I suspect Arnie Walsh had one – probably still does – and that's the one he used to knock Darina unconscious before he strangled her. She must have seen it coming and lashed out at him.

That's how she ended up with traces of blue material under one of her fingernails.

"From his uniform," Bryan said. "He was on duty."

"Right," Aislinn agreed. "Then Walsh sealed her up tight in poly, carried her to the third floor of the building under construction on Center Street, removed some drywall, crammed her in the electrical chase and replaced the drywall. The guys taped and mudded the walls the next day – and Darina was gone – Walsh's third victim."

Stan raised a point. "Everyone and their dog knew that space was under construction. Anyone could have dumped the body."

"Unimportant," she said. "But there's heaps more evidence that ties him directly to the murders."

"Like?"

"Kristin Sanders knew Walsh killed Darina and she started blackmailing him. Every month some of Arnie's cash was going to pay a kid who happened to overhear a telephone conversation, and that must have made him crazy."

"She must have been one tough nut to keep him paying," Stan said.

"I have no doubt she tucked something away that pointed at Walsh and would surface if she died," Aislinn said.

"Makes sense," Bryan said. "That would keep him on the hook."

"Not sure how she did it, but we'll likely find out that Walsh bankrolled her education, paid for everything. When she graduated it appears to have stopped. She was earning a good salary and quit asking for money. Walsh probably just let it go, but then she turned out to have a gambling problem. There may have been a point where she wanted more."

"A lot of conjecture here," Stan said.

"Nothing we can't uncover with a forensic audit, now that we know where we're looking," Curtis said.

Stan shook his head. "I bet Walsh has been looking for a chance to kill Kristen for twenty years. Things were starting to unravel and he jumped on it. Took the risk."

"Yeah," Aislinn agreed. "When Darina's body showed up, everything was back on the table. Kristin is coming to Boston for the reunion and she's broke, so it's back to the piggybank. She calls Walsh's burner cell from the pay phone and he agrees to pay her, probably a lump sum. They meet, he kills her and dumps the car in Rocky Pond with Kristen inside. Walsh uses the birth of his new grandson as an alibi and goes running off the golf course for the hospital. In reality, the child was born the night before and he was heading to meet Kristin. That bought him five or six hours, plenty of time to kill her and drive to Rocky Pond. We got lucky when Bryan tracked the car."

Aislinn leaned forward, just a touch. "This is where we nail it shut. The car windows were tightly sealed and there was still an air pocket inside the driver's compartment. We managed to pull some DNA that matches his from the dry part of the car."

Stan was nodding hard now. "What a piece of crap."

"That's for sure, but also smart and dangerous," Curtis said.

"Are you sure Walsh killed Tony DeMarco?" Bryan asked.

"Positive," Aislinn said. "Aside from all the evidence we've put together, this morning I set Walsh's picture in front of Salvatore and he gave it the nod."

Curtis raised an eyebrow. "You got the old bastard to confirm it was Walsh."

Aislinn nodded. "I did."

"Now *that* is impressive. What else do you have?" Curtis asked.

"Killing Tony was despicable," Aislinn said. "But something bothered me right from the start when I read through the file. It never made sense that Tony's gun would be lying right next to his body. He was in an electronics store during a robbery and would have had his gun out with his arm up and ready to fire. If that was the case, when he was shot the gun would have hit the ground and bounced a few feet away. But it was right next to him. That's because he recognized Walsh when he came around the end of the aisle and Tony lowered his gun. Then Walsh shot him point blank."

"Yeah, yeah, his gun ending up where it did wasn't right," Stan said, then asked, "But how could Walsh know DeMarco would be there? It was a burglary."

Aislinn shook her head. "No, a *burglary in progress* was called in right when Tony was passing the electronics store. Walsh made the call to the precinct about the burglary. He knew when DeMarco left the precinct and he damn sure knew DeMarco's route home. What cop driving past a crime in progress wouldn't stop? Walsh knew DeMarco would respond and he was waiting. It was a classic case of the partner becoming a problem, and Walsh took him out."

Aislinn went three shades of red as she glanced around the room, drawing strength from the pained look on her colleagues faces. "This guy, if he could kill his own partner, he could kill anyone." Her voice cracked on the words.

"Tony was bent," Curtis said with resignation. "It changes things."

"Yeah, a bit." Aislinn waited a minute, then said, "And who better to know where the CCTV coverage is than a cop. That seemed a bit over the top, his ability to evade the cameras. Of course he knew where the cameras were, he'd spent years requesting footage for detectives on active cases."

The room was quiet, and Aislinn added, "Walsh played us all the way through the investigation. He wormed his way in through my dad, then gave us names of businesses that he knew didn't pay money to his and Tony's operation. Misdirected us whenever he could and stayed up to date where we were in the case."

Curtis let out a heavy sigh. "And I gave you the okay to tell them what we had."

"Yeah, well, we got him," Aislinn said. She snapped the file shut.

"What now?" Bryan asked.

"We get a search warrant for his house and we arrest him," Curtis said. "Twenty years late, but better than never."

CHAPTER FIFTY

The cars pulled up in front of the house in unison a few minutes after eleven – three squad cars and two unmarked vehicles. Curtis got out and stood on the sidewalk in front of Arnie Walsh's place.

"Bryan," Curtis said. "Take a couple of guys and cover the back."

They'd pulled the survey of Walsh's lot from the city archives and checked it on Google Maps. The west side of the property had a gate and would provide the best access, but it would have a lock of some sort because of the pool. Bryan was armed with bolt cutters and started down the narrow side yard. Curtis and Aislinn walked up the front sidewalk, two uniformed officers just behind them. Stan waited at the curb, one hand on his radio, the other resting on the gun in his holster.

Curtis rang the bell and the sound of footsteps echoed through the foyer. A moment later Elspeth Walsh opened the door and a brief smile crossed her face when she saw Aislinn. It quickly disappeared when she spotted the additional officers and all the cars parked in front of the house, lights flashing.

"What's going on?" she asked.

Curtis held up the warrant. "Elspeth Walsh, we have a warrant to search your house." He let her take it, then said, "Is Arnie home?"

Her eyes flicked between the warrant and the two cops on her doorstep. Slowly, she moved aside. "Aislinn?"

"Yes, Mrs. Walsh."

"What's this about?" she asked.

"Can't say right now, but we need to know if your husband is here."

She shook her head. "He left this morning, about 7:00. Said he was going golfing."

"Which course?" Aislinn asked.

"Franklin Park, I think. That's where he usually goes."

Aislinn spun on her heels and jogged back to Stan. "He might be at Franklin Park Golf Course. Tee time around 7:30, he should be on the last hole or two. Get some men on it."

"Right." He was on his phone as she ran back up the walk.

The uniforms followed as Curtis and Aislinn moved into the house, cautiously and with their hands close to their guns. Elspeth Walsh backed off, a curious mixture of disbelief and resignation on her face. The living room and kitchen were clear and Aislinn started down the hall toward the bedrooms. The door to the master suite was partially closed and she used her foot to push it open. The bed was made and clean clothes were neatly folded in a pile on a small bench under the window. She stood framed in the doorway, the image of Darina sitting on the bed vivid as the day of the prom.

If we had never come into this room...

That thought was going to stick the rest of her life. Shivers ran down her spine as she surveyed the room, preserved almost exactly as it was twenty years ago, like a time capsule for a day she would never forget. A monster lived here, and they had all been under his spell. Kayla's dad – all of the kids hanging out and laughing with him by the pool, thinking he was the coolest of all the parents, feeling safe because he was a cop. The great deception.

Aislinn pulled herself together and skirted the end of the bed, her eyes on the far edge of the mirror attached to the bureau. It was there.

She picked up the chain – the triangular Celtic Knot dangling on the end, then slipped it into an evidence bag and returned to the living room. Curtis was sitting quietly in a chair, facing Elspeth Walsh who was huddled on one end of the couch.

"Got it." Aislinn held up the pendant. "Any sign of him?"

Curtis shook his head and gestured at Stan, who was at the front door, phone to his ear.

Stan killed the call. "Walsh didn't have a tee time this morning and we found his golf clubs in the garage. He's on the move."

"Aislinn," Elspeth said, her voice shaky and weak. "What is this about?"

"You don't know?" Aislinn looked her in the eye. "You honestly don't know?"

She began to sob. Doubt flashed across her face, haggard and devoid of color. Tears streamed down her cheeks and dripped on her blouse. She wiped at her nose with a tissue.

Aislinn sat on the couch next to Elspeth. "We suspect Arnie of having his fingers in some pretty bad stuff, possibly going back twenty years or more." Aislinn waited, letting the words sink in. "What can you tell us?"

Elspeth stared at her hands, in her lap and tightly clenched. "Arnie talked about work, but it was just regular stuff that was happening at the precinct. Nothing more than that."

"You never suspected there was something else going on?" Aislinn asked.

Nothing for a minute, then Elspeth nodded, a quick couple of motions with her head. "Some days he could be distant – or in a mean mood." She stopped, and there was fear in her eyes. "He never told me what was going on when I asked, so I just stopped asking."

Aislinn waited patiently for her to continue, which she did. "A few days ago he said he was going to trade me in for a new model. Made it sound like a joke, but I knew it wasn't." She was shaking now, close to breaking down completely.

Aislinn clenched her jaw – Walsh was intelligent and controlling with an exaggerated self-worth, and showed no sign of empathy or love – traits of a psychopath. Elspeth had suffered at his hand, as had Kayla. There was little wonder her friend had been a mean and divisive teenager.

"Everyone loved Arnie, but he scared me." Elspeth could barely get the words out. She looked at Aislinn through wet eyes. "I felt like I was crazy."

"Well, you're not," Aislinn said, setting her hand on the woman's arm. She managed a hint of a sympathetic smile. "We're going to need to talk with you at length, Mrs. Walsh, but right now we need to know where Arnie is. Do you have any idea?"

"No, I thought he was golfing."

"Do you have any other property, like a cabin or a piece of land?" Aislinn asked.

"No," she muttered. "Nothing like that."

"Was there any place Arnie liked to go? A fishing lodge, hiking trail, place by the beach?"

She looked bewildered by that, like she was realizing she didn't know her husband. "No."

"Let's set up a proper interview," Curtis said to Aislinn. "When Mrs. Walsh has had some time to process all this."

Aislinn looked at Kayla's mom, staring vacantly at the floor. "How about 2:00 this afternoon? I'll pick you up and we can talk in Lieutenant Westcott's office. Away from the house."

Elspeth nodded, then asked, "What's he done?"

Aislinn tightened the grip on Elspeth's arm. "You've had enough for now."

"We'll have an officer wait at the curb," Curtis said. "To keep away any nosy neighbors."

They left Arnie Walsh's shattered wife on the couch and regrouped outside the back door. Aislinn walked over to the edge of the pool and looked down at the reflections of the sky and trees, tiny ripples in the water moving about.

"She never knew," Aislinn finally said. She looked back at Curtis and Stan. "She never knew she was living with a monster."

"I don't think anyone did," Curtis said.

"My God." Aislinn felt the anger rising. "I was that close to him and never saw what he was."

"Hey, you were a kid," Stan shot back.

She balled her fists and clenched her jaw so tight it hurt. "Not last week I wasn't, sitting across from him at my parents' house, telling him where we were in the investigation." A thought struck her and she said, "That's why he didn't shave."

"Huh?" Bryan said.

"The beard – makes it harder for people to recognize you. He stopped shaving the moment he heard we'd found Darina."

"Getting ready to make a run for it," Curtis said.

"What now?" Bryan asked.

"We get an APB out on him and his car," Curtis said. "Collect CCTV from every camera that might give us an idea which direction he was heading when he left the house. Search land titles for any other property registered to him. Modify his name slightly, a letter or two here and there, something subtle that he could have slipped through when he made the purchase."

"Like Arnald Walsh rather than Arnold," Bryan said, spelling out both versions of Arnold. "Or Welsh rather than Walsh."

"Exactly, like that," Curtis said. "Get a lock on the GPS on his phone. See if his car has a factory-installed GPS tracker. Look back over his phone records for calls made to out-of-state numbers. Talk to the people he called or who called him, maybe he was setting up a place to stay."

"How far back?" Stan asked.

"From the day he got his phone. He's organized and likely had a plan in place."

"Right," Stan said.

"Utilities, telecoms, tax records, VISA and Mastercard statements, bank accounts, parking and speeding tickets, club memberships – any place he may have left a trail – in every state. Canada as well. We'll bring in the FBI if we think he's crossed state lines, but let's try to keep some degree of control over this."

"Massive undertaking," Aislinn said.

"I'll pull some additional help from the bullpen," Curtis said. "You three can each head up a team and decide what everyone is responsible for. My feeling – he is *not* going to be easy to find."

Silence engulfed the still summer air as they all came to grips with what was on their plate. Around them, the lush garden, the designer patio furniture, the inviting pool – had lost its luster. The place was nothing more than home to a monster.

"The bastard killed five people, including a cop," Curtis said. "I'll be busy explaining that to our chief and the commissioner." He managed the tightest of smiles. "Unless one of you wants to switch jobs."

There were no takers.

The three men headed around the side of the house to their cars, but Aislinn hung back waiting for the team that was en route to execute the search warrant. She closed her eyes, picturing the day that had started with such promise. Prom, with all its pomp and pageantry was beckoning, and they were all for it. Excited, feeling like their whole lives were ahead of them, four friends with big dreams.

Except one of them hadn't made it.

CHAPTER FIFTY-ONE

Curtis stood when the commissioner and police chief walked into his office. Perez and Dawson took the chairs facing Curtis's desk and settled in.

"Thanks for coming," Curtis said, closing the door and returning to his seat. "We have a suspect in the Volkov and Sanders murders."

"Good news," Ted Dawson said.

"Maybe not," Curtis replied. "We put an extreme rush on the DNA analysis and got a match from trace evidence on Kristin Sanders' body and other parts of the car she was found in. We're convinced we have our killer."

"And he is..." Perez said.

"Arnie Walsh, a retired BPD sergeant." Curtis let that sink in, then added, "He worked out of District A-1."

Neither man spoke, they just stared at their head of Homicide.

"We've also connected him to the murders of Joey Napier, Alexi Volkov, Darina Volkov, and Tony DeMarco."

Dawson sat bolt upright. "DeMarco was a detective."

All the color had drained from Elian Perez's face.

Curtis nodded. "He was."

Curtis spent the next half hour going over the joint investigations that had led to Arnie Walsh being their man, detailing the evidence trail, and wrapping up with the trip to Walsh's house, warrant in hand.

"So he got away," Perez said. The color in the commissioner's face had returned and it was a blistering shade of red.

"For now," Curtis replied calmly. "We'll get him."

"How do we handle this in the interim?" Perez said. "How do we spin it?"

Curtis was shocked at the comment but didn't let his emotions spill onto his face. "That most of this happened twenty years ago and Kristin Sanders was the result of Walsh panicking as we closed in on him."

"How dangerous is he, Curtis?" Dawson asked.

Curtis took a long, deep breath. "If he's cornered, I would say extremely dangerous. But he'll probably try to blend in somewhere, get low and stay off the radar."

"Is he here, in Boston?" Dawson asked. "Best guess."

Curtis pursed his lips and said, "I don't think so. He's too well known. He went without shaving after we found Darina Volkov's body, which may suggest he was getting ready to run. I can't imagine him staying in town."

Curtis was ready in case one of his superiors broached the issue of how Walsh knew they were getting close, but didn't intend to offer the information unless asked. Admitting Aislinn had unknowingly been feeding Walsh information about the investigation wasn't something that would go over well and Curtis was hoping it never surfaced.

"Does he have another place?" Perez asked.

Curtis shrugged. "We're digging, but we haven't found one yet. We're less than twenty-four hours in so we still have a lot of ground to cover."

"What about the media?" Perez was back on the politics of how this was going to play out with the public.

"Angela Burton is our best bet to break the story," Curtis said. "She knew 99% of what we had and held off at my request. I think we give it to her and then field the blowback as best we can."

"We?" Perez said testily.

Dawson leaned forward and interjected. "Curtis has been on the news many times and he's a known commodity." He gave Perez a knowing nod. "Let's put Westcott under the hot lights on this. It's best if your first press conference as the commissioner is on something more positive."

That settled Perez a bit.

Curtis checked his watch, "Sorry, but I'm expected in a meeting with my detectives." He gave Perez an understanding look as the man stood. "I'll handle it carefully, sir."

Perez nodded and followed Dawson out of the room. Curtis took a moment to reset, including reminding himself that Perez *was* the new guy and having this dumped on his lap was a shitty way to start a high profile job in a new city. He needed to give Perez the respect his title deserved, and being the one to terminate a meeting wasn't the way to do it. He made a mental note to try a bit harder with the new commissioner as he headed into the hallway to link up with his crew.

Stan brightened when he saw Curtis approaching and stood, brandishing a handwritten note. "Bryan found a Heckler & Koch pistol in the house, stashed in a heat vent in the floorboards. He's bringing it in for a ballistics match."

"He left it in the house?" Curtis said, shaking his head in disbelief. This was a gift, Walsh was a professional and should have melted the gun down.

"It was in the master bedroom and his wife was likely still in bed. Maybe he couldn't get to it."

"Think it's the one that killed Tony DeMarco?" Curtis asked. "It's the same caliber bullet."

"That's what we're hoping."

Curtis nodded. "This could tie him to DeMarco's murder."

"Yup."

"Call Bryan and tell him to make sure he follows protocol to a T getting the gun from Walsh's house to the forensics team."

"Bryan was all over that," Stan said. "He had it bagged and photographed at the scene, including the serial number. The seal on the bag will be intact when it arrives."

Curtis dropped into a chair next to Stan's desk and rubbed his temples, a migraine on the way. "We should have gone in the moment Aislinn put it together."

"Listen," Stan said. "It was four in the morning, she wasn't sure at that point, and we had no warrant. A good defense lawyer would have gotten anything we found thrown out."

"Yeah, I know. Still...could have staked out the house."

Stan pointed down the hall. "Aislinn's going to be sitting down with Kayla Walsh in about ten minutes."

Curtis shifted to thinking about the killer's daughter and what it had been like growing up with such a ruthless bastard for a father. "Let's sit in on that."

* * *

AISLINN SETTLED into the chair and looked across the table at Kayla and her fiancé. Mike had taken the plunge knowing what he was getting into – a woman with a sketchy past and three kids – but it was doubtful he'd imagined anything like this.

"You okay to do this?" Aislinn asked. Kayla's eyes were red and puffy, her posture that of someone beaten down. Mike wasn't much better.

"I'll be fine," she said quietly.

Aislinn went through the preamble, then said, "Did you ever suspect your father might be involved in anything illegal?"

She shook her head. "No."

"Was he ever violent at home?"

She squirmed a bit in the chair and stared at the table. "He got angry now and then, and was really rude to Mom sometimes. He seemed disinterested a lot of the time, perked up when our friends came over. We always put it down to the stress of the job." She looked up. "He wasn't abusive."

Aislinn made a quick note on her pad. Playing house was boring for him, but entertaining his daughter's friends pumped up his ego. Aislinn had considered applying to be a profiler before making the decision to push for detective, and had read a lot of department-issued articles on deviant behaviors. By now she was convinced Arnie Walsh had quite a few boxes under *narcissistic psychopath* checked off.

"Did he ever talk about some place he'd like to go – beaches in Florida, the Caribbean, golf courses in the Carolinas? Anything like that?"

"No, the only time he and Mom talked about anything outside Boston was a few times when we went on vacation. If he has another place somewhere I have no idea where that might be."

Aislinn looked down at the list of vacations they had taken as a family that Kayla had prepared. It was a short list – apparently family vacations hadn't been a priority over the years. "Nothing on here that stands out?"

"No."

"No favorites?"

"For Dad you mean?" she asked and Aislinn nodded. "No, he never said."

"Prom night – did he seem different? Stressed? Uptight?"

Tears pooled in her eyes and rolled down her cheeks. She used a tissue to dab them away. "I can't remember, Aislinn," she said, her voice cracking. She took a sip of water to get her voice back. "Did he really do this? Did he kill all those people?"

Aislinn studied the broken woman who had been her friend so many years ago. No one dreamed on prom night that their life would turn out like this. Growing up in the same house with a killer was something that happened on Netflix.

"Yes," Aislinn said calmly. "He did."

* * *

THE FOUR OF them met at Aislinn's desk after the interview was finished and Curtis said, "Anything there?"

"Nope, just another victim." Aislinn finally felt pity for her friend. It had been a long time coming.

"Yeah," Curtis said with resignation. He glanced over at Bryan. "You get Walsh's gun in for ballistics?"

"I did. The guys in the evidence room have already retrieved the bullets from DeMarco's file and ballistics has them. They're working on it now. We should know soon."

"I think we already know," Stan said.

"Well, let's make sure," Curtis reminded him. "Anything on Walsh's car?"

Stan shook his head. "Nope, and nothing on our APB either. He's dropped off the radar."

"Not unexpected," Curtis said. "No CCTV footage that can help us determine which direction he was heading?"

"Nothing," Stan said.

"So we have a suspect with the jump on us who knows exactly how law enforcement works, and who likely set up a safe house years ago. He's going to be hard to find."

Stan snorted. "It took seventeen years to find Whitey Bulger. Seventeen fucking years."

Bryan's phone pinged and all eyes went to him. He held up the incoming message and said, "It's a match. It's the gun that killed DeMarco."

"Cop killer," Aislinn said under her breath. "What a dirtbag."

CHAPTER FIFTY-TWO

The trail was completely cold.

Friday, July 9th – two weeks had passed since Curtis had given Angela Burton the story for *The Globe* and fielded the backlash. To his credit, Elian Perez had stood immediately behind Westcott at the media scrum and stepped forward to answer questions when pressed. As had Ted Dawson, Boston's chief of police. The angry response from the public was predictable, but it had faded in time and things were beginning to get back to normal.

Brandy flew in early on Friday morning and Curtis swung by Logan to pick her up, looking forward to a day off with Brandy and an evening of live theatre. It was his first weekend to himself since they had unmasked Arnie Walsh. The DNA from the rental car and Kristin Sanders' corpse had withstood further, more accurate testing – there was absolutely no doubt they had the right man in their crosshairs. But they still needed to find him.

* * *

"What a place," Brandy enthused as she and Curtis spilled out of the Emerson Colonial Theatre into the warm summer night. Boston's oldest theatre was a jewel box that had been restored to its former glory, and a wonderful venue to see *Twelve Angry Men*.

"It's pretty special," Curtis agreed.

"The actors were brilliant," she said, a lilt in her step. "If it hadn't been for the *one* juror who needed to be convinced, they would have convicted the wrong man."

Curtis smiled and glanced over at her, marveling at how beautiful she looked decked out in her evening wear. "I think as an audience we're supposed to be shocked by the cavalier attitude that the other eleven jurors have to the case, and that's why we immediately side with the holdout. Then the facts start to come into focus."

"And it turns out he's innocent."

Success, Curtis thought, pleased she'd appreciated his favorite play. They headed for home, strolling hand-in-hand through the dark streets, content simply to be in each other's company.

"Hey," Brandy mused. "Are you any closer to finding that Walsh character?"

Curtis grimaced at the mention of his name. "No, and we're running out of options. We found his car three days ago, a neighbor finally called it in after it had been sitting in front of their house for days, but that hasn't helped. Walsh parked it where there were no cameras, so we have no idea what he did after he dumped the car."

"He probably knows all this stuff from being a cop," she said.

"Yeah, he's a crafty one."

When they were almost back, they took a shortcut through the lane and Curtis unlatched the gate to his back yard. He saw the figure when they were halfway between the garage and the house. A man sitting in one of the patio chairs, his form silhouetted against the fence. Curtis's right hand instinctively went for his gun and he yanked Brandy in behind him as he leveled it at the figure.

"No need for that," the man said in a low voice.

Curtis kept the gun leveled and moved forward. He could see the man's hands sitting on the arms of the chair, and there was no weapon in sight. A bit of moonlight played off the man's face, and Curtis said, "Salvatore?"

"Yes."

Curtis glanced around for the gangsters' muscle, but the yard was empty. He kept himself between Brandy and Salvatore and crept closer. "What the hell are you doing here?"

Salvatore didn't move, not with a gun pointed at him. "We need to talk."

Curtis was within five feet now and anger was quickly overtaking the adrenaline rush. "What the fuck are you doing at my house?"

Salvatore merely pointed to a chair.

Curtis could feel his heart thumping in his chest as he tried to figure out where Brandy would be safest. He looked at the back door, Salvatore and his men may have already broken in. There could well be company inside – here, with him, was likely best.

Salvatore wagged a finger at Curtis. "I'm alone, I'm unarmed, and I'm not moving until you sit down and listen."

Curtis took another look at the scene. He didn't like it, not at all, but there was nothing to indicate Salvatore had brought men with him, and the aging gangster wasn't a danger with a gun pointed at him. He relaxed his grip on Brandy's arm and steered her gently toward a chair, then sat down beside her, the gun resting in his lap, still pointing at Salvatore.

"Okay," Curtis said. "I'm listening."

"It's important you understand," Salvatore said. "This conversation never happened. We never met."

Curtis nodded slowly. "Okay, confidential. We never met."

Salvatore pointed a finger at Brandy. "I need to hear that from your friend as well."

Curtis looked at her and nodded. Her voice was surprisingly calm, given the circumstance. "It's confidential. I never saw you."

"Arnie Walsh." Salvatore couldn't keep the emotion, the hate, out of his voice. "You want to find him."

"Of course we do."

Salvatore leaned forward slightly. "I know the name he's using now."

Curtis kept a stoic face, but his heart was racing. He slipped his gun back into its holster. "Who is he?"

Salvatore didn't respond immediately. Instead, he looked around the yard for a minute, then he settled back on Curtis. "Vincenzo had a nice yard. He liked to garden."

Curtis didn't say a word.

"My son should be here, Westcott. He should be alive, tending his flowers, dropping by for dinner."

Again, Curtis waited through another long bout of silence.

"The drugs he got busted with, the drugs that got him sent to jail, those weren't his. They were planted."

"Walsh?" Curtis asked.

Salvatore nodded. "Guys like us, we can do time, I understand that. But not for stuff we didn't do. That's not right."

"No," Curtis agreed. "It's not."

"Vincenzo should have been more careful inside. He shouldn't have messed with those MS-13 guys. They didn't care who he was, who his dad was, they got angry with him and they killed him."

A light went on and a door swung open in the adjacent yard. There were muffled voices, the sound of feet shuffling and a lid on the garbage bin banged open, then shut. The unseen neighbor returned to the house and the light went off.

"My only son, Westcott," Salvatore continued when the interruption was over. "Walsh got him killed."

Curtis looked the Italian in the eyes. "Payback time."

"Yeah, payback time."

The thin layer of cloud had moved off and the moonlight illuminated Salvatore's face. He looked older, frailer, Curtis thought. There was a moment when Curtis felt sympathy for the man, then it passed. Salvatore was, above all else, a gangster.

"We don't help the police," Salvatore said quietly. "Ever."

"Understood," Curtis said.

"Years ago a guy came to me about a cop who wanted fake ID. Really good stuff – expensive. The kind of work that could pass any level of scrutiny."

"Walsh, setting up a new life."

Salvatore nodded.

Curtis curled his fingers around the arm of the chair, he was so close.

Salvatore stood and smoothed his clothing. "Barry Caplan. The address on the ID was in Scottsdale, Arizona." He started for the back gate, then turned and said to Brandy, "I'm sorry if I startled you."

"It's okay," she said, smiling.

He smiled back, then shuffled across the back yard and let himself out into the alley. The gate closed behind him and the yard was silent and calm. Curtis took a few deep breaths and looked over at Brandy.

"You have a crazy life," she said, her eyes sparkling in the moonlight.

CHAPTER FIFTY-THREE

Curtis texted his detectives to meet at his house at seven o'clock on Saturday morning, and promptly on the hour all three of them pulled up to the curb in their respective cars. They sat in his sunny living room, waiting.

"What we talk about today stays here – inside this room." He let that sink in, then continued. "Arnie Walsh found out we were onto him and slipped through our fingers. Maybe he was being proactive, maybe he has a source inside the department. I don't know which, that's why we're meeting here today, not at the office."

"Got it," Stan said. Aislinn and Bryan both nodded.

"I had a visitor last night. I'm not going to say a name and expect the same of you, even if you're sure who it is. Understood?"

Heads bobbed up and down.

"It turns out Arnie Walsh set himself up with fake ID and a safe house years ago – Barry Caplan in Scottsdale, Arizona. We need to confirm his address and that he's still using that identity. I have a contact – AJ Costa – we touched base on a case a few years ago and he's excellent to work with. The kind of guy you can trust with a secret."

"So Walsh is in Phoenix," Aislinn said icily.

"Probably," Curtis replied. "He was all set up for exactly this reason."

"We need to move fast," Stan said.

Curtis nodded. "I'll reach out to AJ and once he's sure Walsh is there, Aislinn and I will head for Scottsdale." He looked at Aislinn and said, "We'll charge our plane tickets to our personal VISA cards, same for hotel reservations. Nothing goes through the department, and we need to be ready to move on a moment's notice."

"What about things on the other end?" Bryan asked. "Will Walsh figure out we're on to him if Costa starts poking around?"

Curtis shook his head. "I doubt it. There's no reason for him to have an inside track with the Phoenix or Scottsdale police. We should be fine, Costa knows how to keep his head down."

"Okay," Bryan said.

"But we need someone in Phoenix to do the legwork and confirm that Walsh is there," Curtis continued. "Until we have that, we keep our wings tucked in and out of sight."

"So we sit on our hands," Stan said.

"Basically, yes." Curtis shifted a bit to get more comfortable. "Go through the motions, keep the investigation moving ahead by following up the leads on Walsh's car and any other threads you have on the go."

"You really think we have a leak? Someone feeding Walsh information?" Stan asked.

Curtis tried to mask his anger, but wasn't very successful. "I don't know. Like I said, we keep things between us for now. Getting Walsh is our priority."

He stood up and pointed to the door. "Go home, enjoy the weekend."

Stan got up, then stopped, his face deadly serious. "What about him?" he said, pointing. "You sure he's not our leak?"

Everyone looked at Barclay, curled up in a large ball in his dog bed. Barclay sensed the attention and lifted his head, saw the smiles and pulled himself up, ready for a treat or a belly rub, whichever came first.

"He's good," Curtis laughed. "Vetted him through PAW Patrol."

They filed out with smiles pasted on their faces, and Curtis sat on the ledge by the window and pulled out his phone. AJ Costa's personal number was in his contacts list and Curtis glanced at his watch. It was too early to call Arizona and he tucked the phone in his pocket. Time to make Brandy some breakfast.

* * *

AJ Costa was relaxing under an umbrella by his pool watching the Arizona sun bake the golfers on the fairway behind his house when his phone rang. He checked the caller ID – Curtis Westcott.

He tapped the green button. "Curtis, how are things in Boston?"

"Excellent," Curtis replied. "And Phoenix?"

"Couldn't be better, my friend. It's been a few years. What's up?"

"Working a case and I could use a bit of help."

AJ grinned at that and sipped his mid-morning coffee. "I'm retired. Called it a day about three years ago."

"How's that going?" Curtis asked, disappointed. Costa was an A-list contact and now he was gone.

"Get up when I want, golf all the time, and hey, I just met this gorgeous woman at the airport. Pretty damn good, I'd have to say."

Curtis laughed. "Oh, I wish."

He watched Brandy as she used her hip to push open the back door, two plates loaded with salad in her hands, Barclay close on her heels. She sat in the chair next to his, her foot tapping to the soft music playing on the deck.

"Careful what you wish for," AJ continued. "It gets boring. I still like to wiggle my toes into things."

"What sort of things?" Curtis asked.

"Long story, my friend. I'll fill you in later. Right now you need someone you can trust in Phoenix."

"Our guy is in Scottsdale, actually."

"Annette Carter," AJ responded. "She's in Scottsdale and there's no one better. I'll make the introduction."

"That would be great," Curtis said.

"She should call this number?" AJ asked. "Your personal cell?"

"Please, discretion is necessary," Curtis said.

"My middle name."

"Thanks, AJ."

"No problem. Hey, maybe we could hook up for a beer when you're in town, if you have time."

Curtis thought about that and said, "It might work, no guarantees though. I could always make another trip. There's a very special friend in Napa and it's a short flight to Phoenix from there." He gave Brandy a wink.

She gave him the nicest smile ever.

"Sure," AJ said.

Curtis wrapped it up. "I'll watch for Carter's call."

He set the phone on the table and touched her arm. Her skin was warm and wonderful and sent a chill up his spine. He looked forward to the weekends that started with a trip to Logan, and that first glimpse of her walking through the arrival doors. Yes, he really loved these weekends.

She picked up her fork but let it dawdle over the plate. "Your life is pretty trippy, and you work crazy hours."

"You think?" he asked, worry creeping in.

She poked a cherry tomato with her fork and popped it in her mouth. "I kinda like it. Never boring."

"That's good – I guess." He dug into lunch, not really sure.

Annette Carter called two hours after Curtis spoke with AJ and listened intently while he gave her the backstory on the case. Presented in bullet points, it was one ugly narrative.

"So Walsh is a cop killer," Carter said after listening and taking notes. "Ballistics was rock solid on the DeMarco murder?"

"One hundred percent," Curtis said. "But keep in mind that DeMarco was dirty. More like Walsh killed his partner in crime than another cop."

"Yeah, I suppose." She paused, then said, "The first thing we need to do is establish whether he's at the address you gave me."

"Right, that's what we're hoping you can help with," Curtis said. "If he is we would really like him back."

"Of course," she said. "I don't want him here."

"Thanks, Detective Carter."

"Annette is fine."

"As is Curtis."

"Let's see," Carter said, thinking through the timeline. The longer she let Walsh move about, the more chance there was for him to do something stupid. And that would be on her if it got out that she knew he was in town and didn't move on him. "It's Saturday. I'll get some eyes on the condo and if he's there we'll take him down. I don't want him pulling some shit on my watch."

"Okay, I'll send you what we have right away," Curtis said. "Walsh likely has a beard or at least some serious stubble. He was letting it grow before he legged it."

"Good to know," she said.

They ended the call and Curtis set his phone on the table. Brandy watched him start in on the salad. "Are you going to Phoenix?"

He shrugged. "Probably. If Walsh is there I'll fly out."

Worry lines creased her brow. "He's killed five people, Curtis."

It wasn't hard to see where her train of thought was going. He shifted his chair closer to hers and held her hand. "We're trained in this sort of thing. And Carter will bring in the SWAT guys to flush him out, so I'll be in the background." He squeezed her hand a bit tighter. "Considering how much time we put in, it's rare that cops get hurt on the job."

"Still..."

He looked down at their hands, entwined and completely comfortable. "I'll be careful."

CHAPTER FIFTY-FOUR

Annette Carter was having trouble confirming whether Arnie Walsh was in Scottsdale.

Her team reported that they had spotted a man leaving the condo mid-morning and followed him to a nearby coffee shop. He sat at a secluded outdoor table drinking a medium dark roast and read the newspaper for forty-five minutes, then returned to the complex and surfed the pool deck, talking to most of the ladies. He had a neatly trimmed beard, never appeared in public without dark sunglasses, and favored designer clothing, including a fedora he kept pulled tight to the glasses. A series of grainy photos taken with a high-power zoom lens accompanied the report.

Carter sent them to Curtis's email on Tuesday afternoon and even Westcott was unable to confirm it was Walsh. The man, if it was him, had changed his look significantly. Curtis followed it up with a phone call to Carter an hour later.

"So you're not sure," Carter said when the call connected.

"No," Curtis said. "Can you get his fingerprints?"

"We're hoping he goes back to the coffee shop. We'll be in position to grab his cup before the server gets it."

"Are you ready to move on him?" Curtis asked.

"Fresh meat," Carter replied. "The SWAT guys are frothing at the mouth on this one."

"Got it," Curtis laughed. The special forces in Boston were high octane as well.

"Do you want to be here when it goes down?" Carter asked.

"I'd like to, if that's possible."

"I can set it up. Just you?" Carter asked.

"I'd like to bring one other detective – Aislinn Byrne."

"Byrne – Aislinn," she repeated as she made a note. "You'll need to move fast once we confirm it's him – get me your flight details and I'll pick you up at Sky Harbor."

"Right," Curtis said. "How's the layout of the condo? Anything that might be a problem?"

"It has some quirks," Carter responded. "There are about thirty apartment-style buildings in the center of the complex, which is surrounded by a golf course, villas and some single family homes. His place is in the middle of the apartments and there are numerous entry and exit doors. I think SWAT wants to go in early, before he's up."

"Got it," Curtis said.

Curtis hung up and headed for Aislinn's cubicle. She was at her desk and lit up when Curtis told her Annette Carter was okay with them being on site when her team moved in on Walsh. All they needed now was confirmation it was him.

"Book your ticket on your own computer and use your personal credit card," Curtis reminded her. "Just in case Walsh has someone inside the department."

"Agreed," Aislinn replied, fuming at the thought that Walsh might have a partner. "Can I tell my dad we found him?"

Curtis nodded. "Just that, and only him. Nothing else. No location. Nothing."

Aislinn checked the time, then packed up and called it a day. She drove to her parents' house, parked on the street and strode up the sidewalk, ready to tell the one person she could trust that they had

Arnie Walsh in their sights. Her father was dozing in a lounger under the shade of a mature elm and she tapped him on the arm.

"Hey, Aislinn," Cian said, waking up and rubbing his eyes. "Must have drifted off."

"Yeah, the rigors of retirement." She dropped into the lounger next to his. "I could get used to afternoon naps."

"Nah, you couldn't." He was awake now. "What's up?"

"Arnie Walsh," she said and watched his face go dark. "Not a word to anyone, Dad, not even Ken and Larry."

"Not a word."

"We might have found him." She sat back and watched the anger and rage build under the thick skin he'd grown from all those years on the job.

"How?" he asked.

"Sorry, can't say."

"You're sure it's him?"

"Just waiting on confirmation." She leaned forward, a hard look on her face. "We're going to get him, Dad."

Aislinn could hear his teeth grinding together. "All those years, sitting with us, drinking, laughing. Pretending he was one of the boys."

Aislinn didn't say a word.

"Son of a bitch used us. Rotten to the core."

"He fooled everyone," Aislinn said. "It's not your fault you didn't see what he was."

"What he *is*," Cian said. "He's not past tense, A. He's still out there."

"Not for long," she said.

He gave her a long look. "Careful what you do if you get him in your sights. Don't let your emotions get the best of you."

She shook her head. "I'm okay. I'm not his executioner." A long silence followed, then she added, "He'll pay."

Cian's face was still a deep shade of red. "I know Tony was dirty, Aislinn, but Walsh gunned him down in cold blood."

Her father's rage for Tony's killing was partially lost on her. In her eyes Tony was equally culpable in his death. Still, she leaned in and grabbed his shoulder and squeezed.

Aislinn's touch calmed him, and after a minute he said, "He's Kayla's dad for Christ's sake. You were at his house, hanging out, swimming in his pool when he was out murdering Alexi and Tony and Darina."

That *wasn't* lost on her. She could have been on a slab if she'd noticed something that threatened him. "Yeah, I know. It's creepy."

"Just get the bastard," he said quietly.

Aislinn drove to Arnold Arboretum, parked near Oak Path and started walking. Summer had settled in and the air was warm and moist, the trees thick with vibrant green leaves. An occasional walker passed by, but mostly she was alone with her thoughts. Dominating them was Darina, who she had been, what she might have done with her life if Arnie Walsh hadn't stolen it. And Kayla – Aislinn wondered if she could ever come to grips with who and what her father was. So many lives torn apart by a man with little, if any, empathy or compassion. A monster hidden in plain sight.

Twenty minutes into her hike she phoned Cody Hall and he answered on the third ring. "Just thought I'd call to see how you're doing."

"Great, actually," he said. "Nice to hear your voice."

"Working on a video game?" she asked.

"You know it." He chuckled, then said, "I'm sketching out the bad guys."

"Well, the user has to hate the bad guy or it's all a waste of time," she said, her mind drifting back to Arnie Walsh.

"Hey, what are you up to on the weekend? Maybe we could hang out, take a walk by the harbor or something."

"I'd love to, but I might be heading out of town on short notice."

"Okay," he said, a touch of disappointment in his voice. "Everything all right?"

"Yeah, all good. I'll take a rain check on that walk. Just called to say hi."

“Excellent.” He sounded pleased by that. “Call me when you’re back.”

“Sure will.”

She slipped the phone in her pocket and forced herself to think of Cody and his infectious smile and kind eyes. Arnie Walsh had been living in her head for too long now and it was time to exorcise him. He faded as she ambled along the path, taking a rare moment just for herself.

CHAPTER FIFTY-FIVE

The wait was excruciating and now it was over. Carter had called – the surveillance team got their hands on a coffee mug Walsh used and the prints matched. SWAT had decided that early Saturday morning would be the best time to kick in Walsh's door – maybe they could catch him sleeping.

Curtis and Aislinn grabbed tickets on a Friday afternoon flight and now Phoenix spread out below them like a patchy brown rug on a sandy floor. Bits of bright green, golf courses and parks, punctuated the desert city like jewels shining through the shimmering heat waves. They landed and retrieved their luggage, then went in search of Annette Carter. They found her waiting near the exit with another detective holding a WESTCOTT sign.

Carter was the same age as Aislinn, with short dark hair and a serious expression. She greeted them and managed a quick smile, then pointed toward the doors. A blast of hot air hit them full on the moment they stepped outside.

"My oven barely gets this hot," Aislinn said as they walked toward a waiting car.

"Summer in Phoenix," Carter said.

"I'll take Boston." Curtis put his suitcase in the open trunk. "Sure would be nice in the winter though."

"Heaven," Carter said.

Once they were moving, Carter said, "We found a nice hotel for you – the Scott Resort – only a few minutes from Walsh's place."

"Nice."

Carter drove with Curtis in the front seat, past rows of palm trees that fronted mile after mile of houses and strip malls, all basking in the evening sun. She accompanied them in to make sure the reservations were in place, and once they were checked in she led them down a short corridor to a meeting room and closed the door.

"Here's what we're up against." Carter spread a map of Walsh's condo development on the table and kept her voice low. "The complex has a large footprint, with numerous four-story buildings surrounding a central pool and cabana area. It's pretty upscale, large units with balconies, and it sides onto a golf course."

"Where is Walsh's unit?" Curtis asked.

Carter stabbed at the map. "He has an interior unit that overlooks the pool. Ground floor, so it's a bit easier for us, but it also gives him one more exit from the unit."

"Out the sliding doors onto the grounds," Curtis said.

"Right, and there's one more possible exit." Carter traced a series of dashed lines with her finger. "These are tunnels running under the complex that house the HVAC and electrical conduits. It's unusual to put mechanical components underground in Phoenix because of the caliche, but that wasn't a problem here."

"Caliche?" Curtis asked.

"Calcium carbonate, and it's all through the soil in the valley. It bonds to gravel and sand – like a natural cement – that's why there are very few basements." She pulled out another page from under the pile that had colorful contour lines on it. "The condo is overtop an area of moderate caliche, so it would have been fairly easy to dig."

"Can he get into the tunnels?" Curtis asked.

Carter shook her head. "Highly unlikely. Access is only through heavy metal doors with solid locks, and we'll be watching the tunnel exits."

"Okay."

Carter tapped the map in three places, where someone had drawn yellow dots. "We have surveillance teams watching him from these vantage points, getting a feel for his routine."

"Any chance he's onto you?" Aislinn asked.

Carter shook her head. "Not yet, and we're being extremely careful to stay out of sight. So far your guy is pretty predictable." A disgusted expression washed over her face. "He's all over the ladies. Goes down to the pool every day with a drink and struts around. He's the pink flamingo at the pool."

"Yeah," Aislinn said. "The one who cleaned out the bank accounts and left a wife and family back in Boston." The look on her face mirrored Carter's.

"He's had some luck with the women, and that complicates things," Carter continued. "We'd like it if he's alone when we go in. We're keeping a close eye on him tonight. The good thing is that he's predictable. If he's home alone by nine, that's it for the night."

"And if he has someone with him?" Aislinn asked.

Carter didn't hesitate. "We ask SWAT – nicely – *not* to take her out."

"Well, let's hope he isn't too charming tonight," Aislinn said, knowing they would do exactly the same thing in Boston. "We're good to go tomorrow morning?"

"We are."

"Anything else we need to run over?"

"No, I think we're good. I'd like to have both of you hang back in case he comes out before we're ready and recognizes you."

"Good thinking," Curtis said.

"Will we have a line of sight on the condo?" Aislinn asked.

"Yes," Carter said slowly, then added. "We want Curtis to stay at the command center, but you could take a position on the far east side of the complex. One of the tunnel doors exits there. I could use the extra manpower."

Aislinn nodded, glad to be part of the team. "Of course."

"Sunrise is 5:31 tomorrow morning," Carter said, rolling up her drawings. "SWAT is moving into place at 4:45 while it's still dark. I'll have a car here to pick you up at 4:30. See you tomorrow." It was clear they were to be ready.

As they waited for the elevator, Aislinn checked out the pool and announced that she was all in for a swim. "Never get to do this in Boston. No pool at my house."

"Okay," Curtis said. "AJ Costa is going to drop by, so I'll be in the bar."

"Who?" Aislinn asked.

Curtis just grinned. "Retired homicide cop from Phoenix. Bit of a character."

* * *

AJ SWAGGERED INTO THE BAR, eyes flicking left then right, sizing up the place. He spotted Curtis, gave a small wave and headed over. He wore faded jeans, sandals, and a Robert Graham shirt. The clothes suited the man, athletic with shoulder-length blond hair and a well-manicured beard.

"Curtis," AJ said, sitting so he had a view of the palm-lined pool where Aislinn was swimming laps.

"AJ, how are things?"

"Couldn't be better." He ordered a beer and eyed up Curtis. "You look good. Boston must be an easy ride."

"Oh, please." Curtis watched as the server, an attractive woman in her thirties, set AJ's beer on the table and gave him a smile. "Thanks for setting me up with Carter."

AJ grinned, a bit like Peter Rabbit eyeing up a carrot patch. "Carter, she's one tough woman. Her and I have had our differences."

"Well, she has everything set to go." Curtis measured AJ for a minute, then asked. "Do you miss it?"

"What? The guns, the bad guys, the lies, the totally unhealthy lifestyle?" He waited a moment, then said, "Of course I do. But not enough to come back."

Aislinn finished her laps, pulled herself out of the pool and adjusted her two piece. She walked over to a chaise lounge, picked up a towel and gave the top of her head a good rub. Her short, red hair popped up like pins in a cushion.

"Now there," AJ said, "is a drip dry girl."

"Um, yeah. Aislinn Byrne, one of my detectives."

AJ wasn't deterred. "I might put in an application."

"Cold in the winter," Curtis said.

"Hmmm." He got a pained look on his face and shook his head. "I'm out."

AJ was gone by the time Aislinn had dressed and checked her email. She sat in the chair overlooking the pool and asked, "Was that Costa?"

Curtis hadn't noticed her looking their way. "Yeah, that was AJ."

"Retired, is he?" she said and he nodded. "Doesn't look like any of the retired cops I know."

"He joined the department at nineteen and put in his twenty-five years." Curtis explained.

"What's he like?" she asked.

Curtis smiled. "Never really learned that the rules apply to him, not just everyone else."

"Interesting guy."

"You have no idea." Curtis waved at the server. "He had some advice before he left."

"What?"

"He said no matter how hot it gets, always wear your vest."

She thought about it. "That probably comes from experience."

"Likely does," Curtis agreed.

The night air was warm and dry, and strings of tiny lights wrapped around palm trunks twinkled in the dusk. It felt tropical, like they were relaxing at a Caribbean resort without a care in the world.

"Budweiser, please," Aislinn said as the server approached.

"Same," Curtis said. He took in Aislinn's beachy look. "A new side to you Detective Byrne."

"I've been to Phoenix before and fried in the heat. I promise not to wear these tomorrow."

Curtis grinned. "I'm not worried."

The drinks arrived and Aislinn nodded a thank you. "Tomorrow," she said. "Tomorrow we take down a very bad hombre."

Curtis held up his drink and they clinked bottles. "Phoenix SWAT takes him down, then we get him."

"Walsh is going to find things rather inhospitable when he gets back to Boston." Aislinn could only imagine what jail was going to look like for him. "My dad feels…" she searched for the right word. "… betrayed. So will Larry and Ken when they find out Walsh was using them."

"I think we were all blindsided," Curtis said.

Aislinn picked at the label on the bottle. "We *all* liked him. He was Kayla's dad and a cop, and he was super friendly. I actually felt safe when I was at her house." She stopped working on the label and looked at Curtis. "He'd always hang out when we were swimming. Then he turns around and *kills* one of us, just like that." She snapped her fingers. "It's so creepy."

"More than creepy," Curtis said. "Much more."

"Yeah." She set her bottle down firmly in the center of a coaster and changed the subject. "On a positive note, I managed to reconnect with a couple of old friends."

"Like Cody Hall," Curtis said without looking at her.

She caught the slight edge in his voice and studied his profile. "You caught that?" she asked.

He nodded. "I had your back – would have stepped in if things started going the wrong direction, but I never pegged him for being involved." He glanced at her. "From what I've seen, he's a good guy."

"I think so too," she said, grinning.

CHAPTER FIFTY-SIX

Arnie Walsh had always been an early riser. It had served him well.

Running the rackets with Tony DeMarco while holding a full-time job as a staff sergeant demanded it, and he used the time before anyone else was awake to total the previous day's take. The numbers were what made everything worthwhile – thousands of dollars in cash every week. After two years building a considerable stash, he'd dumped the lot in a gym bag and driven to Arizona to find a suitable condo in case he had to make a run for it.

It had to be a condo, a place that he could lock the door and leave without having any worries about cutting the grass or fixing a leaking pipe. But not any condo would do – he needed one with a way out in case he was trapped.

He'd found exactly that just off North Hayden Road in Scottsdale – a cluster of upscale apartment-style buildings linked together by an underground system of tunnels. A single locked door on the main floor of his building led to an underground labyrinth filled with pipes, boilers and compressors. There were similar doors from the other buildings, almost thirty of them, some leading directly outside.

Getting a copy of the key to the heavy metal door had been easy once enough cash was on the table.

Today, it looked like that precaution had been a crucial one. Walsh was up at 5:30 with the lights off, brewing the first coffee of the day when he saw a shadow move between the buildings. He froze in the darkness and kept his eyes glued to the spot. A minute later the shadow shifted slightly and for a split second Walsh could see the thick outline of a gun barrel against the light-colored stucco walls.

He knew the gun – a Heckler & Koch MP5 machine gun – preferred weapon for specialized police squads due to its short barrel and 800 rounds per minute fire rate. The figure holding it wasn't moving more than a few inches – he had his position and was holding.

A SWAT team was setting up.

Walsh jogged across the floor and up the stairs to his bedroom and slipped on dark clothes. He shouldered a small pack with stacks of hundred dollar bills and tucked a Glock pistol in his waistband. Less than a minute later he was at the entrance to the suite, his mind racing. *How many boots were on the ground? Were they already in the building? Did they have the perimeter set? Were they watching the exit doors from the tunnels?* Questions he didn't have answers to.

"Fuck," he whispered, anger threatening to take over. He knew exactly who was responsible for this. "Byrne, you fucking bitch."

Walsh sucked in a deep breath, then opened the door noiselessly and took a quick look out into the hallway. The corridor was clear, SWAT was still setting up a perimeter and hadn't moved inside the building yet. He pulled out the Glock and moved fast, pistol leveled and ready to fire. He reached the end of the corridor without making a sound. There was a fire door and he opened it slowly, then peered around the corner. Nothing. Walsh pulled a key out of his trouser pocket, crept the few feet to the maintenance door on his toes and slipped the key in the lock. He swallowed hard – if they had men in the tunnel he would be trapped. The key turned and the door opened. The tunnel ahead was empty and he breathed a bit easier.

Walsh locked the door silently behind him and walked down the narrow passage, arms extended, pistol at chest height, his finger pressing lightly on the trigger. He reached a large room that housed mechanical equipment and wound his way through the machinery to the entrance to the next tunnel, all the while moving toward the edge of the complex.

He wanted to exit the tunnel system at the most northerly point, on the golf course and close to Sundown Drive. Once he crossed a short stretch of fairway he would be into a subdivision with estate homes on large lots. One of them was under construction and it would be easy to cut through the yard and come out on Cortez Road. From there he had a twenty minute walk to where he kept a second car tucked away in a rented garage.

Walsh kept up the quick pace until he came to the final door on the north side of the complex. He inched it open and glanced both ways. The first rays of daylight were pushing through the dark of the night and he could see much better now. The bushes surrounding the building were thick with leaves and it was tough to discern whether there were SWAT troops crouched behind them. Eventually Walsh slipped through the door and it latched behind him. He was committed now, no going back.

He took the stairs one at a time, stepped up into the faint daylight and took a long, hard look around. There was nothing to indicate a police presence. They were focused on the center of the complex, some distance to the south, and he was well out of their line of sight. A couple of residents walked past and said good morning and he responded in kind, then he started across the road and onto the golf course. There were no golfers yet and he walked at a pace that wouldn't draw attention until he reached the open lot where the new house was under construction. He checked his watch – 6:20 – and made his way by the Bobcat and piles of lumber, then scaled the construction fence at the rear of the property and started walking down Cortez Road.

"Take that you stupid fuckers," he hissed under his breath.

* * *

AISLINN WAS WAITING when Curtis came into the hotel lobby at twenty after four. She was dressed in dark pants, black shirt and a snug bulletproof vest. Her gun was in a holster strapped to her belt, as were a set of handcuffs. The desk clerk was keeping his distance from her.

"Nice look," Curtis said as he joined her. "Remember, we're the B-team."

"Just in case," she said.

A car swept up the dark driveway, its lights momentarily blinding them, and pulled up under the lit portico. They could see two uniformed officers in the front seat, one of whom opened the door and asked if they were Westcott and Byrne, then motioned for them to get in. The streets were empty, and Aislinn stared out the window as they drove alongside a long line of palm trees silhouetted against the sky. *So beautiful*, she thought, but here they were with guns strapped on heading to meet a fully armed SWAT team.

"Cities, they all have a dark side," she said quietly.

"Yeah," Curtis responded, like he was thinking the same thing.

Carter was standing beside an unmarked car tucked in behind some bushes next to a fairway on the golf course. Two other cars were parked close by, lights off.

"Morning," she said as they approached. "The SWAT guys closest to Walsh's condo have already moved into position and are waiting. The perimeter force is getting set now. We're moving things up to 6:30, there should be less civilians out then."

"Good thinking," Curtis said.

Carter took a couple of steps out from behind the bushes and pointed to a large conglomeration of three- and four-story buildings a couple of blocks away. "That's the complex. I thought Curtis could stay here at the command center and Aislinn could cover one of the tunnel exits on the north end," she said.

"Where's his unit?" Curtis asked.

Carter pointed to the dark outline of an apartment block. "In the second building from this end, just behind that one."

"Will you and I have a visual on it," Curtis asked.

"No, but we'll be in constant contact with SWAT over the radio."

Carter motioned for one of the officers to come over. She produced a map of the subdivision and pointed to a black circle. "Take Detective Byrne to this location. Lights off, no visual contact with the complex at any time during the drive."

"Got it," the man said.

Carter handed Aislinn a portable radio. "Battery's fully charged and it's set to the right channel."

She clipped it onto her belt. "Thanks."

Aislinn slipped into the car and they drove in silence until they reached the spot Carter had indicated on the map. "That's the north edge of the complex?" she asked, pointing to some multi-story buildings visible over a line of villas and the golf course.

"It is," he said.

"I'm going to move in a bit closer." She slipped her iPhone into her back pocket. He looked like he was going to object, but she gave him a look that shut him down on the spot.

Aislinn lowered the volume on the radio by touch and started walking, taking in the lay of the land as she moved. The villas between her and the apartments were single-story bungalows that impeded her view of the street. She needed to get around them so they didn't obscure Walsh's complex, and she ducked off the road onto the golf course using the shrubs and trees as cover to move closer. The road she was paralleling cut around the villas and led to a gate on the north side with a clear line of sight on the complex. Aislinn kept in the shadows on the golf course and moved as close as possible without exposing herself. She settled in behind a thick shrub when it was impossible to get any closer.

She switched her phone to silent and checked the magazine in her gun, then got into a comfortable position, eyes on the complex. She glanced at her watch – 5:40 – a while yet until SWAT moved in. The sun had crested the horizon, bringing with it early morning shadows that were long and deceiving – possible cover for someone trying to escape. She squinted slightly to bring the building into perfect focus.

A slight motion caught her eye and she concentrated on it. A man appeared from behind a low row of shrubs, his body rising slightly with each step. He was coming up a flight of stairs. Aislinn stiffened and squinted harder, watching him as he started walking away from the building. The angle was wrong and she couldn't see much of his face, just a bit of his profile. He was dressed in dark clothing and had a small backpack, not what a maintenance worker would wear. From what she could see there was no insignia on his shirt and he wasn't wearing work boots. The only reason someone would be coming from the basement area of the building was if they were working on the equipment, and nothing about him indicated that was the case.

The man nodded good morning to a couple he passed, then crossed the road and ducked into the golf course, dropping out of sight as he walked down an incline toward the green. He was definitely not dressed for golf and Aislinn slunk out from behind the bushes and ran in his direction. She kept low, her knees driving hard, back bent. Her legs were burning by the time she reached the point where he had entered the golf course. She slipped behind a bush for cover and peeked over the top of the leaves. Her target was still moving and was off the golf course and crossing a street. He reached the other side, glanced back for a few seconds, then turned and started walking down the sidewalk. The moment he disappeared behind a house, Aislinn unclipped her radio and called it in.

"Possible sighting of suspect," she said and waited for a response. Nothing. She glanced down at the controls and swore under her breath. It was a different model than they used in Boston and when she had tried to decrease the volume she had changed the channel. Carter hadn't told her what channel they were on and it would take too long to figure it out. She considered calling Curtis on his cell, but needed to get moving and decided against it. The radio was useless to her and she dropped it on the grass and started out.

She ran hard, covering the distance between her and the street in less than a minute, slowing as she reached the sidewalk. She took a quick look up the street but he was nowhere in sight. She started walking, taking in the houses on both sides, but concentrating on the far side of the road. There was no reason for him to double back and cut through one of the yards, that would put him back on the golf course. The street was long enough that he would still be in sight if he hadn't ducked in somewhere, which meant he had cut through a yard. A vacant lot with the piles of lumber caught her eye and she cut across the road and tucked up close to the house next door. She peeked around the corner and caught a brief glimpse of him on the other side of a metal construction fence before he turned and was gone.

Aislinn raced through the site and scaled the fence. She grabbed the top and hoisted one leg over, then the other. She let go, her feet solidly under her, but her vest caught on the wobbly metal fence and jerked her sideways. She landed heavily on her hip and heard a sickening crunching sound – her phone. The screen was smashed, broken almost in two, and nothing happened when she hit the power button. She threw it aside and stood, running her hand down her side, feeling for pain. Nothing. Her phone was the only casualty.

Aislinn hustled up to a spot where she could see down the street. The man was a block away and walking at a reasonable clip. She waited until he rounded a slight curve in the road and was out of sight, then started jogging. She reached the bend and looked ahead. The road branched, straightaway was a cul-de-sac and to the right was a stretch of a few hundred yards before a ninety-degree turn. He was nowhere in sight.

"Fuck," she whispered, standing in the middle of the road looking both ways.

A voice cut through the early morning silence. "He went down there."

She spun and saw a woman between two houses putting yard waste in her compost bin. She pointed down the street with the sharp bend. "You just missed him. He went around the corner." Her eyes were on Aislinn's vest and gun.

"Thanks," Aislinn said and started off at a good clip.

Another stretch of road came into view when she reached the bend, but there was no one in sight. She kept walking, looking into the yards on either side, her hand close to her gun and cursing herself for smashing her phone. The houses here were more modest and the lots smaller than by the golf course, providing an almost endless number of nooks and crannies for Walsh to duck into.

If it was Walsh.

She still hadn't got a decent look at the man she was following and was starting to wonder if it was a homeowner out for a morning walk. Ahead of her a garage door began to rise and she angled off to the side of the street. A car backed out and the man driving looked both ways. When he turned toward Aislinn they both froze.

Walsh.

Her hand went for her gun as he hit the gas. The car bounced hard over the curb as it backed out, the bumper scraping on the asphalt. Walsh spun the wheel so he was facing away from Aislinn and she saw the backup lights go off. She dropped to her knees, aimed and fired one round. The rear window exploded, sending bits of tempered glass flying through the car causing Walsh to oversteer as he ducked down. The vehicle veered sharply to one side, coming up on two tires before righting itself. She shifted slightly and fired again, the bullet smashing through the windshield above the steering wheel. Walsh spun the wheel and this time it was too fast for the speed he was traveling. The car went up on two wheels and flipped on its side, then rolled and slid down the road before coming to rest on its roof.

Aislinn was up and running now. Walsh crawled out of the smashed driver's side window, gun in hand. He flopped onto his belly and fired, the shot missing Aislinn by inches. She took aim and squeezed the trigger. There was a puff inches from his head, and Walsh winced in pain as tiny fragments of asphalt peppered his face. He wiped the blood from his eyes, aimed and got off another shot. It hit her square in the chest and she spun sideways and crashed to the ground.

The pain was excruciating and she could barely catch her breath. She took a quick look – no blood. She rolled hard across the asphalt, scraping her bare arms as another bullet screamed by her head. Aislinn crawled behind a bush, out of sight but still vulnerable to his fire. Her body was screaming with pain from the impact of the bullet and even the shallowest breath was a bolt of fire. She flattened herself, hugging the ground, and took a bead on him as he brought the gun around for another shot. She fired and saw his body convulse as the slug tore into him. His gun skittered across the road and she risked a look.

Walsh was lying in a broken heap, his chest rapidly rising and falling. Both his hands were empty and Aislinn jumped up from her cover and closed the distance between them quickly, watching his hands in case he went for a hidden weapon. She got within a few feet and slowed. He was staring up at her, struggling to breathe. Aislinn unclasped her handcuffs and dropped onto him with her knee, flipping him over on his stomach. She snapped on the cuffs, then gave him a rough push and he rolled over onto his back.

People were coming out into the street, watching from a distance. The closest bystander was a woman with a phone and Aislinn pulled out her badge and held it up.

"Police. I need your phone." She pointed at a man close by, also with a phone in hand. "Call 911. Tell them *shots fired* and give them the address."

She met the woman about halfway, all the while keeping an eye on Walsh. "Move back," she said once she had the phone, then dialed Curtis's cell.

"Aislinn," he said when he answered. "We have a report of shots fired and we tried you on the radio but got no response. Are you at the scene?"

"I am. Radio got messed up," she shot back in quick bursts. "I got the son-of-a-bitch. Situation is under control. Send the ambulance."

"We've got your location and we're on our way. TEMS is with us."

"Right." She killed the call. TEMS was the Technical Emergency Medical ambulance that always accompanies a SWAT team. Basically, they were the best there was.

Aislinn lowered the phone and walked the few feet back to Arnie Walsh. Her second shot had caught him between the shoulder and the chest, likely hitting the lung. He was in rough shape, but would probably live. She knelt down and stared in his eyes.

"You fucker," she spat. "You lowlife piece of shit."

He didn't answer, just glared at her with unabashed hate.

Aislinn was inches from him now. "You and your Dean Martin act, always the cool guy." She lowered her knee slightly so it pushed against the bullet wound, and his eyes widened with pain. "I wonder how that's going to play out in jail."

"Oh, fuck, that hurts," he wheezed.

"You're nothing," she whispered. "Just a broken, pathetic, little man."

She let off the pressure on his wound.

"I was aiming for your heart," she said. "But I don't think you have one."

A cacophony of sirens increased as cars came around the corner from both directions, lights on and moving fast. They screeched to a halt a hundred feet back and bodies piled out, some moving directly toward Aislinn, some establishing a perimeter. The cavalry had arrived.

She stood up and held her badge so the approaching cops could see, then holstered her gun and scanned the crowd for Curtis. He was out of his car and jogging, skirting the first line of cars with Annette Carter right beside him. They got within twenty feet and slowed to a walk, intent on watching Walsh being frisked for additional weapons.

"You okay?" Curtis asked, staring at the flattened bullet embedded in her vest.

"Yeah, good thing I had this on." She thought of AJ's advice - *no matter how hot it gets, always wear your vest* – the guy knew what he was talking about.

"Jesus," Carter said. "That was lucky."

The TEMS ambulance navigated its way through the phalanx of squad cars and two EMTs jumped out. They started in on Walsh, first with an IV, then loading him into the vehicle. An armed detective got in the back with the EMTs and the doors slammed shut. It raced off to the hospital, two other cars following close behind.

A modicum of silence settled over the street when the sound of the siren had faded, and Carter turned to Aislinn. "What happened? How did he slip out on us?"

"He came out a maintenance door. It didn't seem right, he wasn't dressed in work clothes, so I followed him. Couldn't call it in, radio got switched to the wrong channel and I smashed my phone going over a fence." She ripped at the Velcro, grasping at her chest as the vest fell away. "Oh, that hurts."

"Do you need an ambulance?" Carter asked.

"No, I need a drink. I don't care if it's six in the morning."

Carter managed a hint of a smile. "One's probably okay, but you have a *shitload* of paperwork to fill out."

"Ohh," Aislinn groaned, thinking of what would happen if a cop from a different city came into Boston and got into a firefight on a residential street. "Well, we didn't have a lot else planned."

Curtis stood back, a look of pride in his eyes. *That,* Aislinn thought as she walked with Carter to a waiting car, *meant almost as much as taking down Walsh.*

CHAPTER FIFTY-SEVEN

It took a week for Walsh to be well enough to travel, which was fine because that was the length of time necessary to put the paperwork in place to transport him back across state lines. Aislinn arrived with her prisoner mid-morning on Monday to a small smattering of media, the time between the shootout and Walsh's return having cooled the story.

Stan and Bryan were at the plane door when it opened and they escorted Walsh out of the twin-engine prop to a waiting paddy wagon. Elian Perez and Curtis stood waiting for Aislinn to deplane, and Curtis motioned for her to join them inside the private terminal.

"Well done, Detective Byrne," the police commissioner said. "Very well done."

"Thank you, sir."

They sat down in a set of lounge chairs and Perez listened intently as Aislinn walked him through how they'd worked the case, stripping away all the layers until Arnie Walsh was standing alone in the limelight. Perez nodded occasionally, but didn't interrupt.

When she was finished, Perez said, "Twenty years, five murders." He had a thoughtful look on his face. "You knew him. Did you ever suspect?"

Aislinn shook her head. "Never. He was a hell of an actor."

Perez got up and gave them a hint of a smile. "Just wanted to be here when you arrived."

Curtis whispered to her as the commissioner headed out to face the cameras. "I think he's got the message that we're pretty well anchored to the deck."

Aislinn chuckled. "And here you thought he was a jerk." She couldn't keep the smile from her face.

He shot her a look as they headed to his car. "Yeah, and I thought you were going to be a good detective."

She settled into the passenger's seat, still grinning from the ribbing. "I think I'll drop in on the folks. Hearing how things played out over the phone isn't going to cut it on this one."

"Right, I can drop you there."

"Nah, home is good. I'll walk over." She watched the streetscape fly past, all for the lush green of Boston after a week in the desert.

"Take the rest of the day off." Curtis glanced at her. "You've earned it."

"Yeah, I might do that," she said. "I will *definitely* do that."

After dropping Aislinn off, Curtis headed back to A-1 and went in search of Bryan Cheung. The precinct was hopping – Stan and Bryan were getting Arnie Walsh settled into his new digs. Curtis left a message on Cheung's desk and spent the next hour going over the caseload with his other detectives, then settled into his office to call Brandy. She was at Frog's Leap working, but stepped outside for a quick chat.

"So he's back in Boston," Brandy said.

"Sure is."

"Would you have found him without the visit from your Italian friend?" she asked.

Curtis gave that some serious thought. "Honestly, unless he did something really stupid and wound up with a DNA sample in the national database, probably not. He was well established under that fake identity."

"Good thing then," she said.

"Yeah, it was," he said, missing her more than usual. "How about I see if I can wiggle some time off. Maybe catch a flight to San Fran."

"Oh, that would be *wonderful*," she said. "Can you?"

"Hey, I *am* the boss."

Bryan Cheung poked his head in and Curtis added, "Sorry, got to go. Can I call you later?"

"Of course, silly," she said.

Curtis hung up and waved Bryan in. Stan was behind him but stopped at the door. Cheung sat and waited.

Curtis dug in his drawer, then handed Bryan Cheung a shiny badge in a leather folder. "Congrats. The guys upstairs didn't even question the application."

Bryan took it, ran his finger across the cool metal and swallowed hard. "Thanks, LT."

"You're going to make a hell of a detective," Curtis said. "Probably as good as him." He looked at Stan, leaning against the door jamb.

"Not a fucking chance," Stan said with a smile.

Curtis grinned and looked back at Bryan. "I heard you paid Danny Zebiak a visit."

Bryan nodded. "I did. I talked to the guys down at Pondville and they have a mentorship program for their ex-cons. They had no problem with me mentoring Danny."

"That's good of you," Curtis said. "Do you think he'll make it?"

"He wants to," Bryan said.

"Okay," Curtis said, indicating they were finished. "Welcome to the team."

"It means a lot," Bryan said.

"Yeah, I know," Curtis said. "Make sure the DA's office has everything they need on the Walsh file then you and Stan can close it."

Bryan nodded.

"The Walsh file," Stan said. "Man, sounds so cold."

"Five victims, gone forever," Curtis said. "Now it's over. Just another case, Stan."

His detectives cleaned out at the end of a hectic workday and Curtis sat alone in the fading daylight. For a lot of people it wasn't over. It would never be over for the Walsh family – Kayla, her mom and her sisters, Kayla's kids. All of them, their lives intertwined with a dirty cop who had murdered without a moment's hesitation. And Aislinn, carrying the memories of her friend – murdered and callously stuffed in a wall for twenty years. This one had cut close to home for her. Still, she'd kept it together and there was never a moment when he had really doubted her ability to lead the investigation.

The lights were off and dusk crept over the office. He stared out the window and thought of Giuseppe Salvatore, sitting alone in a homicide cop's backyard, waiting in the darkness to finally exact revenge on the man who had put his son in jail. And to what Salvatore had said in the interview room - *All these people, on the wrong side of murder* – how he'd thought to himself that there wasn't a right side to any of it. Now he wasn't so sure – maybe there was. Murder was inevitable, people were going to kill each other for a multitude of different motives. Somebody had to be on the other side. Somebody had to solve the cases.

"It's us," he said quietly and snapped his laptop shut.

He left the precinct and headed for home, looking forward to calling Brandy and booking his flight. In fact, he was *very* much looking forward to that.

CURTIS WESTCOTT SERIES

If you enjoyed

The Wrong Side of Murder

Then be sure to visit JEFFBUICK.com and find more titles available and other books in the Curtis Westcott crime series, starting with award winning *A Killing Game.*

Book 1: A Curtis Westcott Crime Thriller

A Killing Game

Renee Charlebois was born into a wealthy and powerful Boston family, but she pushed all that aside and built her own chain of successful restaurants. Beautiful, popular, and intelligent – she has it all. Except for one small detail – she's been abducted without a trace. Who took her, and why, is a complete mystery.

The case gets dropped on Curtis Westcott's desk, but Boston's Chief of Homicide has little to work with. No clues, no body, no motive. Renee had no enemies, no financial skeletons in the closet, no bitter ex-boyfriends. Curtis and Aislinn Byrne, his go-to detective on tough cases, work the file hard but come up empty. Then, while Westcott is at a party, he overhears a story that catches his attention and gives him and Aislinn their first break.

They dig in and unravel a complex series of crimes tied to Renee's disappearance. As the layers peel back they're convinced Renee is alive, but her abductor has every intention of killing her. It's a bizarre and twisted game, and if Curtis and Aislinn can't figure it out in time an innocent woman will die.

A Killing Game is Book One in the Curtis Westcott series, set in Boston.

BOBBY GRECO SERIES

Prequel: Bobby Greco Crime Series

No End of Bad Guys

Get the prequel novella *No End of Bad Guys* free for signing up for Jeff Buick's newsletter! Click here to learn more or visit www.JeffBuick.com!

Book 1: Bobby Greco Crime Series

One is Evil

Set up by dirty cops and then kicked off the Orlando Homicide squad, Bobby Greco lands a job investigating insurance fraud. As he works a file, he notices a detail that seems trivial, but when he follows up on it, a conspiracy to steal US military secrets unfolds.

Armand Cortez is an arms dealer with a brazen plan to steal crucial missile technology, and when Bobby starts poking around, Cortez goes after the one thing Bobby holds dearest – his ex-wife and kids.

Bobby can't go up against Cortez alone, and teams up with June Childers, a scientist working on the missile, and together they try to stop Cortez. If they fail, technology that could trigger a war will be fall into the wrong hands, the reputation of a powerful and honorable man will be destroyed, and a missing woman will never be found.

From the halls of power in Washington DC,

to the frozen wastelands of Siberia,

the chase is on – and the clock is ticking.

ALSO BY JEFF BUICK

If you haven't already, you'll want to grab these free short stories and add them to your Jeff Buick library, available at www.JeffBuick.com!

Sign up at

www.JeffBuick.com/newsletter

to receive all of these titles directly to your email.

ACKNOWLEDGMENTS

While I'm the one who sits in my favorite Starbucks and types for endless hours to create this stuff, my books are a collaborative effort. These are my fellow co-conspirators.

Nothing would get done if it weren't for my incredible wife, Celia. She anchors me (in a good way) and keeps me focused. She is my encouragement, my reality check and my shoulder to rest on. She's also the best editor I've ever had. Lucky me.

Christina Curkovic is my awesome behind the scenes person. She takes care of everything, like those cool links so you can get to Amazon and find my books, and a hundred other things. If Christina suddenly disappeared and I had to do all that stuff, my creative side would shrivel up and die. She lets me write, so I adore her.

Laura Rushford is the BEST proof reader EVER. She is a like a heat-seeking missile for bad grammar (guilty) and misplaced/misused words (guilty again). Thank you, Laura.

Then there are Derek Curtis and Brian Robertson—my crime team. Brian spent 14 years in homicide and worked on over 175 investigations, while Derek is an undercover and surveillance expert. I couldn't have put together *The Wrong Side of Murder* without these two.

Check out The Team page on my website for the rest of the crew. I could never do this alone: https://www.jeffbuick.com/the-team/

ABOUT THE AUTHOR

JEFF BUICK has been writing thrillers since 1998 and he has no plans to stop anytime soon. His first book was a Young Adult story called Download to Disaster that he wrote for one of his sons. It was about a bad guy taking down the Internet (which pretty much no one knew of back then), and it's so hokey it if he released it now, it could be a comedy.

Travel plays a big part in his life, and he's spent time in Africa, South and Central America, Europe, and New Zealand. This love of travel is reflected in where he sets his novels.

Jeff works hard at writing great beach reads that engage, enlighten and entertain the reader.

He lives in Calgary, Canada with his wife Celia.

Find out more about Jeff on his website and sign up for his newsletter to receive exclusive updates and reader bonuses: www.JeffBuick.com

Made in the USA
Columbia, SC
30 July 2021

42315698R00202